Edward Burnet Tylor

Researches into the early history of mankind

Development of civilization

Edward Burnet Tylor

Researches into the early history of mankind
Development of civilization

ISBN/EAN: 9783741176463

Manufactured in Europe, USA, Canada, Australia, Japa

Cover: Foto ©Andreas Hilbeck / pixelio.de

Manufactured and distributed by brebook publishing software
(www.brebook.com)

Edward Burnet Tylor

Researches into the early history of mankind

RESEARCHES

INTO THE

EARLY HISTORY OF MANKIND.

RESEARCHES

INTO THE

EARLY HISTORY OF MANKIND

AND THE

DEVELOPMENT OF CIVILIZATION.

By EDWARD BURNET TYLOR,
AUTHOR OF 'MEXICO AND THE MEXICANS.'

LONDON:
JOHN MURRAY, ALBEMARLE STREET.
1865.

JOHN EDWARD TAYLOR, PRINTER,
LITTLE QUEEN STREET, LINCOLN'S INN FIELDS.

CONTENTS.

CHAPTER I.

INTRODUCTION 1

CHAPTER II.

THE GESTURE-LANGUAGE 14

CHAPTER III.

THE GESTURE-LANGUAGE—(*continued*) 34

CHAPTER IV.

GESTURE-LANGUAGE AND WORD-LANGUAGE 55

CHAPTER V.

PICTURE-WRITING AND WORD-WRITING 83

CHAPTER VI.

IMAGES AND NAMES 107

CHAPTER VII.

GROWTH AND DECLINE OF CULTURE 150

CHAPTER VIII.

THE STONE AGE—PAST AND PRESENT 191

CHAPTER IX.

FIRE, COOKING, AND VESSELS 228

CHAPTER X.

SOME REMARKABLE CUSTOMS 279

CHAPTER XI.

HISTORICAL TRADITIONS AND MYTHS OF OBSERVATION . . 298

CHAPTER XII.

GEOGRAPHICAL DISTRIBUTION OF MYTHS 325

CHAPTER XIII.

CONCLUDING REMARKS 361

RESEARCHES

INTO THE

EARLY HISTORY OF MANKIND.

CHAPTER I.

INTRODUCTION.

In studying the phenomena of knowledge and art, religion and mythology, law and custom, and the rest of the complex whole which we call Civilization, it is not enough to have in view the more advanced races, and to know their history so far as direct records have preserved it for us. The explanation of the state of things in which we live has often to be sought in the condition of rude and early tribes; and without a knowledge of this to guide us, we may miss the meaning even of familiar thoughts and practices. To take a trivial instance, the statement is true enough as it stands, that the women of modern Europe mutilate their ears to hang jewels in them, but the reason of their doing so is not to be fully found in the circumstances among which we are living now. The student who takes a wider view thinks of the rings and bones and feathers thrust through the cartilage of the nose; the weights that pull the slit ears in long nooses to the shoulder; the ivory studs let in at the corners of the mouth; the wooden plugs as big as table-spoons put through slits in the under lip; the teeth of animals stuck point outwards through holes in the cheeks; all familiar things among the lower races up and down in the world. The modern earring of the higher nations stands not as a product of our own times, but as a relic of a ruder mental condition, one of the many cases in which the result of progress has been not positive in adding, but negative in taking away, something belonging to an earlier state of things.

It is indeed hardly too much to say that Civilization, being a process of long and complex growth, can only be thoroughly understood when studied through its entire range; that the past is continually needed to explain the present, and the whole to explain the part. A feeling of this may account in some measure for the eager curiosity which is felt for descriptions of the life and habits of strange and ancient races, in Cook's Voyages, Catlin's 'North American Indians,' Prescott's 'Mexico' and 'Peru,' even in the meagre details which antiquaries have succeeded in recovering of the lives of the Lake-dwellers of Switzerland and the Reindeer Tribes of Central France. For matters of practical life these people may be nothing to us; but in reading of them we are consciously or unconsciously completing the picture, and tracing out the course of life, of what has been so well said to be after all our most interesting object of study, mankind.

Though, however, the Early History of Man is felt to be an attractive subject, and great masses of the materials needed for working it out have long been forthcoming, they have as yet been turned to but little account. The opinion that the use of facts is to illustrate theories, the confusion between History and Mythology, which is only now being partly cleared up, an undue confidence in the statements of ancient writers, whose means of information about times and places remote from themselves were often much narrower than those which are, ages later, at our own command, have been among the hindrances to the growth of sound knowledge in this direction. The time for writing a systematic treatise on the subject does not seem yet to have come; certainly nothing of the kind is attempted in the present series of essays, whose contents, somewhat miscellaneous as they are, scarcely come into contact with great part of the most important problems involved, such as the relation of the bodily characters of the various races, the question of their origin and descent, the development of morals, religion, law, and many others. The matters discussed have been chosen, not so much for their absolute importance, as because, while they are among the easiest and most inviting parts of the subject, it is possible so to work them as to bring into view certain general lines of argument, which apply not only to them, but also to the more complex and difficult problems involved in a complete treatise on the History of Civilization. These lines of argument, and their relation to the different essays, may be briefly stated at the outset.

In the first place, when a general law can be inferred from a group of facts, the use of detailed history is very much superseded. When we see a magnet attract a piece of iron, having come by experience to the general law that magnets attract iron, we do not take the trouble to go into the history of the particular magnet in question. To some extent this direct reference to general laws may be made in the study of Civilization. The four next chapters of the present book treat of the various ways in which man utters his thoughts, in Gestures, Words, Pictures, and Writing. Here, though Speech and Writing must be investigated historically, depending as they do in so great measure on the words and characters which were current in the world thousands of years ago, on the other hand the Gesture-Language and Picture-Writing may be mostly explained without the aid of history, as direct products of the human mind. In the following chapter on "Images and Names," an attempt is made to refer a great part of the beliefs and practices included under the general name of magic, to one very simple mental law, as resulting from a condition of mind which we of the more advanced races have almost outgrown, and in doing so have undergone one of the most notable changes which we can trace as having happened to mankind. And lastly, a particular habit of mind accounts for a class of stories which are here grouped together as "Myths of Observation," as distinguished from the tales which make up the great bulk of the folk-lore of the world, and which latter are now being shown by the new school of Comparative Mythologists in Germany and England to have come into existence also by virtue of a general law, but a very different one.

But it is only in particular parts of Human Culture where the facts have not, so to speak, travelled far from their causes, that this direct method is practicable. Most of its phenomena have grown into shape out of such a complication of events, that the laborious piecing together of their previous history is the only safe way of studying them. It is easy to see how far a theologian or a lawyer would go wrong who should throw history aside, and attempt to explain, on abstract principles, the existence of the Protestant Church or the Code Napoléon. A Romanesque or an Early English cathedral is not to be studied as though all that the architect had to do was to take stone and mortar and set up a building for a given purpose. The development of the architecture of Greece, its passage into the architecture of Rome, the growth of Christian ceremony and symbolism, are only part of the elements which went to form the state of things in which the genius of the builder had to work out the requirements of the moment. The late Mr. Buckle did good service in urging students to look through the details of history to the great laws of Human Development which lie behind; but his attempt to explain, by a few rash generalizations, the complex phases of European history, is a warning of the danger of too hasty an appeal to first principles.

As, however, the earlier civilization lies very much out of the beaten track of history, the place of direct records has to be supplied in great measure by indirect evidence, such as Antiquities, Language, and Mythology. This makes it generally difficult to get a sound historical basis to work on, but there happens to be a quantity of material easily obtainable, which bears on the development of some of the more common and useful arts. Thus in the eighth and ninth chapters, the transition from implements of stone to those of metal is demonstrated to have taken place in almost every district of the habitable globe, and a progress from ruder to more perfect modes of making fire and boiling food is traced in many different countries; while in the seventh, evidence is collected on the important problem of the relation which Progress has borne to Decline in art and knowledge in the history of the world.

In the remote times and places where direct history is at

fault, the study of Civilization, Culture-History as it is conveniently called in Germany, becomes itself an important aid to the historian, as a means of re-constructing the lost records of early or barbarous times. But its use as contributing to the early history of mankind depends mainly on the answering of the following question, which runs through all the present essays, and binds them together as various cases of a single problem.

When similar arts, customs, or legends are found in several distant regions, among peoples not known to be of the same stock, how is this similarity to be accounted for? Sometimes it may be ascribed to the like working of men's minds under like conditions, and sometimes it is a proof of blood relationship or of intercourse, direct or indirect, between the races among whom it is found. In the one case it has no historical value whatever, while in the other it has this value in a high degree, and the ever-recurring problem is how to distinguish between the two. An example on each side may serve to bring the matter into a clearer light.

The general prevalence of a belief in the continuance of the soul's existence after death, does not prove that all mankind have inherited such a belief from a common source. It may have been so, but the historical argument is made valueless by the fact that certain natural phenomena may have suggested to the mind of man, while in a certain stage of development, the idea of a future state, and this not once only, but again and again in different regions and at different times. These phenomena may prove nothing of the kind to us, but that is not the question. The reasoning of the savage is not to be judged by the rules which belong to a higher education; and what the ethnologist requires in such a case, is not to know what the facts prove to his own mind, but what inference the very differently trained mind of the savage may draw from them.

The belief that man has a soul capable of existing apart from the body it belongs to, and continuing to live, for a time at least, after that body is dead and buried, fits perfectly in such a mind with the fact that the shadowy forms of men and women

do appear to others, when the men and women themselves are
at a distance, and after they are dead. We call these apparitions dreams or phantasms, according as the person to whom
they appear is asleep or awake, and when we hear of their
occurrence in ordinary life, set them down as subjective processes of the mind. We do not think that the phantom of the
dark Brazilian who used to haunt Spinoza was a real person;
that the head which stood before a late distinguished English
peer, whenever he was out of health, was a material object; that
the fiends which torment the victim of delirium tremens, are
what and where they seem to him to be; that any real occurrence corresponds to the dreams of the old men who tell us
they were flogged last night at school. It is only a part of
mankind, however, who thus disconnect dreams and visions
from the objects whose forms they bear. Among the less
civilized races, the separation of subjective and objective impressions, which in this, as in several other matters, makes the
most important difference between the educated man and the
savage, is much less fully carried out. This is indeed true to
some extent among the higher nations, for no Greenlander or
Kafir ever mixed up his subjectivity with the evidence of his
senses into a more hopeless confusion than the modern spiritualist. As the subject is only brought forward here as an illustration, it is not necessary to go at length into its details. A
few picked examples will bring into view the two great theories
of dreams and visions, current among the lower races. One is,
that when a man is asleep or seeing visions, the figures which
appear to him come from their places and stand over against
him; the other, that the soul of the dreamer or seer goes out
on its travels, and comes home with a remembrance of what it
has seen.

The Australians, says Sir George Grey, believe that the
nightmare is caused by an evil spirit. To get rid of it they
jump up, catch a lighted brand from the fire, and with various
muttered imprecations fling it in the direction where they think
the spirit is. He simply came for a light, and having got it,
he will go away.[1]   Others tell of the demon Koin, a creature

<hr>

[1] Grey, 'Journals;' London, 1841, vol. ii. p. 339.

who has the appearance of a native, and like them is painted
with pipe-clay and carries a fire-stick. He comes sometimes
when they are asleep and carries a man off as an eagle does its
prey. The shout of the victim's companions makes the demon
let him drop, or else he carries him off to his fire in the bush.
The unfortunate black tries to cry out, but feels himself all but
choked and cannot. At daylight Koin disappears, and the
native finds himself brought safely back to his own fireside.[1]
Even in Europe, such expressions as being ridden by a hag or
by the devil, preserve the recollection of a similar train of
thought. In the evil demons who trouble people in their sleep,
the Incubi and Succubi, the belief in this material and personal
character of the figures seen in dreams comes strongly out,
perhaps nowhere more strikingly than among the natives of the
Tonga Islands.[2] "Whoso seeth me in his sleep," said Mohammed, "seeth me truly, for Satan cannot assume the simili-
tude of my form."

Mr. St. John says that the Dayaks regard dreams as actual
occurrences. They think that in sleep the soul sometimes remains in the body, and sometimes leaves it and travels far
away, and that both when in and out of the body it sees and
hears and talks, and altogether has a prescience given to it,
which, when the body is in its natural state, it does not enjoy.
Fainting fits, or a state of coma, are thought to be caused by
the departure or absence of the soul on some distant expedition
of its own. When a European dreams of his distant country,
the Dayaks think his soul has annihilated space, and paid a
flying visit to Europe during the night.[3] Very many tribes believe in this way that dreams are incidents which happen to
the spirit in its wanderings from the body, and the idea has
even expressed itself in a superstitious objection to waking a
sleeper, for fear of disturbing his body while his soul is out.[4]
Father Charlevoix found both the theories in question current

[1] Backhouse, 'Visit to the Australian Colonies;' London, 1843, p. 555.
[2] Mariner, 'Tonga Islands;' 2nd ed., London, 1818, vol. ii. p. 112.
[3] St. John, 'Forests of the Far East;' London, 1862, vol. i. p. 189.
[4] Bastian, 'Der Mensch in der Geschichte;' Leipzig. 1860, vol. ii. p. 819,
etc. etc.

among the Indians of North America. A dream might either
be a visit from the soul of the object dreamt of, or it might be
one of the souls of the dreamer going about the world, while
the other—for every man has two—stayed behind with the body.
Dreams, they think, are of supernatural origin, and it is a religious duty to attend to them. That the white men should look
upon a dream as a matter of no consequence is a thing they
cannot understand.[1]

How like a dream is to the popular notion of a soul, a shade,
a spirit, or a ghost, need not be said. But there are facts
which bring the dream and the ghost into yet closer connexion
than follows from mere resemblance. Thus the belief is found
among the Finnish races that the spirits of the dead can plague
the living in their sleep, and bring sickness and harm upon
them.[2] Herodotus relates that the Nasamones practise divination in the following manner:—they resort to the tombs of
their ancestors, and after offering prayers, go to sleep by them,
and whatever dream appears to them they take for their answer.[3]
In modern Africa, the missionary Casalis says of the Basuto,
" Persons who are pursued in their sleep by the image of a deceased relation, are often known to sacrifice a victim on the
tomb of the defunct, in order, as they say, to calm his dis-
quietude."[4] Clearly, then, a man who thinks he sees in sleep
the apparitions of his dead relatives and friends has a reason
for believing that their spirits outlive their bodies, and this
reason lies in no far-fetched induction, but in what seems to
be the plain evidence of his senses. I have set the argument
down as belonging especially to the lower stages of mental development, though indeed I have been startled by hearing it
myself urged in sober earnest very far outside the range of
savage life.

It is interesting to read how Lucretius, reasoning against

<hr>

[1] Charlevoix, Hist. et Descr. Gén. de la Nouvelle-France; Paris, 1744, vol.
vi. p. 74.

[2] Castrén, 'Vorlesungen über die Finnische Mythologie;' (Tr. and Ed.
Schiefner,) St. Petersburg, 1853, p. 120.

[3] Herod. iv. 172. See Mela i. 8.

[4] Casalis, 'The Basutos;' London, 1861, p. 245.

the belief in a future life, takes notice of the argument from
dreams as telling against him, and states, in opposition to it,
his doctrine that not dreams only, but even ordinary appearances and imaginations, are caused by film-like images which
fly off from the surfaces of real objects, and come in contact
with our minds and senses,—

> "Touching these matters, let me now explain,
> How there are so-called images of things
> Which, like films torn from bodies' outmost face
> Hither and thither flutter through the air.
> These scare us, meeting us in waking hours,
> And in our dreams, when oftentimes we see
> Marvellous shapes, and phantoms of the dead
> Which oft have roused us horror-struck from sleep.
> Lest we should judge perchance that souls escape
> From Acheron, shades flit 'mid living men,
> Or aught of us can after death endure."[1]

Never, perhaps, has the train of thought which the Epicurean
poet so ingeniously combats been more clearly drawn out than
in Madge Wildfire's rambling talk of her dead baby, " Whiles
I think my puir bairn's dead—ye ken very weel it's buried—
but that signifies naething. I have had it on my knee a hundred times, and a hundred till that, since it was buried—and
how could that be were it dead, ye ken—it's merely impossible."

It appears then, from these considerations, that when we find
dim notions of a future state current in the remotest regions
of the world, we must not thence assume that they were all

---

[1] Lucret.:—'De Rerum Natura,' iv. 29-39:—

> " Nunc agere incipiam tibi, quod vementer ad has res
> Attinet, esse ea quæ rerum simulacra vocamus ;
> Quæ, quasi membranæ summo de corpore rerum
> Dereptæ, volitant ultroque citroque per auras,
> Atque eadem nobis vigilantibus obvia mentes
> Terrificant atque in somnis, cum sæpe figuras
> Contuimur miras simulacraque luce carentum,
> Quæ non horrifice languentis sæpe sopore
> Excierunt ; ne forte animas Acherunte reamur
> Effugere aut umbras inter vivos volitare,
> Neve aliquid nostri post mortem posse relinqui."

diffused from a single geographical centre. The case is one in which any one plausible explanation from natural causes is sufficient to bar the argument from historical connection. On the other hand, there is nothing to hinder such an argument in the following case, which is taken as showing the opposite side of the problem.

The great class of stories known as Beast Fables have of late risen much in public estimation. In old times they were listened to by high and low with the keenest enjoyment for their own sake. Then they were wrested from their proper nature into means of teaching little moral lessons, and at last it came to be the most contemptuous thing that could be said of a silly, pointless tale, to call it a "cock and bull story." In our own day, however, a generation among whom there has sprung up a new knowledge of old times, and with it a new sympathy with old thoughts and feelings, not only appreciate the beast fables for themselves, but find in their diffusion over the world an important aid to early history. Thus Dr. Dasent, in his Introduction to the Norse Tales, has shown that popular stories found in the west and south of Africa must have come from the same source with old myths current in distant regions of Europe. Still later, Dr. Bleek has published a collection of Hottentot Fables,[1] which shows that other mythic episodes, long familiar in remote countries, have established themselves among these rude people as household tales.

A Dutchman found a Snake, who was lying under a great stone, and could not get away. He lifted up the stone, and set her free, but when he had done it she wanted to eat him. The Man objected to this, and appealed to the Hare and the Hyena, but both said it was right. Then they asked the Jackal, but he would not even believe the thing could have happened unless he saw it with his two eyes. So the Snake lay down, and the Man put the stone upon her, just to show how it was. "Now let her lie there," said the Jackal. This is only another version of the story of the Ungrateful Crocodile, which the sage Dûbân declined to tell the king while the executioner was standing ready to cut his head off. It is given by Mr. Lane in his Notes

[1] Bleek, 'Reynard the Fox in South Africa;' London, 1864, pp. 11-13, 16, 19, 23.

to the Arabian Nights,[1] and I am not sure that the simpler
Hottentot version is not the neater of the two. Again, the
name of Reynard in South Africa, given by Dr. Bleek to his
Hottentot tales, is amply justified by their containing familiar
episodes belonging to the mediæval "Reynard the Fox."[2] The
Jackal shams death and lies in the road till the fish-waggon
comes by, and the waggoner throws him in to make a kaross
of his skin, but the cunning beast throws a lot of fish out into
the road, and then jumps out himself. In another place, the
Lion is sick, and all the beasts go to see him but the Jackal.
His enemy the Hyena fetches him to give his advice, so he
comes before the Lion, and says he has been to ask the witch
what was to be done for his sick uncle, and the remedy is for
the Lion to pull the Hyena's skin off over his ears, and put it
on himself while it is warm. Again, the trick by which Chan-
ticleer gets his head out of Reynard's mouth by making him
answer the farmer, reminds one of the way in which, in the
Hottentot tale, the Cock makes the Jackal say his prayers, and
when the outwitted beast folds his hands and shuts his eyes,
flies off and makes his escape. Of course these tales, though
adapted to native circumstances and with very clever native
turns, may be all of very recent introduction. Such a story as
that which introduces a fish-waggon, would be naturally referred
to the Dutch boers, from whom indeed all the Reynard stories
are likely to have come. One curious passage tends to show
that the stories are taken, not from the ancient versions of
Reynard, but from some interpolated modern rendering. A
proof that Jacob Grimm brings forward of the independent,
secluded course of the old German Beast-Saga, is, that it did
not take up into itself stories long current elsewhere, which would
have fitted admirably into it,—thus, for instance, Æsop's story
of the Fox who will not go into the Lion's den because he only
sees the footsteps going in, but none coming out, is nowhere to
be found in the mediæval Reynard. But we find in the Hottentot tales that this very episode has found its way in, and

---

[1] Lane, 'The Thousand and One Nights,' new edit., London, 1859, vol. i.
pp. 84, 114.

[2] Jacob Grimm, 'Reinhart Fuchs;' Berlin, 1834, pp. cxxii. l. 80, cclxxii.

exactly into its fitting place. "The Lion, it is said, was ill, and they all went to see him in his suffering. But the Jackal did not go, because the traces of the people who went to see him did not turn back."

As it happens, we know from other sources enough to explain the appearance in South Africa of stories from Reynard and the Arabian Nights by referring them to European or Moslem influence. But even without such knowledge, the tales themselves prove an historical connection, near or remote, between Europe, Egypt, and South Africa. To try to make such evidence stand alone is a more ambitious task. In a chapter on the Geographical Distribution of Myths, I have compared a series of stories collected on the American Continent with their analogues elsewhere, endeavouring thereby to show an historical connection between the mythology of America and that of the rest of the world, but with what success the reader must decide. In another chapter, some remarkable customs, which are found spread over distant tracts of country, are examined in order to ascertain, if possible, whether any historical argument may be grounded upon them.

For the errors which no doubt abound in the present essays, and for the superficial working of a great subject, a word may be said in apology. In discussing questions in which sometimes the leading facts have never before been even roughly grouped, it is very difficult not only to reject the wrong evidence, but to reproduce the right with accuracy, and the way in which new information comes in, which quite alters the face of the old, does not tend to promote over-confidence in first results. For instance, after having followed other observers in setting down as peculiar to the South Sea Islands, in or near the Samoan group, an ingenious little drilling instrument which will be hereafter described, I found it kept in stock in the London tool shops; mistakes of this kind must be frequent till our knowledge of the lower civilization is much more thoroughly collected and sifted. More accuracy might indeed be obtained by keeping to a very small number of subjects, but our accounts of the culture of the lower races, being mostly unclassified, have to be gone through as a whole, and up to a certain point it is a question whether the student of a very limited field might not lose more in largeness of view than he gained by concentration. Whatever be the fate of my arguments, any one who collects and groups a mass of evidence, and makes an attempt to turn it to account which may lead to something better, has, I think, a claim to be exempt from any very harsh criticism of mistakes and omissions. As the Knight says in the beginning of his Tale:—

> "I have, God wot, a largë feeld to ere ;
> And weykë ben the oxen in my plough."

[Beside ordinary references, I wish to acknowledge separately some particular obligations. My friend Mr. Henry Christy has given me, for years past, not only the benefit of his wide knowledge of ethnography, but also the opportunity of studying the productions of the lower races from the carefully chosen specimens in his great collection. I am indebted to Dr. W. H. Scott, the Director of the Deaf and Dumb Institution, at Exeter, for much of the assistance which has enabled me to write about the Gesture-Language with something of the confidence of an "expert;" and I have to thank Prof. Pott, of Halle, and Prof. Lazarus, of Berne, for personal help in several difficult questions. Among books, I have drawn largely from the philological works of Prof. Steinthal, of Berlin, and from the invaluable collection of facts bearing on the history of civilisation in the 'Allgemeine Cultur-Geschichte der Menschheit,' and 'Allgemeine Culturwissenschaft,' of Dr. Gustav Klemm, of Dresden.]

CHAPTER II.

THE GESTURE-LANGUAGE.

THE power which man possesses of uttering his thoughts is one of the most essential elements of his civilization. Whether he can even think at all without some means of outward expression is a metaphysical question which need not be discussed here. Thus much will hardly be denied by any one, that man's power of utterance, so far exceeding any that the lower animals possess, is one of the principal causes of his immense pre-eminence over them.

Of the means which man has of uttering or expressing that which is in his mind, speech is by far the most important, so much so that when we speak of *uttering* our thoughts, the phrase is understood to mean expressing them in words. But when we say that man's power of utterance is one of the great differences between him and the lower animals, we must attach to the word utterance a sense more fully conformable to its etymology. As Steinthal admits, the deaf-and-dumb man is the living refutation of the proposition, that man cannot think without speech, unless we allow the understood notion of speech as the utterance of thought by articulate sounds to be too narrow.[1] To *utter* a thought is literally to put it outside us, as to *express* it is to squeeze it out. Grossly material as these metaphors are, they are the best terms we have for that wonderful

---

[1] Steinthal, 'Ueber die Sprache der Taubstummen' (in Prutz's 'Deutsches Museum,' Jan. to June, 1851, p. 904, etc.).

process by which a man, by some bodily action, can not only make other men's minds reproduce more or less exactly the workings of his own, but can even receive back from the outward sign an impression similar to theirs, as though not he himself, but some one else, had made it.

Besides articulate speech, the principal means by which man can express what is in his mind are the Gesture-Language, Picture-Writing, and Word-Writing. If we knew now, what we hope to know some day, how Language sprang up and grew in the world, our knowledge of man's earliest condition and history would stand on a very different basis from what it now does. But we know so little about the Origin of Language, that even the greatest philologists are forced either to avoid the subject altogether, or to turn themselves into metaphysicians in order to discuss it. The Gesture-Language and Picture-Writing, however, insignificant as they are in practice in comparison with Speech and Phonetic Writing, have this great claim to consideration, that we can really understand them as thoroughly as perhaps we can understand anything, and by studying them we can realize to ourselves in some measure a condition of the human mind which underlies anything which has as yet been traced in even the lowest dialect of Language, if taken as a whole. Though, with the exception of words which are evidently imitative, like "peewit" and "cuckoo," we cannot at present tell by what steps man came to express himself by words, we can at least see how he still does come to express himself by signs and pictures, and so get some idea of the nature of this great movement, which no lower animal is known to have made or shown the least sign of making. There is, however, no proof that man passed through any intermediate stage, such as the use of gestures, before he spoke. This theory, though by no means contemptible, has, so far as at present appears, no sufficient support from observed facts.

The Gesture-Language, or Language of Signs, is in great part a system of representing objects and ideas by a rude outline-gesture, imitating their most striking features. It is, as has been well said by a deaf-and-dumb man, "a picture-language." Here at once its essential difference from speech becomes evident. Why the words *stand* and *go* mean what they do is a question to which we cannot as yet give the shadow of an answer, and if we had been taught to say "stand" where we now say "go," and "go" where we now say "stand," it would be practically all the same to us. No doubt there was a sufficient reason for these words receiving the meanings they now bear, as indeed there is a sufficient reason for everything; but so far as we are concerned, there might as well have been none, for we have quite lost sight of the connection between the word and the idea. But in the gesture-language the relation between idea and sign not only always exists, but is scarcely lost sight of for a moment. When a deaf-and-dumb child holds his two first fingers forked like a pair of legs, and makes them stand and walk upon the table, we want no teaching to show us what this means, nor why it is done.

This definition of the gesture-language is, however, not complete. Such objects as are actually in the presence of the speaker, or may be supposed so, are brought bodily into the conversation by touching, pointing, or looking towards them, either to indicate the objects themselves or one of their characteristics. Thus if a deaf and dumb man touches his underlip with his forefinger, the context must decide whether he means to indicate the lip itself or the colour "red," unless, as is sometimes done, he shows by actually taking hold of the lip with finger and thumb, that it is the lip itself, and not its quality, that he means. Under the two classes " pictures in the air " and things brought before the mind by actual pointing out, the whole of the sign-language may be included.

It is in Deaf and Dumb Institutions that the gesture-language may be most conveniently studied, and what slight practical knowledge I have of it has been got in this way in Germany and in England. In these institutions, however, there are grammatical signs used in the gesture-language which do not fairly belong to it. These are mostly signs adapted, or perhaps invented, by teachers who had the use of speech, to express ideas which do not come within the scope of the very limited natural grammar and dictionary of the deaf-and-dumb. But it is to be observed that though the deaf-and-dumb have been taught to understand these signs and use them in school, they ignore them in their ordinary talk, and will have nothing to do with them if they can help it.

By dint of instruction, deaf-mutes can be taught to communicate their thoughts, and to learn from books and men in nearly the same way as we do, though in a more limited degree. They learn to read and write, to spell out sentences with the finger-alphabet, and to understand words so spelt by others; and besides this, they can be taught to speak in articulate language, though in a hoarse and unmodulated voice, and when another speaks, to follow the motions of his lips almost as though they could hear the words uttered.

It may be remarked here, once for all, that the general public often confuses the real deaf-and-dumb language of signs, in which objects and actions are expressed by pantomimic gestures, with the deaf-and-dumb finger-alphabet, which is a mere substitute for alphabetic writing. It is not enough to say that the two things are distinct; they have nothing whatever to do with one another, and have no more resemblance than a picture has to a written description of it. Though of little scientific interest, the finger-alphabet is of great practical use. It appears to have been invented in Spain, to which country the world owes the first systematic deaf-and-dumb teaching, by Juan Pablo Bonet, in whose work a one-handed alphabet is set forth differing but little from that now in use in Germany, or perhaps by his predecessor, Pedro de Ponce. The two-handed or French alphabet, generally used in England, is of newer date.[1]

The mother-tongue (so to speak) of the deaf-and-dumb is the language of signs. The evidence of the best observers tends to prove that they are capable of developing the gesture-language out of their own minds without the aid of speaking men. Indeed the deaf-mutes in general surpass the rest of the world in their power of using and understanding signs, and for this simple reason, that though the gesture-language is the common property of all mankind, it is seldom cultivated and

---

[1] Bonet, ' Reduction de las Letras, y Arte para enseñar á ablar los Mudos;' Madrid, 1620; pp. 128, etc. Schmalz, ' Ueber die Taubstummen;' Dresden and Leipzig, 1848; pp. 214, 352.

developed to so high a degree by those who have the use of
speech, as by those who cannot speak, and must therefore have
recourse to other means of communication. The opinions of
two or three practical observers may be cited to show that the
gesture-language is not, like the finger-alphabet, an art learnt
in the first instance from the teacher, but an independent process originating in the mind of the deaf-mute, and developing
itself as his knowledge and power of reasoning expand under
instruction.

Samuel Heinicke, the founder of deaf-and-dumb teaching in
Germany, remarks :—" He (the deaf-mute) prefers keeping to
his pantomime, which is simple and short, and comes to him
fluently as a mother-tongue."[1] Schmalz says :—" Not less com-
prehensible are many signs which we indeed do not use in ordinary life, but which the deaf-and-dumb child uses, having no
means of communicating with others but by signs. These
signs consist principally in drawing in the air the shape of
objects to be suggested to the mind, indicating their character,
imitating the movement of the body in an action to be described, or the use of a thing, its origin, or any other of its
notable peculiarities."[2] " With regard to signs," says Dr.
Scott, of Exeter, " the (deaf-and-dumb) child will most likely
have already fixed upon signs by which it names most of the
objects given in the above lesson (pin, key, etc.), and which it
uses in its intercourse with its friends. These signs had always
better be retained (by the child's family), and if a word has not
received such a sign, endeavour to get the child to fix upon
one. It will do this most probably better than you."[3]

The Abbé Sicard, one of the first and most eminent of the
men who have devoted their lives to the education and " hu-
manizing " of these afflicted creatures, has much the same account to give. " It is not I," he says, " who am to invent
these signs. I have only to set forth the theory of them under
the dictation of their true inventors, those whose language
consists of these signs. It is for the deaf-and-dumb to make
them, and for me to tell how they are made. They must be

<hr>

[1] Heinicke, ' Beobachtungen über Stumme,' etc. ; Hamburg, 1778, p. 56.
[2] Schmalz, p. 317.   [3] Scott, ' The Deaf and Dumb ;' London, 1844, p. 81.

drawn from the nature of the objects they are to represent. It is only the signs given by the mute himself to express the actions which he witnesses, and the objects which are brought before him, which can replace articulate language." Speaking of his celebrated deaf-and-dumb pupil, Massieu, he says :— "Thus, by a happy exchange, as I taught him the written signs of our language, Massieu taught me the mimic signs of his." "So it must be said that it is neither I nor my admirable master (the Abbé de l'Épée) who are the inventors of the deaf-and-dumb language. And as a foreigner is not fit to teach a Frenchman French, so the speaking man has no business to meddle with the invention of signs, giving them abstract values."[1] All these are modern statements; but long before the days of Deaf and Dumb Institutions, Rabelais' sharp eye had noticed how natural and appropriate were the untaught signs made by born deaf-mutes. When Panurge is going to try by divination from signs what his fortune will be in married life, Pantagruel thus counsels him :—"Pourtant, vous fault choisir ung mut sourd de nature, affin que ses gestes vous soyent naïfuement propheticques, non fainctz, fardez, ne affectez."

Nor are we obliged to depend upon the observations of ordinary speaking men for our knowledge of the way in which the gesture-language developes itself in the mind of the deaf-and-dumb. The educated deaf-mutes can tell us from their own experience how gesture-signs originate. The following account is given by Kruse, a deaf-mute himself, and a well-known teacher of deaf-mutes, and author of several works of no small ability :—"Thus the deaf-and-dumb must have a language, without which no thought can be brought to pass. But here nature soon comes to his help. What strikes him most, or what ... makes a distinction to him between one thing and another, such distinctive signs of objects are at once signs by which he knows these objects, and knows them again; they become tokens of things. And whilst he silently elaborates the signs he has found for single objects, that is, whilst he describes their forms for himself in the air, or imitates them in

<hr>

[1] Sicard, 'Cours d'Instruction d'un Sourd-muet,' Paris, 1803, pp. xlv, 18.

thought with hands, fingers, and gestures, he developes for himself suitable signs to represent ideas, which serve him as a means of fixing ideas of different kinds in his mind and re-calling them to his memory. And thus he makes himself a language, the so-called gesture-language (*Geberden-sprache*); and with these few scanty and imperfect signs, a way for thought is already broken, and with his thought as it now opens out, the language cultivates and forms itself further and further."[1]

I will now give some account of the particular dialect (so to speak) of the gesture-language, which is current in the Berlin Deaf and Dumb Institution.[2] I made a list of about 500 signs, taking them down from my teacher, Carl Wilke, who is himself deaf-and-dumb. They talk of 5000 signs being in common use there, but my list contains the most important. First, as to the signs themselves, the following, taken at random, will give an idea of the general principle on which all are formed.

To express the pronouns "I, thou, he," I push my fore-finger against the pit of my stomach for "I;" push it towards the person addressed for "thou;" point with my thumb over my right shoulder for "he;" and so on.

When I hold my right hand flat with the palm down, at the level of my waist, and raise it towards the level of my shoulder, that signifies "great;" but if I depress it instead, it means "little."

The sign for "man" is the motion of taking off the hat; for "woman," the closed hand is laid upon the breast; for "child," the right elbow is dandled upon the left hand.

The adverb "hither" and the verb "to come" have the same sign, beckoning with the finger toward oneself.

To hold the first two fingers apart, like a letter V, and dart the finger tips out from the eyes, is to "see." To touch the

<hr>

[1] Kruse, 'Ueber Taubstummen,' etc.; Schleswig. 1853, p. 61.

[2] Whether the "dialects" of the different deaf-and-dumb institutions have received any considerable proportion of natural signs from one another, as, for instance, by the spreading of the system of teaching from Paris, I am unable to say; but there is so much in each that differs from the others in detail, though not in principle, that they may, I think, be held as practically independent, except as regards grammatical signs.

ear and tongue with the fore-finger, is to "hear" and to "taste." Whatever is to be pointed out, the fore-finger, so appropriately called "index," has to point out or indicate.

> ". . . atque ipsa videtur
> Protrahere ad gestum pueros infantia linguæ
> Quom facit ut digito quæ sint præsentia monstrent."[1]

To "speak" is to move the lips as in speaking (all the deaf-and-dumb are taught to speak in articulate words in the Berlin establishment), and to move the lips thus, while pointing with the fore-finger out from the mouth, is "name," or "to name," as though one should define it to "point out by speaking."

The outline of the shape of roof and walls done in the air with two hands is "house;" with a flat roof it is "room." To smell as at a flower, and then with the two hands make a horizontal circle before one, is "garden."

To pull up a pinch of flesh from the back of one's hand is "flesh" or "meat." Make the steam curling up from it with the fore-finger, and it becomes "roast meat." Make a bird's bill with two fingers in front of one's lips and flap with the arms, and that means "goose;" put the first sign and these together, and we have "roast goose."

How natural all these imitative signs are. They want no elaborate explanation. To seize the most striking outline of an object, the principal movement of an action, is the whole secret, and this is what the rudest savage can do untaught, nay, what is more, can do better and more easily than the educated man. "None of my teachers here who can speak," said the Director of the Institution, "are very strong in the gesture-language. It is difficult for an educated speaking man to get the proficiency in it which a deaf-and-dumb child attains to almost without an effort. It is true that I can use it perfectly; but I have been here forty years, and I made it my business from the first to become thoroughly master of it. To be able to speak is an impediment, not an assistance, in acquiring the gesture-language. The habit of thinking in words, and translating these words into signs, is most difficult to shake off; but until this is done, it is hardly possible to place the signs in the

[1] Lucretius, v. 1029.

logical sequence in which they arrange themselves in the mind of the deaf-mute."

As new things come under the notice of the deaf-and-dumb, of course new signs immediately come up for them. So to express "railway" and "locomotive," the left hand makes a chimney, and the steam curling almost horizontally out is imitated with the right fore-finger. The tips of the fingers of the half-closed hand coming towards one like rays of light, is "photograph."

But the casual observer, who should take down every sign he saw used in class by masters and pupils, as belonging to the natural gesture-language, would often get a very wrong idea of its nature. Teachers of the deaf-and-dumb have thought it advisable for practical purposes, not merely to use the independent development of the language of signs, but to add to it and patch it so as to make it more strictly equivalent to their own speech and writing. For this purpose signs have to be introduced, for many words of which the pupil mostly learns the meaning through their use in writing, and is taught to use the sign where he would use the word. Thus, the clenched fists, pushed forward with the thumbs up, mean "yet." To throw the fingers gently open from the temple means "when." To move the closed hands with the thumbs out, up and down upon one's waistcoat, is to "be." All these signs may, it is true, be based upon natural gestures. Dr. Scott, for instance, explains the sign "when" as formed in this way. But this kind of derivation does not give them a claim to be included in the pure gesture-language; and it really does not seem as though it would make much difference to the children if the sign for "when" were used for "yet," and so on.

The Abbé Sicard has left us a voluminous account of the sign-language he used, which may serve as an example of the curious hybrid systems which grow up in this way, by the grafting of the English, or French, or German grammar and dictionary on the gesture-language. Sicard was strongly impressed with the necessity of using the natural signs, and even his most arbitrary ones may have been based on such; but he had set himself to make gestures do whatever words can do, and was thereby often driven to strange shifts. Yet he either drew so directly from his deaf-and-dumb scholars, or succeeded so well in learning to think in their way, that it is often very hard to say exactly where the influence of spoken or written language comes in. For instance, the deaf-mute borrows the signs of space, as we do similar words, to express notions of time; and Sicard, keeping to these real signs, and only using them with a degree of analysis which has hardly been attained to but by means of words, makes the present tense of his verb by indicating "here" with the two hands held out, palm downward, the past tense by the hand thrown back over the shoulder, "behind," the future by putting the hand out, "forward." But when he takes on his conjugation to such tenses as "I should have carried," he is merely translating words into more or less appropriate signs. Again, by the aid of two fore-fingers hooked together,—to express, I suppose, the notion of dependence or connection,—he distinguishes between *moi* and *me*, and by translating two abstract grammatical terms from words into signs, he introduces another conception quite foreign to the pure gesture-language. If something that has been signed is a substantive, he puts the right hand under the left, to show that it is that which stands underneath; while if it is an adjective, he puts the right hand on the top, to show that it is the quality which lies upon or is added to the substantive below.[1]

These partly artificial systems are probably very useful in teaching, but they are not the real gesture-language, and what is more, the foreign element so laboriously introduced seems to have little power of holding its ground there. So far as I can learn, few or none of the factitious grammatical signs will bear even the short journey from the schoolroom to the playground, where there is no longer any verb "to be," where the abstract conjunctions are unknown, and where mere position, quality, action, may serve to describe substantive and adjective alike.

At Berlin, as in all deaf-and-dumb institutions, there are numbers of signs which, though most natural in their character, would not be understood beyond the limits of the circle in

[1] Sicard, 'Théorie des Signes pour l'Instruction des Sourds-muets,' Paris, 1808, vol. ii. p. 562, etc. A really possible distinction appears in "lip," "red," *ante*, p. 16.

which they are used. These are signs which indicate an object by some accidental peculiarity, and are rather epithets than names. My deaf-and-dumb teacher, for instance, was named among the children by the action of cutting off the left arm with the edge of the right hand; the reason of this sign was, not that there was anything peculiar about his arms, but that he came from Spandau, and it so happened that one of the children had been at Spandau, and had seen there a man with one arm; thence this epithet of "one-armed" came to be applied to all Spandauers, and to this one in particular. Again, the Royal residence of Charlottenburg was named by taking up one's left knee and nursing it, in allusion apparently to the late king having been laid up with the gout there.

In like manner, the children preferred to indicate foreign countries by some characteristic epithet, to spelling out their names on their fingers. Thus England and Englishmen were aptly alluded to by the action of rowing a boat, while the signs of chopping off a head and strangling were used to describe France and Russia, in allusion to the deaths of Louis XVI. and the Emperor Paul, events which seem to have struck the deaf-and-dumb children as the most remarkable in the history of the two countries. These signs are of much higher interest than the grammatical symbols, which can only be kept in use, so to speak, by main force, but these, too, never penetrate into the general body of the language, and are not even permanent in the place where they arise. They die out from one set of children to another, and new ones come up in their stead.

The gesture-language has no grammar, properly so called; it knows no inflections of any kind, any more than the Chinese. The same sign stands for "walk," "walkest," "walking," "walked," "walker." Adjectives and verbs are not easily distinguished by the deaf-and-dumb; "horse-black-handsome-trot-canter," would be the rough translation of the signs by which a deaf-mute would state that a black handsome horse trots and canters. Indeed, our elaborate systems of "parts of speech" are but little applicable to the gesture-language, though, as will be more fully said in another chapter, it may perhaps be possible to trace in spoken language a Dualism, in some measure resembling that of the gesture-language, with its two constituent parts, the bringing forward objects and actions in actual fact, and the mere suggestion of them by imitation.

It has however a syntax, which is worthy of careful examination. The syntax of speaking man differs according to the language he may learn, "equus niger," "a black horse;" "hominem amo," "j'aime l'homme." But the deaf-mute strings together the signs of the various ideas he wishes to connect, in what appears to be the natural order in which they follow one another in his mind, for it is the same among the mutes of different countries, and is wholly independent of the syntax which may happen to belong to the language of their speaking friends. For instance, their usual construction is not "black horse," but "horse black;" not "bring a black hat," but "hat black bring;" not "I am hungry, give me bread," but "hungry me bread give." The essential independence of the gesture-language may indeed be brought very clearly into view, by noticing that ordinary educated men, when they first begin to learn the language of signs, do not come naturally to the use of its proper syntax, but, by arranging their gestures in the order of the words they think in, make sentences which are unmeaning or misleading to a deaf-mute, unless he can reverse the process, by translating the gestures into words, and considering what such a written sentence would mean. Going once into a deaf-and-dumb school, and setting a boy to write words on the black board, I drew in the air the outline of a tent, and touched the inner part of my under-lip to indicate "red," and the boy wrote accordingly "a red tent." The teacher remarked that I did not seem to be quite a beginner in the sign-language, or I should have translated my English thought *verbatim*, and put the "red" first.

The fundamental principle which regulates the order of the deaf-mute's signs seems to be that enunciated by Schmalz, "that which seems to him the most important he always sets before the rest, and that which seems to him superfluous he leaves out. For instance, to say, 'My father gave me an apple,' he makes the sign for 'apple,' then that for 'father,' and that for 'I,' without adding that for 'give.'[1]   The following remarks, sent to me by Dr. Scott, seem to agree with this view.   "With regard to the two sentences you give (I struck Tom with a stick, Tom struck me with a stick), the sequence in the introduction of the particular parts would, in some measure, depend on the part that most attention was wished to be drawn towards.   If a mere telling of the fact was required, my opinion is that it would be arranged so, 'I-Tom-struck-a-stick,' and the passive form in a similar manner, with the change of Tom first.   But these sentences are not generally said by the deaf-and-dumb without their having been interested in the fact, and then, in coming to tell of them, they first give that part they are most anxious to impress upon their hearer.   Thus if a boy had struck another boy, and the injured party came to tell us; if he was desirous to impress us with the idea that a particular boy did it, he would point to the boy first.   But if he was anxious to draw attention to his own suffering, rather than to the person by whom it was caused, he would point to himself and make the sign of striking, and then point to the boy; or if he was wishful to draw attention to the cause of his suffering, he might sign the striking first, and then tell afterwards by whom it was done."

Dr. Scott is, so far as I know, the only person who has attempted to lay down a set of distinct rules for the syntax of the gesture-language.[2]   "The subject comes before the attribute, ... the object before the action."   A third construction is common, though not necessary, "the modifier after the modified."   The first construction, by which the horse is put before the "black," enables the deaf-mute to make his syntax supply, to some extent, the distinction between adjective and substantive, which his imitative signs do not themselves express. The other two are well exemplified by a remark of the Abbé Sicard's.   "A pupil, to whom I one day put this question, 'Who made God?' and who replied, 'God made nothing,' left me in no doubt as to this kind of inversion, usual to the deaf-and-dumb, when I went on to ask him, 'Who made the shoe?' and he answered, 'The shoe made the shoemaker.'"[3]

[1] Schmalz, p. 274.   [2] Scott, 'The Deaf and Dumb,' p. 63.
[3] Sicard, 'Théorie,' p. xxviii.

So when Laura Bridgman, who was blind as well as deaf-and-dumb, had learnt to communicate ideas by spelling words on her fingers, she would say "Shut door," "Give book;" no doubt because she had learnt these sentences whole, but when she made sentences for herself, she would go back to the natural deaf-and-dumb syntax, and spell out "Laura bread give," to ask for bread to be given her, and "water drink Laura," to express that she wanted to drink water.[1]

It is to be observed that there is one important part of construction which Dr. Scott's rules do not touch, namely, the relative position of the actor and the action, the nominative case and the verb. Dr. Schmalz attempts to lay down a partial rule for this. "If the deaf-mute connects the sign for an action with that for a person, to say that the person did this or that, he places, as a general rule, the sign of the action before that of the person. For example, to say, "I knitted," he moves his hands as in knitting, and then points with his fore-finger to his breast.[2] Thus, too, Heinicke remarks that to say, "The carpenter struck me on the arm," he would strike himself on the arm, and then make the sign of planing,[3] as if to say, "I was struck on the arm, the planing-man did it." But though these constructions are, no doubt, right enough as they stand, the rule of precedence according to importance often reverses them. If the deaf-mute wished to throw the emphasis not upon the knitting, but upon himself, he would probably point to himself first. Kruse gives the construction of "The ship sails on the water" like our own, "ship sail water;" and of "I must go to bed," as "I bed go."[4]

A look of inquiry converts an assertion into a question, and fully serves to make the difference between "The master is come," and "Is the master come?" The interrogative pronouns, "who?" "what?" are made by looking or pointing about in an inquiring manner; in fact, by a number of unsuccessful attempts to say, "he," "that." The deaf-and-dumb child's way of asking, "Who has beaten you?" would be, "You beaten; who was it?" Though it is possible to render

[1] Steinthal, Spr. der T., p. 923.
[2] Schmalz, pp. 274, 58.   [3] Meinicke, p. 56.   [4] Kruse, p. 57.

a great mass of simple statements or questions, almost gesture
for word, the concretism of thought which belongs to the deaf-
mute whose mind has not been much developed by the use of
written language, and even to the educated one when he is
thinking and uttering his thoughts in his native signs, commonly requires more complex phrases to be re-cast. A question so common amongst us as, "What is the matter with
you?" would be put, "You crying? you been beaten?" and so
on. The deaf-and-dumb child does not ask, "What did you
have for dinner yesterday?" but "Did you have soup? did you
have porridge?" and so forth. A conjunctive sentence he expresses by an alternative or contrast; "I should be punished
if I were lazy and naughty," would be put, "I lazy, naughty,
no!—lazy, naughty, I punished, yes!" Obligation may be
expressed in a similar way; "I must love and honour my
teacher," may be put, "teacher, I beat, deceive, scold, no!—I
love, honour, yes!" As Steinthal says in his admirable essay,
it is only the certainty which speech gives to a man's mind in
holding fast ideas in all their relations, which brings him to the
shorter course of expressing only the positive side of the idea,
and dropping the negative.[1]

What is expressed by the genitive case, or a corresponding
preposition, may have a distinct sign of holding in the gesture-
language. The three signs to express "the gardener's knife,"
might be the knife, the garden, and the action of grasping the
knife, pressing it to his breast, putting it into his pocket, or
something of the kind. But the mere putting together of the
possessor and the possessed may answer the purpose, as is well
shown by the way in which a deaf-and-dumb man designates
his wife's daughter's husband and children in making his will
by signs. The following account is taken from the 'Justice of
the Peace,' October 1, 1864 :—

John Gealo, of Yateley, yeoman, deaf, dumb, and unable
to read or write, died leaving a will which he had executed by
putting his mark to it. Probate of this will was refused by
Sir J. P. Wilde, Judge of the Court of Probate, on the ground
that there was no sufficient evidence of the testator's under-

<hr>

[1] Kruse, p. 56, etc. Steinthal, Spr. der T., p. 323.

standing and assenting to its provisions. At a later date,
Dr. Spinks renewed the motion upon the following joint affi-
davit of the widow and the attesting witnesses :—" The signs
by which deceased informed us that the will was the instrument
which was to deal with his property upon his death, and that
his wife was to have all his property after his death in case she
survived him, were in substance, so far as we are able to describe the same in writing, as follows, viz.:—The said John
Geale first pointed to the said will itself, then he pointed to
himself, and then he laid the side of his head upon the palm of
his right hand with his eyes closed, and then lowered his right
hand towards the ground, the palm of the same hand being upwards. These latter signs were the usual signs by which he
referred to his own death or the decease of some one else. He
then touched his trousers pocket (which was the usual sign by
which he referred to his money), then he looked all round
and simultaneously raised his arms with a sweeping motion all
round (which were the usual signs by which he referred to all
his property or all things). He then pointed to his wife, and
afterwards touched the ring-finger of his left hand, and then
placed his right hand across his left arm at the elbow, which
latter signs were the usual signs by which he referred to his
wife. The signs by which the said testator informed us that
his property was to go to his wife's daughter, in case his wife
died in his lifetime, were . . . as follows :—He first referred to his
property as before, he then touched himself, and pointed to
the ring-finger of his left hand, and crossed his arm as before
(which indicated his wife); he then laid the side of his head on
the palm of his right hand (with his eyes closed), which indicated his wife's death ; he then again, after pointing to his
wife's daughter, who was present when the said will was executed, pointed to the ring-finger of his left hand, and then
placed his right hand across his left arm at the elbow as before.
He then put his forefinger to his mouth, and immediately touched
his breast, and moved his arms in such a manner as to indicate
a child, which were his usual signs for indicating his wife's
daughter. He always indicated a female by crossing his arm,
and a male person by crossing his wrist. The signs by which

the said testator informed us that his property was to go to William Wigg (his wife's daughter's husband), in case his wife's daughter died in his lifetime, were ... as follows :—He repeated the signs indicating his property and his wife's daughter, then laid the side of his head on the palm of his right hand with his eyes closed, and lowered his hand towards the ground as before (which meant her death); he then again repeated the signs indicating his wife's daughter, and crossed his left arm at the wrist with his right hand, which meant her husband, the said William Wigg. He also communicated to us by signs, that the said William Wigg resided in London. The said William Wigg is in the employ of and superintends the goods department of the North-Western Railway Company at Camden Town. The signs by which the said testator informed us that his property was to go to the children of his wife's daughter and son-in-law, in case they both died in his lifetime, were ... as follows, namely :—He repeated the signs indicating the said William Wigg and his wife, and their death before him, and then placed his right hand open a short distance from the ground, and raised it by degrees, and as if by steps, which were his usual signs for pointing out their children, and then swept his hand round with a sweeping motion, which indicated that they were all to be brought in. The said testator always took great notice of the said children, and was very fond of them. After the testator had in manner aforesaid expressed to us what he intended to do by his said will, the said R. T. Dunning, by means of the before-mentioned signs, and by other motions and signs by which we were accustomed to converse with him, informed the said testator what were the contents and effect of the said will.

"Sir J. P. Wilde granted the motion."

The deaf-mute commonly expresses past and future time in a concrete form, or by implication. To say "I have been ill," he may convey the idea of his being ill by looking as though he were so, pressing in his cheeks with thumb and finger to give himself a lantern-jawed look, putting his hand to his head, etc., and he may show that this event was "a day behind," "a week behind," that is to say yesterday or a week ago, and so

he may say that he is going home "a week forward." That
he would of himself make the abstract past or future, as the
Abbé Sicard has it, by throwing the hand back or forward, without specifying any particular period, I am not prepared to
say. The difficulty may be avoided by signing "my brother
sick done" for "My brother has been sick," as to imply that
the sickness is a thing finished and done with. Or the expression of face and gesture may often tell what is meant.
The expression with which the sign for eating dinner is made
will tell whether the speaker has had his dinner or is going
to it. When anything pleasant or painful is mentioned by
signs, the look will commonly convey the distinction between
remembrance of what is past, and anticipation of what is to
come.

Though the deaf and dumb has, much as we have, an idea of
the connection of cause and effect, he has not, I think, any direct means of distinguishing causation from mere sequence or
simultaneity, except a way of showing by his manner that two
events belong to one another, which can hardly be described in
words, though if he sees further explanation necessary, he has
no difficulty in giving it. Thus he would express the statement
that a man died of drinking, by saying that he "died, drank,
drank, drank." If the inquiry were made, "died, did he?" he
could put the causation beyond doubt by answering, "yes, he
drank, and drank, and drank!" If he wished to say that the
gardener had poisoned himself, the order of his signs would be,
"gardener dead, medicine bad drank."

To "make" is too abstract an idea for the deaf-mute; to
show that the tailor makes the coat, or that the carpenter
makes the table, he would represent the tailor sewing the coat,
and the carpenter sawing and planing the table. Such a proposition as "Rain makes the land fruitful" would not come into
his way of thinking; "rain fall, plants grow," would be his
pictorial expression.[1]

As an example of the structure of the gesture-language, I
give the words roughly corresponding to the signs by which
the Lord's Prayer is acted every morning at the Edinburgh In-

[1] Steinthal, Spr. der. T., p. 022.

stitution. They were carefully written down for me by the
Director, and I made notes of the signs by which the various
ideas were expressed in this school. "Father" is represented
in the prayer as "man old," though in ordinary matters he is
generally "the man who shaves himself;" "name" is, as I have
seen it elsewhere, touching the forehead and imitating the
action of spelling on the fingers, as to say, "the spelling one is
known by." To "hallow" is to "speak good of" ("good"
being expressed by the thumb, while "bad" is represented by
the little finger, two signs of which the meaning lies in the
contrast of the larger and more powerful thumb with the
smaller and less important little finger). "Kingdom" is shown
by the sign for "crown;" "will," by placing the hand on the
stomach, in accordance with the natural and wide-spread
theory that desire and passion are located there, to which
theory such expressions belong as "to have no stomach to it."
"Done" is "worked," shown by hands as working. The
phrase "on earth as it is in heaven" was, I believe, put by
signs for "on earth" and "in heaven," and then by putting
out the two fore-fingers side by side, the sign for sameness and
similarity all the world over, so that the whole would stand,
"earth on, heaven in, just the same." "Trespass" is "doing
bad;" to "forgive" is to rub out, as from a slate; "temptation" is plucking one by the coat, as to lead him slily into
mischief. The alternative "but" is made with the two fore-
fingers, not alongside of one another as in "like," but opposed
point to point, Sicard's sign for "against." "Deliver" is
to "pluck out," "glory" is "glittering," "for ever" is shown
by making the fore-fingers held horizontally turn round and
round one another.

The order of the signs is much as follows :—"Father our,
heaven in—name thy hallowed—kingdom thy come—will thy
done—earth on, heaven in, as. Bread give us daily—trespasses
our forgive us, them trespass against us, forgive, as. Temptation lead not—but evil deliver from—kingdom power glory
thine for ever."

When I write down descriptions in words of the deaf-and-
dumb signs, they seem bald and weak, but it must be remem-

bered that I can only write down the skeletons of them. To
see them is something very different, for these dry bones have
to be covered with flesh. Not the face only, but the whole
body joins in giving expression to the sign. Nor are the sober,
restrained looks and gestures to which we are accustomed in
our daily life sufficient for this. He who talks to the deaf-and-
dumb in their own language, must throw off the rigid covering
that the Englishman wears over his face like a tragic mask,
that never changes its expression while love and hate, joy and
sorrow, come out from behind it.

Religious service is performed in signs in many deaf-and-
dumb schools. In the Berlin Institution, the simple Lutheran
service, a prayer, the gospel for the day, and a sermon, is acted
every Sunday morning in the gesture-language for the children
in the school and the deaf-and-dumb inhabitants of the city,
and it is a very remarkable sight. No one could see the
parable of the man who left the ninety and nine sheep in the
wilderness, and went after that which was lost, or of the woman who lost the one piece of silver, performed in expressive
pantomime by a master in the art, without acknowledging that
for telling a simple story and making simple comments on it,
spoken language stands far behind acting. The spoken narrative must lose the sudden anxiety of the shepherd when he
counts his flock and finds a sheep wanting, his hurried penning
up the rest, his running up hill and down dale, and spying
backwards and forwards, his face lighting up when he catches
sight of the missing sheep in the distance, his carrying it home
in his arms, hugging it as he goes. We hear these stories
read as though they were lists of generations of antediluvian
patriarchs. The deaf-and-dumb pantomime calls to mind the
"action, action, action!" of Demosthenes.

CHAPTER III.

THE GESTURE-LANGUAGE—(CONTINUED).

THERE is another department of the gesture-language which
has reached nearly as high a development as that in use among
the deaf-mutes. Men who do not know one another's language
are to each other as though they were dumb. Thus Sophocles
uses ἄγλωσσος, "tongueless," for "barbarian," as contrasted
with "Greek;" and the Russians, to this day, call their neighbours the Germans, "Njemez,"—that is, speechless, njemoy
meaning dumb. When men who are thus dumb to one
another have to communicate without an interpreter, they
adopt all over the world the very same method of communication by signs, which is the natural language of the deaf-
mutes.

Alexander von Humboldt has left on record, in the following
passage, his experiences of the gesture-language among the
Indians of the Orinoco, in districts where it often happens that
small, isolated tribes speak languages of which even their nearest neighbours can hardly understand a word:—"'After you
leave my mission,' said the good monk of Uruana, 'you will
travel like mutes.' This prediction was almost accomplished;
and, not to lose all the advantage that is to be had from intercourse even with the most brutalized Indians, we have sometimes preferred the language of signs. As soon as the native
sees that you do not care to employ an interpreter, as soon as
you ask him direct questions, pointing the object out to him,

he comes out of his habitual apathy, and displays a rare intelligence in making himself understood. He varies his signs, pronounces his words slowly, and repeats them without being asked. His *amour-propre* seems flattered by the consequence you accord to him by letting him instruct you. This facility of making himself understood is above all remarkable in the independent Indian, and in the Christian missions I should recommend the traveller to address himself in preference to those of the natives who have been but lately *reduced*, or who go back from time to time to the forest to enjoy their ancient liberty."[1]

It is well known that the Indians of North America, whose nomade habits and immense variety of languages must continually make it needful for them to communicate with tribes whose language they cannot speak, carry the gesture-language to a high degree of perfection, and the same signs serve as a medium of converse from Hudson's Bay to the Gulf of Mexico. Several writers make mention of this "Indian pantomime," and it has been carefully described in the account of Major Long's expedition, and more recently by Captain Burton.[2] The latter traveller considers it to be a mixture of natural and conventional signs, but so far as I can judge from the one hundred and fifty or so which he describes, and those I find mentioned elsewhere, I do not believe that there is a really arbitrary sign among them. There are only about half-a-dozen of which the meaning is not at once evident, and even these appear on close inspection to be natural signs, perhaps a little abbreviated or conventionalized. I am sure that a skilled deaf-and-dumb talker would understand an Indian interpreter, and be himself understood at first sight, with scarcely any difficulty. The Indian pantomime and the gesture-language of the deaf-and-dumb are but different dialects of the same language of nature. Burton says that an interpreter who knows all the signs is preferred by the whites even to a good speaker. "A story is

<hr>

[1] Humboldt and Boupland, 'Voyage;' Paris, 1814, etc. vol. ii. p. 278.

[2] Edwin James, Major Stephen H. Long's Exped. Rocky Moun.; Philadelphia, 1823, i. p. 378, etc. Capt. R. F. Burton, 'The City of the Saints,' London, 1861, p. 160, etc. See also Prince Maximilian von Wied-Neuwied, ' Voyage dans l'Intérieur de l'Amérique du Nord;' Paris, 1840-3, vol. iii. p. 359, etc.

told of a man, who, being sent among the Cheyennes to qualify himself for interpreting, returned in a week and proved his competence: all that he did, however, was to go through the usual pantomime with a running accompaniment of grunts."

In the Indian pantomime, actions and objects are expressed very much as a deaf-mute would show them. The action of beckoning towards oneself represents to "come;" darting the two first fingers from the eyes is to "see;" describing in the air the form of the pipe and the curling smoke is to "smoke;" thrusting the hand under the clothing of the left breast is to "hide, put away, keep secret." "Enough to eat" is shown by an imitation of eating, and the forefingers and thumb forming a C, with the points towards the body, are raised upward as far as the neck; "fear," by putting the hands to the lower ribs, and showing how the heart flutters and seems to rise to the throat; "book," by holding the palms together before the face, opening and reading, quite in deaf-and-dumb fashion, and as the Moslems often do while they are reciting prayers and chapters of the Koran.

One of our accounts says that "fire" is represented by the Indian by blowing it and warming his hands at it; the other that flames are imitated with the fingers. The latter sign was in use at Berlin, but I noticed that the children in another school did not understand it till the sign of blowing was added. The Indian and the deaf-mute indicate "rain" by the same sign, bringing the tips of the fingers of the partly-closed hand downward, like rain falling from the clouds, and the Indian makes the same sign do duty for "year," counting years by annual rains. The Indian indicates "stone," if light, by picking it up, if heavy, by dropping it. The deaf-mute taps his teeth with his finger-nail to show that it is something hard, and then makes the gesture of flinging it. The Indian sign for mounting a horse is to make a pair of legs of the two first fingers of the right hand, and to straddle them across the left fore-finger; a similar sign among the deaf-and-dumb means to "ride."

Among the Indians the sign for "brother" or "sister" is, according to Burton, to put the two first finger-tips (that is, I suppose, the fore-fingers of both hands) into the mouth, to show that both fed from the same breast; the deaf-mute makes the mere sign of likeness or equality suffice, holding out the fore-fingers, of both hands close together, a sign which, according to James, also does duty to indicate "husband" or "companion." This sign of the two fore-fingers is understood everywhere, and some very curious instances of its use in remote parts of the world are given by Marsh[1] in illustration of Fluellen's "But 'tis all one, 'tis so like as my fingers is to my fingers." It belongs, too, to the sign-language of the Cistercian monks.

Animals are represented in the Indian pantomime very much as the deaf-and-dumb would represent them, by signs characterizing their peculiar ears, horns, etc., and their movements. Thus the sign for "stag" among the deaf-and-dumb, namely, the thumbs to both temples, and the fingers widely spread out, is almost identical with the Indian gesture. For the dog, however, the Indians have a remarkable sign, which consists in trailing the two first fingers of the right hand, as if they were poles dragged along the ground. Before the Indians had horses, the dogs were trained to drag the lodge-poles on the march in this way, and in Catlin's time the work was in several tribes divided between the dogs and the horses; but it appears that in tribes where the trailing is now done by horses only, the sign for "dog" derived from the old custom is still kept up.

One of the Indian signs is curious as having reflected itself in the spoken language of the country. "Water" is represented by an imitation of scooping up water with the hand and drinking out of it, and "river" by making this sign, and then waving the palms of the hands outward, to denote an extended surface. It is evident that the first part of the sign is translated in the western Americanism which speaks of a river as a "drink," and of the Mississippi, *par excellence*, as the "Big Drink."[2] It need hardly be said that spoken language is full of such translations from gestures, as when one is said to wink at another's faults, an expression which shows us the act of

<hr>

[1] Marsh, 'Lectures on the English Language;' London, 1862, p. 486.

[2] J. R. Bartlett, 'Dictionary of Americanisms,' 2nd edit., Boston, 1859, s. v. "Drink."

winking accepted as a gesture-sign, meaning to pretend not to see. But the Americanism is interesting as being caught so near its source.

I noted down a few signs from Burton as not self-evident, but it will be seen that they are all to be explained. They are, "yes," wave the hands straight forward from the face; "no," wave the hand from right to left as if motioning away. Those signs correspond with the general practice of mankind, to nod for "yes," and shake the head for "no." The idea conveyed by nodding seems to correspond with the deaf-and-dumb sign for "truth," made by moving the finger straightforward from the lips, apparently with the sense of "straightforward speaking," while the finger is moved to one side to express "lie," as "sideways speaking." The understanding of nodding and shaking the head as signs of assent and denial appears to belong to uneducated deaf-and-dumb children, and even to those who are only one degree higher than idiots. In a very remarkable dissertation on the art of thrusting knowledge into the minds of such children, Schmalz assumes that they can always make and understand these signs.[1] It is true they may have learnt them from the people who take care of them.

This explanation is, however, somewhat complicated by the Indian signs for "truth" and "lie," given by Burton, who says that the fore-finger extended from the mouth means to "tell truth," "one word;" but two fingers mean to tell lies," "double tongue." So to move two fingers before the left breast means, "I don't know," that is to say, "I have two hearts." I found that deaf-and-dumb children understood this Indian sign for "lie" quite as well as their own.

"Good," wave the hand from the mouth, extending the thumb from the index, and closing the other three fingers. This is like kissing the hand as a salutation, or what children call "blowing a kiss," and it is clearly a natural sign, as it is recognized by the deaf-and-dumb language. Dr. James gives the Indian sign as waving the hand with the back upward, in a horizontal curve outwards, the well-known gesture of benediction. At Berlin, a gesture like that of patting a child on

<hr>

[1] Schmalz, pp. 267-277. But see Bastian, vol. i. p. 835.

the head, accompanied, as of course all these signs are, with
an approving smile, is in use. Possibly the ideas of stroking
or patting may lie at the bottom of all these signs of approving
and blessing.

"Think," pass the fore-finger sharply across the breast from
right to left, meaning of course that a thought passes through
one's heart.

"Trade, exchange, swop," cross the fore-fingers of both hands
before the breast. This sign is also used, Captain Burton says,
to denote Americans, or indeed any white men, who are generally called by the Indians west of the Rocky Mountains,
"shwop," from their trading propensities. As given by Burton,
the sign is hardly intelligible. But Dr. James describes the
gesture of which this is a sort of abridgement, which consists
in holding up the two fore-fingers, and passing them by each
other transversely in front of the breast so that they change
places, and nothing could be clearer than this.

The sign in the Berlin gesture-language for "day" is made
by opening out the palms of the hands. I supposed it to be
an arbitrary and meaningless sign, till I found the Indian sign
for "this morning" to consist in the same gesture. It refers,
perhaps, to awaking from sleep, or to the opening out of
the day.

As a means of communication, there is no doubt that the
Indian pantomime is not merely capable of expressing a few
simple and ordinary notions, but that, to the uncultured savage,
with his few and material ideas, it is a very fair substitute for
his scanty vocabulary. Stansbury mentions a discourse delivered in this way in his presence, which lasted for some hours
occupied in continuous narration. The only specimen of a
connected story I have met with is a hunter's simple history
of his day's sport, as Captain Burton thinks that an Indian
would render it in signs. The story to be told is as follows:—
"Early this morning, I mounted my horse, rode off at a gallop,
traversed a kanyon or ravine, then over a mountain to a plain
where there was no water, sighted bison, followed them, killed
three of them, skinned them, packed the flesh upon my pony,
remounted, and returned home." The arrangement of the

signs described is as follows:—"I—this morning—early—mounted my horse—galloped—a kanyon—crossed—a mountain—a plain—drink—no!—sighted—bison—killed—three—skinned—packed flesh—mounted—hither." There is perhaps nothing which would strike a deaf-and-dumb man as peculiar in the sequence of these signs; but it would be desirable for a real discourse, delivered by an Indian in signs, to be taken down, especially if its contents were of a more complex nature.

Among the Cistercian monks there exists, or existed, a gesture-language. As a part of their dismal system of mortifying the deeds of the body, they held speech, except in religious exercises, to be sinful. But for certain purposes relating to the vile material life that they could not quite shake off, communication among the brethren was necessary, so the difficulty was met by the use of pantomimic signs. Two of their written lists or dictionaries are printed in the collected edition of Leibnitz's works,[1] one in Latin, the other in Low German; they are not identical, but appear to be mostly or altogether derived from a list drawn up by authority.

A great part of the Cistercian gesture-signs are either just what the deaf-and-dumb would make, or are so natural that they would at once understand them. Thus, to make a roof with the fingers is "house;" to grind the flats together is "corn;" to "sing" is indicated by beating time; to "bathe" is to imitate washing the breast with the hollow of the hand; "candle," or "fire," is shown by holding up the fore-finger and blowing it out like a candle; a "goat" is indicated by the fingers hanging from the chin like a beard; "salt," by taking an imaginary pinch and sprinkling it; "butter," by the action of spreading it in the palm of the hand. The deaf-and-dumb sign used at Berlin and other places to indicate "time" by drawing the tip of the forefinger up the arm, is in the Cistercian list "a year;" it is Sicard's sign for "long," and the idea it conveys is plainly that of "a length" transferred from space to time. To "go" is to make the two first fingers walk hanging in the air (Hengestu se dahl and rörest se,

<hr>

[1] Leibnitz, Opera Omnia, ed. Dutens; Geneva, 1768, vol. vi. part ii., p. 207, etc.

betekend *Gahen*), while the universal sign of the two fore-fingers stands for "like" (Hölstu so even thosamen, dat betekent *like*). The sign for "beer" is to put the hand before the face and blow into it, as if blowing off the froth (Thustu do hand vor dem anschlabo dat du darin pustest, dat bedüdt *yut Bier*). Wiping your mouth with the whole hand upwards (cum omnibus digitis tergo buccam sursum), means a country clown (rusticus).

To put the fore-finger against the closed lips is "silence," but the finger put in the mouth means a "child." These are two very natural and distinct signs; but then the finger to the lips for "silence" may serve also quite fitly to show that a child so represented is an *infant*, that is, that it cannot speak. The confusion of the signs of "childhood" and "silence" once led to a curious misunderstanding. The infant Horus, god of the dawn, was appropriately represented by the Egyptians as a child with his fingers to his lips, and his name as written in the hieroglyphics (Fig. 1) may be read Har-(p)-chrot, "Horus-(the)-son."[1] The Greeks mistook the meaning of the gesture, and (as it seems) Græcizing this name into Harpocrates, adopted him as the god of silence.

Fig. 1.

To conclude, the Cistercian lists contain a number of signs which at first sight seem conventional, but yet a meaning may be discerned in most or all of them. Thus, it seems foolish to make two fingers at the right side of one's nose stand for "friend;" but when we see that placed on the left side, they stand for "enemy," it becomes clear that it is the opposition of right and left that is meant. So the little finger to the tip of the nose means "fool," which seemingly poor sign is explained by the fore-finger being put there for "wise man." The fact of such a contrast as wise and foolish being made between the fore-finger and the little finger, corresponds with the use of the thumb and little finger for "good" and "bad" by the deaf-and-dumb, and makes it likely that both pairs of signs

[1] Coptic *khroti* (ni) = filii, liberi, *krati* = cognatus, filius. Old Eg. in Rosetta Ins. Compare S. Sharpe, Hist. of Egypt, 4th ed. vol. ii. p. 148. Wilkinson, 'Popular Account of the Ancient Egyptians;' London, 1854, vol. ii. p. 182.

may be natural, and independent of one another. The sign of grasping the nose with the crooked fore-finger for "wine," suggests that the thought of a jolly red nose was present even in so unlikely a place. The sign for "the devil," gripping one's chin with all five fingers, shows the enemy seizing a victim, and compares curiously with a passage in an Indian tale, where it is not an evil demon, but Old Age in person, who comes to claim his own. "In time then, when I had grown grey with years, Old Age took me by the chin, and in his love to me said kindly, 'My son, what doest thou yet in the house?'"[1]

There is yet another development of the gesture-language to be noticed, the stage performances of the professional mimics of Greece and Rome, the Pantomime *par excellence*. To judge by two well-known anecdotes, the old mimes had brought their art to great perfection. Macrobius says it was a well-known fact that Cicero used to try with Roscius the actor which of them could express a sentiment in the greater variety of ways, the player by mimicry or the orator by speech, and that these experiments gave Roscius such confidence in his art, that he wrote a book comparing oratory with acting.[2] Lucian tells a story of a certain barbarian prince of Pontus, who was at Nero's court, and saw a pantomime perform so well, that, though he could not understand the songs which the player was accompanying with his gestures, he could follow the performance from the acting alone. When Nero afterwards asked the prince to choose what he would have for a present, he begged to have the player given to him, saying that it was difficult to get interpreters to communicate with some of the tribes in his neighbourhood who spoke different languages, but that this man would answer the purpose perfectly.[3]

It would seem from these stories that the ancient pantomimes generally used gestures so natural that their meaning was self-evident, but a remark of St. Augustine's intimates that

[1] 'Mährchensammlung des Somadeva Bhatta' (trans. by Dr. H. Brockhaus); Leipzig, 1843, ii. p. 96.
[2] Macrob. Saturn. lib. ii. c. x.   [3] Lucian. De Saltatione, 64.

signs understood only by regular playgoers were also used.
"For all those things which are valid among men, because it
pleases them to agree that they shall be so, are human institutions. . . . So if the signs which mimes make in their performances had their meaning from nature, and not from the
agreement and ordinance of men, the crier in old times would
not have given out to the Carthaginians at the play what
the actor meant to express, a thing still remembered by many
old men by whom we use to hear it said; which is readily
to be believed, seeing that even now, if any one who is not
learned in such follies goes into the theatre, unless some one
else tells him what the signs mean, he can make nothing of
them. All men, indeed, desire a certain likeness in sign-making,
that the signs should be as like as may be to that which is
signified; but seeing that things may be like one another in
many ways, such signs are not constant among men, unless
by common consent."[1]

Knowing what we do of mimic performances from other
sources, we can, I think, only understand by this that natural
gestures were very commonly conventionalized and abridged
to save time and trouble, and not that arbitrary signs were
used; and such abridgments, like the simplified sign for
trading or swopping among the Indians, as well as the whole
class of epithets and allusions which would grow up among
mimics addressing their regular set of playgoers, would not
be intelligible to a stranger. Christians, of course, did not
frequent such performances in St. Augustine's time, but looked
upon them as utterly abominable and devilish; nor can we
accuse them of want of charity for this, when we consider the
class of scenes that were commonly chosen for representation.

There seem to have been written lists of signs used to learn
from, which are now lost.[2] The mimic, it should be observed,
had not the same difficulties to contend with as an Indian interpreter. In the first place, the stories represented were
generally mythological, very usually love-passages of the gods
and heroes, with which the whole audience was perfectly fami-

<hr>

[1] Aug. Doct. Chr. ii 25.
[2] Grysar, in Ersch and Gruber, art. " Pantomimische Kunst der Alten."

liar; and, moreover, appropriate words were commonly sung
while the mimic acted, so that he could apply all his skill to
giving artistic illustrations of the tale as it went on. The pantomimic performances of Southern Europe may be taken as
representing in some degree the ancient art, but it is likely
that the mimicry in the modern ballet and the Eastern pantomimic plays falls much below the classical standard of
excellence.

I have now noticed what I venture to call the principal
dialects of the gesture-language. It is fit, however, that,
gesture-signs having been spoken of as forming a complete
and independent language by themselves, something should
be said of their use as an accompaniment to spoken language.
We in England make comparatively little use of these signs,
but they have been and are in use in all quarters of the world
as highly important aids to conversation. Thus, Captain Cook
says of the Tahitians, after mentioning their habit of counting
upon their fingers, that "in other instances, we observed that,
when they were conversing with each other, they joined signs
to their words, which were so expressive that a stranger might
easily apprehend their meaning;"[1] and Charlevoix describes,
in almost the same words, the expressive pantomime with
which an Indian orator accompanied his discourse.[2]

Gesticulation goes along with speech, to explain and em-
phasize it, among all mankind. Savage and half-civilized
races accompany their talk with expressive pantomime much
more than nations of higher culture. The continual gesticulation of Hindoos, Arabs, Neapolitans, as contrasted with the
more northern nations of Europe, strikes every traveller who
sees them. But we cannot lay down a rule that gesticulation
decreases as civilization advances, and say, for instance, that a
Southern Frenchman, because his talk is illustrated with gestures, as a book with pictures, is less civilized than a German
or an Englishman.

We English are perhaps poorer in the gesture-language than
any other people in the world. We use a form of words to

---

[1] Cook, First Voyage, in Hawkesworth's Voyages; London, 1773, vol. ii. p. 225.
[2] Charlevoix, vol. i. p. 113.

denote what a gesture or a tone would express. Perhaps it is because we read and write so much, and have come to think and talk as we should write, and so let fall those aids to speech which cannot be carried into the written language.

The few gesture-signs which are in common use among ourselves are by no means unworthy of examination; but we have lived for so many centuries in a highly artificial state of society, that some of them cannot be interpreted with any certainty, and the most that we can do is to make a good guess at their original meaning. Some, it is true, such as beckoning or motioning away with the hand, shaking the fist, etc., carry their explanation with them; and others may be plausibly explained by a comparison with analogous signs used by speaking men in other parts of the world, and by the deaf-and-dumb. Thus, the sign of "snapping one's fingers" is not very intelligible as we generally see it; but when we notice that the same sign made quite gently, as if rolling some tiny object away between the finger and thumb, or the sign of flipping it away with the thumb-nail and fore-finger, are usual and well-understood deaf-and-dumb gestures, denoting anything tiny, insignificant, contemptible, it seems as though we had exaggerated and conventionalized a perfectly natural action so as to lose sight of its original meaning. There is a curious mention of this gesture by Strabo. At Anchiale, he writes, Aristobulus says there is a monument to Sardanapalus, and a stone statue of him as if snapping his fingers, and this inscription in Assyrian letters:— "Sardanapallus, the son of Anacyndaraxes, built in one day Anchiale and Tarsus. Eat, drink, play; the rest is not worth that!"[1]

Shaking hands is not a custom which belongs naturally to all mankind, and we may sometimes trace its introduction into countries where it was before unknown. The Fijians, for instance, who used to salute by smelling or sniffing at one another, have learnt to shake hands from the missionaries.[2] The Wa-nika, near Mombas, grasp hands; but they use the

[1] Strabo, xiv. 5, 9.
[2] Rev. Thos. Williams, 'Fiji and the Fijians,' 2nd ed.; London, 1860, vol. i. p. 153.

Moslem variety of the gesture, which is to press the thumbs against one another as well,[1] and this makes it all but certain that the practice is one of the many effects of Moslem influence in East Africa.

It is commonly thought that the Red Indians adopted the custom of shaking hands from the white men.[2] This may be true; but there is reason to suppose that the expression of alliance or friendship by clasping hands was already familiar to them, so that they would readily adopt it as a form of salutation, if they had not used it so before the arrival of the Europeans. More than a century ago, Charlevoix noticed in the Indian picture-writing the expression of alliance by the figure of two men holding each other by one hand, while each grasped a calumet in the other hand.[3] In one of the Indian pictures given by Schoolcraft, close affection is represented by two bodies united by a single arm (see Fig. 6); and in a pictorial message sent from an Indian tribe to the President of the United States, an eagle, which represents a chief, is holding out a hand to the President, who also holds out a hand.[4] The last of these pictured signs may be perhaps ascribed to European influence, but hardly the first two.

We could scarcely find a better illustration of the meaning of the gesture of joining hands than in its use as a sign of the marriage contract. One of the ceremonies of a Moslem wedding consists in the bridegroom and the bride's proxy sitting upon the ground, face to face, with one knee on the ground, and grasping each other's right hands, raising the thumbs and pressing them against each other,[5] or in the almost identical ceremony in the Pacific Islands, in which the bride and bridegroom are placed on a large white cloth, spread on the pavement of a marae, and join hands.[6] This as evidently means that

[1] Krapf, 'Travels, etc., in East Africa;' London, 1860, p. 138.

[2] H. R. Schoolcraft, 'Historical and Statistical Information respecting the History, etc., of the Indian Tribes of the U. S.;' Philadelphia, 1851, etc., part iii. pp. 213, 214. Burton, 'City of the Saints,' p. 144. But see also Schoolcraft, part iii. p. 203.

[3] Charlevoix, vol. v. p. 410.   [4] Schoolcraft, part i. pp. 403, 418.

[5] E. W. Lane, 'Modern Egyptians;' London, 1837, vol. i. p. 218.

[6] Rev. W. Ellis, 'Polynesian Researches;' London, 1830, vol. ii. p. 569.

the man and wife are joined together, as the corresponding
ceremony in the ancient Mexican and the modern Hindoo
wedding, in which the clothes of the parties are tied together
in a knot. Among our own Aryan race, the taking hands was
a usual ceremony in marriage in the Vedic period.[1] The idea
which shaking hands was originally intended to convey, was
clearly that of fastening together in peace and friendship; and
the same thought appears in the probable etymology of *peace,
pax,* Sanskrit *paç,* to bind, and in *league* from *ligare.*

Cowering or crouching is so natural an expression of fear or
inability to resist, that it belongs to the brutes as well as to
man. Among ourselves this natural sign of submission is
generally used in the modified forms of bowing and kneeling;
but the analogous gestures found in different countries not
only give us the intermediate stages between an actual prostration and a slight bow, but also a set of gestures and ceremonies which are merely suggestive of a prostration which is
not actually performed. The extreme act of lying with the
face in the dust is not only usual in China, Siam, etc., but
even in Siberia the peasant grovels on the ground and kisses
the dust before a man of rank. The Arab only suggests such
a humiliation by bending his hand to the ground and then
putting it to his lips and forehead,—a gesture almost identical
with that of the ancient Mexican, who touched the ground with
his right hand and put it to his mouth.[2] Captain Cook describes the way of doing reverence to chiefs in the Tonga Islands, which was in this wise:—When a subject approached to
do homage, the chief had to hold up his foot behind, as a horse
does, and the subject touched the sole with his fingers, thus
placing himself, as it were, under the sole of his lord's foot.
Every one seemed to have the right of doing reverence in this
way when he pleased; and chiefs got so tired of holding up
their feet to be touched, that they would make their escape at
the very sight of a loyal subject.[3] Other developments of the
idea are found in the objection made to a Polynesian chief

[1] Ad. Pictet, 'Origines Indo-Européennes,' Paris, 1859–63, part ii. p. 336.
[2] A. v. Humboldt, 'Vues des Cordillères,' Paris, 1810, p. 83.
[3] Cook, Third Voyage, 2nd ed.; London, 1785, vol. i. pp. 257, 409.

going down into the ship's cabin,[1] and to images of Buddha
being kept there[2] in Siam, namely, that they were insulted by
the sailors walking over their heads, and in the custom, also
among the Tongans, of sitting down when a chief passed.[3]
The ancient Egyptian may be seen in the sculptures abbreviat-
ing the gesture of touching the ground by merely putting one
hand down to his knee in bowing before a superior. A slight
inclination of the body indicates submission or reverence, and
becomes at last a mere act of politeness, not involving any
sense of inferiority at all. This is brought about by that
common habit of civilized man, of pretending to a humility
that he does not feel, which leads the Chinese to allude to
himself in conversation as "the blockhead" or "the thief,"
and makes our own high official personages write themselves,
Sir, your most obedient humble servant, to persons whom they
really consider their inferiors.

With regard to the position of the hands in prayer, there
seems to have been a confusion of two gestures quite distinct
in their origin. The upturned hands seem to expect some de-
sired object to be thrown down, while when clasped or set together they seem to ward off an impending blow. It is not
unnatural that mercy or protection should be looked upon as a
gift, and that the rustic Phidyle should hold out her supine
hands to ask that her vines should *not* feel the pestilent south-
west wind; but the conventionalizing process is carried much
further when the hands clasped or with the finger-tips set together can be used, not only to avert an injury, as seems their
natural office, but also to ask for a benefit which they cannot
even catch hold of when it comes.

It is easy enough to give a plausible reason for the custom
of taking off the hat as an expression of reverence or politeness, by referring it to times when armour was generally worn.
To take off the helmet would be equivalent to disarming, and
would indicate, in the most practical manner, either submission
or peace. The practice of laying aside arms on entering a
house appears in a quotation from the 'Boke of Curtayse,'

[1] Cook, Third Voyage, vol. I. p. 265.
[2] Sir J. Bowring, 'Siam,' London, 1857, vol. i. p. 125.   [3] Cook, ib. p. 400.

which shows that in the middle ages visitors were expected to
leave their weapons with the porter at the outer gate, and when
they came to the hall door to take off hoods and gloves.

> " When thou come the hall dor to,
> Do of thy hode, thy gloves also."[1]

That women are not required to uncover their heads in church
or on a visit, is quite consistent with such an origin of the
custom, as their head-dresses were not armour; and the same
consistency may be observed in the practice of ladies keeping
the glove on in shaking hands, while men very commonly remove it. When a knight's glove was a steel gauntlet, such a
distinction would be reasonable enough.

This may indeed be fanciful. The practice of women having
the head covered in church belongs to the earliest period of
Christianity, and the reasons for adopting it were clearly speci-
fied. And the usage of men praying with the head uncovered,
may have been an intentional reversal of the practice of covering the head in offering sacrifice among the Romans, and by
the Jews in their prayers then and now. It does not seem to
have been universal, and is even now not followed in the Coptic and Abyssinian churches, in which the Semitic custom of
uncovering not the head but the feet is still kept up. This
latter ceremony is of high antiquity, and may be plausibly explained as having been done at first merely for cleanliness, as
it is now among the Moslems in their baths and houses, as
well as in their mosques, that the ground may not be defiled.

There are, moreover, a number of practices found in different
parts of the world, which throw doubt on these off-hand explanations of the customs of uncovering the head and feet, and
would almost lead us to include both, as particular cases of a
general class of reverential uncoverings of the body. Saul
strips off his clothes to prophesy, and lies down so all that day
and night.[2] Tertullian speaks against the practice of praying with cloaks laid aside, as the heathen do.[3] There was a
well-known custom in Tahiti, of uncovering the body down to
the waist in honour of gods or chiefs, and even in the neigh-

---

[1] Wright, 'History of Domestic Manners,' etc.; London, 1862, p. 141.
[2] 1 Sam. xix. 24.　　　[3] Tert., De Orationo, xii.

E

bourhood of a temple, and on the sacred ground set apart for
royalty, with which may be classed a very odd ceremony,
which was performed before Captain Cook on his first visit to
the island.[1]

The regulations concerning the *foro* or turban in the Tonga
Islands are very curious, from their partial resemblance to
European usages. The turban, Mariner says, may only be
worn by warriors going to battle, or at sham fights, or at
night-time by chiefs and nobles, or by the common people
when at work in the fields or in canoes. On all other occasions, to wear a head-dress would be disrespectful, for although
no chief should be present, some god might be at hand unseen.
If a man were to wear a turban except on those occasions, the
first person of superior rank who met him would knock him
down, and perhaps even an equal might do it. Even when
the turban is allowed to be worn, it must be taken off when a
superior approaches, unless in actual battle, but a man who is
not much higher in rank will say, "Toogo ho fow," that is,
Keep on your turban.[2]

During the administration of the ordeal by poison in Madagascar, Ellis says that no one is allowed to sit on his long
robe, nor to wear the cloth round the waist, and females must
keep their shoulders uncovered.[3] A remarkable statement is
made by Ibn Batuta, in his account of his journey into the
Soudan, in the fourteenth century. He mentions as an evil
thing which he has observed in the conduct of the blacks, that
women may only come unclothed into the presence of the Sultan of Melli, and even the Sultan's own daughters must conform to the custom. He notices also, that they throw dust
and ashes on their heads as a sign of reverence,[4] which makes
it appear that the stripping was also a mere act of humiliation.
With regard to the practice of uncovering the feet, when we

[1] Cook, First Voy. II., vol. ii. pp. 125, 163. Ellis, Polyn. Res., vol. ii. pp.
171, 352-3.
[2] Mariner, 'Tonga Islands;' vol. i. p. 158.
[3] Rev. W. Ellis, Hist. of Madagascar; London, 1838, vol. I. p. 461.
[4] Ibn Batuta, in 'Journal Asiatique,' 4me Série, vol. I. p. 221. Waitz, Introd.
to Anthropology, E. Tr. ed. by J. F. Collingwood; part i., London, 1863, p. 301.

find the Damaras, in South Africa, taking off their sandals before entering a stranger's house,[1] the idea of connecting the practice with the ancient Egyptian custom, or of ascribing it to Moslem influence, at once suggests itself, but the taking off the sandals as a sign of respect seems to have prevailed in Peru. No common Indian, it is said, dared go shod along the Street of the Sun, nor might any one, however great a lord he might be, enter the houses of the sun with shoes on, and even the Inca himself went barefoot into the Temple of the Sun.[2]

In this group of reverential uncoverings, the idea that the subject presents himself naked, defenceless, poor, and miserable before his lord, seems to be dramatically expressed, and this view is borne out by the practice of stripping, or uncovering the head and foot, as a sign of mourning,[3] where there can hardly be anything but destitution and misery to be expressed.

The lowest class of salutations, which merely aim at giving pleasant bodily sensations, merge into the civilities which we see exchanged among the lower animals. Such are patting, stroking, kissing, pressing noses, blowing, sniffing, and so forth. The often described sign of pleasure or greeting of the Indians of North America, by rubbing each other's arms, breasts, and stomachs, and their own,[4] is similar to the Central African custom, of two men clasping each other's arms with both hands, and rubbing them up and down,[5] and that of stroking one's own face with another's hand or foot, in Polynesia;[6] and the pattings and slappings of the Fuegians belong to the same class. Darwin describes the way in which noses are pressed in New Zealand, with details which have escaped less accurate observers.[7] It is curious that Linnæus found the salutation by touching noses in the Lapland Alps. People did

<hr>

[1] C. J. Andersson, 'Lake Ngami,' etc., 2nd ed.; London, 1856, p. 231.

[2] Prescott, History of the Conquest of Peru, 2nd ed.; London, 1847, vol. l. pp. 57, 78.

[3] Micah i. 8. Ezekiel xxiv. 17. Herod. ii. 85. Rev. J. Roberts, 'Oriental Illustrations of the Sacred Scriptures,' 2nd ed.; London, 1844, p. 492, etc.

[4] Charlevoix, vol. iii. p. 16; vol. vi. p. 189, etc.

[5] Burton, 'Lake Regions of Central Africa;' London, 1860, vol. ii. p. 69.

[6] Cook, Third Voy., vol. i. p. 176.

[7] Darwin, Journal of Res., etc.; London, 1860, pp. 205, 422.

not kiss, but put noses together.[1]   The Andaman Islanders salute by blowing into another's hand with a cooing murmur.[2] Charlevoix speaks of an Indian tribe on the Gulf of Mexico, who blow into one another's ears;[3] and Du Chaillu describes himself as having been blown upon in Africa.[4]   Natural expressions of joy, such as clapping hands in Africa,[5] and jumping up and down in Tierra del Fuego,[6] are made to do duty as signs of friendship or greeting.

There are a number of well-known gestures which are hard to explain.   Such are various signs of hatred and contempt, such as lolling out the tongue, which is a universal sign, though it is not clear why it should be so, biting the thumb, making the sign of the stork's bill behind another's back (*ciconiam facere*), and the sign known as "taking a sight," which was as common at the time of Rabelais as it is now.

In modern India, as in ancient Rome, only a part of the signs we find described are such as can be set down at once to their proper origin.[7]   One of the common gestures in India, especially, has puzzled many Europeans.   This is the way of beckoning with the hand to call a person, which looks as though it were the reverse of the movement which we use for the purpose.   I have heard, on native authority, that the apparent difference consists in the palm being outwards instead of inwards, but a remark made about the natives of the south of India by Mr. Roberts, who seems to have been an extremely good observer, suggests another explanation : "The way in which the people beckon for a person, is to lift up the right hand to its extreme height, and then bring it down with a sudden sweep to the ground."[8]   It is evident that to make a sort of abbreviation of this movement, as by doing it from the wrist or elbow instead of from the shoulder, would be a natural

[1] Linnæus, 'Tour in Lapland ;' London, 1811, vol. i. p. 316.
[2] Mouat, 'Andaman Islanders ;' London, 1863, pp. 279–80.
[3] Charlevoix, vol. iii p. 16.
[4] Du Chaillu, 'Equatorial Africa ;' London, 1861, pp. 303, 430.
[5] Burton, 'Central Africa,' vol. ii. p. 69.
[6] Wilkes, U. S. Exploring Exp. ; London, 1845, vol. i. p. 127.
[7] Plin. ii. 103.   Roberts, Oriental Illustr., pp. 87, 90, 285, 293, 461, 475, 491.
[8] Id. p. 396.

sign, and yet would be liable to be taken for our gesture of
motioning away. It is possible that something of this kind
has led to the following description of the way of beckoning in
New Zealand :—" In signals for those some way off to come near
the arm is waved in an exactly opposite direction to that
adopted by Englishmen for similar purposes, and the natives
in giving silent assent to anything, elevate the head and chin
in place of nodding acquiescence."[1] The latter sign of acquiescence seems as natural as our own, as contrasting with
the sideways movement of negation.

Of signs used to avert the evil eye, some are connected with
the ancient counter-charms, and others are of uncertain meaning, such as the very common one represented in old Greek and
Roman amulets, the hand closed all but the fore-finger and
little finger, which are held out straight. When King Fer-
dinand I. of Naples used to appear in public, he might be seen
to put his hand from time to time into his pocket. Those who
understood his ways knew that he was clenching his fist with
the thumb struck out between the first and second fingers, to
avert the effect of a glance of the evil eye that some one in the
street might have cast on him.

Enough has now been said to show that gesture-language is
a natural mode of expression common to mankind in general.
Moreover, this is true in a different sense to that in which we
say that spoken language is common to mankind, including
under the word language many hundreds of mutually unintelligible tongues, for the gesture-language is essentially one and
the same in all times and all countries. It is true that the
signs used in different places, and by different persons, are
only partially the same ; but it must be remembered that the
same idea may be expressed in signs in very many ways, and
that it is not necessary that all should choose the same. How
the choice of gesture-signs is influenced by education and
habit of life is well shown by a story told somewhere of a boy,
himself deaf-and-dumb, who paid a visit to a Deaf and Dumb
Asylum. When he was gone, the inmates expressed to the

<hr>

[1] A. S. Thomson, 'The Story of New Zealand,' London, 1859, vol. i. p. 209.
See Cook, First Voy. ll., vol. ii. p. 811.

master their disgust at his ways. He talked an ugly language,
they said; when he wanted to show that something was black,
he pointed to his dirty nails.

The best evidence of the unity of the gesture-language is
the ease and certainty with which any savage from any country
can understand and be understood in a deaf-and-dumb school.
A native of Hawaii is taken to an American Institution, and
begins at once to talk in signs with the children, and to tell
about his voyage and the country he came from. A Chinese,
who had fallen into a state of melancholy from long want of
society, is quite revived by being taken to the same place,
where he can talk in gestures to his heart's content. A deaf-
and-dumb lad named Collins is taken to see some Laplanders,
who were carried about to be exhibited, and writes thus to
his fellow-pupils about the Lapland woman:—"Mr. Joseph
Humphreys told me to speak to her by signs, and she understood me. When Cunningham was with me, asking Lapland
woman, and she frowned at him and me. She did not know
we were deaf-and-dumb, but afterwards she knew that we
were deaf-and-dumb, then she spoke to us about reindeers and
elks and smiled at us much."[1]

The study of the gesture-language is not only useful as
giving us some insight into the workings of the human mind.
We can only judge what other men's minds are like by observing their outward manifestations, and similarity in the
most direct and simple kind of utterance is good evidence of
similarity in the mental processes which it communicates to
the outer world. As, then, the gesture-language appears not
to be specifically affected by differences in the race or climate
of those who use it, the shape of their skulls and the colour of
their skins, its evidence, so far as it goes, bears against the
supposition that specific differences are traceable among the
various races of man, at least in the more elementary processes
of the mind.

<hr>

[1] Dr. Orpen, 'The Contrast,' p. 177.

CHAPTER IV.

GESTURE-LANGUAGE AND WORD-LANGUAGE.

WE know very little about the origin of language, but the subject has so great a charm for the human mind that the want of evidence has not prevented the growth of theory after theory; and all sorts of men, with all sorts of qualifications, have solved the problem, each in his own fashion. We may read, for instance, Dante's treatise on the vulgar tongue, and wonder, not that, as he lived in mediæval times, his argument is but a mediæval argument, but that in the 'Paradiso,' seemingly on the strength of some quite futile piece of evidence, he should have made Adam enunciate a notion which even in this nineteenth century has hardly got fairly hold of the popular mind, namely, that there is no primitive language of man to be found existing on earth.

> " La lingua ch' io parlai fu tutta spenta
>> Innanzi che all' ovra inconsumabile
>> Fosse la gente di Nembrotte attenta.
> Chè nullo affetto mai raziocinabile
>> Per lo piacere uman che rinnovella,
>> Seguendo 'l cielo, sempre fu durabile.
> Opera naturale è ch' uom favella;
>> Ma così, o così, natura lascia
>> Poi fare a voi secondo che v' abbella.
> Pria ch' io scendessi all' Infernale ambascia
>> EL s' appellava in terra il sommo Bene
>> Onde vien la letizia che mi fascia;
> ELI si chiamò poi: e ciò conviene:
>> Chè l' uso de' mortali è come fronda
>> In ramo, che sen va, ed altra viena."

In Mr. Pollock's translation :—

> "The language, which I spoke, was quite worn out
> Before unto the work impossible
> The race of Nimrod had their labour turned ;
> For no production of the intellect
> Which is renewed at pleasure of mankind,
> Following the sky, was durable for aye.
> It is a natural thing that man should speak ;
> But whether this or that way, nature leaves
> To your election, as it pleases you.
> Ere I descended on the infernal road,
> Upon earth, EL was called the Highest Good,
> From whom the enjoyment flows that me surrounds ;
> And was called ELI after ; as was meet :
> For mortal usages are like a leaf,
> Upon a bough, which goes, and others come."

Since Dante's time, how many men of genius have set the whole power of their minds against the problem, and to how little purpose. Steinthal's masterly summary of these speculations in his 'Origin of Language' is quite melancholy reading. It may indeed be brought forward as evidence to prove something that matters far more to us than the early history of language, that it is of as little use to be a good reasoner when there are no facts to reason upon, as it is to be a good bricklayer when there are no bricks to build with.

At the root of the problem of the origin of language lies the question, why certain words were originally used to represent certain ideas, or mental conditions, or whatever we may call them. The word may have been used for the idea because it had an evident fitness to be used rather than another word, or because some association of ideas, which we cannot now trace, may have led to its choice. That the selection of words to express ideas was ever purely arbitrary, that is to say, such that it would have been consistent with its principle to exchange any two words as we may exchange algebraic symbols, or to shake up a number of words in a bag and re-distribute them at random among the ideas they represented, is a supposition opposed to such knowledge as we have of the formation of language. And not in language only, but in the study of the whole range of art and belief among mankind, the principle is continually coming more and more clearly into view, that man has not only a definite reason, but very commonly an assignable one, for everything that he does and believes.

In the only departments of language of whose origin we have any clear notion, as for instance in the class of pure imitative words such as "*curkoo*," "*peewit*," and the like, the connection between word and idea is not only real but evident. It is true that different imitative words may be used for the same sound, as for instance the *tick* of a clock is called also *pick* in Germany; but both these words have an evident resemblance to the unwriteable sound that a clock really makes. So the Tahitian word for the crowing of cocks, *aaoa*, might be brought over as a rival to "cock-a-doodle-doo!" There is, moreover, a class of words of undetermined extent, which seem to have been either chosen in some measure with a view to the fitness of their sound to represent their sense, or actually modified by a reflection of sound into sense. Some such process seems to have made the distinction between to *crush*, to *crash*, to *crunch*, and to *craunch*, and to have differenced to *flip*, to *flap*, to *flop* and to *flump*, out of a common root. Some of these words must be looked for in dictionaries of "provincialisms," but they are none the less English for that. In pure interjections, such as *oh! ah!* the connection between the actual pronunciation and the idea which is to be conveyed is perceptible enough, though it is hardly more possible to define it than it is to convey in writing their innumerable modulations of sound and sense.

But if there was a living connection between word and idea outside the range of these classes of words, it seems dead now. We might just as well use "inhabitable" in the French sense as in that of modern English. In fact Shakspeare and other writers do so, as where Norfolk says in ' Richard the Second,'

> " Even to the frozen ridges of the Alps,
> Or any other ground inhabitable."

It makes no practical difference to the world at large, that our word to "rise" belongs to the same root as Old German *risan*, to fall, French *arriser*, to let fall, whichever of the two meanings may have come first, nor that *black, blanc, bleich,* to bleach, to *blacken,* Anglo-Saxon *blæc, blac*=black, *blác*=pale, white, come so nearly together in sound. It has been plausibly conjectured that the reversal of the meaning of to "rise" may have happened through a preposition being prefixed to change the sense, and dropping off again, leaving the word with its altered meaning,[1] while if *black* is related to German *bluken,* to burn, and has the sense of "charred, burnt to a coal," and *blanc* has that of shining,[2] a common origin may possibly be forthcoming for both sets among the family of words, which includes *blaze, fulgeo, flagro,* φλέγω, φλόξ, Sanskrit *bhrág,* and so forth. But explanations of this kind have no bearing on the practical use of such words by mankind at large, who take what is given them and ask no questions. Indeed, however much such a notion may vex the souls of etymologists, there is a great deal to be said for the view that much of the accuracy of our modern languages is due to their having so far "lost consciousness" of the derivation of their words, which thus become like counters or algebraic symbols, good to represent just what they are set down to mean. Archæology is a very interesting and instructive study, but when it comes to exact argument, it may be that the distinctness of our apprehension of what a word means, is not always increased by a misty recollection hovering about it in our minds, that it or its family once meant something else. For such purposes, what is required is not so much a knowledge of etymology, as accurate definition, and the practice of checking words by realizing the things and actions they are used to denote.

It is as bearing on the question of the relation between idea and word that the study of the gesture-language is of particular interest. We have in it a method of human utterance independent of speech, and carried on through a different medium, in which, as has been said, the connection between idea and sign has hardly ever been broken, or even lost sight of for a moment. The gesture-language is in fact a system of

<hr>

[1] Jacob Grimm, 'Geschichte der Deutschen Sprache;' Leipzig, 1848, p. 604.

[2] See J. and W. Grimm, 'Deutsches Wörterbuch,' s. vv. *black, blaken, blick,* etc. Diez, Wörterb., s. v. *bianco.*

utterance to which the description of the primæval language in the Chinese myth may be applied; "Suy-jin first gave names to plants and animals, and these names were so expressive, that by the name of a thing it was known what it was."[1]

To speak first of the comparison of gesture-signs with words, it has been already observed that the gesture-language uses two different processes. It brings objects and actions bodily into the conversation, by pointing to them or looking at them, and it also suggests by imitation of actions, or by "pictures in the air," and these two processes may be used separately or combined. This division may be clumsy and in some cases inaccurate, but it is the best I have succeeded in making. I will now examine more closely the first division, in which objects are brought directly before the mind.

When Mr. Lemuel Gulliver visited the school of languages in Lagado, he was made acquainted with a scheme for improving language by abolishing all words whatsoever. Words being only names for things, people were to carry the things themselves about, instead of wasting their breath in talking about them. The learned adopted the scheme, and sages might be seen in the streets bending under their heavy sacks of materials for conversation, or unpacking their loads for a talk. This was found somewhat troublesome. "But for short conversations, a man may carry implements in his pockets, and under his arms, enough to supply him; and in his house, he cannot be at a loss. Therefore the room where the company meet who practise this art, is full of all things, ready at hand, requisite to furnish matter for this kind of artificial converse."

The traveller records that this plan did not come into general use, owing to the ignorant opposition of the women and the common people, who threatened to raise a rebellion if they were not allowed to speak with their tongues after the manner of their forefathers. But this system of talking by objects is in sober earnest an important part of the gesture-language, and in its early development among the deaf-and-dumb, perhaps the most important. Is there then anything in spoken

[1] Goguet, 'De l'Origine des Lois,' etc., Paris, 1758, vol. iii. p. 322.

language that can be compared with the gestures by which
this process is performed?   Quintilian incidentally answers the
question.   "As for the hands indeed, without which action
would be maimed and feeble, one can hardly say how many
movements they have, when they almost follow the whole stock
of words; for the other members help the speaker, but they,
I may almost say, themselves speak." ... "*Do they not in
pointing out places and persons, fulfil the purpose of adverbs
and pronouns?* so that in so great a diversity of tongues among
all peoples and nations this seems to me the common language
of all mankind?"—"Manus vero, sine quibus trunca esset
actio ac debilis, vix dici potest, quot motus habeant, quum
pæne ipsam verborum copiam persequantur; nam cæteræ
partes loquentem adjuvant, hæ, prope est ut dicam, ipsæ lo-
quuntur. ... *Non in demonstrandis locis ac personis adverbio-
rum atque pronominum obtinent vicem?* ut in tanta per omnes
gentes nationesque linguæ diversitate hic mihi omnium homi-
num communis sermo videatur."[1]

Where a man stands is to him the centre of the universe,
and he refers the position of any object to himself, as before or
behind him, above or below him, and so on; or he makes his
fore-finger issue, as it were, as a radius from this imaginary
centre, and, pointing in any direction into space, says that the
thing he points out is *there*.   He defines the position of an object somewhat as it is done in Analytical Geometry, using either
a radius vector, to which the demonstrative pronoun may partly
be compared, or referring it to three axes, as, in front or behind, to the right or left, above or below.   His body, however,
not being a point, but a structure of considerable size, he often
confuses his terms, as when he uses *here* for some spot only
comparatively near him, instead of making it come towards
the same imaginary centre whence *there* started.   He can in
thought shift his centre of co-ordinates and the position of his

[1] Quint., Inst. Orat., lib. xi. 3, 85, seqq.   "Luther führt an *das ist meja teib* und
bemerkt dabei folgendes, ' das ist ein pronomen und lautet der buchstab a drinnen
stark und lang, als ware es geschrieben also, dahes, wie ein schwäbisch oder algau-
wisch dass lautet, und wer es höret, dem ist als stehe ein finger dabei der darauf
zeige'"   (Grimm, D. W., s. v. "der").

axes, and imagining himself in the place of another person, or even of an inanimate object, can describe the position of himself or anything else with respect to them. Movement and direction come before his mind as a real or imaginary going from one place to another, and such movement gives him the idea of time which the deaf-and-dumb man expresses by drawing a line with his finger along his arm from one point to another, and the speaker by a similar adaptation of prepositions or adverbs of place.

I do not wish to venture below the surface of this difficult subject, for an elaborate examination of which I would especially refer to the researches of Professor Pott, of Halle.[1] But it may be worth while to call attention to an apparent resemblance of two divisions of the root-words of our Aryan languages to the two great classes of gesture-signs. Professor Max Müller divides the Sanskrit root-forms into two classes, the *predicative* roots, such as to *shine*, to *extend*, and so forth; and the *demonstrative* roots, "a small class of independent radicals, not predicative in the usual sense of the word, but simply pointing, simply expressive of existence under certain more or less definite, local or temporal prescriptions."[2] If we take from among the examples given, *here*, *there*, *this*, *that*, *thou*, *he*, as types, we have a division of the elements of the Sanskrit language to which a division of the signs of the deaf-mute into *predicative* and *demonstrative* would at least roughly correspond. Many centuries ago the Indian grammarians made desperate efforts to bring pronouns and verbs, as the Germans say, "under one hat." They deduced the demonstrative *ta* from *tan*, to stretch, and the relative *ya* from *yaj*, to worship. Unity is pleasant to mankind, who are often ready to sacrifice things of more consequence than etymology for it. But perhaps, after all, the world may not have been constructed for the purpose of providing for the human mind just what it is pleased to ask for. Of course, any full comparison of speech and the gesture-language would have to go into the hard problem of the relation of prepositions to adverbs and pronouns on the one hand,

<hr>

[1] Pott, 'Etymologische Forschungen,' new ed.; Lemgo and Detmold, 1859, etc., vol. I.   [2] Müller, Lectures, 3rd ed., London, 1862, p. 372.

and to verb-roots on the other. As to this matter, I can only say that the deaf-mute puts his right fore-finger into the palm of his left hand to say " in," takes it out again to say " out," puts his right hand above or below his left to say " above" or " below," etc., signs which are merely imitative and suggestive. But the gestures with which he shows that anything is "above me," " behind me," and so on, are of a more direct character, and are rather demonstrative than predicative.

The class of imitative and suggestive signs in the gesture-language corresponds in some measure with the Chinese words which are neither verbs, substantives, adjectives, nor adverbs, but answer the purpose of all of them, as, for instance, *ta*, meaning great, greatness, to make great, to be great, greatly ;[1] or they may be compared with what Sanskrit roots would be if they were used as they stand in the dictionaries, without any inflections. In the gesture-language there seems no distinction between the adjective, the adverb which belongs to it, the substantive, and the verb. To say, for instance, " The pear is green," the deaf-and-dumb child first eats an imaginary pear, and then using the back of the flat left hand as a ground, he makes the fingers of the right hand grow up on the edge of it like blades of grass. We might translate these signs as " pear-grass ;" but they have quite as good a right to be classed as verbs, for they are signs of eating in a peculiar way, and growing.

It is not necessary to have recourse to Asiatic languages for analogies of this kind with the gesture-language. The substantive-adjective is common enough in English, and indeed in most other languages. In such compounds as *chestnut-horse, spoon-bill, iron-stone, feather-grass,* we have the substantive put to express a quality which distinguishes it. Our own language, which has gone so far towards assimilating itself to the Chinese by dropping inflection and making syntax do its work, has developed to a great extent a concretism which is like that of the Chinese, who makes one word do duty for " stick" and to " beat with a stick," or of the deaf-mute, whose sign for "butter" or the act of " buttering" is

[1] Endlicher, Chin. Gramm.; Vienna, 1845, p. 168.

the same, the imitation of spreading with his finger on the palm of his hand. To *butter* bread, to *cudgel* a man, to *oil* machinery, to *pepper* a dish, and scores of such expressions, involve action and instrument in one word, and that word a substantive treated as the root or crude form of a verb. Such expressions are concretisms, picture-words, gesture-words, as much as the deaf-and-dumb man's one sign for " butter" and " buttering." To separate these words, and to say that there is one *butter*, a noun, and another *butter*, a verb, may be convenient for the dictionary; but to pretend that there is a real distinction between the words is a mere grammatical juggle, like saying that the noun *man* has a nominative case *man*, and an objective case which is also *man*, and much of the rest of the curious system of putting new wine into old bottles, and stretching the organism of a live language upon a dead framework, which is commonly taught as English Grammar.

The reference of substantives to a verb-root in the Aryan languages and elsewhere is thoroughly in harmony with the spirit of the gesture-language. Thus, the horse is the *neigher*; stone is what *stands*, is *stable*; water is that which *waves, undulates*; the mouse is the *stealer*; an age is what *goes on*; the oar is what *makes to go*; the serpent is the *creeper*; and so on; that is to say, the etymologies of these words lead us back to the actions of neighing, standing, waving, stealing, etc. Now, the deaf-and-dumb Kruse tells us that even to the mute who has no means of communication but signs, " the bird is what flies, the fish what swims, the plant what sprouts out of the earth."[1] It may be said that action, and form resulting from action, form the staple of that part of the gesture-language which occupies itself with suggesting to the mind that which it does not bring bodily before it. But, though there is so much similarity of principle in the formation of gesture-signs and words, there is no general correspondence in the particular idea chosen to name an object by in the two kinds of utterance.

In the second place, with regard to the syntax of the gesture-language, it is hardly possible to compare it with

that of inflected languages such as Latin, which can alter the
form of words to express their relation to one another. With
Chinese and some other languages of Eastern Asia, and with
English and French, etc., where they have thrown off inflection,
it may be roughly compared, though all these languages use
at least grammatical particles which have nothing corresponding to them in the gesture-language. Now, it is remarkable
to what an extent Chinese and English agree in doing just
what the gesture-language does not. Both put the attribute
before the subject, *pe ma*, "white horse;" *shing jin*, "holy
man;" both put the action before the object, *ngo ta ni*, "I
strike thee," *tien sang in*, "heaven destroys me." The frequent practice of the gesture-language in putting the modifier
after the modified is opposed both to Chinese and English
construction, as these examples show; and even where the
antagonism is not so absolute, and the deaf-mute says in
signs "boy ball threw," as well as "ball threw boy," there is
still an important difference. "It seems," says Steinthal, "that
the speech of the Chinese hastens toward the conclusion, and
brings the end prominently forward. In the described position
of the three relations of speech the more important member
stands last."[1] A more absolute contradiction of the leading
principle of the gesture-syntax could hardly have been formu-
lated in words.

The theory that the gesture-language was the original language of man, and that speech came afterwards, has been
already mentioned. We have no foundation to build such a
theory upon, but there are several questions bearing upon the
matter which are well worth examining. Before doing so,
however, it will be well to look a little more closely into the
claim of the gesture-language to be considered as a means of
utterance independent of speech.

In the first place, an absolute separation between the two
things is not to be found within the range of our experience.
Though the deaf-mute may not speak himself, yet the most of
what he knows, he only knows by means of speech, for he

<hr>

[1] Steinthal, 'Charakteristik der hauptsächlichsten Typen des Sprachbaues;' Berlin, 1860, p. 114, etc.

learns from the gestures of his parents and companions what they learnt through words. We speak conventionally of the uneducated deaf-and-dumb, but every deaf-and-dumb child is educated more or less by living among those who speak, and this education begins in the cradle. And on the other hand, no child attains to speech independently of the gesture-language, for it is in great measure by means of such gestures as pointing, nodding, and so forth, that language is first taught.

In old times, when the mental capacity of the deaf-and-dumb was little known, it was thought by the Greeks that they were incapable of education, since hearing, the sense of instruction, was wanting to them. Quite consistent with this notion is the confusion which runs through language between mental stupidity, and deafness, dumbness, and even blindness. *Surdus* means " deaf," and also " stupid ;" a hollow nut is a *deaf-nut*, *taube Nuss*; κωφός means dumb, deaf, stupid. " Speech-less " (*infans*, νήπιος) being a natural term for a child, in a similar way " dumb " (*tump*, *tumb*) becomes in Old German a common word for young, giddy, thoughtless, till at last " dumb and wise " come to mean nothing more than " lads and grown men," as where in the tournament many a shock is heard of wise and of dumb, and the breaking of the lances sounds up towards the sky,

> " Von *wisen* und von *tumben*   man hôrte manegen stôz,
> Dâ der schefte brechen   gein der hœhe dôs." [1]

Even Kant is to be found committing himself to the opinion, so amazing, one would think, to anybody who has ever been inside a deaf-and-dumb Institution, that a born mute can never attain to more than something analogous to reason (einem Analogon der Vernunft). [2]

The evidence of teachers of the deaf-and-dumb goes to prove, that in their untaught state, or at least with only such small teaching as they get from the signs of their relatives and friends, their thought is very limited, but still it is human thought, while when they have been regularly instructed and taught to read and write, their minds may be developed up to

[1] Nibel. Not, 87.
[2] Kant, 'Anthropologie,' Königsberg, 1798, p. 49. Schmalz, p. 46.

about the average cultivation of those who have had the power
of speech from childhood. Even in a low state of education,
the deaf-mute seems to conceive general ideas, for when he
invents a sign for anything, he applies it to all other things of
the same class, and he can also form abstract ideas in a certain way, or at least he knows that there is a quality in which
snow and milk agree, and he can go on adding other white
things, such as the moon and whitewash, to his list. He can
form a proposition, for he can make us understand, and we
can make him understand, that "this man is old, that man
is young." Nor does he seem incapable of reasoning in something like a syllogism, even when he has no means of communication but the gesture-language, and certainly as soon as he
has learnt to read that "All men are mortal, John is a man,
therefore John is mortal," he will show by every means of
illustration in his power, that he fully comprehends the argument.

There is detailed evidence on record as to the state of mind
of the deaf-and-dumb who have had no education but what
comes with mere living among speaking people. Thus Massieu, the Abbé Sicard's celebrated pupil, gave an account of
what he could remember of his untaught state. He loved his
father and mother much, and made himself understood by them
in signs. There were six deaf-and-dumb children in the
family, three boys and three girls. "I stayed," he said, "at
my home till I was thirteen years and nine months old, and
never had any instruction; I had darkness for the letters
(j'avois ténèbres pour les lettres). I expressed my ideas by
manual signs or gesture. The signs which I used then, to
express my ideas to my relatives and my brothers and sisters,
were very different from those of the educated deaf-and-dumb.
Strangers never understood us when we expressed our ideas
to them by signs, but the neighbours understood us." He
noticed oxen, horses, vegetables, houses, and so forth, and
remembered them when he had seen them. He wanted to
learn to read and write, and to go to school with the other
boys and girls, but was not allowed to; so he went to the
school and asked by signs to be taught to read and write, but

the master refused harshly, and turned him out of the school. His father made him kneel at prayers with the others, and he imitated the joining of their hands and the movement of their lips, but thought (as other deaf-and-dumb children have done), that they were worshipping the sky. "I knew the numbers," he said, "before my instruction, my fingers had taught me them. I did not know the figures; I counted on my fingers, and when the number was over ten, I made notches in a piece of wood." When he was asked what he used to think people were doing when they looked at one another and moved their lips, he replied that he thought they were expressing ideas, and in answer to the inquiry why he thought so, he said he remembered people speaking about him to his father, and then his father threatened to have him punished.[1]

Kruse tells a very curious story of an untaught deaf-and-dumb boy. He was found by the police wandering about Prague, in 1805. He could not make himself understood, and they could find out nothing about him, so they sent him to the deaf-and-dumb Institution, where he was taught. When he had been sufficiently educated to enable him to give accurate answers to questions put to him, he gave an account of what he remembered of his life previously to his coming to the Institution. His father, he said, had a mill, and of this mill, the furniture of the house, and the country round it, he gave a precise description. He gave a circumstantial account of his life there, how his mother and sister died, his father married again, his step-mother ill-treated him, and he ran away. He did not know his own name, nor what the mill was called, but he knew it lay away from Prague towards the morning. On inquiry being made, the boy's statement was confirmed. The police found his home, gave him his name, and secured his inheritance for him.[2]

Even Laura Bridgman, who was blind as well as deaf-and-dumb, expressed her feelings by the signs we all use, though she had never seen them made, and could not tell that the by-standers could observe them. She would stamp with delight, and shudder at the idea of a cold bath. When astonished, she

[1] Sicard, 'Théorie,' vol. ii. p. 632, etc.   [2] Kruse, p. 54.

would protrude her lips, and hold up her hands with fingers wide spread out, and she might be seen "biting her lips with an upward contraction of the facial muscles when roguishly listening at the account of some ludicrous mishap, precisely as lively persons among us would do." While speaking of a person, she would point to the spot where he had been sitting when she last conversed with him, and where she still believed him to be.[1]

Though, however, the deaf-and-dumb prove clearly to us that a man may have human thought without being able to speak, they by no means prove that he can think without any means of physical expression. Their evidence tends the other way. We may read with profit an eloquent passage on this subject by a German professor, as, transcendental as it is, it is put in such clear terms, that wo may almost think we understand it.

"Herein lies the necessity of utterance, the representation of thought. Thought is not even present to the thinker, till he has set it forth out of himself. Man, as an individual endowed with sense and with mind, first attains to thought, and at the same time to the comprehension of himself, in setting forth out of himself the contents of his mind, and in this his free production, he comes to the knowledge of himself, his thinking 'I.' He comes first to himself in uttering himself."[2]

This view is not contradicted, but to some extent supported, by what we know of the earliest dawnings of thought among the deaf-and-dumb. But wo must take the word "utterance" in its larger sense, to include not speech alone, as Heyse seems to do, but all ways by which man can express his thoughts. *Man* is essentially, what the derivation of his name among our Aryan race imports, not "the speaker," but he who thinks, he who *means*.

The deaf-and-dumb Kruse's opinion as to the development of thought among his own class, by and together with gesture-signs, has been already quoted; how the qualities which make

<hr>

[1] Lieber, On the Vocal Sounds of Laura Bridgman, in Smithsonian Contrib., vol. ii.; Washington, 1851.

[2] Heyse, 'System der Sprachwissenschaft;' Berlin, 1850, p. 39.

a distinction to him between one thing and another, become, when he imitates objects and actions in the air with hands, fingers, and gestures, suitable signs, which serve him as a means of fixing ideas in his mind, and recalling them to his memory, and that thus he makes himself signs, which, scanty and imperfect as they may be, yet serve to open a way for thought, and those thoughts and signs develope themselves further and further. Very similar is Professor Steinthal's opinion, which, to some extent, agrees with the theory of the manifestation of the Ego adopted by Heyse, but gives a larger definition to "utterance." Man, "even when he has no perception of sound, can yet manifest to himself through any other sense that which is contained in his sensible certainty, can set forth an object out of himself, and separate himself, his Ego, as something permanent and universal, from that which is transitory and particular, even if he does not at once comprehend this universal something in the form of the Ego." The same writer, after asserting that mind and speech are developed together; that the mind does not originally *make* speech, but that it *is* speech; that language shapes itself in mind, or mind shapes itself in language, goes on to qualify these assertions. "We recognize the power of language not so much in the sound, as in the inward process. But it is as certain that this goes forward in the deaf-mute, as it is that he is a human being, flesh of human flesh and spirit of infinite spirit. But it goes forward in him in a somewhat different form," etc.[1]

Whether the human mind is capable of exercising at all any of its peculiarly human functions without any means of utterance, or not, we shall all admit that it could have gone but very little way, could only just have passed the line which divides beast from man. All experience concurs to prove, that the mental powers and the stock of ideas of those human beings who have but imperfect means of utterance, are imperfect and scanty in proportion to those means. The manner in which we can see such persons accompanying their thought with the utterance which is most convenient to them, shows to how great a degree thought is "talking to oneself." The

[1] Steinthal, Spr. der T., pp. 007, 909.

deaf-and-dumb gesticulate as they think.   Laura Bridgman's fingers worked, making the initial movements for letters of the finger-alphabet, not only during her waking thought, but even in her dreams.

Spoken language, though by no means the exclusive medium of thought and expression, is undoubtedly the best.   In default of this, it is only by means of a substitute for it, namely, alphabetic writing, that we succeed in giving more than a very low development to the minds of the deaf-and-dumb; and they of course connect the idea directly with the written word, not as we do, the writing with the sound, and then the sound with the idea.   When they think in writing, as they often do, the image of the written words which correspond to their ideas, must rise up before them in the "mind's eye."   The Germans, who are strong advocates of the system of teaching the deaf-and-dumb to articulate, believe that the power of connecting ideas with actual or imaginary movements of the organs of speech, gives an enormous increase of mental power, which I am however inclined to think is a good deal exaggerated.   Heinicke gives a description of the results of his teaching his pupils to articulate, their delight at being able to communicate their ideas in this new way, and the increased intelligence which appeared in the expression of their faces.   As soon, he says, as the born-mute is sufficiently taught to enable him to increase his stock of ideas by the power of naming them, he begins to talk aloud in his sleep, and when this happens, it shows that the power of thinking in words has taken root.[1] Heinicke was, however, an enthusiast for his system of teaching, and in practice, it is I believe generally found, that articulation does not displace gesture-signs and written language as a medium of thought; and certainly, the deaf-and-dumb who can speak, very much prefer the sign language for practical use among themselves.   Instructors of the deaf-and-dumb in England and America seem to have generally decided, that with ordinary pupils, articulation is not worth the time and trouble it costs, and they use it but little.   Of course, no one doubts that it is desirable that the children should be taught

<hr>

[1] Heinicke, p. 102, etc.

to speak, and to read from the lips, especially when the deafness is not total; but the question is, whether it is worth while
to devote a large proportion of the few years' instruction which
is given to the poorer pupils, to this object. It is asserted in
Germany, that a want of the natural use of the lungs promotes
the tendency to consumption, which is very common among the
deaf-and-dumb, and that teaching them to articulate tends to
counteract this. This sounds probable enough, though I do
not find, even in Schmalz, any sufficient evidence to prove it,
but at any rate, there is no doubt that the deaf-and-dumb
should be encouraged to use their lungs in shouting at their
play, as they naturally do.

It is quite clear that the loss of the powers of hearing and
speech is a loss to the mind which no substitute can fully replace. Children who have learnt to speak and afterwards become deaf, lose the power of thinking in inward language, and
become to all intents and purposes the same as those who
could never hear at all, unless great pains are taken to keep
up and increase their knowledge by other means. "And thus
even those who become hard of hearing at an age when they
can already speak a little, by little and little lose all that they
have learnt. Their voices lose all cheerfulness and euphony,
every day wipes a word out of the memory, and with it the
idea of which it was the sign." [1]

Spoken words appear to be, in the minds of the deaf-mutes
who have been artificially taught to speak, merely combined
movements of the throat and other vocal organs, and the initial
movement made by them in calling words to mind has been
compared to a tickling in the throat. People wanting a sense
often imagine to themselves a resemblance between it and one
of the senses which they possess. The old saying of the blind
man, that he thought scarlet was like the sound of a trumpet,
is somewhat like a remark made by Kruse, that though he is
"stock-deaf," he has a bodily feeling of music, and different
instruments have different effects upon him. Musical tones
seem to his perception to have much analogy with colours.
The sound of the trumpet is yellow to him, that of the drum

[1] Schmalz, pp. 2, 32.

rod; while the music of the organ is green, and of the bass-viol blue, and so on. Such comparisons are, indeed, not confined to those whose senses are incomplete. Language shows clearly that men in general have a strong feeling of such analogies among the impressions of the different senses. Expressions such as "schreiend roth," and the use of "loud," as applied to colours and patterns, are superficial examples of analogies which have their roots very deep in the human mind.

It is a very notable fact bearing upon the problem of the Origin of Language, that even born-mutes, who never heard a word spoken, do of their own accord and without any teaching make vocal sounds more or less articulate, to which they attach a definite meaning, and which, when once made, they go on using afterwards in the same unvarying sense. Though these sounds are often capable of being written down more or less accurately with our ordinary alphabets, their effect on those who make them can, of course, have nothing to do with the sense of hearing, but must consist only in particular ways of breathing, combined with particular positions of the vocal organs.

Teuscher, a deaf-mute, whose mind was developed by education to a remarkable degree, has recorded that, in his uneducated state, he had already discovered the sounds which were inwardly blended with his sensations (innig verschmolzen mit meiner Empfindungsweise.) So, as a child, he had affixed a special sound to persons he loved, his parents, brothers and sisters, to animals, and things for which he had no sign (as water); and called any person he wished with one unaltered voice.[1] Heinicke gives some remarkable evidence, which we may, I think, take as given in entire good faith, though the reservation should be made, that through his strong partiality for articulation as a means of educating the deaf-and-dumb, he may have given a definiteness to these sounds in writing them down which they did not really possess. The following are some of his remarks:—"All mutes discover words for themselves for different things. Among over fifty whom I have partly instructed or been acquainted with,

<hr>

[1] Steinthal, Spr. der T., p. 917.

there was not one who had not uttered at least a few spoken names, which he had discovered himself, and some were very clear and well defined. I had under my instruction a born deaf-mute, nineteen years old, who had previously invented many writeable words for things, some three, four, and six syllables long." For instance, he called to eat "mumm," to drink "schipp," a child "tutten," a dog "beyer," money "patten." He had a neighbour who was a grocer, and him he called "patt" [a name, no doubt, connected with his name for money, for buying and selling is indicated by the deaf and dumb by the action of counting out coin]. The grocer's son he called by a simple combination "pattutten." For the two first numerals, he had words—1, "gä;" 2, "schuppatter." In his language, "riecko" meant "I will not;" and when they wanted to force him to do anything, he would cry "naffet riecko schito." An exclamation which he used was "heschhofa," in the sense of God forbid.[1]

Some of these sounds, as "mumm" and "schipp," for eating and drinking, and perhaps "beyer," for the dog, are mere vocalizations of the movements of the mouth, which the deaf-and-dumb make in imitating the actions of eating, drinking, and barking, in their gesture-language. Besides, it is a common thing for even the untaught deaf-and-dumb to speak and understand a few words of the language spoken by their associates. Though they cannot hear them, they imitate the motions of the lips and teeth of those who speak, and thus make a tolerable imitation of words containing labial and dental letters, though the gutturals, being made quite out of sight, can only be imparted to them by proper teaching, and then only with difficulty and imperfectly. It is scarcely necessary to say that when the deaf-and-dumb are taught to speak in articulate language, this is done merely by developing and systematizing the lip-imitation which is natural to them. As instances of the power which deaf-mutes have of learning words by sight without any regular teaching, may be given the cases mentioned by Schmalz of children born stone-deaf, who learnt in this way to say "papa," "mamma," "muhmo" (cousin), "puppe"

[1] Heinicke, p. 137, etc.

(doll), " bitte" (please).[1] All the sounds in these words are such as deaf persons may imitate by sight.

An extraordinary story of this kind is told by Eschwege, who was a scientific traveller of high standing, and upon whom the responsibility for the truth of the narrative must rest. The scene is laid in a place in the interior of Brazil, where he rested on a journey, and his account is as follows :—" I was occupied the rest of the day in quail-hunting, and in making philosophical observations on a deaf-and-dumb idiot negro boy about thirteen years old, with water on the brain, and upon whom nothing made any impression except the crowing of a cock, whose voice he could imitate to the life. Just as people teach the deaf-and-dumb to speak, so this beast-man, by observing and imitating the movements of the neck and tongue of the cock, had in time learnt to crow, and this seemed the only pleasure he had beyond the satisfaction of his natural wants. He lay most part of the day stark naked on the ground, and crowed as if for a wager against the cock."[2]

Returning to the list of words given by Heinicke, it does not seem easy to set down any of them as lip-imitations, unless it be " heschbefa" " Gott bewahre !" in which befa may be an imitation of bewahre. We have, then, left several articulate sounds, such as " patten," money, " tutten," child, etc., which seem to have been used as real words, but of which it seems impossible to say why the dumb lad selected them to bear the meanings which he gave them.

The vocal sounds used by Laura Bridgman are of great interest from the fact that, being blind as well as deaf-and-dumb, she could not even have imitated words by seeing them made. Yet she would utter sounds, as " *ho-o-ph-ph* " for wonder, and a short of chuckling or grunting as an expression of satisfaction. When she did not like to be touched, she would say, *f !* Her teachers used to restrain her from making inarticulate sounds, but she felt a great desire to make them, and would sometimes shut herself up and " indulge herself in a surfeit of sounds." But this vocal faculty of hers was chiefly

<hr>

[1] Schmalz, p. 210 a.

[2] Eschwege, ' Brasilien ;' Brunswick, 1830, part i. p. 69.

exercised in giving what may be called name-sounds to persons whom she knew, and which she would make when the persons to whom she had given them came near her, or when she wanted to find them, or even when she was thinking of them. She had made as many as fifty or sixty of these name-sounds, some of which have been written down, as *foo, too, pn, fif, pig, ts*, but many of them were not capable of being written down even approximately.

Even if Laura's vocal sounds are not classed as real words, a distinction between the articulate sounds used by the deaf-and-dumb for child, water, eating, and drinking, etc., and the words of ordinary language, could not easily be made, whether the deaf-mutes invented these sounds or imitated them from the lips of others. To go upon the broadest ground, the mere fact that teachers can take children who have no means of uttering their thoughts but the gesture-language, and teach them to articulate words, to recognize them by sight when uttered by others, to write them, and to understand them as equivalents for their own gestures, is sufficient to bridge over the gulf which lies between the gesture-language and, at least, a rudimentary form of word-language. These two kinds of utterance are capable of being translated with more or less exactness into one another; and it seems more likely than not that there may be a similarity between the process by which the human mind first uttered itself in speech, and that by which the same mind still utters itself in gestures.

To turn to another subject. We have no evidence of man ever having lived in society without the use of spoken language; but there are some myths of such races, and, moreover, statements have been made by modern writers of eminence as to an intermediate state between gesture-language and word-language, which deserve careful examination.

In Ethiopia, across the desert, says the geographer Pomponius Mela, there dwell dumb people, and such as use gestures instead of language; others, whose tongues give no sound; others, who have no tongues (muti populi, et quibus pro eloquio nutus est; alii sine sono linguæ; alii sine linguis, etc.)[1]. Pliny

<hr>

[1] Mela, iii. 9.

gives much the same account. Some of these Ethiopian tribes are said to have no noses, some no upper lips, some no tongues. Some have for their language nods and gestures (quibusdam pro sermone nutus motusque membrorum est).[1]

To go thoroughly into the discussion of these stories would require an investigation of the whole subject of the legends of monstrous tribes; but an off-hand rationalizing explanation may be sufficient here. The frequent use of the gesture-language by savage tribes in intercourse with strangers may combine with the very common opinion of uneducated men that the talk of foreigners is not real speech at all, but a kind of inarticulate chirping, barking, or grunting. Moreover, from using the words "speechless," "tongueless," with the sense of "foreigner," "barbarian," and talking of tribes who have no tongue (no lingo, as our sailors would say), to the point-blank statement that there are races of men without speech and without tongues, is a transition quite in the spirit of mythology.

In modern times we hear little of dumb races, at least from authors worthy of credit; but we find a number of accounts of people occupying as it were a halfway house between the mythic dumb nations and ourselves, and having a speech so imperfect that even if talking of ordinary matters they have to eke it out by gestures. To begin in the last century, Lord Monboddo says that a certain Dr. Peter Greenhill told him that there was a nation east of Cape Palmas in Africa, who could not understand one another in the dark, and had to supply the wants of their language by gestures.[2] Had Lord Monboddo been the only or the principal authority for stories of this class, we might have left his half-languaged men to keep company with his human apes and tailed men in the regions of mythology; but in this matter it will be seen that, right or wrong, he is in very good company.

Describing the Puris and Coroados of Brazil, Spix and Martius, having remarked that different tribes converse in

<hr>

[1] Plin. vi. 35.

[2] Lord Monboddo, 'Origin and Progress of Language,' 2nd ed., Edinburgh, 1774, vol. i. p. 253.

signs, and explained the difficulty they found in making them
understand by signs the objects or ideas for which they wanted
the native names, go on to say how imperfect and devoid of
inflexion or construction these languages are. Signs with
hand or mouth, they say, are required to make them intelligible. To say, " I will go into the wood," the Indian uses the
words " wood-go," and points his mouth like a snout in the
direction he means.[1] Madame Pfeiffer, too, visited the Puris,
and says that for " to-day," " to-morrow," and " yesterday,"
they have only the word " day;" the rest they express by
signs. For " to-day" they say " day," and touch themselves
on the head, or point straight upward; for " to-morrow " they
say also " day," pointing forward with the finger; and for
" yesterday," again " day," pointing behind them.[2]

Mr. Mercer, describing the low condition of some of the
Veddah tribes of Ceylon, stated that not only is their dialect
incomprehensible to a Singhalese, but that even their commu-
nications with one another are made by signs, grimaces, and
guttural sounds, which bear little or no resemblance to distinct
words or systematized language.[3]

Dr. Milligan, speaking of the language of Tasmania, and the
rapid variation of its dialects, says " The habit of gesticulation,
and the use of signs to eke out the meaning of monosyllabic
expressions, and to give force, precision, and character to
vocal sounds, exerted a further modifying effect, producing, as
it did, carelessness and laxity of articulation, and in the application and pronunciation of words." " To defects in orthoepy
the aborigines added short-comings in syntax, for they observed no settled order or arrangement of words in the construction of their sentences, but conveyed in a supplementary
fashion by tone, manner, and gesture those modifications of
meaning which we express by mood, tense, number, etc."[4]

We find a similar remark made about a tribe of North
American Indians, by Captain Burton. " Those natives who,

<hr>

[1] Spix and Martius, ' Reise in Brasilien,' Munich, 1823, etc., vol. i. p. 385, etc.
[2] Ida Pfeiffer, ' Eine Frauenfahrt um die Erde,' Vienna, 1850, p. 102.
[3] Sir J. Emerson Tennent, 'Ceylon,' 3rd ed. ; London, 1859, vol. ii. p. 441.
[4] Milligan, in Papers and Proc. of Roy. Soc. of Tasmania, 1859 ; vol. iii.
part ii.

like the Arapahos, possess a very scanty vocabulary, pronounced in a quasi-unintelligible way, can hardly converse with one another in the dark; to make a stranger understand them they must always repair to the camp-fire for 'pow-wow.' "[1]

Mr. Schoolcraft, whose opinion on the matter would have been valuable, knew of the question, and inserted it in the list of inquiries to be answered by Indian agents, etc. Asking for information about the language of any tribe, he puts the inquiry, No. 345, " Is gesticulation essential to carry out some of its meanings ? "[2]

The array of evidence in favour of the existence of tribes whose language is incomplete without the help of gesture-signs, even for things of ordinary import, is very remarkable. The matter is important, ethnologically, for could it be taken as proved, that there are really people whose language does not suffice to speak of the common subjects of every-day life without the aid of gesture, the fact would either furnish about the strongest case of degeneration known in the history of the human race, or would supply a telling argument in favour of the theory that the gesture-language is the original utterance of mankind, out of which speech has developed itself more or less fully among different tribes. But the evidence does not in any case give all that would be required to prove the fact. Spix and Martius make no claim to having mastered the Puri and Coroado languages. The Coroado words for " to-morrow " and " the day after to-morrow," viz. *herinanta* and *hinó herinanta*, make it unlikely that their neighbours the Puris, who are so nearly on the same level of civilization, have no such words. (I have not had access to a Puri vocabulary, which would probably settle the question.) Mr. Mercer seems to have adopted the common view of foreigners about the Vodduhs, but it has happened here, as in many other accounts of savage tribes, that closer acquaintance has shown them to have been wrongly accused. Mr. Bailey, who has had good opportunities of studying them, shows them to be low in culture, but by no means exceptionally so, and he contradicts their supposed deficiency in language with the remark, " I never

<hr>

[1] Burton, 'City of the Saints,' p. 151.   [2] Schoolcraft, part i. p. 561.

knew one of them at a loss for words sufficiently intelligible to
convey his meaning, not to his fellows only, but to the Singhalese of the neighbourhood, who are all, more or less, acquainted with the Veddah patois."[1] Dr. Milligan is, I believe,
our best authority as to the Tasmanians and their language,
but he probably had to trust in this matter to native information, which is far from being always safe.[2] Lastly, Captain
Burton only paid a flying visit to the Western Indians, and his
interpreters could hardly have given him scientific information
on such a subject.

The point in question is one which it is not easy to bring to
a perfectly distinct issue, seeing that all people, savage and
civilized, do use signs more or less. As has been remarked
already, many savage tribes accompany their talk with gestures to a great extent, and in conversation with foreigners,
gestures and words are usually mixed to express what is to be
said. It is extremely likely that Madame Pfeiffer's savages
suffered the penalty of being set down as wanting in language,
for no worse fault than using a combination of words and signs
in order to make what they meant as clear as possible to her
comprehension. But the existence of a language incomplete,
even for ordinary purposes, without the aid of gesture-signs,
could only be proved by the evidence of an educated man so
familiar with the language in question, as to be able to say
from absolute personal knowledge not only what it can, but
what it cannot do, an amount of acquaintance to which I think
none of the writers quoted would lay claim. In the case of
languages spoken by very low races, like the Puris and the
Tasmanians, the difficulty of deciding such a point must be
very great.

There is a point of some practical importance involved in
the question, whether gestures or words are, so to speak, most
natural. If signs form an easier means for the reception and
expression of ideas than words, then idiots ought to learn to
understand and use gestures more readily than speech. I
have only been able to get a distinct answer to the question,

[1] J. Bailey, in Tr. Eth. Soc.; London, 1863, p. 300.
[2] The objection to trusting native information as to grammatical structure, may

whether they do so or not, from one competent judge in such a matter, Dr. Scott, of Exeter, who assures me that semi-idiotic children, to whom there is no hope of teaching more than the merest rudiments of speech, are yet capable of receiving a considerable amount of knowledge by means of signs, and of expressing themselves by them.   It is well known that a certain class of children are dumb from deficiency of intellect, rather than from want of the sense of hearing, and it is to these that the observation applies.[1]

The idea of solving the problem of the origin of language by actual experiment, must have very often been started. There are several stories of such an experiment having been tried, the first being Herodotus's well-known tale of Psammi-tichus, King of Egypt, who had the two children brought up by a silent keeper, and suckled by goats.   The first word they said, *bekos*, meaning bread in the Phrygian language, of course proved that the Phrygians were the oldest race of mankind. It is a very trite remark that there is nothing absolutely incredible in the story, and that *bek, bek*, is a good imitative word for bleating, as in βληχάομαι, μηκάομαι, *blöken, meckern*, etc.   But the very name of Psammitichus, who has served as a lay-figure for so many tales to be draped upon, is fatal to any claim to the historical credibility of such a story.   He sounds the springs of the Nile with a cord thousands of fathoms long, and finds no bottom; he accomplishes the prediction of one oracle by pouring a libation out of a brazen helmet, and of another, concerning cocks, by leading an army of Carians, with crested helmets, against Tementhes, king of Egypt, and he figures in the Greek version of the story of Cinderella's slipper. It is interesting to see how naturally mythology takes to the bekos-legend, and brings it out in a new place.   Miss Goodman says, " A Scotch lady staying in the house, informed me that one of the early kings of her country, anxious to discover the

be seen in the difficulty, so constantly met with in investigating the languages of rude tribes, of getting a substantive from a native without a personal pronoun tacked to it.   Thus in Dr. Milligan's vocabulary, the expressions *puggan arraa, googalmarra*, given for " husband " and " father," seem really to mean " your husband," " my father," or something of the kind.

[1] See W. R. Scott, ' Remarks on the Education of Idiots ;' London, 1847.

primitive language, placed two infants on an uninhabited island in the Hebrides, under the care of a dumb old woman," etc.[1]

The third story is told of the great Mogul, Akbar Khan. It is mentioned by Purchas, only twenty years after Akbar's death,[2] and told in detail by the Jesuit Father Catrou, as follows:—

"Indeed it may be said that desire of knowledge was Akbar's ruling passion, and his curiosity induced him to try a very strange experiment. He wished to ascertain what language children would speak without teaching, as he had heard that Hebrew was the natural language of those who had been taught no other. To settle the question, he had twelve children at the breast shut up in a castle six leagues from Agra, and brought up by twelve dumb nurses. A porter, who was dumb also, was put in charge and forbidden on pain of death to open the castle door. When the children were twelve years old [there is a decided feeling for duodecimals in the story], he had them brought before him, and collected in his palace men skilled in all languages. A Jew who was at Agra was to judge whether the children spoke Hebrew. There was no difficulty in finding Arabs and Chaldeans in the capital. On the other hand the Indian philosophers asserted that the children would speak the Hanscrit[3] language, which takes the place of Latin among them, and is only in use among the learned, and is learnt in order to understand the ancient Indian books of Philosophy and Theology. When however the children appeared before the Emperor, every one was astonished to find that they did not speak any language at all. They had learnt from their nurses to do without any, and they merely expressed their thoughts by gestures which answered the purpose of words. They were so savage and so shy that it was a work of some trouble to tame them and to loosen their tongues, which they had scarcely used during their infancy."[4]

[1] Margaret Goodman, 'Experiences of an English Sister of Mercy;' London, 1862, p. 61.

[2] Purchas, His Pilgrimes; London, 1625–6, vol. v. (1626) p. 516.

[3] I.e. Sanskrit, after the Persian form of the word.

[4] Catrou, Hist. Gén. de l'Empire du Mogol; Paris, 1705, p. 260, etc.

There may possibly be a foundation of fact for this story, which fits very well with what is known of Akbar's unscrupulous character, and his greediness for knowledge. Moreover it tells in its favour, that had a story-teller invented it, he would hardly have brought it to what must have seemed to him such a lame and impotent conclusion, as that the children spoke no language at all.

CHAPTER V.

PICTURE-WRITING AND WORD-WRITING.

THE art of recording events, and sending messages, by means of pictures representing the things or actions in question, is called Picture-Writing.

The deaf-and-dumb man's remark, that the gesture-language is a picture-language, finds its counterpart in an observation of Wilhelm von Humboldt's, that "In fact, gesture, destitute of sound, is a species of writing." There is indeed a very close relation between these two ways of expressing and communicating thought. Gesture can set forth thought with far greater speed and fulness than picture-writing, but it is inferior to it in having to place the different elements of a sentence in succession, in single file, so to speak; while by a picture the whole of an event may be set in view at one glance, and that permanently, so as to serve as a message to a distant place or a record to a future time. But the imitation of visible qualities as a means of expressing ideas, is common to both methods, and both belong to similar conditions of the human mind. Both are found in very distant countries and times, and spring up naturally under favourable circumstances, provided that a higher means of supplying the same wants has not already occupied the place which they can only fill very partially and rudely.

There being so great a likeness between the conditions which cause the use of the gesture-language and of picture-writing, it is not surprising to find the natives of North America as great proficients in the one as in the other. Their pictures, as drawn and interpreted by Schoolcraft and other writers, give the best information that is to be had of the lower development of the art.[1]

Fig. 2.

Fig. 2 is an Indian record on a blazed pine-tree (to blaze a tree is to wound (*blesser*) its side with an axe, so as to mark it with a conspicuous white patch). On the right are two canoes (2 and 4), with a cat-fish (1) in one of them, and a fabulous animal, known as the copper-tailed bear (3), in the other. On the left are a bear and six catfish; and the sense of the picture is simply that two hunters, whose names, or rather totems or clan-names, were "Copper-tailed Bear" and "Catfish," went out on a hunting expedition in their canoes, and took a bear and six catfish.

Fig. 3.

Fig. 3 is a picture on the face of a rock on the shore of Lake Superior, and records an expedition across the lake, which was led by Myeengun, or "Wolf," a celebrated Indian chief. The canoes with the upright strokes in them represent the force of the party in men and boats, and Wolf's chief ally, Kishke-munnasee, that is, "Kingfisher," goes in the first canoe. The

[1] Figs. 2 to 7, and their interpretations, are from Schoolcraft, part i.

arch with three circles below it shows that there were three suns under heaven, that is, that the voyage took three days. The tortoise seems to indicate their getting to land, while the representation of the chief himself on horseback shows that the expedition took place since the time when horses were introduced into Canada.

The Indian grave-posts, Fig. 4, tell their story in the same childlike manner. Upon one is a tortoise, the dead warrior's totem, and a figure beside it representing a headless man, which shows he is dead. Below are his three marks of honour. On the other post there is no separate sign

Fig. 4.

for death, but the chief's totem, a crane, is reversed. Six marks of honour are awarded to him on the right, and three on the left. The latter represent three important general treaties of peace which he had attended; the former would seem to stand for six war-parties or battles. The pipe and hatchet are symbols of influence in peace and war.

The great defect of this kind of record is that it can only be understood within a very limited circle. It does not tell the story at length, as is done in explaining it in words; but it merely suggests some event, of which it only gives such details as are required to enable a practised observer to construct a complete picture. It may be compared in this respect to the elliptical forms of expression which are current in all societies whose attention is given specially to some narrow subject of interest, and where, as all men's minds have the same framework set up in them, it is not necessary to go into an elaborate description of the whole state of things; but one or two details are enough to enable the hearer to understand the whole. Such expressions as "new white at 48," "best selected at 92," though perfectly understood in the commercial circles where they are current, are as unintelligible to any one who is not familiar with the course of events in those circles, as an Indian record of a war-party would be to an ordinary Londoner.

Though, however, familiarity with the picture-writing of the Indians, as well as with their habits and peculiarities, might enable the student to make a pretty good guess at the meaning of such documents as the above, which are meant to be understood by strangers, there is another class of picture-writings, used principally by the magicians or medicine-men, which cannot be even thus interpreted. The songs and charms used among the Indians of North America are repeated or sung by memory, but, as an assistance to the singer, pictures are painted upon sticks, or pieces of birch-bark or other material, which serve to suggest to the mind the successive verses. Some of these documents, with the songs to which they refer, are given in Schoolcraft, and one or two examples will show sufficiently how they are used, and make it evident that they

Fig. 5.

can only convey their full meaning to those who know by heart already the compositions they refer to. They are mere Samson's riddles, only to be guessed by those who have ploughed with his heifer. Thus, a drawing of a man with two marks on his breast and four on his legs (Fig. 5) is to remind the singer that at this place comes the following verse:—

" Two days must you fast, my friend,—
Four days must you sit still."

Fig. 6.

Fig. 6 is the record of a love-song—(1) represents the lover in (2) he is singing, and beating a magic drum ; in (3) he surrounds himself with a secret lodge, denoting the effects of his necromancy; in (4) he and his mistress are shown joined by a single arm, to indicate the union of their affections; in (5) she is shown on an island; in (6) she is asleep, and his voice is shown, while his magical powers are reaching her heart; and the heart itself is shown in (7).   To each of these figures a verse of the song corresponds.

1. It is my painting that makes me a god.
2. Hear the sounds of my voice, of my song; it is my voice.
3. I cover myself in sitting down by her.
4. I can make her blush, because I hear all she says of me.
5. Were she on a distant island, I could make her swim over.
6. Though she were far off, even on the other hemisphere.
7. I speak to your heart.

Fig. 7.

Fig. 7 is a war-song.   The warrior is shown in (1); he is drawn with wings, to show that he is active and swift of foot. In (2) he stands under the morning star; in (3) he is standing under the centre of heaven, with his war-club and rattle; in (4) the eagles of carnage are flying round the sky; in (5) he lies slain on the field of battle; and in (6) he appears as a spirit in the sky.   The words are these:—

1. I wish to have the body of the swiftest bird.
2. Every day I look at you, the half of the day I sing my song.
3. I throw away my body.
4. The birds take a flight in the air.
5. Full happy am I to be numbered with the slain.
6. The spirits on high repeat my name.

Catlin tells how the chief of the Kickapoos, a man of great ability, generally known as the " Shawnee Prophet," having, as was said, learnt the doctrines of Christianity from a missionary, taught them to his tribe, pretending to have received a supernatural mission. He composed a prayer, which he wrote down on a flat stick, " in characters somewhat resembling Chinese letters." When Catlin visited the tribe, every man, woman, and child used to repeat this prayer morning and evening, placing the fore-finger under the first character, repeating a sentence or two, and so going on to the next, till the prayer, which took some ten minutes to repeat, was finished.[1] I do not know whether any of these curious prayer-sticks are now to be seen, but they were probably made on the same principle as the suggestive pictures used for the native Indian songs.

Picture-writing is found among savage races in all quarters of the globe, and, so far as we can judge, its principle is the same everywhere. The pictures on the Lapland magic drums, of which we have interpretations, serve much the same purpose as the American writing. Savage paintings, or scratchings, or carvings on rocks, have a family likeness, whether we find them in North or South America, in Siberia or Australia. The interpretation of rock-pictures, which mostly consist of few figures, is in general a hopeless task, unless a key is to be had. Many are, no doubt, mere pictorial utterances, drawings of animals and things without any historical sense; some are names, as the totems carved by those who sprang upon the dangerous leaping-rock at the Red Pipestone Quarry.[2] Dupaix noticed in Mexico a sculptured eagle, apparently on the boundary of Quauhnahuac, " the place *near the eagle*," now called Cuernavaca,[3] and the fact suggests that rock-sculptures may often be, like this, symbolic boundary-marks. But there is seldom a key to be had to the reading of rock-sculptures, which the natives generally say were done by the people long

---

[1] Catlin, ' North American Indians,' 7th ed.; London, 1848, vol. ii. p. 99.

[2] Catlin, vol. ii. p. 170.

[3] Lord Kingsborough, ' Antiquities of Mexico;' London, 1830, etc., vol. iv. part i., no. 31, and vol. v. Expl.

ago. I have seen them in Mexico on cliffs where one can
hardly imagine how the savage sculptors can have climbed.
When Humboldt asked the Indians of the Oronoko who it
was that sculptured the figures of animals and symbolic signs
high up on the face of the crags along the river, they answered
with a smile, as relating a fact of which only a stranger, a
white man, could possibly be ignorant, "that at the time of the
great waters their fathers went up to that height in their canoes."[1]

As the gesture-language is substantially the same among
savage tribes all over the world, and also among children who
cannot speak, so the picture-writings of savages are not only
similar to one another, but are like what children make untaught even in civilized countries. Like the universal language
of gestures, the art of picture-writing tends to prove that the
mind of the uncultured man works in much the same way at
all times and everywhere. As an example of the way in which
it is possible for an observer who has never realized this fact
to be led astray by such a general resemblance, the celebrated
"Livre des Sauvages" may be adduced.

This book of pictures had been lying for many years in a
Paris library, before the Abbé Domenech unearthed it and
published it in facsimile, as a native American document of
high ethnological value. It contains a number of rude drawings
done in black lead and red chalk, in great part enormously indecent, though perhaps not so much with the grossness of the
savage as of the European blackguard. Many of the drawings
represent Scripture scenes, and ceremonies of the Roman Catholic church, often accompanied by explanatory German words
in the cursive hand, one or two of which, as the name
"Maria" written close to a rude figure of the Virgin Mary,
the Abbé succeeded in reading, though most of them were a
deep mystery to him. There are an evident Adam and Eve in
the garden, with "betruger" (deceiver) written against them;
Adam and Eve sent out of Paradise, with the description
"gebant" (banished); a priest offering mass; figures with the
well-known rings of bread in their hands, explained as "fass-
dag" (fast-day), and so on. There is no evidence of any con-

<hr>

[1] Humboldt and Bonpland, vol. ii. p. 239.

nexion with America in the whole matter, except that the document is said to have come into the hands of a collector, in company with an Iroquois dictionary, and that the editor says it is written on Canadian paper, but he gives no reason for thinking so. So far as one can judge from the published copy, it may have been done by a German boy in his own country. One of the drawings shows a man with what seems a mitre on his head, speaking to three figures standing reverently before him. This personage is entitled " grosshud " (great-hat), a common term among the German Jews, who speak of their rabbis, in all reverence, as the " great hats."

The Abbé Domenech had spent many years in America, and was, no doubt, well acquainted with Indian pictures. Moreover, the resemblance which struck him as existing between the pictures he had been used to see among the Indians, and those in the " Book of the Savages," is quite a real one. A great part of the pictures, if painted on birch-bark or deerskins, might pass as Indian work. The mistake he made was that his generalization was too narrow, and that he founded his argument on a likeness which was only caused by the similarity of the early development of the human mind.

Map-making is a branch of picture-writing with which the savage is quite familiar, and he is often more skilful in it than the generality of civilized men. In Tahiti, for instance, the natives were able to make maps for the guidance of foreign visitors.[1] Maps made with raised lines are mentioned as in use in Peru before the Conquest,[2] and there is no doubt about the skill of the North American Indians and Esquimaux in the art, as may be seen by a number of passages in Schoolcraft and elsewhere.[3] The oldest map known to be in existence is the map of the Æthiopian gold-mines, dating from the time of Sethos I., the father of Rameses II.,[4] long enough

---

[1] Gustav Klemm, 'Allgemeine Cultur-Geschichte der Menschheit,' Leipzig, 1843-52, vol. iv. p. 306.

[2] Rivero and v. Tschudi, 'Antigüedades Peruanas,' Vienna, 1851, p. 124. Prescott, 'Peru,' vol. I. p. 116.

[3] Schoolcraft, part i. pp. 334, 353; part iii. pp. 256, 485. Harmon, 'Journal,' Andover, 1820, p. 371. Klemm, C. G., vol. ii. pp. 169, 280.

[4] Birch, in 'Archæologia,' vol. xxxiv. p. 382.

before the time of the bronze tablet of Aristagoras, on which was inscribed the circuit of the whole earth, and all the sea and all rivers.[1]

The highest development of the art of picture-writing is to be found among the ancient Mexicans. Their productions of this kind are far better known than those of the Red Indians, and are indeed much more artistic, as well as being more systematic and copious. Some of the most characteristic specimens have been drawn and described by Alexander von Humboldt, and Lord Kingsborough's great work contains a huge mass of them, which he published in facsimile in support of his views upon that philosopher's stone of ethnologists, the Lost Tribes of Israel.

The bulk of the Mexican paintings are mere pictures, directly representing migrations, wars, sacrifices, deities, arts, tributes, and such matters, in a way not differing in principle from that of the lowest savages. But in the historical records and calendars, the events are accompanied by a regular notation of years, and sometimes of divisions of years, which entitles them to be considered as regularly dated history. The art of dating events was indeed not unknown to the Northern Indians. A resident among the Kristinaux (generally called for shortness, Crees), who knew them before they were in their present half-civilized state, says that they had names for the moons which make up the year, calling them "whirlwind moon," "moon when the fowls go to the south," "moon when the leaves fall off from the trees," and so on. When a hunter left a record of his chase pictured on a piece of birch-bark, for the information of others who might pass that way, he would draw a picture which showed the name of the month, and make beside it a drawing of the shape of the moon at the time, so accurately, that an Indian could tell within twelve or twenty-four hours, the month and the day of the month, when the record was set up.[2]

It is even related of the Indians of Virginia, that they recorded time by certain hieroglyphic wheels, which they called "Sagkokok Quiacosough," or "record of the gods." These wheels had sixty spokes, each for a year, as if to mark the

<hr>

[1] Herod. v. 49.   [2] Harmon, p. 371.

ordinary age of man, and they were painted on skins kept by
the principal priests in the temples. They marked on each
spoke or division a hieroglyphic figure, to show the memorable
events of the year. John Lederer saw one in a village called
Pommacomck, on which the year of the first arrival of the
Europeans was marked by a swan spouting fire and smoke
from its mouth. The white plumage of the bird and its living
on the water indicated the white faces of the Europeans and
their coming by sea, while the fire and smoke coming from
its mouth meant their firearms.[1] Thus the ancient Mexicans
(as well as the civilized nations of Central America, who used
a similar system) can only claim to have dated their records
more generally and systematically than the ruder North American tribes.

The usual way of recording series of years among the Mexicans has been often described. It consists in the use of four
symbols—tochtli, acatl, tecpatl, calli, *i. e. rabbit, cane, cutting-
stone, house,* each symbol being numbered by dots from 1 to 13,
making thus 52 distinct signs. Each year of a cycle of 52 has
thus a distinct numbered symbol belonging to it alone, the
numbering of course not going beyond 13. These numbered
symbols are, however, not arranged in their reasonable order,
but the signs change at the same time as the numbers, till all
the 52 combinations are exhausted, the order being 1 rabbit,
2 cane, 3 knife, 4 house, 5 rabbit, 6 cane, and so on. I have
pointed out elsewhere the singular coincidence of a Mexican
cycle with an ordinary French or English pack of playing-cards,
which, arranged on this plan, as for instance ace of hearts, 2
of spades, 3 of diamonds, 4 of clubs, 5 of hearts again, and so
on, forms an exact counterpart of an Aztec cycle of years. The
account of days was kept by series combined in a similar way,
but in different numbers.[2]

The extraordinary analogy between the Mexican system of
reckoning years in cycles, and that still in use over a great part

---

[1] 'Journal des Sçavans,' 1681, p. 46. Sir W. Talbot, 'The Discoveries of John
Lederer;' London, 1672, p. 4. Humboldt, 'Vues des Cordillères,' Paris,
1810-12, pl. xiii.

[2] Tylor, 'Mexico and the Mexicans;' London, 1861, p. 239.

of Asia, forms the strongest point of Humboldt's argument for
the connexion of the Mexicans with Eastern Asia, and the remarkable character of the coincidence is greatly enforced by
the fact, that this complex arrangement answers no useful purpose whatever, inasmuch as mere counting by numbers, or by
signs numbered in regular succession, would have been a far
better arrangement.   It may perhaps have been introduced for
some astrological purpose.

The historical picture-writings of the Mexicans seem for the
most part very bare and dull to us, who know and care so little
about their history.   They consist of records of wars, famines,
migrations, sacrifices, and so forth, names of persons and places
being indicated by symbolic pictures attached to them, as King
Itzcoatl, or "knife-snake," by a serpent with stone knives on
its back; Tzompanco, or "the place of a skull," now Zum-
pango, by a picture of a skull skewered on a bar between two
upright posts, as enemies' skulls used to be set up; Chapulte-
pec, or "grasshopper-hill," by a hill and a grasshopper, and so
on, or by more properly phonetic characters, such as will be
presently described.   The positions of footprints, arrows, etc.,
serve as guides to the direction of marches and attacks, in very
much the same way as may be seen in Catlin's drawing of the
pictured robe of Ma-to-toh-pa, or "Four Bears."   The mystical
paintings which relate to religion and astrology are seldom
capable of any independent interpretation, for the same reasons which make it impossible to read the pictured records of
songs and charms used further north, namely, that they do not
tell their stories in full, but only recall them to the minds of
those who are already acquainted with them.   The paintings
which represent the methodically arranged life of the Aztecs
from childhood to old age, have more human interest about
them than all the rest put together.   In judging the Mexican
picture-writings as a means of record, it should be borne in
mind that though we can understand them to a considerable
extent, we should have made very little progress in deciphering
them, were it not that there are a number of interpretations
made in writing from the explanations given by Indians, so
that the traditions of the art have never been wholly lost. Some

few of the Mexican pictures now in existence may perhaps be
original documents made before the arrival of the Spaniards,
and great part of those drawn since are certainly copied, wholly
or in part, from such original pictures.

It is to M. Aubin, of Paris, a most zealous student of Mexican antiquities, that we owe our first clear knowledge of a phenomenon of great scientific interest in the history of writing.
This is a well-defined system of phonetic characters, which
Clavigero and Humboldt do not seem to have been aware of,
as it does not appear in their descriptions of the art.[1] Humboldt indeed speaks of vestiges of phonetic hieroglyphics among
the Aztecs, but the examples he gives are only names in which
meaning, rather than mere sound, is represented, as in the
pictures of a face and water for Axayacatl, or " Water-Face,"
five dots and a flower for Macuilxochitl, or " Five-Flowers." So
Clavigero gives in his list the name of King Itzcoatl, or " Knife-
Snake," as represented by a picture of a snake with stone
knives upon its back, a more genuine drawing of which is
given here (Fig. 8), from the Le Tellier Codex. This is mere

Fig. 8.   Fig. 9.

picture-writing, but the way in which the same king's name is
written in the Vergara Codex, as shown in Fig. 9, is something
very different. Here the first syllable, itz, is indeed represented by a weapon armed with blades of obsidian, itz (tli);
but the rest of the word, coatl, though it means snake, is
written, not by a picture of a snake, but by an earthen pot, co
(mitl), and above it the sign of water, a (tl). Here we have
real phonetic writing, for the name is not to be read, according
to sense, " knife-kettle-water," but only according to the sound

¹ Clavigero, 'Storia Antica del Messico ;' Cesena, 1780-1, vol. ii. pp. 101, etc.,
249, etc. Humboldt, Vues des Cord., pl. xiii.

of the Aztec words, Itz-co-atl.   Again, in Fig.
10, in the name of Teocaltitlan, which means
"the place of the god's house," the different
syllables (with the exception of the *ti*, which
is only put in for euphony) are written by (*b*)
lips, (*c*) a path (with footmarks on it), (*a*) a
house, (*d*) teeth.   What this combination of

Fig. 10.

pictures means is only explained by knowing that lips, path,
house, teeth, are called in Aztec *te* (ntli), *o* (tli), *cal* (li) *tlan*
(tli), and thus come to stand for the word To-o-cal-(ti)-tlan.
The device is perfectly familiar to us in what is called a
"rebus," as where Prior Burton's name is sculptured in St.
Saviour's Church as a cask with a thistle on it, "burr-tun."
Indeed, the puzzles of this kind in children's books keep alive
to our own day the great transition stage from picture-writing
to word-writing, the highest intellectual effort of one period in
our history coming down, as so often happens, to be the child's
play of a later time.

M. Aubin may be considered as the discoverer of these phonetic signs in the Mexican pictures, or at least he is the first
who has worked them out systematically and published a list
of them.[1]   But the ancient written interpretations have been
standing for centuries to prove their existence.   Thus, in the
Mendoza Codex, the name of a place pictured as
in Fig. 11 by a fishing-net and teeth, is interpre-
tated Matlatlan, that is "Net-Place."   Now,
matla (tl) means a net, and so far the name is
a picture, but the teeth, *tlan* (tli), are used, not
pictorially but phonetically, for *tlan*, place.
Other more complicated names, such as Acolma,

Fig. 11.

Quauhpanoayan, etc., are written in like manner in phonetic
symbols in the same document:[2]

There is no sufficient reason to make us doubt that this

[1] Aubin, in 'Revue Orientale et Américaine,' vols. iii.–v.   Brasseur, Hist. des
Nat. Civ. du Mexique et de l'Amérique Centrale; Paris, 1857–9, vol. i.   An
attempt to prove the existence of something more nearly approaching alphabetic
signs (Rev., vol. iv. p. 276–7; Brasseur, p. lxviii.) requires much clearer evidence.
[2] Kingsborough, vol. I, and Expl. in vol. vi.

purely phonetic writing was of native Mexican origin, and after
the Spanish Conquest they turned it to account in a new and
curious way. The Spanish missionaries, when embarrassed by
the difficulty of getting the converts to remember their Ave
Marias and Paternosters, seeing that the words were of course
mere nonsense to them, were helped out by the Indians themselves, who substituted Aztec words as near in sound as might
be to the Latin, and wrote down the pictured equivalents for
these words, which enabled them to remember the required
formulas. Torquemada and Las Casas have recorded two instances of this device, that *Pater noster* was written by a flag
(*pantli*) and a prickly pear (*nochtli*), while the sign of water, *a*
(*tl*) combined with that of aloe, *me* (*tl*) made a compound word
ametl, which would mean "water-aloe," but in sound made
a very tolerable substitute for Amen.[1] But M. Aubin has actually found the beginning of a Paternoster of this kind in the

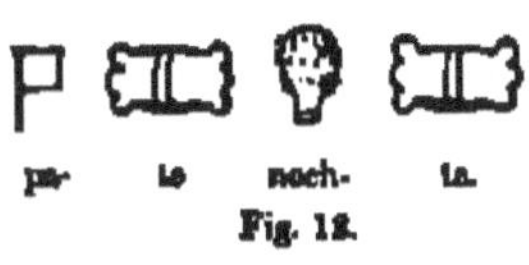

Fig. 12.

metropolitan library of Mexico
(Fig. 12), made with a flag, *pa*
(ntli), a stone, *te* (tl), a prickly
pear, *noch* (tli), and again a stone,
te (tl), and which would read
Pa-to noch-to, or perhaps Pa-tetl noch-tetl.[2]

After the conquest, when the Spaniards were hard at work
introducing their own religion and civilization among the conquered Mexicans, they found it convenient to allow the old
picture-writing still to be used, even in legal documents. It
disappeared in time, of course, being superseded in the long-
run by the alphabet ; but it is to this transition-period that we
owe many, perhaps most, of the picture-documents still preserved. Copies of old historical paintings were made and continued to dates after the arrival of Cortes, and the use of records written in pictures, or in a mixture of pictures and Spanish
or Aztec words in ordinary writing, relating to lawsuits, the
inheritance of property, genealogies, etc., were in constant use
for many years later, and special officers were appointed under
government to interpret such documents. To this transition-
period, the writing whence the name of Teocaltitlan (Fig. 10)

[1] Brasseur, vol. I. p. xli.   [2] Aubin, Rev. O. and A., vol. iii. p. 265.

is taken, clearly belongs, as appears by the drawing of the house with its arched door.

A genealogical table of a native family in the possession of Mr. Christy is as good a record of this time of transition as could well be cited. The names in it are written, but are accompanied by male and female heads drawn in a style that is certainly Aztec. The names themselves tell the story of the change that was going on in the country. One branch of the family, among whom are to be read the names of Citlalmecatl, or " Star-Necklace," and Cohuacihuatl, or " Snake-Woman," ends in a lady with the Spanish name of Justa ; while another branch, beginning with such names as Tlapalxilotzin and Xiuh-cozcatzin, finishes with Juana and her children Andres and Francisco. The most thoroughly native thing in the whole is a figure referring to an ancestor of Justa's, and connected with his name by a line of footprints to show how the line is to be followed, in true Aztec fashion. The figure itself is a head drawn in native style, with the eye in full front, though the face is in profile, in much the same way as an Egyptian would have drawn it, and it is set in a house as a symbol of dignity, having written over against it the high title of Ompamozcalti-totzaqualtzineo, which, if I may trust the imperfect dictionary of Molina, and my own weak knowledge of Aztec, means " His excellency our twice skilful gaoler."

The importance of this Mexican phonetic system in the History of the Art of Writing may be perhaps made clearer by a comparison of the Aztec pictures with the Egyptian hieroglyphics.

Egyptian hieroglyphic inscriptions consist of figures of objects, animate and inanimate, men and animals, and parts of them, plants, the heavenly bodies, and an immense number of different weapons, tools, and articles of the most miscellaneous character. These figures are arranged in upright columns or horizontal bands, and are to be read in succession, but they are not all intended to act upon the mind in the same way. When an ordinary inscription is taken to pieces, it is found that the figures composing it fall into two great classes. Part of them are to be read and understood as pictures, a drawing of

a horse for "horse," a branch for "wood," etc., upon the same
principle as in any savage picture-writing. The other part of the
figures are phonetic. Thus the figure of a strap, the name of
which is *m-s*, becomes a phonetic sign to write the sound *m-s*
with. (The – stands for some vowel, which is represented by
ou in the Coptic form of the word, *mous*.) Again, there are
many characters which Champollion held to be pure consonants, *p*, *r*, and so forth. They are certainly so in the spelling
of Ptolemy and Cleopatra, Tiberius and Hadrian, and such foreign names, and even in writing pure Egyptian words at a
much earlier date, where they come at the ends of words, as
where the mouth, *ro* or *ru*, ends the word *kar* (under, with),
being there nothing but the letter *r*. Modern Egyptologists,
however, hold Champollion to have gone too far in reducing
phonetic characters to mere letters; for instance, Mr. Birch
reads as *ka* and *pu* the *k*- and *p*- sounds which Champollion
set down as mere letters *k* and *p* in his alphabet. For practical purposes in interpreting Egyptian inscriptions, the distinction is of very little consequence, for vowels are very hazy
things in the ancient Egyptian, as in its successor the Coptic,
and it may be allowable to go on writing Egyptian words
whose vowels are indefinite, as though they had none at all.
But the syllabic theory (it is not a new view, for Dr. Young
held it before Champollion went away from it) is of great interest in the history of writing, as giving the whole course of
development, by which a picture, of a mouth for instance,
meant first simply mouth, then the name of mouth *ro*, and
lastly dropped its vowel and became the letter *r*. Of these
three steps, the Mexicans made the first two.

In Egyptian hieroglyphics, special figures are not always set
apart for phonetic use. At least, a number of signs are used
sometimes as letters, and sometimes as pictures, in which
latter case they are often marked with a stroke. Thus the
mouth, with a stroke to it, is usually (though not always)
pictorial, as it were, "one mouth," while without the stroke it
is *r* or *ro*, and so on. The words of a sentence are generally
written by a combination of these two methods, that is, by
spelling the word first, and then adding a picture sign to re-

move all doubt as to its meaning. Thus the letters read as
futi in an inscription, followed by a drawing of a worm, mean
"worm" (Coptic, *fent*), and the letters *kk*, followed by the
picture of a star hanging from heaven, mean "darkness" (Coptic, *kake*). There may even be words written in ancient hieroglyphics which are still alive in English. Thus *hbn*, followed
by two signs, one of which is the determinative for wood, is
ebony; and *tb*, followed by the drawing of a brick, is a sun-
dried brick, Coptic *tôbe*, *tôbi*, which seems to have passed into
the Arabic *tub*, or with the article, *attob*, thence into Spanish
through the Moors, as *adobe*, in which form, and as *dobie*, it
is current among the English-speaking population of America.

The Egyptians do not seem to have entirely got rid of their
determinative pictures even in the latest form of their native
writing, the demotic character. How it came to pass that,
having come so early to the use of phonetic writing, they were
later than other nations in throwing off the crutches of picture-signs, is a curious question. No doubt the poverty of their
language, which expressed so many things by similar combinations of consonants, and the indefiniteness of their vowels, had
to do with it, just as we see that poverty of language, and the
consequent necessity of making similar words do duty for many
different ideas, has led the Chinese to use in their writing determinative signs, the so-called keys or radicals, which were
originally pictures, though now hardly recognizable as such.
Nothing proves that the Egyptian determinative signs were
not mere useless lumber, so well as the fact that if there had
been none, the deciphering of the hieroglyphics in modern
times could hardly have gone a step beyond the first stage,
the reading of the kings' names.

We thus see that the ancient Egyptians and the Aztecs
made in much the same way the great step from picture-
writing to word-writing. To have used the picture of an
object to represent the sound of the root or crude-form of
its name, as the Mexicans did in drawing a hand, *ma* (itl), to
represent, not a hand, but the sound *ma*; and teeth, *tlan* (tli),
to represent, not teeth, but the sound *tlan*, though they do
not seem to have applied it to anything but the writing of

proper names and foreign words, is sufficient to show that they had started on the road which led the Egyptians to a system of syllabic, and to some extent of alphabetic writing. There is even evidence that the Maya nation of Yucatan, the ruins of whose temples and palaces are so well known from the travels of Catherwood and Stephens, not only had a system of phonetic writing, but used it for writing ordinary words and sentences. A Spanish MS., 'Relacion de las Cosas de Yucatan,' bearing the date of 1561, and the name of Diego de Landa, Bishop of Merida, has just been published by the Abbé Brasseur,[1] and contains not only a set of chronological signs resembling the figures of the Central American sculptures and the Dresden Codex, but a list of over thirty characters, some alphabetic, as *a, i, m, n;* some syllabic, as *ku, ti;* and a sentence, *ma in kati,* "I will not," written with them. The genuineness of this information, and its bearing on the interpretation of the inscriptions on the monuments, are, of course, matters for future investigation.

Yet another people, the Chinese, made the advance from pictures to phonetic writing, and it was perhaps because of the peculiar character of their spoken language that they did it in so different a way. The whole history of their art of writing still lies open to us. They began by drawing the plainest outlines of sun, moon, tortoise, fish, boy, hatchet, tree, dog, and so forth, and thus forming characters which are still extant, and are known as the *Ku-wăn,* or "ancient pictures."[2] Such pictures, though so much altered that, were not their ancient forms still to be seen, it would hardly be safe to say they had ever been pictures at all, are still used to some extent in Chinese writing, as in the characters for man, sun, moon, tree, etc. There are also combined pictorial signs, as water and eye for "tears," and other kinds of purely symbolic characters. But the great mass of characters at present in use are double, consisting of two signs, one for sound, the other for sense. They

<hr>

[1] Brasseur, 'Relation des Choses de Yucatan de Diego de Landa,' etc.; Paris and London, 1864.

[2] J. M. Callery, 'Systema Phoneticum Scripturæ Sinicæ,' part i.; Macao, 1841, p. 29. Endlicher, Chin. Gramm., p. 3, etc.

are called *hing-shing*, that is, "pictures and sounds."   In one
of the two signs the transition from the picture of the object
to the sound of its name has taken place ; in the other it has
not, but it is still a picture, and its use (something like that of
the determinative in the Egyptian hieroglyphics) is to define
which of the meanings belonging to the spoken word is to be
taken.   Thus a ship is called in Chinese *chow*, so a picture of a
ship stands for the sound *chow*.   But the word *chow* means
several other things ; and to show which is intended in any
particular instance, a determinative sign or key is attached to
it.   Thus the ship joined with the sign of water stands for
chow, " ripple," with that of speech for *chow*, " loquacity,"
with that of fire, for *chow*, " flickering of flame ;" and so on for
" waggon-pole," " fluff," and several other things, which have
little in common but the name of *chow*.   If we agreed that
pictures of a knife, a tree, an O, should be determinative signs
of things which have to do with cutting, with plants, and with
numbers, we might make a drawing of a pear to do duty, with
the assistance of one of these determinative signs, for *parr*, *pear*,
pair.   In a language so poverty-stricken as the Chinese, which
only allows itself so small a stock of words, and therefore has
to make the same sound stand for so many different ideas, the
use of such a system needs no explanation.

Looking now at the history of purely alphabetic writing, it
has been shown that there is one alphabet, that of the Egyptian
hieroglyphics, the development of which (and of course of its
derived forms) is clearly to be traced from the stage of pure
pictures to that of pure letters.   Some few of these interesting
characters are even now in use.   The Coptic Christians still keep
up in their churches their sacred language, which is a direct
descendant of the ancient Egyptian ; and the Coptic alphabet,
in which it is written and printed, was formed in early Christian
times by adding to the Greek alphabet certain new characters
to express articulations not properly belonging to the Greek.
Among these additional letters, at least four seem clearly to be
taken from the old hieroglyphics, probably from their hieratic
or cursive form, and thus to preserve an unbroken tradition at
once from the period of picture-writing to that of the alphabet,

and from times earlier than the building of the pyramids up to
the present day.

But as to the ultimate origin of most of the alphabets which
are or have been in use in the world, we have no such satis-
factory information as this. Thus, though the great family
of alphabets to which the Roman letters belong with the Greek,
the Gothic, the Northern Runes, etc., may be easily traced
back into connection with the Phœnician and Old Hebrew
characters, it is a very different question to tell how these
ancient Semitic letters came to be made. The theory main-
tained by Gesenius, that the Phœnician and Old Hebrew letters
are rude pictures of Aleph the Ox, Beth the House, Gimel the
Camel, etc., may, I think, be shown to be unsafe. Some of
the resemblances may possibly be real, though they are mostly
very slight and indefinite ; and while (after setting aside words
of very doubtful or fanciful etymology, as Zayin, Koph, He)
there appear to be some eleven letters which are more or less
like the meanings of their names, pure chance may be shown
to produce nearly as many coincidences as this. At least, if
we turn the list upside down, and put Tau against the letter
Aleph, and so on, it seems to me that there will be found something like eight resemblances of about the same strength, or
weakness. Again, the theory that the names of the letters
date from the time when these letters were first formed, and
thus record the very process of their formation, is a very bold
one, considering that we know by experience how slight the
bond is which may attach the name to the letter. Two alphabets, which are actually descended from that which is also
represented by the Phœnician and Hebrew, have taken to
themselves new sets of names belonging to the languages they
were used to write, simply choosing for each letter a word
which began with it. The names of our Anglo-Saxon Runes
are Feoh (cattle, fee), Úr (urus, wild ox), Thorn (thorn), Hägl
(hail), Nead (need), and so on, for F, Ú, Th, H, N, etc., this
English list corresponding in great measure with those belonging to the Scandinavian and German forms of the Runic alphabet. Again, in the old Slavonic alphabet, the names of Dobro,
(good), Zemlja (land), Liudi (people), Slovo (word), are given
to D, Z, L, S.

If it be granted that there is an amount of resemblance between the letters and their names in the old Semitic alphabets, which is wanting in these later ones, it does not follow from thence that the shape of the Hebrew letters was taken from their names. Letters may be named in two ways, acrostically, by names chosen because they begin with the right letters, or descriptively, as when we speak of certain characters as pothooks and hangers. A combination of the two methods, by choosing out of the words beginning with the proper letter such as had also some suitability to describe its shape, would produce much such a result as we see in the names of the Hebrew letters, and would moreover serve a direct object in helping children to learn them. It is easy to choose such names in English, as Arch or Arrowhead for A, Bow or Butterfly for B, Curve or Crescent for C; and we may even pick out of the Hebrew lexicon other names which fit about as well as the present set.

Whatever may be the real origin, syllabic or other, of the Semitic characters, the argument so confidently put forth in the Hebrew grammars is not strong enough for the weight laid upon it, seeing that the coincidences on which it rests may be explained as being not primary and essential, but secondary and superficial. The list of names of letters, Aleph, Beth, Gimel, and the rest, is certainly a very ancient and interesting record; but its value may lie not in its taking us back to the pictorial origin of the Hebrew letters, but in its preserving for us among the Semitic race the earliest known version of the "A was an Archer."

Mr. Samuel Sharpe has made an attempt to derive the Hebrew letters from Egyptian hieroglyphs, and in his list there are certainly two letters, both also belonging to the Coptic supplement, namely, *f* and *sh*, which run through the whole series of hieroglyphic, hieratic, Phœnician, old and new Hebrew (in Van and Shin), in very similar forms, a point which deserves careful investigation.[1] With respect to these speculations, however, it may be suggested that, though it is likely enough that the Jews or Phœnicians may have got the art of writing from the Egyptians, whose possession of it is proved to go back to so

<hr>

[1] Sharpe, 'Egyptian Hieroglyphics;' London, 1861, p. 17.

early a period, it does not necessarily follow from such a supposition that the characters of their alphabet should be traceable, letter for letter, to Egyptian originals. The possibility of one people getting the art of writing from another, without taking the characters they used for particular letters, is not a matter of theory, but of fact. Two systems of letters, or rather of characters representing syllables, have been invented in modern times, by men who had got the idea of representing sound by written characters, from seeing the books of civilized men, and applied it in their own way to their own languages.

Some forty years ago a halfbreed Cherokee Indian, named Sequoyah (otherwise George Guess), invented an ingenious system of writing his language in syllabic signs, which were adopted by the missionaries, and came into common use. In the table given by Schoolcraft there are eighty-five such signs, in great part copied or modified from those Sequoyah had learnt from print; but the letter D is to be read a; the letter M, lu; the figure 4, se; and so on through R, T, i, A, and a number more.[1]

The syllabic system invented by a West African negro, Momoru Doalu Bukere, that is to say, Mohammed Doalu the Bookman, was found in use in the Vei country, about fifteen years since.[2] When Europeans inquired into its origin, Doalu said that the invention was revealed to him in a dream by a tall venerable white man in a long coat, who said he was sent by other white men to bring him a book, and who taught him some characters to write words with. Doalu awoke, but never learnt what the book was about. So he called his friends together, and one of them afterwards had another dream, in which a white man appeared to him, and told him that the book had come from God. It appears that Doalu, when he was a boy, had really seen a white missionary, and had learnt verses from the English Bible from him, so that it is pretty clear that the sight of a printed book gave him the original idea which he worked out into his very complete and original phonetic

[1] Schoolcraft, part ii. p. 228.   Bastian, vol. i. p. 423.
[2] Koelle, 'Grammar of the Vei Language,' London, 1854, p. 239, etc.

system. It is evident from Fig. 13 that some part of the characters he adopted were taken, of course without any reference

$$\text{Ʀ Ɛ B } \underline{\text{X, T}} \text{ K I } \underline{\text{Ꙃ, N}} \quad \underline{\text{H , N}}$$
be fen gba gbe mbe na po re(le)

Fig. 13.

to their sound, from the letters he had seen in print. His system numbers 162 characters, representing mostly syllables, as *a, be, bo, dao, fen, gbu*; but sometimes longer articulations, as *adi, aediya, taro.* Though it is almost entirely and purely phonetic, it is interesting to observe that it includes three genuine picture-signs, ∘∘ *gba,* "money;" ∘°∘ *bu,* "gun," (represented by bullets,) and ～～ *chi,* "water," this last sign being identical with that which stands for water in the Egyptian hieroglyphs.

It appears from these facts that the transmission of the art of writing does not necessarily involve a detailed transmission of the particular signs in use, and the difficulty in tracing the origin of the Semitic characters may result from their having been formed, in great part or wholly, in the same way as the American and African syllabaria. If this be the case, there is an end of all hope of tracing them any further.

In conclusion, it may be observed that the art of picture-writing soon dwindles away in all countries when word-writing is introduced; yet there are a few isolated forms in which it holds its own, in spite of writing and printing, at this very day. The so-called Roman numerals are still in use, and I II III are as plain and indisputable picture-writing as any sign on an Indian scroll of birch-bark. Why V and X mean five and ten is not so clear, but there is some evidence in favour of the view that it may have come by counting fingers or strokes up to nine, and then making a stroke with another across to mark it, somewhat as the deaf-and-dumb Massieu tells us that, in his untaught state, his fingers taught him to count up to ten, and then he made a mark. Loskiel, the Moravian missionary, says of the Iroquois, "They count up to ten, and make a cross; then ten again, and so on, till they have finished; then they take the tens together, and make with them hundreds, thousands, and hundreds of thousands."[1]   A more modern observer says of the distant tribe of the Creeks, that they reckon by tens, and that in recording on grave-posts the years of age of the deceased, the scalps he has taken, or the war-parties he has led, they make perpendicular strokes for units, and a cross for ten.[2]   The Chinese character for ten is an upright cross; and in an old Chinese account of the life of Christ, it is said that " they made a very large and heavy machine of wood, resembling the character ten," which he carried, and to which he was nailed.[3]   The Egyptians, in their hieroglyphic character, counted by upright strokes up to nine, and then made a special sign for ten, in this respect resembling the modern Creek Indians; and the fact that the Chinese only count I II III in strokes, and go on with an X for four, and then with various other symbols till they come to + or ten, does not interfere with the fact, that in three or four systems of numeration, so far as we know independent of one another, in Italy, China, and North America, more or less of the earlier numerals are indicated by counted strokes, and ten by a crossed stroke.   Such an origin for the Roman X is quite consistent with a half X or V, being used for five, to save making a number of strokes which would be difficult to count at a glance.[4]

However this may be, the pictorial origin of I II III is beyond doubt.   And in technical writing, such terms as T-square and S-hook, and phrases such as " ⊙ before clock 4 min.," and " ☽ rises at 8h. 35m.," survive to show that even in the midst of the highest European civilization, the spirit of the earliest and rudest form of writing is not yet quite extinct.

[1] Loskiel, Gesch. der Mission der evangelischen Brüder; Darby, 1789. p. 50.

[2] Schoolcraft, part I. p. 273.

[3] Davis, 'The Chinese;' London, 1851, vol. ii. p. 170.

[4] A dactylic origin of V, as being a rude figure of the open hand, with thumb stretched out, and fingers close together, succeeding the I II III IIII, made with the upright fingers, has been propounded by Grotefend, and has occurred to others. It is plausible, but wants actual evidence.

CHAPTER VI.

IMAGES AND NAMES.

THE trite comparison of savages to "grown-up children," is in the main a sound one, though not to be carried out too strictly. In the uncivilized American or Polynesian, the strength of body and force of character of a grown man are combined with a mental development in many respects not beyond that of a young child of a civilized race. It has been already noticed how naturally children can appreciate and understand such direct expressions of thought as the gesture-language and picture-writing. In like manner, the use of dolls or images as an assistance to the operations of the mind, is familiar to all children, though among those who grow up under the influences of civilized society, it is mostly superseded and forgotten in after life. Few educated Europeans ever thoroughly realize the fact, that they have once passed through a condition of mind from which races at a lower stage of civilization never fully emerge; but this is certainly the case, and the European child playing with its doll, furnishes the key to several of the mental phenomena which distinguish the more highly cultivated races of mankind from those lower in the scale.

When a child plays with a doll or plaything, the toy is commonly made to represent in the child's mind some imaginary object which is more or less like it. Wooden soldiers, for instance, or the beasts in a Noah's ark, have a real resemblance which any one would recognize at once to soldiers and beasts,

and all that the child has to do is to suppose them bigger,
and alive, and to consider them as walking of themselves when
they are pushed about.   But an imaginative child will be content with much less real resemblance than this.   It will bring
in a larger subjective element, and make a dog do duty for a
horse, or a soldier for a shepherd, till at last the objective resemblance almost disappears, and a bit of wood may be dragged
about, representing a ship on the sea, or a coach on the road.
Here the likeness of the bit of wood to a ship or a coach is
very slight indeed; but it is a thing, and can be moved about
in an appropriate manner, and placed in a suitable position
with respect to other objects.   Unlike as the toy may be to
what it represents in the child's mind, it still answers a purpose, and is an evident assistance to the child in enabling it to
arrange and develope its ideas, by working the objects and
actions and stories it is acquainted with, into a series of dra-
matic pictures.   Of how much use the material object is in setting the mind to work, may be seen by taking it away and leaving the child to play, with nothing to play with.

At an early age, children learn more from play than from
teaching; and the use of toys is very great in developing their
minds by giving them the means of, as it were, taking a scene
or an event to pieces, and putting its parts together in new
combinations, a process which immensely increases the definiteness of the children's ideas and their power of analysis.   It
is because the use of toys is principally in developing the subjective side of the mind, that the elaborate figures and models
of which the toy-shops have been full of late years are of so
little use.   They are carefully worked out into the nicest details; but they are models or pictures, not playthings, and
children, who know quite well what it is they want, tire of
them in a few hours, unless, indeed, they can break them up
and make real toys of the bits.   What a child wants is not one
picture, but the means of making a thousand.   Objective knowledge, such as is to be gained from the elaborate doll's houses
and grocer's shops, with their appurtenances, may be got in
plenty elsewhere by mere observation; but toys, to be of value
in early education, should be separate, so as to allow of their

being arranged in any variety of combination, and not too servile and detailed copies of objects, so that they may not be mere pictures, but symbols, which a child can make to stand for many objects with the aid of its imagination.

In later years, and among highly educated people, the mental process which goes on in a child playing with wooden soldiers and horses, though it never disappears, must be sought for in the midst of more complex phenomena. Perhaps nothing in after life more closely resembles the effect of a doll upon a child, than the effect of the illustrations of a tale upon a grown-up reader. Here the objective resemblance is very indefinite; two artists would make pictures of the same scene that were very unlike one another, the very persons and places depicted are imaginary, and yet what reality and definiteness is given to the scene by a good picture. But in this case the direct action of an image on the mind complicates itself with the deepest problems of painting and sculpture. The comparison of the workings of the mind of the uncivilized man, and of the civilized child, is much less difficult.

Mr. Backhouse one day noticed in Van Diemen's Land a native woman arranging several stones that were flat, oval, and about two inches wide, and marked in various directions with black and red lines. These he learned represented absent friends, and one larger than the rest stood for a fat native woman on Flinders Island, known by the name of Mother Brown.[1] Similar practices are found among far higher races than the ill-fated Tasmanians. Among some North American tribes, a mother who has lost a child keeps its memory ever present to her by filling its cradle with black feathers and quills, and carrying it about with her for a year or more. When she stops anywhere, she sets up the cradle and talks to it as she goes about her work, just as she would have done if the dead baby had been still alive within it.[2] Here we have no image; but in Africa we find a rude doll, representing the child, kept as a memorial. It is well known that over a great

[1] Backhouse, 'Narrative of a Visit to the Australian Colonies;' London, 1843, p. 104.

[2] Catlin, vol. ii. p. 133.

part of Africa the practice prevails, that whenever twin children are born, one or both of them are immediately killed. Among the Wanyamwezi, one of the two is always killed; and, strange to say, "the universal custom amongst these tribes, is for the mother to wrap a gourd or calabash in skins, to place it to sleep with, and feed it like, the survivor."[1] Among the Bechuanas, it is a custom for married women to carry a doll with them till they have a child, when the doll is discarded. There is one of these dolls in the London Missionary Museum, consisting simply of a long calabash, like a bottle, wound round with strings of beads. The Basuto women use clay dolls in the same way, giving them the names of tutelary deities, and treating them as children.[2] Among the Ostyaks of Eastern Siberia, there is found a still more instructive case, in which we see the transition from the image of the dead man to the actual idol. When a man dies, they set up a rude wooden image of him, which receives offerings and has honours paid to it, and the widow embraces and caresses it. As a general rule, these images are buried at the end of three years or so, but sometimes the image of a shaman[3] is set up permanently, and remains as a saint for ever.[4]

The principal use of images to races in the lower stages of civilization is that to which their name of "the visible," εἴδωλον, idol, has come to be in great measure restricted in modern language. The idol answers to the savage in one province of thought the same purpose that its analogue the doll does to the child. It enables him to give a definite existence and a personality to the vague ideas of higher beings, which his mind can hardly grasp without some material aid. How these ideas came into the minds of even the lowest savages, need not be discussed here; it is sufficient to know that, so far as we have accurate information, they seem to be present everywhere in at least a rudimentary state.

[1] Burton, 'Central Africa,' vol. ii. p. 23.   [2] Casalis, p. 251.

[3] A shaman is a native sorcerer or medicine-man. His name is corrupted from Sanskrit çramana, a Buddhist ascetic, a term which is one of the many relics of Buddhism in Northern Asia, having been naturalized into the grovelling fetish-worship of the Ostyaks and Tunguses. See Weber, 'Indische Skizzen,' p. 66.

[4] Erman, 'Reise um die Erde,' Berlin, 1833–48, vol. ii. p. 677.

It does not appear that idols accompany religious ideas down to the lowest levels of the human race, but rather that they belong to a period of transition and growth. At least this seems the only reasonable explanation of the fact, that in America, for instance, among the lowest races, the Fuegians and the Indians of the southern forests, we hear little or nothing of idols. Among the so-called Red Indians of the North, we sometimes find idols worshipped and sacrificed to, but not commonly, while in Mexico and Peru the whole apparatus of idols, temples, priests, and sacrifices is found in a most complex and elaborate form. It does not seem, indeed, that the growth of the use of images may be taken as any direct measure of the growth of religious ideas, which is complicated with a multitude of other things. But it seems that when man has got some way in developing the religious element in him, he begins to catch at the device of setting a puppet or a stone as the symbol and representative of the notions of a higher being which are floating in his mind. He sees in it, as a child does in a doll, a material form which his imagination can clothe with all the attributes of a being which he has never seen, but of whose existence and nature he judges by what he supposes to be its works. He can lodge it in the place of honour, cover it up in the most precious garments, propitiate it with offerings such as would be acceptable to himself. The Christian missionary goes among the heathen to teach the doctrines of a higher religion, and to substitute for the crude superstition of the savage a belief in a God so far beyond human comprehension, that no definition of the Deity is possible to man beyond vague predications, as of infinite power, duration, knowledge, and goodness. It is not perhaps to be wondered at, that the missionary should see nothing in idol-worship but hideous folly and wickedness, and should look upon an idol as a special invention of the devil. He is strengthened, moreover, in such a view by the fact that by the operation of a certain law of the human mind (of which more will be said presently), the idol, which once served a definite and important purpose in the education of the human race, has come to be confounded with the idea of which it was the symbol, and has thus become the parent of the grossest superstition and delusion. But the student who occupies himself in tracing the early stages of human civilization, can see in the rude image of the savage an important aid to early religious development, while it often happens that the missionary is as unable to appreciate the use and value of an idol, as the grown-up man is to realize the use of a doll to a child.

Man being the highest living creature that can be seen and imitated, it is natural that idols should mostly be imitations, more or less rude, of the human form. To show that the beings they represent are greater and more powerful than man, they are often huge in size, and sometimes, by a very natural expedient, several heads and pairs of arms and legs show that they have more wisdom, strength, and swiftness than man. The sun and moon, which, in the physical system of the savage, are often held to be living creatures of monstrous power, are represented by images. The lower animals, too, are often mixed to the honour of personating supernatural powers, a practice which need not surprise us, when we consider that the savage does not set the lower animals at so great a depth below him as the civilized man does, but allows them the possession of language, and after his fashion, of souls, while we perhaps err in the opposite direction, by stretching the great gap which separates the lowest man from the highest animal, into an impassable gulf. Moreover, as animals have some powers which man only possesses in a less degree, or not at all, these powers may be attributed to a deity by personating him under the forms of the animals which possess them, or by giving to an image of human form parts of such animals; thus the feet of a stag, the head of a lion, or the wings of a bird, may serve to express the swiftness or ferocity of a god, or to show that he can fly into the upper regions of the air, or, like the goat's feet of Pan, they may be mere indications of his character and functions.

It is not necessary that the figure of a deity should have the characteristics of the race who worship it; the figure of another race may seem fitter for the purpose. Mr. Catlin, for instance, brought over with him a tent from the Crow Indians, which he describes as having the Great or Good Spirit painted on one side of it, and the Bad Spirit on the other. His drawing, unfortunately, only shows clearly one figure, in the unmistakable uniform of a white soldier with a musket in the one hand and a pipe in the other,[1] and this may very likely be the figure of the Good Spirit, for the pipe is a known symbol of peace.[2] But the white man stands also to the savage painter for the portrait of the Evil Demon, especially in Africa, where we find the natives of Mozambique drawing their devil in the likeness of a white man,[3] while Römer, speaking of the people of the Guinea coast, says that they say the devil is white, and paint him with their whitest colours. The pictures of him are lent on hire for a week or so by the old woman who makes them, to people whom the devil visits at night. When he sees his image, he is so terrified that he never comes back.[4] This impersonation need not, however, be intended by any means as an insult to the white man. As Captain Burton says of his African name of *Muzungu Mbaya*, "the wicked white man," it would have been but a sorry compliment to have called him a good white man. Much of the reverence of the savage is born rather of fear than of love, and the white colonist has seldom failed to make out that title to the respect of the savage, which lies in the power, not unaccompanied by the will, to hurt him.

The rudeness and shapelessness of some of the blocks and stones which serve as idols among many tribes, and those not always the lowest, is often surprising. There seems to be but one limit to the shapelessness of an idol, which is yet to represent the human form, and this is the same which a child would unconsciously apply, namely, that its length, breadth, and thickness must bear a proportion not too far different from the proportions of the human body. A wooden brick or a cotton-reel, set up or lying down, will serve well enough for a child to

[1] Catlin, vol. I. p. 44.
[2] Sir G. Simpson, Narrative of a Journey round the World; London, 1847, vol. I. p. 75.
[3] Purchas, vol. v. p. 768. See Livingstone, Missionary Travels, etc., in South Africa; London, 1857, p. 468.
[4] L. F. Römer, Nachr. von der Küste Guinea's; Copenhagen, Leipzig, 1769, p. 43.

represent a man or woman standing or lying, but a cube or
a ball would not answer the purpose so well, and if put for a
man, could hardly be supposed even by the imagination of a
child, to represent more than position and movement, or relative size when compared with larger or smaller objects. Much
the same test is applied by the uncivilized man in a particular
class of myths or legends, which come to be made on this wise.
We all have more or less of the power of seeing forms of men
and animals in inanimate objects, which sometimes have in fact a
considerable likeness of outline to what they suggest, but which,
in some instances, have scarcely any other resemblance to the
things into which fancy shapes them, than a rough similarity
in the proportions of their longer and shorter diameters. Myths
which have been applied to such fancied resemblances, or have
grown up out of them, may be collected from all parts of the
world, and from races high and low in the scale of culture.

Among the Riccaras, there was once a young Indian who
was in love with a girl, but her parents refused their consent to
the marriage, so the youth went out into the prairie, lamenting
his fate, and the girl wandered out to the same place, and the
faithful dog followed his master. There they wandered with
nothing to live on but the wild grapes, and at last they were
turned into stone, first their feet, and then gradually the upper
part of their bodies, till at last nothing was left unchanged but
a bunch of grapes, which the girl holds in her hand to this day.
And all this story has grown out of the fancied likeness of three
stones to two human figures and a dog. There are many
grapes growing near, and the Riccaras venerate these figures,
leaving little offerings for them when they pass by.[1]

There was a Maori warrior named Hau, and his wife Wairaka
deserted him. So he followed her, going from one river to
the next, and at last he came to one, where he looked out slyly
from the corner of his eye to see if he could discover her. He
breathed hard when he reached the place where Wairaka was
sitting with her paramour. He said to her, "Wairaka, I am
thirsty, fetch me some water." She got up and walked down
to the sea with a calabash in each hand. He made her go on

<hr>

[1] Lewis and Clarke, Expedition; Philadelphia, 1814, p. 107.

until the waves flowed over her shoulders, when he repeated a charm, which converted her into a rock that still bears her name. Then he went joyfully on his way.[1]

So the figure of the weeping Niobe turned into a rock, might be seen on Mount Sipylus.[2] So the circles of upright stones, set up long ago, on downs and hilltops in England and elsewhere, we cannot tell certainly for what purpose, have suggested the idea of a ring-dance, and the story has shaped itself, perhaps in Puritan times, that such a ring was a party of girls who were turned into stone for dancing carols on a Sunday.

There is a tradition, probably still current in Palestine, of a city between Petra and Hebron, whose inhabitants were turned into stone for their wickedness. This tradition may have been embodied in the Arabian Nights story of the city of fire-worshippers, who refused to embrace Islam, and were turned into stone. Seetzen, the traveller, visited the spot where the remains of the petrified inhabitants of the wicked city are still to be seen, and he found their heads, a number of stony concretions, lying scattered on the ground.[3]

The myths of footprints stamped into the rock by gods or mighty men are not the least curious of this class, not only from the power of imagination required to see footprints in mere round or long cavities, but also from the unanimity with which Egyptians, Greeks, Brahmans, Buddhists, Christians, and Moslems have adopted them as relics, each from their own point of view. The typical case is the sacred footprint of Ceylon, which is a cavity in the rock, 5 feet long by 2½ feet wide, at the top of Adam's Peak, made into something like a huge footstep by mortar divisions for the toes. Brahmans, Buddhists, and Moslems still climb the mountain to do reverence to it; but to the Brahman it is the footstep of Siva, to the Buddhist of the great founder of his religion, Gautama Buddha, and to the Moslem it is the spot where Adam stood when he was driven from Paradise; while the Gnostics have

[1] W. D. Baker, On Maori Popular Poetry, Trans. Eth. Soc., London, 1867, p. 49.

[2] Pausanias, i. 21.

[3] Kenrick, 'Essay on Primæval History,' London, 1846, p. 41.

held it to be the footprint of Icû, and Christians have been
divided between the conflicting claims of St. Thomas and the
Eunuch of Candace, Queen of Ethiopia.[1] The followers of
these different faiths have found holy footprints in many countries of the Old World, and the Christians have carried the
idea into various parts of Europe, where saints have left their
footmarks; while, even in America, St. Thomas left his footsteps on the shores of Bahia, as a record of his mythic
journey.[2]

For all we know, the whole mass of the Old World footprint-
myths may have had but a single origin, and have travelled
from one people to another. The story is found, too, in the
Pacific Islands, for in Samoa two hollow places, near six feet
long, in a rock, are shown as the footprints of Tiitii, where he
stood when he pushed the heavens up from the earth.[3] But
there are reasons which may make us hesitate to consider the
great Polynesian mythology as independent of Asiatic influence. Even in North America, at the edge of the Great
Pipestone Quarry, where the Great Spirit stood when the
blood of the buffalos he was devouring ran down upon the
stone and turned it red, there his footsteps are to be seen
deeply marked in the rock, in the form of the track of a great
bird.[4]

There are three kinds of prints in the rock which may have
served as a foundation for such tales as these. In many parts
of the world there are fossil footprints of birds and beasts,
many of huge size. The North American Indians also, whose
attention is specially alive to the footprints of men and animals,
very often carve them on rocks, sometimes with figures of the
animals to which they belong. These footprints are sometimes so naturally done as to be mistaken for real ones. The
rock of which Andersson heard in South Africa, "in which the
tracks of all the different animals indigenous to the country

[1] Tennent, 'Ceylon;' vol. ii. p. 132. Scherzer, Voy. of the Novara, E. Tr.; London, 1861, etc., vol. i. p. 413.
[2] Southey, 'History of Brazil;' London, 1822, vol. i.; Sup. p. xx.
[3] Rev. G. Turner, 'Nineteen Years in Polynesia;' London, 1861, p. 245.
[4] Catlin, vol. ii. p. 165, etc.

are distinctly visible,"[1] is probably such a sculptured rock. Thirdly, there are such mere shapeless holes as those to which most or all of the Old World myths seem to be attached. Now the difficulty in working out the problem of the origin of these myths is this, that if the prints are real fossil ones, or good sculptures, stories of the beings that made them might grow up independently anywhere; but one can hardly fancy men in many different places coming separately upon the quaint notion of mere hollows, six feet long, being monstrous footprints, unless the notion of monstrous footprints being found elsewhere were already current. At the foot of the page are references to some passages relating to the subject.[2]

It has just been remarked that there is a certain process of the human mind through which, among men at a low level of education, the use of images leads to gross superstition and delusion. No one will deny that there is an evident connexion between an object, and an image or picture of it; but we civilized men know well that this connexion is only *subjective*, that is, in the mind of the observer, while there is no *objective* connexion between them. By an objective connexion, I mean such a connexion as there is between the bucket in the well and the hand that draws it up,—when the hand stops, the bucket stops too; or between a man and his shadow,—when the man moves, the shadow moves too; or between an electro-magnet and the iron filings near it,—when the current passes through the coil, a change takes place in the condition of the iron filings. These are, of course, crude examples; but if more nicety is necessary, it might be said that the connexion is in some degree what a mathematician expresses in saying that y is a function of x, when, if x changes, y changes too. The connexion between a man and his portrait is not objective, for what is done to the man has no effect upon the portrait, and *vice versâ*.

[1] C. J. Andersson, Lake Ngami, etc., p. 327.

[2] Lyell, Second Visit to U. S., London, 1850, vol. ii. p. 313. C. Hamilton Smith, Nat. Hist. of Human Species; Edinburgh, 1848, p. 35. Schoolcraft, part iii. p. 74. Burton, 'Central Africa,' vol. i. p. 284. Squier and Davis, Anct. Mon. of Missi. Valley, vol. i. of Smithsonian Contr.; Washington, 1818, p. 253. Rawlinson, Herodotus, book ii. 91. iv. 82.

To an educated European nowadays this sounds like a mere truism, so self-evident that it is not necessary to make a formal statement of it ; but it may nevertheless be shown that this is one of the cases in which the accumulated experience and the long course of education of the civilized races, have brought them not only to reverse the opinion of the savage, but commonly to think that their own views are the only ones that could naturally arise in the mind of any rational human being. It needs no very large acquaintance with the life and ways of thought of the savage, to prove that there is to be found all over the world, especially among races at a low mental level, a view as to this matter which is very different from that which a more advanced education has impressed upon us. Man, in a low stage of culture, very commonly believes that between the object and the image of it there is a real connexion, which does not arise from a mere subjective process in the mind of the observer, and that it is accordingly possible to communicate an impression to the original through the copy. We may follow this erroneous belief up into periods of high civilization, its traces becoming fainter as education advances, and not only is this confusion of subjective and objective relation the prime cause of most of the delusions of idolatry, but even so seemingly obscure a subject as magic and sorcery may be brought in great measure into clear daylight, by looking at it as evolved from this process of the mind.

It is related by an early observer of the natives of Australia, that in one of their imitative dances they made use of a grass-figure of a kangaroo, and the ceremony was held to give them power over the real kangaroos in the bush.[1] In North America, when an Algonquin wizard wishes to kill a particular animal, he makes a grass or cloth image of it, and hangs it up in his wigwam. Then he repeats several times the incantation, "See how I shoot," and lets fly an arrow at the image. If he drives it in, it is a sign that the animal will be killed next day. Again, while an arrow touched by the magical medáwin, and afterwards fired into the track of an animal, is believed to arrest his course, or otherwise affect him, till the hunter can come

[1] Collins, 'New South Wales,' London, 1798, vol. i. p. 569.

up, a similar virtue is believed to be exerted, if but the figure
of the animal sought be drawn on wood or bark, and afterwards submitted to the influences of the magic medicine and
incantation.[1] In their picture-writings, a man or beast is
shown to be under magic influence by drawing a line from the
mouth to the heart, as in the annexed figure, which represents
a wolf under the charm of the
magician, and corresponds to the
incantation sung by the medicine-
man, "Run, wolf, your body's
mine."[2] Writing in the last century, Charlevoix remarks, that
the Illinois and some other tribes
make little marmouzets or puppets to represent those whose

Fig. 11.

lives they wish to shorten, and pierce these images to the
heart.[3]

We find thus among the Indians of North America one of
the commonest arts of magic practised in Europe in ancient
and mediæval times. The art of making an image and melting it away, drying it up, shooting at it, sticking pins or thorns
into it, that some like injury may befall the person it is to represent, is too well known to need detailed description here,[3]
and it is still to be found existing in various parts of the world.
Thus the Peruvian sorcerers are said still to make rag dolls and
stick cactus-thorns into them, and to hide them in secret holes
in houses, or in the wool of beds or cushions, thereby to cripple
people, or turn them sick or mad.[4] In Borneo the familiar
European practice still exists, of making a wax figure of the
enemy to be bewitched, whose body is to waste away as the
image is gradually melted,[5] as in the story of Margery Jordane's
waxen image of Henry VI. The Hindoo arts are thus described by the Abbé Dubois:—"They knead earth taken from
the sixty-four most unclean places, with hair, clippings of hair,

<hr>

[1] Schoolcraft, part i. pp. 372, 380–382.   [2] Charlevoix, vol. vi. p. 68.
[3] Jacob Grimm, 'Deutsche Mythologie,' Göttingen, 3rd edit.; 1854, p. 1045, etc.
Brand, 'Popular Antiquities,' Bohn's Series; London, 1855, vol. iii. p. 10, etc.
[4] Rivero and Tschudi, p. 181.   [5] St. John, vol. ii. p. 260.

bits of leather, etc., and with this they make little figures, on the breasts of which they write the name of the enemy; over these they pronounce magical words and mantrams, and consecrate them by sacrifices. No sooner is this done, than the *grahas*, or planets, seize the hated person, and inflict on him a thousand ills. They sometimes pierce these figures right through with an awl, or cripple them in different ways, with the intention of killing or crippling in reality the object of their vengeance."[1] Again, the Karens of Burmah model an image of a person from the earth of his footprints, and stick it over with cottonseeds, intending thereby to strike the person represented with dumbness.[2] Here we have the making of the figure combined with the ancient practice in Germany known as the "earth-cutting" (erdschnitt), cutting out the earth or turf where the man who is to be destroyed has stood, and hanging it in the chimney, that he may perish as his footprint dries and shrivels.[3]

In these cases the object in view is to hurt the original through the image, but it is also possible to make an image, transfer to it the evil spirit of the disease which has attacked the person it is to represent, and then send it out like a scapegoat into the wilderness. They conjure devils into puppets in West Africa;[4] in Siam the doctor makes an image of clay, sends his patient's disease into it, and then takes it away to the woods and buries it;[5] while the Tunguz cures his leg or his heart by wearing a carved model of the part affected about him.[6]

The transfer of life or the qualities of a living being to an image may be made by giving it a name, or by the performance of a ceremony over it. Thus, at the festival of the Durga Pûja, the officiating Brahman touches the cheeks, eyes, breast, and forehead of each of the images that have been prepared, and says, "Let the soul of Durga long continue in happiness in this image."

[1] Dubois, Mœurs, etc., des Peuples de l'Inde; Paris, 1825, vol. ii. p. 63.
[2] Mrs. Mason, 'Civilising Mountain Men;' London, 1862, p. 121.
[3] Grimm, D. M., p. 1017.
[4] Hutchinson, in Tr. Eth. Soc., London, 1861, p. 330.
[5] Bowring, 'Siam;' London, 1857, vol. i. p. 139.
[6] Ravenstein, 'The Russians on the Amur;' London, 1861, p. 351.

Till life is thus given to them, they may not be worshipped.[1] But the mere making of the image of a living creature is very commonly sufficient to set up at once its connexion with life, among races who have not thoroughly passed out of the state of mind to which these practices belong. Looking at the matter from a very different point of view, and yet with the same feeling of a necessary connexion between life and the image of the living creature, the Moslem holds that he who makes an image in this world will have it set before him on the day of judgment, and will be called upon to give it life, but he will fail to finish the work he has thus left half done, and will be sent to expiate his offence in hell.

With such illustrations to show how widely spread and deeply rooted is the belief that there is a real connexion between the object and its image, we can see how almost inevitable it is, that the man at a low stage of education should come to confound the image with that which it was made to represent. The strong craving of the human mind for a material support to the religious sentiment, has produced idols and fetishes over most parts of the world, and at most periods in its history; and while the more intelligent, even among many low tribes, have often seen clearly enough that the images were mere symbols of superhuman beings, the vulgar have commonly believed that the idols themselves had life and supernatural powers. Missionaries have remarked this difference in the views of more and less intelligent members of the same tribe; and it is emphatically true of a large part of Christendom, that the images and pictures, which, to the more instructed, serve merely as a help to realize religious ideas and to suggest devotional thoughts, are looked upon by the uneducated and superstitious crowd, as beings endowed not only with a sort of life, but with miraculous influences.

The line between the cases in which the connexion between object and figure is supposed to be real, and those in which it is known to be imaginary, is often very difficult to draw. Thus idols and figures of saints are beaten and abused for not granting the prayers of their worshippers, which may be a mere

[1] Coleman, 'The Mythology of the Hindus,' London, 1832, p. 93.

expression of spite towards their originals, but then two rival
gods may be knocked together when their oracles disagree,
that the one which breaks first may be discarded, and here a
material connection must certainly be supposed to exist.   To
the most difficult class belong the symbolic sacrifices of models
of men and animals in Italy and Greece, and the œconomical
paper-offerings of Eastern Asia.   The Chinese perform the rite
of burning money and clothes for the use of the dead; but the
real things are too valuable to be wasted by a thrifty people,
so paper figures do duty for them.   Thus they set burning
junks adrift as sacrifices to get a favourable wind, but they are
only paper ones.   Perhaps the neatest illustration of this kind
of offerings, and of the state of mind in which the offerer makes
them, is to be found in Huc and Gabet's story of the Tibetan
lamas, who sent horses flying from the mountain-top in a gale
of wind, for the relief of worn-out pilgrims who could get no
further on their way.   The horses were bits of paper, with a
horse printed on each, saddled, bridled, and galloping at full
speed.[1]

Hanging and burning in effigy is a proceeding which, in
civilized countries at any rate, at last comes fairly out into pure
symbolism.   The idea that the burning of the straw and rag
body should act upon the body of the original, perhaps hardly
comes into the mind of any one who assists at such a performance.   But it is not easy to determine how far this is the case
with the New Zealanders, whose minds are full of confusion
between object and image, as we may see by their witchcraft,
and who also hold strong views about their effigies, and fero-
ciously revenge an insult to them.   One very curious practice
has come out of their train of thought about this matter.   They
were very fond of wearing round their necks little hideous
figures of green jade, with their heads very much on one side,
which are called *tiki*, and are often to be seen in museums.
It seems likely that they are merely images of Tiki, the god of
the dead.   They are carried as memorials of dead friends, and
are sometimes taken off and wept and sung over by a circle of
natives; but a *tiki* commonly belongs, not to the memory of a

[1] Huc and Gabet, Voy. dans la Tartarie, etc.; Paris, 1850, vol. ii. p. 136.

single individual, but of a succession of deceased persons who have worn it in their time, so that it cannot be considered as having in it much of the nature of a portrait.[1] Some New Zealanders, however, who were lately in London, were asked why these *tikis* usually, if not always, have but three fingers on their hands, and they replied that if an image is made of a man, and any one should insult it, the affront would have to be revenged, and to avoid such a contingency the *tikis* were made with only three fingers, so that, not being any one's image, no one was bound to notice what happened to them.

In medicine, the notion of the real connexion between object and image has manifested itself widely in both ancient and modern times. Pliny speaks of the folly of the magicians in using the catanance ($\kappa\alpha\tau\alpha\nu\acute{\alpha}\gamma\kappa\eta$, compulsion) for love-potions, because it shrinks in drying into the shape of the claws of a dead kite (and so, of course, holds the patient fast); but it does not strike him that the virtues of the lithospermum or "stone-seed" in curing calculus were no doubt deduced in just the same way.[2] In more modern times, such notions as these were elaborated into the old medical theory known as the "Doctrine of Signatures," which supposed that plants and minerals indicated by their external characters the diseases for which nature had intended them as remedies. Thus the Euphrasia or eye-bright was, and is, supposed to be good for the eyes, on the strength of a black pupil-like spot in its corolla, the yellow turmeric was thought good for jaundice, and the blood-stone is probably used to this day for stopping blood.[3] By virtue of a similar association of ideas, the ginseng, which is still largely used in China, was also employed by the Indians of North America, and in both countries its virtues were deduced from the shape of the root, which is supposed to resemble the human body. Its Iroquois name, *abesoutchenzu*, means "a child," while in China it is called *jin-seng*, that is to say, "resemblance of man."[4]

<hr>

[1] Hale, in U. S. Exploring Exp.; Philadelphia, vol. vi., 1846, p. 23. Rev. W. Yate, 'Account of New Zealand;' London, 1835, p. 151.

[2] Plin., xxvii. 35, 74.   [3] Paris, 'Pharmacologia;' London, 1843, p. 47.

[4] Charlevoix, vol. vi. p. 24. For a similar case, see the 'Penny Cyclopædia,' art. "Atropa Mandragora" (mandrake).

Such cases as these bring clearly into view the belief in a real and material connexion existing between an object and its image. By virtue of their resemblance, the two are associated in thought, and being thus brought into connexion in the mind, it comes to be believed that they are also in connexion in the outside world. Now the association of an object with its name is made in a very different way, but it nevertheless produces a series of very similar results. Except in imitative words, the objective resemblance between thing and word, if it ever existed, is not discernible now. A word cannot be compared to an image or a picture, which, as everybody can see, is like what it stands for; but it is enough that idea and word come together by habit in the mind, to make men think that there is some real bond of connexion between the thing, and the name which belongs to it in their mother-tongue. Professor Lazarus, in his "Life of the Soul," tells a good story of a German who went to the Paris Exhibition, and remarked to his companion what an extraordinary people the French were, "For bread, they say *du pain!*" "Yes," said the other, "and we say *bread.*" "To be sure," replied the first, "*but it is bread, you know.*"[1]

As, then, men confuse the word and the idea, in much the same way as they confuse the image with that which it represents, there springs up a set of practices and beliefs concerning names, much like those relating to images. Thus it is thought that the utterance of a word ten miles off has a direct effect on the object which that word stands for. A man may be cursed or bewitched through his name, as well as through his image. You may lay a smock frock on the door-sill, and pronounce over it the name of the man you have a spite against, and then when you beat that smock, your enemy will feel every blow as well as if he were inside it in the flesh.[2] Thus, too, when the root of the devil-nettle was plucked to be worn as a charm against intermittent fevers, it was necessary to say for what purpose, and for whom, and for whose son it was pulled up,

[1] Lazarus, 'Leben der Serle;' Berlin, 1856–7, vol. ii. p. 77.

[2] Kuhn, 'Die Herabkunft des Feuers und des Göttertranks;' Berlin, 1859, p. 227.

and other magical plants required also a mention of the patient's name to make them work.[1]

How the name is held to be part of the very being of the man who bears it, so that by it his personality may be carried away, and, so to speak, grafted elsewhere, appears in the way in which the sorcerer uses it as a means of putting the life of his victim into the image upon which he practises. Thus King James, in his 'Dæmonology,' says that "the devil teacheth how to make pictures of wax or clay, that by roasting thereof, the persons that they bear the name of may be continually melted or dried away by continual sickness."[2] A mediæval sermon speaks of baptizing a "wax" to bewitch with; and in the eleventh century, certain Jews, it was believed, made a waxen image of Bishop Eberhard, set about with tapers, bribed a clerk to baptize it, and set fire to it on that sabbath, the which image burning away at the middle, the bishop fell grievously sick and died.[3]

A similar train of thought shows itself in the belief, that the utterance of the name of a deity gives to man a means of direct communication with the being who owns it, or even places in his hands the supernatural power of that being, to be used at his will. The Moslems hold that the "great name" of God (not Allah, which is a mere epithet), is known only to prophets and apostles, who, by pronouncing it, can transport themselves from place to place at will, can kill the living, raise the dead, and do any other miracle.[4]

The concealment of the name of the tutelary deity of Rome, for divulging which Valerius Soranus is said to have paid the penalty of death, is a case in point. As to the reason of its being kept a secret, Pliny says that Verrius Flaccus quotes authors whom he thinks trustworthy, to the effect that when the Romans laid siege to a town, the first step was for the priests to summon the god under whose guardianship the place was, and to offer him the same or a greater place or worship among the Romans. This practice, Pliny adds, still remains in the pontifical discipline, and it is certainly for this reason that it has

<hr>

[1] Plin., xxii. 16, 21; xxiii. 54.
[2] Brand, vol. iii. p. 10.
[3] Grimm, D. M., p. 1047.
[4] Lane, Mod. Eg., vol. i. p. 361.

been kept secret under the protection of what god Rome itself has been, lest its enemies should use a like proceeding.[1]

Moreover, as man puts himself into communication with spirits through their names, so they know him through his name. In Borneo, they will change the name of a sickly child to deceive the evil spirits that have been tormenting it.[2] In South America, among the Abipones and Lenguas, when a man died, his family and neighbours would change their own names[3] to cheat Death when he should come to look for them. It is perhaps a falling off from these extreme instances of the intimacy with which name and object have grown together in the savage mind, to cite the practice of exchanging names in evidence of identity of mind and feeling, which was found in the West Indies at the time of Columbus,[4] and in the South Seas by Captain Cook, who was called Oree, while his friend Oree went by the name of Cookee.[5]

But Cadwallader Colden's account of his new name, is admirable evidence of what there is in a name in the mind of the savage. "The first Time I was among the *Mohawks*, I had this Compliment from one of their old *Sachems*, which he did, by giving me his own Name, *Cayenderongue*. He had been a notable Warrior; and he told me, that now I had a Right to assume to myself all the Acts of Valour he had performed, and that now my Name would echo from Hill to Hill over all the *Five Nations*." When Colden went back into the same part ten or twelve years later, he found that he was still known by the name he had thus received, and that the old chief had taken another.[6]

Taking a still wider stretch, the power of association grasps not only the spoken word, but its written representative. It

<hr>

[1] Plin., xxviii. 4. Plut., Q. R. Macrob. Sat., iii. 9. See Bayle, art. "Soranus."

[2] St. John, 'Borneo,' vol. i. p. 107.

[3] Dobrizhoffer, 'The Abipones,' E. Tr.; London, 1822, vol. ii. p. 273. Southey, 'History of Brazil,' London, 1819, vol. iii. p. 394.

[4] 'Letters of Columbus' (Hakluyt Soc.); London, 1847, p. 217.

[5] Cook, First Voy. II., vol. ii. p. 251. Second Voyage; London, 2nd edit., 1777, vol. i. p. 167.

[6] Colden, Hist. of the Five Indian Nations of Canada; London, 1747, part I. p. 10.

has been seen how the Hindoo sorcerers wrote the name of their victim on the breast of the image made to personate him. A Chinese physician, if he has not got the drug he requires for his patient, will write the prescription on a piece of paper, and let the sick man swallow its ashes, or an infusion of the writing, in water.[1] This practice is no doubt very old, and may even descend from the time when the picture-element in Chinese writing, now almost effaced, was still clearly distinguishable, so that the patient would at least have the satisfaction of eating a picture, not a mere written word. Whether the Moslems got the idea from them or not, I do not know, but among them a verse of the Koran washed off into water and drunk, or even water from a cup in which it is engraved, is an efficacious remedy.[2] Here the connexion between the two ends of the chain is very remote indeed. The arbitrary characters, which represent the sound of the word, which represents the idea, have to do duty for the idea itself. The example is a striking one, and will serve to measure the strength of the tendency of the uneducated mind to give an outward material reality to its own inward processes.

This confusion of objective with subjective connexion, which shows itself so uniform in principle, though so various in details, in the practices upon images and names, done with a view of acting through them on their originals or their owners, may be applied to explain one branch after another of the arts of the sorcerer and diviner, till it almost seems as though we were coming near the end of his list, and might set down practices not based on this mental process, as exceptions to a general rule.

When a lock of hair is cut off as a memorial, the subjective connexion between it and its former owner, is not severed. In the mind of the friend who treasures it up, it recalls thoughts of his presence, it is still something belonging to him. We know, however, that the objective connexion was cut by the scissors, and that what is done to that hair afterwards, is not

<hr>

[1] Davis, vol. ii. p. 215.
[2] Lane, Mod. Eg., vol. i. p. 347-8. Petherick, Egypt, etc.; Edinburgh, 1861, p. 221.

felt by the bond on which it grew.   But this is exactly what
the savage has not come to know.   He feels that the subjective
bond is unbroken in his own mind, and he believes that the
objective bond, which his mind never gets clearly separate from
it, is unbroken too.   Therefore, in the remotest parts of the
world, the sorcerer gets clippings of the hair of his enemy,
parings of his nails, leavings of his food, and practises upon
them, that their former possessor may fall sick and die.   This
is why South Sea Island chiefs had servants always following
them with spittoons, that the spittle might be buried in some
secret place, where no sorcerer could find it, and why even
brothers and sisters had their food in separate baskets.   In the
island of Tanna, in the New Hebrides, there was a colony of
disease-makers who lived by their art.   They collected any
nahak or rubbish that had belonged to any one, such as the
skin of a banana he had eaten, wrapped it in a leaf like a cigar,
and burnt it slowly at one end.   As it burnt, the owner got
worse and worse, and if it was burnt to the end, he died.   When
a man fell ill, he knew that some sorcerer was burning his
rubbish, and shell-trumpets, which could be heard for miles,
were blown to signal to the sorcerers to stop, and wait for the
presents which would be sent next morning.   Night after night,
Mr. Turner used to hear the melancholy too-tooing of the
shells, entreating the wizards to stop plaguing their victims.
And when a disease-maker fell sick himself, he believed that
some one was burning his rubbish, and had his shells too blown
for mercy.[1]   It is not needful to give another description after
this, the process is so perfectly the same in principle wherever
it is found, all over Polynesia,[1] in Africa,[3] in India,[4] in North
and South America,[5] in Australia.[6]   It is alive to this day in
Italy, where a man does not like to trust a lock of his hair in
the hands of any one, lest he should be bewitched or enamoured
against his will.[7]

[1] Turner. 'Polynesia,' pp. 15, 89, 424.

[2] Polack, 'Manners and Customs of the New Zealanders ;' London, 1840, vol.
i. p. 281.   Ellis, vol. ii. p. 229.   Williams, 'Fiji,' vol. i. p. 249.   Purchas, vol. ii.
p. 1052, etc.   [3] Casalis, p. 276.   [4] Roberts, Or. Illustr. p. 470.

[5] Klemm, C. G., vol. ii. p. 168.   Fitz Roy, in Tr. Eth. Soc. ; London, 1861, p. 6.

[6] Stanbridge, Id., p. 229.

[7] Story, 'Roba di Roma ;' London, 1863, vol. ii. p. 342.

One of the best accounts we have of the art of procuring death by sorcery, is given in Sir James Emerson Tennent's great work on Ceylon. It is not that there is much that is peculiar in the processes it describes, but just the contrary; its importance lies in its presenting, among a somewhat isolated race, a system of sorcery, which is quite a little museum of the arts practised among the most dissimilar tribes in the remotest regions of the world. The account is as follows:—"The vidahn stated to the magistrate that a general belief existed among the Tamils [of Ceylon] in the fatal effects of a ceremony, performed with the skull of a child, with the design of producing the death of an individual against whom the incantation is directed. The skull of a male child, and particularly of a first-born, is preferred, and the effects are regarded as more certain if it be killed expressly for the occasion; but for ordinary purposes, the head of one who had died a natural death is presumed to be sufficient. The form of the ceremony is to draw certain figures and cabalistic signs upon the skull, after it has been scraped and denuded of the flesh; adding the name of the individual upon whom the charm is to take effect. A paste is then prepared, composed of sand from the footprints of the intended victim, and a portion of his hair moistened with his saliva, and this, being spread upon a leaden plate, is taken, together with the skull, to the graveyard of the village, where for forty nights the evil spirits are invoked to destroy the person so denounced. The universal belief of the natives is, that as the ceremony proceeds, and the paste dries up on the leaden plate, the sufferer will waste away and decline, and that death, as an inevitable consequence, must follow."[1] Here we have at once the name, the earth-cutting, the hair and saliva, the cursing, and the drying up. The use of the skull lies in its association with death, and we shall presently find it used in the same way in a very different place.

Even the spirits of the dead may be acted on through the remains of their bodies. Though the savage commonly holds that after death the soul goes its own way, for the most part independently of the body to which it once belonged, yet in his

[1] Tennent, 'Ceylon,' vol. ii. p. 545.

mind the soul and the body of his enemy or his friend are inseparably associated, and thus he comes to hold, in his inconsistent way, that a bond of connexion must after all survive between them. Therefore, the African fastens the jaw of his slain enemy to a tabor or a horn, and his skull to the big drum, that every crash and blast may send a thrill of agony through the ghost of their dead owner.[1]

The connexion between a cut lock of hair and its former owner is, in the mind at least, much closer than is necessary for these purposes. As has been seen, the remains of a person's food are sufficient to bewitch him by. In a witchcraft case in the seventeenth century, the supposed sorceress confessed that " there was a glove of the said Lord Henry buried in the ground, and as that glove did rot and waste, so did the liver of the said lord rot and waste."[2] Indeed, any association of ideas in a man's mind, the vaguest similarity of form or position, even a mere coincidence in time, is sufficient to enable the magician to work from association in his own mind, to association in the material world. Nor is there any essential difference in the process, whether his art is that of the diviner or of the sorcerer, that is, whether his object is merely to foretell something that will happen to a person, or actually to make that something happen; or if he is only concerned with the searching out of the hidden past, the process remains much the same, the intention only is different.

Out of the endless store of examples, I will do no more than take a few typical cases. They hung up charms in the Pacific Islands to keep thieves and trespassers out of plantations; a few cocoa-nut leaves, plaited into the form of a shark, will cause the thief who disregards it to be eaten by a real one; two sticks, set one across the other, will send a pain right across his body, and the very sight of these tabus will send thieves and trespassers off in terror.[3] In Kamchatka, when something had been stolen, and the thief could not be discovered, they would throw nerves or sinews into the fire, that as they shrank and wriggled with the heat, the like might happen to the body

[1] Römer, 'Guinea,' p. 112.   Klemm, C. G., vol. iii. p. 352.
[2] Brand, vol. iii. p. 29.   [3] Turner, p. 291.

of the thief.[1] In New Zealand, when a male child had been baptized in the native manner, and had received its name, they thrust small pebbles, the size of a large pin's head, down its throat, to make its heart callous, hard, and incapable of pity.[2] The Red Indian hunter wears ornaments of the claws of the grizzly bear, that he may be endowed with its courage and ferocity,[3] a simpler charm than that whereby the magicians made men invincible in Pliny's time, in which the head and tail of a dragon, marrow of a lion and hair from his forehead, foam of a victorious racehorse, and claws of a dog, were bound together in a piece of deerskin, with alternate sinews of a deer and a gazelle.[4] Many of the food-prejudices of savage races depend on the belief which belongs to this class of superstitions, that the qualities of the eaten pass into the eater. Thus, among the Dayaks, young men sometimes abstain from the flesh of deer, lest it should make them timid, and before a pig-hunt they avoid oil, lest the game should slip through their fingers,[5] and in the same way the flesh of slow-going and cowardly animals is not to be eaten by the warriors of South America; but they love the meat of tigers, stags, and boars, for courage and speed.[6] An English merchant in Shanghai, at the time of the Taeping attack, met his Chinese servant carrying home a heart, and asked him what he had got there. He said it was the heart of a rebel, and that he was going to take it home and eat it to make him brave.

When a Maori war-party is to start, the priests set up sticks in the ground to represent the warriors, and he whose stick is blown down is to fall in the battle.[7] In the Fiji Islands, the diviner will shake a bunch of dry cocoa-nuts to see whether a sick child will die; if all fall off, it will recover; if any remain on, it will die. He will spin a cocoa-nut, and decide a question according to where the eye of the nut looks towards when at rest again, or he will sit on the ground and take omens from his legs; if the right leg trembles first, it is good; if the left, it is

---

[1] Krascheninnikow, Descr. du Kamtchatka, Paris, 1768, p. 22. Klemm, C. G., vol. ii. p. 207. [2] Yate, p. 83. [4] Schoolcraft, part iii. p. 60.
[3] Plin., xxix. 20. [5] St. John, vol. i. p. 170.
[5] Dobrizhoffer, vol. i. p. 258. [7] Polack, vol. i. p. 270.

evil; or he will decide by whether a leaf tastes sweet or bitter, or whether he bites it clean through at once, or whether drops of water will run down his arm to the wrist and give a good answer, or fall off by the way and give a bad one.[1] In British Guiana, when young children are betrothed, trees are planted by the respective parties in witness of the contract, and if either tree should happen to wither, the child it belongs to is sure to die.[2] A slightly different idea appears north of the Isthmus, in the Central American tale, where the two brothers, starting on their dangerous journey to the land of Xibalba, where their father had perished, plant each a cane in the middle of their grandmother's house, that she may know by its flourishing or withering whether they are alive or dead.[3] And again, to take stories from the Old World, when Devasmita would not let Guhasena leave her to go with his merchandise to the land of Cathay, Siva appeared to them in a dream, and gave to each a red lotus that would fade if the other were unfaithful;[4] and so, in the German tale, when the two daughters of Queen Wilowitte were turned into flowers, the two princes who were their lovers had each a sprig of his mistress's flower, that was to stay fresh while their love was true.[5]

On this principle of association, it is easy to understand how, in the Old World, the names of the heavenly bodies, and their position at the time of a man's birth, should have to do with his character and fate; while, in the astrology of the Aztecs, the astronomical signs have a similar connexion with the parts of the human body, so that the sign of the Skull has to do with the head, and the sign of the Flint with the teeth.[6] Why fish may be caught in most plenty when the Sun is in the sign of Pisces, is as clear as the reason why trees are to be felled, or vegetables gathered, or manure used, while the moon is on the wane, for these things have to fall, or be consumed, or rot;

---

[1] Williams, 'Fiji,' p. 228.

[2] Rev. J. H. Bernau, 'Missionary Labours in British Guiana;' London, 1847, p. 59.   [3] Brasseur, 'Popol Vuh;' Paris, 1861, p. 141.

[4] Somadeva Bhatta, vol. i. p. 139.

[5] J. and W. Grimm, 'Kinder- und Hausmärchen;' Göttingen, 1857–6, vol. iii. p. 328.   [6] Kingsborough, Vatican MS., vol. ii. pl. 75; vols. v. and vi. Expl.

while, on the other hand, grafts are to be set while the moon is waxing,[1] and it is only lucky to begin an undertaking when the moon is on the increase, as has been held even in modern times. It is as clear why the Chinese doctor should administer the heads, middles, and roots of plants, as medicine for the heads, bodies, and legs of his patients respectively, and why passages in books looked at while some thought is in the reader's mind, should be taken as omens, from Western Europe to Eastern Asia, in old times and now. When it is borne in mind that the Tahitians ascribe their internal pains to demons who are inside them, tying their intestines in knots, it becomes easy to understand why the Laplanders, under certain circumstances, object to knots being tied in clothes, and so on from one phase to another of witchcraft and superstition.

It would be quite intelligible on this principle, that the sorcerer should think it possible to impress his own mind upon the outer world, even without any external link of communication. The mere presence of the thought in his mind might be enough to cause, as it were by reflection, a corresponding reality. He is usually found, however, working his will by some material means, or at least by an utterance of it into the world. This seems to be the case with the rainmaker, or weather-changer, wherever he is met with, that is to say, among most races of man below the highest culture. Sometimes he works by clear association of ideas, as the Samoan rainmakers with their sacred stone, which they wet when they want rain, and put to the fire to dry when they want to dry the weather,[2] or the Lapland wizards, with the winds they used to sell to our sea-captains in a knotted cord, to be let out by untying it knot by knot. In the notable practice of killing an enemy by prophesying that he will die, or by uttering a wish that he may, the outward act of speech comes between the thought and the reality, but perhaps a mere unspoken wish may be held sufficient. This kind of bewitching is found over almost as wide a range as the practices of the rainmaker, and extends like them into the upper regions of our race.

---

[1] Plin., ix. 85; xviii. 75; xvii. 24. [2] Turner, p. 347, and see p. 428.

> " There dwelt a weaver in Moffat toun,
>   That said the minister wad dee sune ;
>   The minister dee'd ; and the fouk o' the toun,
>   They brant the weaver wi' the wudd o' his lume,
>   And ca'd it weel-warrd on the warlock loon." [1]

As has been so often said, these two arts are encouraged by
the unfailing test of success, if they have but time enough,
and the latter justifies itself by killing the patient through his
own imagination. When he hears that he has been "wished,"
he goes home and takes to his bed at once. It is impossible
to realize the state of mind into which the continual terror of
witchcraft brings the savage. It is held by many tribes to be
the necessary cause of death. Over great part of Africa, in
South America and Polynesia, when a man dies, the question
is at once, " who killed him ?" and the soothsayer is resorted
to to find the murderer, that the dead man may be avenged.
The Abipones held that there was no such thing as natural
death, and that if it were not for the magicians and the Spaniards, no man would die unless he were killed. The notion
that, after all, a man might perhaps die of himself, comes out
curiously in the address of an old Australian to the corpse at a
funeral, "If thou comest to the other black-fellows and they
ask thee who killed thee, answer, 'No one, but I died.'" [2]

There are of course branches of the savage wizard's art that
are not connected with the mental process to which so many
of his practices may be referred. He is often a doctor with
some skill in surgery and medicine, and an expert juggler ; and
often, though knavery is not the basis of his profession, a cunning knave. One of the most notable superstitions of the
human race, high and low, is the belief in the Evil Eye.
Knowing, as we all do, the strange power which one mind has
of working upon another through the eye, a power which is not
the less certain for being wholly unexplained, it seems not unreasonable to suppose that the belief in the mysterious influences of the Evil Eye flows from the knowledge of what the
eye can do as an instrument of the will, while experience has

[1] R. Chambers, ' Popular Rhymes of Scotland ;' Edinburgh, 1826, p. 23.
[2] Lang, ' Queensland ;' London, 1861, p. 360.

not yet set such limits as we recognize to the range of its action. The horror which savages so often have of being looked full in the face, is quite consistent with this feeling. You may look at him or his, but you must not stare, and above all, you must not look him full in the face, that is to say, you must not do just what the stronger mind does when it uses the eye as an instrument to force its will upon the weaker.

It is clear that the superstitions which have been cursorily described in this chapter, are no mere casual extravagances of the human mind. The way in which the magic arts have taken to themselves the verb to "do," as claiming to be "doing" *par excellence*, sometimes gives us an opportunity of testing their importance in the popular mind. As in Madagascar the sorcerers and diviners of Mâtitânana go by the name of *mpiasa*,[1] that is "workers," so words in the languages of our Aryan race show a like transition. In Sanskrit, magic has possessed itself of a whole family of words derived from *kṛ*, to "do," *kṛtya*, sorcery, *kṛtvas*, enchanting, (literally, working), *kârmaṇa*, enchantment (from *karman*, a deed, work), and so on, while Latin *facere* has produced in the Romance languages, Italian *fattura*, enchantment, old French *faiture*, Portuguese *feitiço* (whence *fetish*), and a dozen more, and Grimm holds that the most probable derivation of *zauber*, Old High German *zoupar*, is from *zouran*, Gothic *táujan*, to *do*,[2] and other like etymologies are to be found. The belief and practices to which such words refer form a compact and organic whole, mostly developed from a state of mind in which subjective and objective connexions are not yet clearly separated. What then does this mass of evidence show from the ethnologist's point of view; what is the position of sorcery in the history of mankind?

When Dr. Martius, the Bavarian traveller, was lying one night in his hammock in an Indian hut in South America, and all the inhabitants seemed to be asleep, each family in its own place, his reflexions were interrupted by a strange sight. "In a

<hr>

[1] Ellis, 'Madagascar,' vol. i. p. 73.

[2] Pictet, 'Origines,' part ii. p. 641. Diez, Wörterb. s. v. "fattizio." Grimm, D. M. p. 984, etc. See Diefenbach, Vergl. Wörterb. i. 12; ii. 659.

dark corner there arose an old woman, naked, covered with dust
and ashes, a miserable picture of hunger and wretchedness; it
was the slave of my hosts, a captive taken from another tribe.
She crept cautiously to the hearth and blew up the fire, brought
out some herbs and bits of human hair, murmured something in an earnest tone, and grinned and gesticulated strangely
towards the children of her masters. She scratched a skull,
threw herbs and hair rolled into balls into the fire, and so on.
For a long while I could not conceive what all this meant, till
at last springing from my hammock and coming close to her, I
saw by her terror and the imploring gesture she made to me
not to betray her, that she was practising magic arts to destroy
the children of her enemies and oppressors." "This," he
continues, "was not the first example of sorcery I had met with
among the Indians. When I considered what delusions and
darkness must have been working in the human mind before
man could come to fear and invoke dark unknown powers for
another's hurt,—when I considered that so complex a superstition was but the remnant of an originally pure worship of
nature, and what a chain of complications must have preceded
such a degradation," etc. etc.[1]

I cannot but think that Dr. Martius's deduction is the absolute reverse of the truth. Looking at the practices of sorcery
among the lower races as a whole, they have not the appearance of mutilated and misunderstood fragments of a higher
system of belief and knowledge. Among savage tribes we
find families of customs and superstitions in great part traceable to the same principle, the confusion of imagination and
reality, of subjective and objective, of the mind and the outer
world. Among the higher races we find indeed many of the
same customs, but they are scattered, practised by the vulgar
with little notion of their meaning, looked down upon with
contempt by the more instructed, or explained as mystic sym-
bolisms, and at last dropped off one by one as the world grows
wiser. There is a curious handful of plain savage superstitions
among the rules to which the Roman Flamen Dialis had to

<hr>

[1] Dr. v. Martius, 'Vergangenheit and Zukunft der Amerikanischen Menschheit;' 1839.

conform. He was not only prohibited from touching a dog, a she-goat, raw meat, beans, and ivy, but he might not even name them, he might not have a knot tied in his clothes, and the parings of his nails and the clippings of his hair were collected and buried under a lucky tree.[1] So little difference does the mere course of time make in such things as these, that a modern missionary to a savage tribe may learn to understand them better than the Romans who practised them two thousand years ago.

It is quite true that there are anomalies among the superstitious practices of the lower races, proceedings of which the meaning is not clear, signs of the breaking-down or stiffening into formalism of beliefs carried down by tradition to a distance from their source; and besides, the rites of an old religion, carried down through a new one, may mix with such practices as have been described here, while the adherents of one religion are apt to ascribe to magic the beliefs and wonders of another, as the Christians held Odin, and the Romans Moses, to have been mighty enchanters of ancient times. But when we see the whole system of sorcery and divination comparatively compact and intelligible among savage tribes, less compact and less intelligible among the lower civilized races, and still less among ourselves, there seems reason to think that such imperfection and inconsistency as are to be found among this class of superstitions in the lower levels of our race, are signs of a degeneration (so to speak) from a system of error that was more perfect and harmonious in a yet lower condition of mankind, when man had a less clear view of the difference between what was in him and what was out of him, than the lowest savages we have ever studied,—when his life was more like a long dream than even the life that the Puris are leading at this day, deep in the forests of South America.

There is a remarkable peculiarity by which the sorcery of the savage seems to repudiate the notion of its having come down from something higher, and to date itself from the childhood of the human race. There is one musical instrument (if the name may be allowed to it) which we give over to young

<hr>

[1] Aulus Gellius, 'Noctes Atticæ,' x. 15. Plut., Q. R., cis. etc.

children, who indeed thoroughly appreciate and enjoy it,—the
rattle.

> " Behold the child, by Nature's kindly law,
> Pleased with a rattle, tickled with a straw."

When the dignity of manhood is to be conferred on a Sia-
mese prince by cutting his hair and giving him a new dress,
they shake a rattle before him as he goes, to show that till the
ceremony is performed, he is still a child. As if to keep us
continually in mind of his place in history, the savage magician
clings with wonderful pertinacity to the same instrument. It
is a bunch of hoofs tied together, a blown bladder with peas in
it, or, more often than anything else, a calabash with stones or
shells or bones inside. It is his great instrument in curing the
sick, the accompaniment of his medicine-songs, and the symbol
of his profession, among the Red Indians, among the South
American tribes, and in Africa. For the magician's work, it
holds its own against far higher instruments, the whistles and
pipes of the American, and even the comparatively high-class
flutes, harmonicons, and stringed instruments of the negro.[1]
Next above the rattle in the scale of musical instruments is the
drum, and it too has been to a great extent adopted by the
sorcerer, and, often painted with magic figures, it is an important implement to him in Lapland, in Siberia, among some
North American and some South American tribes.[2] The
clinging together of savage sorcery with these childish instruments, is in full consistency with the theory that both belong to
the infancy of mankind. With less truth to nature and history, the modern spirit-rapper, though his bringing up the
spirits of the dead by doing hocus-pocus under a table or in a
dark room is so like the proceedings of the African mganga
or the Red Indian medicine-man, has cast off the proper ac-
companiments of his trade, and juggles with fiddles and ac-
cordions.

<hr>

[1] Catlin, vol. i. p. 39, 100. Schoolcraft, part i. p. 310; part ii. p. 179. Char-
levoix, vol. vi. p. 187. Burton, 'Central Africa,' vol. i. p. 41; vol. ii. p. 295.
Purchas, vol. iv. p. 1339, 1520, etc. etc. Dobrizhoffer, vol. ii. p. 72. Klemm,
C.G., vol. ii. p. 109, 171-2. See Strabo, xv. 1, 22.

[2] Regnard, 'Lapland,' in Pinkerton, vol. i. p. 168, 140. Ravenstein, p. 89.
Molina, Hist. of Chile, E. Tr.; London, 1809, vol. ii. p. 100, etc. etc.

Tho question whether there is any historical connexion among the superstitious practices of tho lower races, is distinct from that of their development from the human mind. On tho whole, the similarity that runs through the sorcerer's art in tho most remote countries, not only in principle, but so often in details, as for instance in the wide prevalence of tho practice of bewitching by locks of hair and rubbish which once belonged to the victim, often favours tho view that these coincidences are not independent growths from the same principle, but practices which have spread from one geographical source. I have put together in another place some accounts of one of tho most widely spread phenomena of sorcery, the pretended extraction of bits of wood, stone, hair, and such things, from the bodies of the sick, which is based upon the belief that disease is caused by such objects having been conjured into them. The value of this belief to the ethnologist depends much on its being difficult to explain it, and therefore also difficult to look upon it as having often arisen independently in the human mind. But from the intelligible, and to a particular state of mind one might almost say reasonable, beliefs and practices which have been described in the present chapter, it seems hardly prudent to draw inferences as to the descent and communication of the races among whom they are found, at least while the ethnological argument from beliefs and customs is still in its infancy.

To turn now to a different subject, the same state of mind which has had so large a share in the development of sorcery, has also manifested itself in a very remarkable series of observances regarding spoken words, prohibiting tho mention of the names of people, or even sometimes of animals and things. A man will not utter his own name; husband and wife will not utter one another's names ; the son or daughter-in-law will not mention the name of the father or mother-in-law, and *vice versâ* ; the names of chiefs may not be uttered, nor the names of certain other persons, nor of superhuman beings, nor of animals and things to which supernatural powers are ascribed. These various prohibitions are not found all together, but one tribe may hold to several of them. A few details will suffice to give an idea of the extent and variety of this series of superstitions.

The intense aversion which savages have from uttering their own names, has often been noticed by travellers. Thus Captain Mayne says of the Indians of British Columbia, that " one of their strangest prejudices, which appears to pervade all tribes alike, is a dislike to telling their names—thus you never get a man's right name from himself; but they will tell each other's names without hesitation." [1]   So Dobrizhoffer says that the Abipones of South America think it a sin to utter their own names, and when a man was asked his name, he would nudge his neighbour to answer for him,[2] and in like manner, the Fijians and the Sumatrans are described as looking to a friend to help them out of the difficulty, when this indiscreet question is put to them.[3]

Nor does the dislike to mentioning ordinary personal names always stop at this limit. Among the Algonquin tribes, children are generally named by the old woman of the family, usually with reference to some dream, but this real name is kept mysteriously secret, and what usually passes for the name is a mere nickname, such as " Little Fox," or " Red-Head." The real name is hardly ever revealed even by the grave-post, but the totem or symbol of the clan is held sufficient. The true name of La Belle Sauvage was not Pocahontas, " her true name was Matokes, which they concealed from the English, in a superstitious fear of hurt by the English, if her name was known." [4]   " It is next to impossible to induce an Indian to utter personal names; the utmost he will do, if a person implicated is present, is to move his lips, without speaking, in the direction of the person."   Schoolcraft saw an Indian in a court of justice, pressed to identify a man who was there, but all they could get him to do was to push his lips towards him.[5] So Mr. Backhouse describes how a native woman of Van Diemen's Land threw sticks at a friendly Englishman, who in his ignorance of native manners, mentioned her son, who was at school at Newtown.[6]

[1] Mayne, ' British Columbia,' etc.; London, 1862, p. 276.

[2] Dobrizhoffer, vol. ii. p. 445.

[3] Siemann, ' Viti;' London, 1862, p. 190. Marsden, Hist. of Sumatra; London, 1811, p. 288.   [4] Schoolcraft, part ii. p. 65.

[5] Id. p. 453. See also Burton, ' City of the Saints,' p. 141.

[6] Backhouse, ' Australia,' p. 93.

In various parts of the world, a variety of remarkable customs are observed between men and women, and their fathers- and mothers-in-law. These will be noticed elsewhere, but it is necessary to mention here, that among the Dayaks of Borneo, a man must not pronounce the name of his father-in-law;[1] among the Omahas of North America, the father- and mother-in-law do not speak to their son-in-law, or mention his name,[2] nor do they call him or he them by name among the Dacotahs.[3] Again, the wife is in some places prohibited from mentioning her husband's name. "A Hindoo wife is never, under any circumstances, to mention the name of her husband. 'He,' 'The Master,' 'Swamy,' etc., are titles she uses when speaking of, or to her lord. In no way can one of the sex annoy another more intensely and bitterly, than by charging her with having mentioned her husband's name. It is a crime not easily forgiven."[4] In East Africa, among the Barea, the wife never utters the name of her husband, or eats in his presence, and even among the Beni Amer, where the women have extensive privileges and great social power, the wife is still not allowed to eat in the husband's presence, and only mentions his name before strangers.[5] The Kafir custom prohibits wives from speaking the names of relatives of their husbands and fathers-in-law. In Australia, among the names which in some tribes must not be spoken, are those of a father- or mother-in-law, of a son-in-law, and of persons in some kind of connexion by marriage. Another of the Australian prohibitions is not only very curious, but is curious as having apparently no analogue elsewhere. Among certain tribes in the Murray River district, the youths undergo, instead of circumcision, an operation called *wharepin*, and afterwards, the natives who have officiated, and those who have been operated upon, though they may meet and talk, must never mention one another's names, nor must the name of one even be spoken by a third person in the presence of the other.[6]

---

[1] St. John, vol. I. p. 51.　　　[2] Long's Exp., vol. i. p. 253.

[3] Schoolcraft, part ii. p. 196.

[4] F. de W. Ward, 'India and the Hindoos;' London, 1853, p. 189.

[5] Munzinger, 'Ostafrikanische Studien;' Schaffhausen, 1864, pp. 325, 528.

[6] Eyre, vol. ii. pp. 336–0. The wharepin is a ceremonial depilation.

It is especially in Eastern Asia and Polynesia, that we find the names of kings and chiefs held as sacred, and not to be lightly spoken.   In Siam, the king must be spoken of by some epithet;[1] in India and Burmah, the royal name is avoided as something sacred and mysterious; and in Polynesia, the prohibition to mention chiefs' names has even impressed itself deeply in the language of the islands where it prevails.[2]

But it is among the most distant and various races that we find one class of names avoided with mysterious horror, the names of the dead.   In North America, the dead are to be alluded to, not mentioned by name, especially in the presence of a relative.[3]   In South America, he must be mentioned among the Abipones as "the man who does not now exist," or some such periphrasis;[4] and the Fuegians have a horror of any kind of allusion to their dead friends, and when a child asks for its dead father or mother, they will say, "Silence! don't speak bad words."[5]   The Samoied only speaks of the dead by allusion, for it would disquiet them to utter their names.[6]   The Australians, like the North Americans, will set up the pictured crest or symbol of the dead man's clan, but his name is not to be spoken.   Dr. Lang tried to get from an Australian the name of a native who had been killed.   "He told me who the lad's father was, who was his brother, what he was like, how he walked when he was alive, how he held the tomahawk in his left hand instead of his right (for he had been left-handed), and with whom he usually associated; but the dreaded name never escaped his lips; and I believe no promises or threats could have induced him to utter it."[7]   The Papuans of the Eastern Archipelago avoid speaking the names of the dead, and in Africa, a like prejudice is found among the Masai.[8]   In the Old World, Pliny says of the Roman custom, "Why, when we mention the dead, do we declare that we do not vex their memory?"[9] and indeed, the superstition is still to be found in

[1] Bowring, p. 38.   [2] Polack, vol. i. p. 38.
[3] Simpson, Journey, vol. i. p. 130.   Schoolcraft, part iii. p. 234.
[4] Dobrizhoffer, vol. ii. p. 273.
[5] Shepard, 'Fireland,' ('Sunday at Home,' Oct. 31, 1863).
[6] Klemm, C. G., vol. ii. p. 226.
[7] Lang, 'Queensland,' pp. 367, 367.   Eyre, l. c.
[8] Bastian, vol. ii. p. 270, etc.   [9] Plin., xxviii. 5.

modern Europe, and better marked than in ancient Rome; perhaps nowhere more notably than in Shetland, where it is all but impossible to get a widow, at any distance of time, to mention the name of her dead husband, though she will talk about him by the hour. No dead person must be mentioned, for his ghost will come to him who speaks his name.[1]

To conclude the list, the dislike to mentioning the names of spiritual or superhuman beings, and everything to which supernatural powers are ascribed, is, as every one knows, very general. The Dayak will not speak of the small-pox by name, but will call it "the chief" or "jungle leaves," or say "Has he left you?"[2] The euphemism of calling the Furies the Eumenides, or 'gracious ones,' is the stock illustration of this feeling, and the euphemisms for fairies and for the devil are too familiar to quote. The Yezidis, who worship Satan, have a horror of his name being mentioned. The Laplanders will call the bear "the old man with the fur coat," but they do not like to mention his name. In Asia, the same dislike to speak of the tiger is found in Siberia, among the Tunguz;[3] and in Annam, where he is called "Grandfather" or "Lord,"[4] while in Sumatra, they are spoken of as the "wild animals" or "ancestors."[5] The name of Brahma is a sacred thing in India, as that of Jehovah is to the Jews, not to be uttered but on solemn occasions. The Moslem, it is true, has the name of Allah for ever on his lips, but this, as has been mentioned, is only an epithet, not the "great name."

Among this series of prohibitions, several cases seem, like the burning in effigy among the practices with images, to fall into mere association of ideas, devoid of any superstitious thought. The names of husbands, of chiefs, of supernatural beings, or of the dead, may be avoided from an objection to liberties being taken with the property of a superior, from a dislike to associate names of what is sacred with common life, or to revive hateful thoughts of death and sorrow. But in other instances,

---

[1] Mrs. Edmondston, 'Shetland Islands;' Edin., 1856, p. 50.
[2] St. John, vol. i. p. 62.　　　[3] Ravenstein, p. 382.
[4] Mouhot, 'Travels in Indo-China,' etc.; London, 1864, vol. I. p. 263.
[5] Marsden, p. 292.

the notion comes out with great clearness, that the mere speaking of a name acts upon its owner, whether that owner be man, beast, or spirit, whether near or far off. Sometimes it may be explained by considering supernatural creatures as having the power of hearing their names wherever they are uttered, and as sometimes coming to trouble the living when they are thus disturbed. Where this is an accepted belief, such sayings as "Talk of the Devil and you see his horns," "Parlez du loup," etc., have a far more serious meaning than they bear to us now. Thus an aged Indian of Lake Michigan explained why the native wonder-tales must only be told in the winter, for then the deep snow lies on the ground, and the thick ice covers up the waters, and so the spirits that dwell there cannot hear the laughter of the crowd listening to their stories round the fire in the winter lodge. But in spring the spirit-world is all alive, and the hunter never alludes to the spirits but in a sedate, reverent way, careful lest the slightest word should give offence.[1] In other cases, however, the effect of the utterance of the name on the name's owner would seem to be different from this. The explanation does not hold in the case of a man refusing to speak his own name, nor would he be likely to think that his mother-in-law could hear whenever he mentioned hers.

Some of these prohibitions of names have caused a very curious phenomenon in language. When the prohibited name is a word in use, and often when it is only something like such a word, that word has to be dropped and a new one found to take its place. Several languages are known to have been specially affected by this proceeding, and it is to be remarked that in them the causes of prohibition have been different. In the South Sea Islands, words have been tabued, from connexion with the names of chiefs; in Australia, Van Diemen's Land, and among the Abipones of South America, from connexion with the names of the dead; while in South Africa, the avoidance of the names of certain relatives by marriage has led to a result in some degree similar.

Captain Cook noticed in Tahiti that when a chief came to the royal dignity, any words resembling his name were changed.

[1] Schoolcraft, part iii. pp. 314, 492.

Even to call a horse or a dog " Prince " or " Princess " was disgusting to the native mind.[1] Polack says that from a New Zealand chief being called " Wai," which means " water," a new name had to be given to water. A chief was called " Maripi," or " knife ; " and knives were called, in consequence, by another name, " nekrn."[2] Hale, the philologist to the U. S. Exploring Expedition, gives an account of the similar Tahitian practice known as *te pi*, by virtue of which, for instance, the syllable *tu* was changed even in indifferent words, because there was a king whose name was Tu. Thus *fetu* (star) was changed to *fetia*, *tui* (to strike) became *tiai*, and so on.[3]

Mentioning the Australian prohibition of uttering the names of the dead, Mr. Eyre says :—" In cases where the name of a native has been that of some bird or animal of almost daily recurrence, a new name is given to the object, and adopted in the language of the tribe. Thus at Moorunde, a favourite son of the native Tenberry was called Torpool, or the Toal ; upon the child's death the appellation of tilquaitch was given to the teal, and that of torpool altogether dropped among the Moorunde tribe."[4] The change of language in Tasmania, which has resulted from dropping the names of the dead, is thus described by Mr. Milligan :—" The elision and absolute rejection and disuse of words from time to time has been noticed as a source of change in the Aboriginal dialects. It happened thus :—The names of men and women were taken from natural objects and occurrences around, as, for instance, a kangaroo, a gum-tree, snow, hail, thunder, the wind, the sea, the Waratah—or Blandifordia or Boronia when in blossom, etc., but it was a settled custom in every tribe, upon the death of any individual, most scrupulously to abstain ever after from mentioning the name of the deceased,—a rule, the infraction of which would, they considered, be followed by some dire calamities : they therefore used great circumlocution in referring to a dead person, so as to avoid pronunciation of the name,—if, for

<hr>

[1] Cook, Third Voyage, vol. ii. p. 170.
[2] Polack, vol. i. p. 39 ; vol. ii. p. 126.
[3] Hale, in U. S. Exp., vol. vi. p. 288. Max Müller, 'Lectures,' 2nd series ; London, 1864, pp. 34–41.
[4] Eyre, vol. ii. p. 354.

instance, William and Mary, man and wife, were both deceased,
and Lucy, the deceased sister of William, had been married to
Isaac, also dead, whose son Jemmy still survived, and they
wished to speak of Mary, they would say 'the wife of the
brother of Jemmy's father's wife,' and so on. Such a practice
must, it is clear, have contributed materially to reduce the
number of their substantive appellations, and to create a necessity for new phonetic symbols to represent old ideas, which new
vocables would in all probability differ on each occasion, and
in every separate tribe; the only chance of fusion of words between tribes arising out of the capture of females for wives from
hostile and alien people,—a custom generally prevalent, and
doubtless as beneficial to the race in its effects as it was savage
in its mode of execution."[1]

Martin Dobrizhoffer, the Jesuit missionary, gives the following account of the way in which this change was going on in
the language of the Abipones in his time. "The Abiponian
language is involved in new difficulties by a ridiculous custom
which the savages have of continually abolishing words common
to the whole nation, and substituting new ones in their stead.
Funeral rites are the origin of this custom. The Abipones do
not like that anything should remain to remind them of the
dead. Hence appellative words bearing any affinity with the
names of the deceased are presently abolished. During the
first years that I spent amongst the Abipones, it was usual to
say *Heymalkam kahamátek?*, 'When will there be a slaughtering of oxen?' On account of the death of some Abipone,
the word *kahamátek* was interdicted, and, in its stead, they
were all commanded, by the voice of a crier, to say, *Heymalkam négerkatà?* The word *nihirenak*, a tiger, was exchanged
for *apañigehak*; *peñe*, a crocodile, for *kaeprhak*, and *kuámar*,
Spaniards, for *Rikil*, because these words bore some resemblance to the names of Abipones lately deceased. Hence it is
that our vocabularies are so full of blots, occasioned by our
having such frequent occasion to obliterate interdicted words,
and insert new ones."[2]

[1] Milligan, in Papers, etc., of Roy. Soc. of Tasmania, vol. iii. part ii. 1859,
p. 281.   [2] Dobrizhoffer, vol. ii. p. 203.

In South Africa, it appears that some Kafir tribes drop from their language words resembling the names of their former chiefs. Thus the Ama-Mbalu do not call the sun by its ordinary Zulu name *i-langa*, but their first chief's name having been Ulanga, they use the word *i-sota* instead. It is also among the Kafirs that the peculiar custom of *uku-hlonipa* is found, which is remarked upon by Professor Max Müller in his second course of lectures.[1] The following account of it is from another source, the Rev. J. L. Döhne, who thus speaks of it under the verb *hlonipa*, which means to be bashful, to keep at a distance through timidity, to shun approach, to avoid mentioning one's name, to be respectful. "This word describes a custom between the nearest relations, and is exclusively applied to the female sex, who, when married, are not allowed to call the names of the relatives of their husbands nor of their fathers-in-law. They must keep at a distance from the latter. Hence they have the habit of inventing new names for the members of the family, which is always resorted to when those names happen to be either derived from, or are equivalent to some other word of the common language, as, for instance, if the father or brother-in-law is called Umehlo, which is derived from amehlo, eyes, the isifazi [female sex] will no longer use amehlo but substitute amakangelo (lookings), etc., and hence, the izwi lozifazi, *i.e.* : women-word or language has originated."[2]

Other instances of change of language by interdicting words are to be found. The Yezidis, who worship the devil, not only refuse to speak the name of *Sheitan*, but they have dropped the word *shat*, "river," as too much like it, and use the word *nahr* instead. Nor will they utter the word *keitan*, "thread" or "fringe," and even *naal*, "horse-shoe," and *naal-band*, "farrier," are forbidden words, because they approach to *laun*, "curse," and *maloun*, "accursed."[3] It is curious to observe that a "disease of language" belonging to the same family has shown itself in English-speaking countries and in modern

<hr>

[1] Max Müller, *l. c.*

[2] Döhne, 'Zulu-Kafir Dictionary ;' Cape Town, 1857, *s.v.* hlonipa.

[3] Layard, 'Nineveh ;' London, 1849, vol. *i.* p. 297.

times. In America especially, a number of very harmless words have been "tabooed" of late years, not for any offence of their own, but for having a resemblance in sound to words looked upon as indelicate, or even because slang has adopted them to express ideas ignored by a somewhat over-fastidious propriety. We in England are not wholly clear from this offence against good taste, but we have been fortunate in seeing it developed into its full ugliness abroad, and may hope that it is checked once for all among ourselves.

It may be said in concluding the subject of Images and Names, that the effect of an inability to separate, so clearly as we do, the external object from the mere thought or idea of it in the mind, shows itself very fully and clearly in the superstitious beliefs and practices of the untaught man, but its results are by no means confined to such matters. It is not too much to say that nothing short of a history of Philosophy and Religion would be required to follow them out. The accumulated experience of so many ages has indeed brought to us far clearer views in these matters than the savage has, though after all we soon come to the point where our knowledge stops, and the opinions which ordinary educated men hold, or at least act upon, as to the relation between ideas and things, may come in time to be superseded by others taken from a higher level. But between our clearness of separation of what is in the mind from what is out of it, and the mental confusion of the lowest savages of our own day, there is a vast interval. Moreover, as has just been said, the appearance even in the system of savage superstition, of things which seem to have outlived the recollection of their original meaning, may perhaps lead us back to a still earlier condition of the human mind. Especially we may see, in the superstitions connected with language, the vast difference between what a name is to the savage and what it is to us, to whom "words are the counters of wise men and the money of fools." Lower down in the history of culture, the word and the idea are found sticking together with a tenacity very different from their weak adhesion in our minds, and there is to be seen a tendency to grasp at the word as though it were the object it stands for, and to hold that to be able to

speak of a thing gives a sort of possession of it, in a way that
we can scarcely realize. Perhaps this state of mind was hardly
ever so clearly brought into view as in a story told by Dr.
Lieber. "I was looking lately at a negro who was occupied
in feeding young mocking-birds by the hand. 'Would they
eat worms?' I asked. The negro replied, 'Surely not, they
are too young, they would not know what to call them.'"[1]

[1] Lieber, 'Laura Bridgman;' Smiths. C., 1851, p. 0.

CHAPTER VII.

GROWTH AND DECLINE OF CULTURE.

DIRECT record is the mainstay of History, and where this fails us in remote places and times, it becomes much more difficult to make out where civilization has gone forward, and where it has fallen back. As to progress in the first place; when any important movement has been made in modern times, there have usually been well-informed contemporary writers, only too glad to come before the public with something to say that the world cared to hear. But in going down to the lower levels of traditional history, this state of things changes. It is not only that real information becomes more and more scarce, but that the same curiosity that we feel about the origin and growth of civilization, unfortunately combined with a disposition to take any semblance of an answer rather than live in face of mere blank conscious ignorance, has favoured the growth of the crowd of mythic inventors and civilizers, who have their place in the legends of so many distant ages and countries. Their stories often give us names, dates, and places, even the causes which led to change,—just the information wanted, if only it were true. And, indeed, recollections of real men and their inventions may sometimes have come to be included among the tales of these gods, heroes, and sages; and sometimes a mythic garb may clothe real history, as when Cadmus, קדם, " The East," brings the Phœnician letters to Greece. But, as a rule, not history, but mythology fallen cold

and dead, or even etymology, allusion, fancy, are their only
basis, from Sol, the son of Oceanus, who found out how to
mine and melt the brilliant, sun-like gold, and Pyrodes, the
"Fiery," who discovered how to get fire from flint, and the
merchants who invented the art of glass-making (known in
Egypt in such remote antiquity) by making fires on the sandy
Phœnician coast, with their kettles set to boil over them on
lumps of natron, brought for this likely purpose from their
ship,—across the world to Kahukura, who got the fairies'
fishing-net from which the New Zealanders learnt the art of
netting, and the Chinese pair, Hoei and Y-men, of whom the
one invented the bow, and the other the arrow.

As the gods Ceres and Bacchus become the givers of corn
and wine to mortals, so across the Atlantic there has grown
out of a simple mythic conception of nature, the story of the
great enlightener and civilizer of Mexico. When the key
which Professor Müller and Mr. Cox have used with such success in unlocking the Indo-European mythology is put to the
mass of traditions of the Mexican Quetzalcohuatl, collected by
the Abbé Brasseur,[1] the real nature of this personage shows
out at once.

He was the son of Camaxtli, the great Toltec conqueror
who reigned over the land of Anahuac. His mother died at
his birth, and in his childhood he was cared for by the virgin
priestesses who kept up the sacred fire, emblem of the sun.
While yet a boy he was bold in war, and followed his father on
his marches. But while he was far away, a band of enemies
rose against his father, and with them joined the Mixcohuas,
the "Cloud-Snakes," and they fell upon the aged king and
choked him, and buried his body in the temple of Mixcoate-
petl, the "Mountain of the Cloud-Snakes." Time passed on,
and Quetzalcohuatl knew not what had happened, but at last
the Eagle came to him and told him that his father was slain
and had gone down into the tomb. Then Quetzalcohuatl rose
and went with his followers to attack the temple of the Cloud-
Snakes' Mountain, where the murderers had fortified themselves, mocking him from their battlements. But he mined in

<hr>

[1] Brasseur, 'Histoire,' vol. i. books ii. and iii. See vol. iii. book xi. chapter iii.

a way from below, and rushed into the temple among them
with his Tigers. Many he slew outright, but the bodies of
the guiltiest he hewed and hacked, and throwing red pepper
on their wounds, left them to die.

After this there comes another story. Quetzalcohuatl appeared at Panuco, up a river on the Eastern Coast. He had
landed there from his ship, coming no man knew from whence.
He was tall, of white complexion, pleasant to look upon, with
fair hair and bushy beard, dressed in long flowing robes. Received everywhere as a messenger from heaven, he travelled
inland across the hot countries of the coast to the temperate
regions of the interior, and there he became a priest, a lawgiver, and a king. The beautiful land of the Toltecs teemed
with fruit and flowers, and his reign was their Golden Age.
Poverty was unknown, and the people revelled in every joy of
riches and well-being. The Toltecs themselves were not like
the small dark Aztecs of later times; they were large of stature and fair almost as Europeans, and (sun-like) they could
run unresting all the long day. Quetzalcohuatl brought with
him builders, painters, astronomers, and artists in many other
crafts. He made roads for travel, and favoured the wayfaring
merchants from distant lands. He was the founder of history,
the lawgiver, the inventor of the calendar of days and years,
the composer of the Tonalamatl, the "Sun-Book," where the
Tonalpouhqui, "he who counts by the sun," read the destinies
of men in astrological predictions, and he regulated the times
of the solemn ceremonies, the festival of the new year and of
the fifty-two years' cycle. But after a reign of years of peace
and prosperity, trouble came upon him too. His enemies
banded themselves against him, and their head was a chief
who bore a name of the Sun, Tetzcatlipoca, the "Smoking
Mirror," a splendid youth, a kinsman of Quetzalcohuatl, but
his bitter enemy. They rose against Quetzalcohuatl, and he
departed. The kingdom, he said, was no longer under his
charge, he had a mission elsewhere, for the master of distant
lands had sent to seek him, and this master was the Sun. He
went to Cholullan, "the place of the fugitive," and founded
there another empire, but his enemy followed him with his

armies, and Quetzalcohuatl said he must begone to the land of
Tlapallan, for Heaven willed that he should visit other countries, to spread there the light of his doctrine; but when his
mission was done, he would return and spend his old age with
them.   So he departed and went down a river on his ship to
the sea, and there he disappeared.   The sunlight glows on the
snow-covered peak of Orizaba long after the lands below are
wrapped in darkness, and there, some said, his body was carried, and rose to heaven in the smoke of the funeral pile, and
when he vanished, the sun for a time refused to show himself
again.

How dim the meaning of these tales had grown among the
Mexicans, when Montezuma thought he saw in Cortes and the
Spanish ships the return of the great ruler and his age of gold.
Quetzalcohuatl had come back already many a time, to bring
light, and joy, and work, upon the earth, for he was the Sun.
We may even find him identified with the Sun by name, and
his history is perhaps a more compact and perfect series of
solar myths than hangs to the name of any single personage
in our own Aryan mythology.   His mother, the Dawn or the
Night, gives birth to him, and dies.   His father Camaxtli is
the Sun, and was worshipped with solar rites in Mexico, but
he is the old Sun of yesterday.   The clouds, personified in the
mythic race of the Mixcohuas, or "Cloud-Snakes" (the Nibe-
lungs of the western hemisphere), bear down the old Sun and
choke him, and bury him in their mountain.   But the young
Quetzalcohuatl, the Sun of to-day, rushes up into the midst of
them from below, and some he slays at the first onset, and
some he leaves, rift with red wounds, to die.   We have the
Sun-boat of Helios, of the Egyptian Ra, of the Polynesian
Maui.   Quetzalcohuatl, his bright career drawing towards its
close, is chased into far lands by his kinsman Tetzcatlipoca,
the young Sun of to-morrow.   He, too, is well-known as a Sun-
god in the Mexican theology.   Wonderfully fitting with all
this, one incident after another in the life of Quetzalcohuatl
falls into its place.   The guardians of the sacred fire tend him,
his funeral pile is on the top of Orizaba, he is the helper of
travellers, the maker of the calendar, the source of astrology,

the beginner of history, the bringer of wealth and happiness. He is the patron of the craftsman, whom he lights to his labour; as it is written in an ancient Sanskrit hymn, " He steps forth, the splendour of the sky, the wide-seeing, the far-aiming, the shining wanderer; surely, enlivened by the sun, do men go to their tasks and do their work."[1] Even his people the Toltecs catch from him solar qualities. Will it be even possible to grant to this famous race, in whose story the legend of Quetzalcohuatl is the leading incident, anything more than a mythic existence?

The student, then, may well look suspiciously on statements professing to be direct history of the early growth of civilization, and may even find it best to err on the safe side and not admit them at all, unless they are shown to be probable by other evidence, or unless the tradition is of such a character that it could hardly have arisen but on a basis of fact. For instance, both these tests seem to be satisfied by the Chinese legend concerning quipus. In the times of Yung-ching-che, it is related, people used little cords marked by different knots, which, by their numbers and distances, served them instead of writing. The invention is ascribed to the Emperor Suy-jin, the Prometheus of China.[2] Putting names and dates out of the question, this story embodies the assertion that in old times the Chinese used quipus for records, till they were superseded by the art of writing. Now in the first place, it is not easy to imagine how such a story could come into existence, unless it were founded on fact ; and in the second place, an examination of what is known of this curious art in other countries, shows that just what the Chinese say once happened to them, is known to have happened to other races in various parts of the world.

The quipu is a near relation of the rosary and the wampum-string. It consists of a cord with knots tied in it for the purpose of recalling or suggesting something to the mind. When a farmer's daughter ties a knot in her handkerchief to re-

<hr>

[1] Müller, Lectures, 2nd series, p. 497.

[2] Goguet, vol. iii. p. 323. De Mailla, Histoire Gén. de la Chine; Paris, 1777, vol. i. p. 4.

member a commission at market by, she makes a rudimentary quipu. Darius made one when he took a thong and tied sixty knots in it, and gave it to the chiefs of the Ionians, that they might untie a knot each day, till, if the knots were all undone, and he had not returned, they might go back to their own land.[1] Such was the string on which Lo Boo tied a knot for each ship he met on his voyage, to keep in mind its name and country, and that one on which his father, Abba Thulle, tied first thirty knots, and then six more, to remember that Captain Wilson was to come back in thirty moons, or at least in six beyond.[2]

This is so simple a device that it may, for all we know, have been invented again and again, and its appearance in several countries does not prove it to have been transmitted from one country to another. It has been found in Asia,[3] in Africa,[4] in Mexico, among the North American Indians;[5] but its greatest development was in South America.[6] The word *quipu*, that is, "knot," belongs to the language of Peru, and quipus served there as the regular means of record and communication for a highly-organized society. Von Tschudi describes them as consisting of a thick main cord, with thinner cords tied on to it at certain distances, in which the knots are tied. The length of the quipus varies much, the main trunk being often many ells long, sometimes only a single foot, the branches seldom more than two feet, and usually much less. He has dug up a quipu, he says, towards eight pounds in weight, a portion of which is represented in the woodcut from which the accompanying (Fig. 15) is taken. The cords are often of various colours, each with its own proper meaning; red for soldiers, yellow for gold, white for silver, green for corn, and so on. This knot-writing was especially suited for reckonings and statistical tables; a

[1] Herod., iv. 98.   See Plin., ii. 34.

[2] Keate, 'Pelew Islands;' London, 1788, pp. 367, 392.

[3] Erman (E. Tr.); London, 1848, vol. i. p. 412.

[4] Goguet, vol. i. pp. 161, 212.   Klemm, C. G., vol. i. p. 3.   Bastian, vol. i. p. 412.

[5] Charlevoix, vol. vi. p. 161.   Long's Exp., vol. i. p. 235 (a passage which suggests a reason for Lucina being the patroness of child-birth).   Talbot, Disc. of Laborer, p. 4.   [6] Humboldt and Bonpland, vol. iii. p. 20.

single knot meant ten, a double one a hundred, a triple one a
thousand, two singles side by side twenty, two doubles two
hundred.   The distances of the knots from the main cord were
of great importance, as was the sequence of the branches, for
the principal objects were placed on the first branches and near
the trunk, and so in decreasing order.   This art of reckoning,

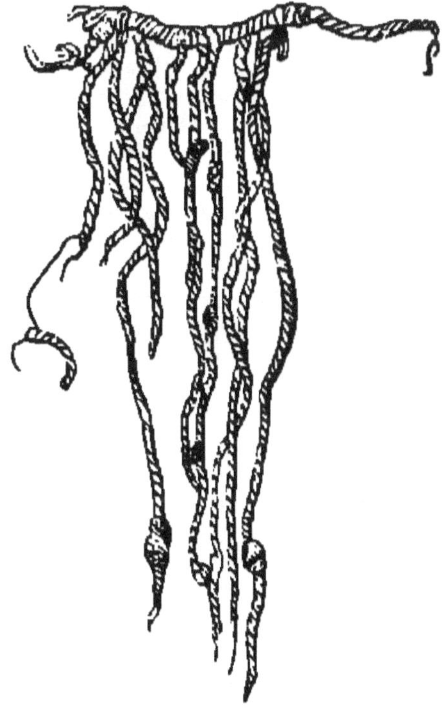

Fig. 15.

continues Von Tschudi, is still in use among the herdsmen of
the Puna (the high mountain plateau of Peru), and he had it
explained to him by them, so that with a little trouble he could
read any of their quipus.   On the first branch they usually
register the bulls, on the second the cows, these again they
divide into milch-cows and those that were dry; the next

branches contain the calves, according to age and sex, then the sheep in several subdivisions, the number of foxes killed, the quantity of salt used, and, lastly, the particulars of the cattle that have died. On other quipus is set down the produce of the herd in milk, cheese, wool, etc. Each heading is indicated by a special colour or a differently twined knot.

It was in the same way that in old times the army registers were kept; on one cord the slingers were set down, on another the spearmen, on a third those with clubs, etc., with their officers; and thus also the accounts of battles were drawn up. In each town were special functionaries, whose duty was to tie and interpret the quipus; they were called Quipucamayocuna, or Knot-officers. Insufficient as this kind of writing was, the official historians had attained, during the flourishing of the kingdom of the Incas, to great facility in its interpretation. Nevertheless, they were seldom able to read a quipu without the aid of an oral commentary; when one came from a distant province, it was necessary to give notice with it whether it referred to census, tribute, war, and so forth. In order to indicate matters belonging to their own immediate district, they made at the beginning of the main cord certain signs only intelligible to themselves, and they also carefully kept the quipus in their proper departments, so as not, for instance, to mistake a tribute-cord for one relating to the census. By constant practice, they so far perfected the system as to be able to register with their knots the most important events of the kingdom, and to set down the laws and ordinances. In modern times, all the attempts made to read the ancient quipus have been in vain. The difficulty in deciphering them is very great, since every knot indicates an idea, and a number of intermediate notions are left out. But the principal impediment is the want of the oral information as to their subject-matter, which was needful even to the most learned decipherers. However, should we even succeed in finding the key to their interpretation, the results would be of little value; for what would come to light would be mostly census-records of towns or provinces, taxation-lists, and accounts of the property of deceased persons. There are still some Indians, in the southern provinces of Peru, who are perfectly familiar with the contents of certain historical quipus preserved from ancient times; but they keep their knowledge a profound secret, especially from the white men.[1]

Coming nearer to China, quipus are found in the Eastern Archipelago and in Polynesia proper,[2] and they were in use in Hawaii forty years ago, in a form seemingly not inferior to the most elaborate Peruvian examples. "The tax-gatherers, though they can neither read nor write, keep very exact accounts of all the articles, of all kinds, collected from the inhabitants throughout the island. This is done principally by one man, and the register is nothing more than a line of cordage from four to five hundred fathoms in length. Distinct portions of this are allotted to the various districts, which are known from one another by knots, loops, and tufts, of different shapes, sizes, and colours. Each tax-payer in the district has his part in this string, and the number of dollars, hogs, dogs, pieces of sandal-wood, quantity of taro, etc., at which he is rated, is well defined by means of marks of the above kinds, most ingeniously diversified."[3]

The fate of the quipu has been everywhere to be superseded, more or less entirely, by the art of writing. Even the picture-writing of the ancient Mexicans appears to have been strong enough to supplant it. Whether its use in Mexico is mentioned by any old chronicler or not, I do not know; but Boturini placed the fact beyond doubt by not only finding some specimens in Tlascala, but also recording their Mexican name, *nepohualtzitzin*,[4] a word derived from the verb *tlapohua*, to count. When, therefore, the Chinese tell us that they once upon a time used this contrivance, and that the art of writing superseded it, the analogy of what has taken place in other countries makes it extremely probable that the tradition is a true one, and this probability is reinforced by the unlikeliness of such a story having been produced by mere fancy.

[1] J. J. v. Tschudi, 'Peru;' St. Gall, 1846, vol. ii. p. 383.
[2] Marsden, p. 192. Kmio, *loc. cit.* Klemm, C. G., vol. iv. p. 306.
[3] Tyerman and Bennet, Journal; London, 1831, vol. I. p. 455.
[4] Boturini, 'Idea de una nueva Historia,' etc.; Madrid, 1746, p. 85.

Moreover, the historical value of early tradition does not lie exclusively in the fragments of real history it may preserve. Even the myths which it carries down to later times may become important indirect evidence in the hands of the ethnologist. And ancient compositions handed down by memory from generation to generation, especially if a poetic form helps to keep them in their original shape, often give us, if not a sound record of real events, at least a picture of the state of civilization in which the compositions themselves had their origin. Perhaps no branch of indirect evidence, bearing on the history of culture, has been so well worked as the memorials of earlier states of society, which have thus been unintentionally preserved, for instance, in the Homeric poems. Safer examples than the following might be quoted; but as so much has been said of the history of the art of writing, the place may serve to cite what seems to be a memorial of a time when, among the ancient Greeks, picture-writing had not as yet been superseded by word-writing, in the tale of Bellerophon, whom Prœtus would not kill, but he sent him into Lycia, and gave him baneful signs, graving on a folded tablet many soul-destroying things, and bade him show them to the king, that he might perish at his hands.

Πέμπε δέ μιν Λυκίηνδε, πόρεν δ' ὅ γε σήματα λυγρά,
Γράψας ἐν πίνακι πτυκτῷ θυμοφθόρα πολλά,
Δεῖξαι δ' ἠνώγει ᾧ πενθερῷ, ὄφρ' ἀπόλοιτο.[1]

It happens unfortunately that but little evidence as to the early history of civilization is to be got by direct observation, that is, by contrasting the condition of a low race at different times, so as to see whether its culture has altered in the meanwhile. The contact requisite for such an inspection of a savage tribe by civilized men, has usually had much the same effect as the experiment which an inquisitive child tries upon the root it put in the ground the day before, by digging it up to see whether it has grown. It is a general rule that original and independent progress is not found among a people of low civiliza-

---

[1] Il., vi. 168. Wolf, Proleg. in Hom.; Halle, 1859, 2nd ed. vol. i. p. 48, etc. Liddell and Scott, s. v. σῆμα.

tion in presence of a higher race. It is natural enough that this should be the case, and it does not in the least affect the question whether the lower race was stationary or progressing before the arrival of the more cultivated foreigners. Even when the contact has been but slight and temporary, it either becomes doubtful whether progress made soon afterwards is original, or certain that it is not so. It has been asserted, for instance, that the Andaman Islanders had no boats in the ninth century, and that the canoe with an outrigger has only lately appeared among them.[1] If these statements should prove correct, we cannot assume, upon the strength of them, that the islanders made these inventions themselves, seeing that they could easily have copied them from foreigners. Moreover, the fact that they now use bits of glass-bottles, and iron from wrecks, in making their tools and weapons, proves that, slight as their intercourse has been with foreigners, and bitter as is their hostility to them, their condition has, nevertheless, been materially changed by foreign influence.

Though direct evidence thus generally fails us in tracing the history of the lower culture of mankind, there are many ways of bringing indirect evidence to bear on the problem. The early Culture-History of Mankind is capable of being treated as an Inductive Science, by collecting and grouping facts. It is true that very little has as yet been done in this way, as regards the lower races at least; but the evidence has only to a very slight extent been got into a state to give definite results, and the whole argument is extremely uncertain and difficult: a fact which sufficiently accounts for writers on the Origin of Civilization being able to tell us all about it, with that beautiful ease and confidence which belong to the speculative philosopher, whose course is but little obstructed by facts.

In a Lecture on the Origin of Civilization, since reprinted with a Preface,[2] the late Archbishop Whately thus summarily disposes of any claim of the lower races to a power of self-improvement. " For, all experience proves that men, left in

[1] Mouat, 'Andaman Islanders,' pp. 7, 11, 315.
[2] Whately, 'Miscellaneous Lectures and Reviews;' London, 1856.

the lowest, or even anything approaching to the lowest, degree
of barbarism in which they can possibly subsist at all, never did
and never can raise themselves, unaided, into a higher condition." This view, it may be remarked in passing, serves as
basis for a theory that, though races arrived already at a mode-
rate state of culture may make progress of themselves, such
races must have been started on their way upwards by a supernatural revelation, to bring them to the point where independent progress became possible. Now, the denial to the low
savage of the power of self-improvement is a broad statement,
requiring, to justify it, at least a good number of cases of tribes
who have had a fair trial under favourable circumstances, and
have been found wanting. As definite statements of this nature, the two following are considered by Archbishop Whately
as sufficient to give substance to his argument.

"The New Zealanders, . . . whom Tasman first discovered
in 1642, and who were visited for the second time by Cook,
127 years after, were found by him exactly in the same condition." Tasman, however, never set foot in New Zealand. The
particulars he recorded of the civilization of the natives occupy
the space of a page or so in his journal.[1] He mentions fires
seen on shore; a sort of trumpet blown upon by the natives;
their dressing their hair in a bunch behind the top of the
head, with a white feather stuck in it; their double canoes,
joined above with a platform; their paddles and sails; their
clothing, which was (as it seemed) sometimes of matting,
and sometimes of cotton (he was wrong as to this last point, but
very excusably so, considering how little opportunity he had
of close examination); their spears and clubs; a white flag
carried by a man in a boat; and the square garden-enclosures
seen on Three Kings' Island. The evidence to be got from
this account, that the civilization of the New Zealanders had
not considerably advanced when Cook afterwards visited the
country, or, for the matter of that, that it had not as considerably declined, does not seem very forcible.

The other statement lies in the citing of a remark of Dar-

---

[1] Swart, 'Journaal van de Reis naar het onbekende Zuidland, door Abel Jansz.
Tasman;' Amsterdam, 1860, pp. 80–93.

win's about the Fuegians, which runs thus:[1]—"Their skill in some respects may be compared to the instinct of animals; for it is not improved by experience: the canoe, their most ingenious work, poor as it is, has remained the same, for the last two hundred and fifty years." But it must be noticed, that neither is the wretched hand-to-mouth life of the Fuegians favourable to progress, nor can a bark canoe ten feet long, holding four or five grown persons, beside children, dogs, implements, and weapons, and in which a fire can be kept burning on a hearth in the rough sea off Tierra del Fuego, be without tolerable sea-going qualities. As to workmanship, the modern Fuegian bark canoes are intermediate between the very rude ones of the Australian coast and the highly finished ones of North America, and it does not appear that their build may not be considerably better (or worse) than at the time of the visit of Sarmiento de Gamboa, in the sixteenth century. But the most remarkable thing in the whole matter, is the fact that the Fuegians should have had canoes at all, while coast-tribes across the straits made shift with rafts. This was of course a fact familiar to Mr. Darwin, and in the very next sentence after that quoted above, he actually goes on to ascribe to the Fuegian race the invention of their art of boat-building. "Whilst beholding these savages, one asks, whence have they come? What could have tempted, or what change compelled a tribe of men to leave the fine regions of the north, to travel down the Cordillera or backbone of America, to invent and build canoes, and then to enter on one of the most inhospitable countries within the limits of the globe?" Of this part of Mr. Darwin's remarks, however, Archbishop Whately did not think it necessary to take notice.

I have brought forward these statements of his, not for the purpose of discussing his particular views, but of illustrating the unsound relation in which theory has so often been placed to fact. But far more profitable work than the criticism and construction of speculative theories, may be done by collecting facts or groups of facts leading to direct inferences. When

[1] Fitz Roy and Darwin. Narrative of Voyage of 'Adventure' and 'Beagle.' London, 1839, vol. iii. p. 230. See vol. i. p. 137.

both fact and inference are sound, every such argument is a step gained, while if either be unsound, a distinct statement of fact and issue is the best means of getting them corrected, or, if needful, discarded altogether. A principal object of the present chapter, is to bring forward a variety of instances drawn from sources where indirect evidence bearing on our early history is to be sought.

As examples of evidence from language, a few cases may be given. The word *calculation*, indicating the primitive art of reckoning by pebbles or *calculi*, has passed on with the growth of science to designate the working of problems far beyond the reach of the abacus. So, though the Mexicans, when they were discovered, had a high numerical system and were good reckoners, the word *tetl*, "stone," remained as an integral part of one of their sets of numerals for counting animals and things; *centetl* "one stone," *ontetl* "two stone," *etetl* "three stone," etc., meaning nothing more than one, two, three. Nor is Mexico the only country where this curious phenomenon occurs. The Malays say for "one" not only *sa*, but also *sa-watu*, that is literally "one stone," and the Javans say not only *sa* but *sawiji*, that is, "one corn, or seed," and in like manner the Nias language calls one and two *sambua* and *dumbua*, that is, apparently, "one fruit," "two fruits."[1]

Still more notable is the Aztec term for an eclipse. The idea that the sun and moon are swallowed or bitten by dragons, or great dogs, or other creatures, is not only very common in the Old World, but it is even found in North and South America, and Polynesia.[2] But there is evidence that the ancient Mexicans understood the real cause of eclipses. They are represented in the picture-writings by a figure of the moon's disc covering part of the sun's, and this symbol, Humboldt remarks, "proves exact notions as to the cause of eclipses; it reminds us of the allegorical dance of the Mexican

<hr>

[1] Crawfurd, Gr. and Dic. of Malay Language; London, 1852, vol. I. pp. lvi. lviii. lxvii., and see cccxviii.

[2] Jacob Grimm, 'Deutsche Mythologie;' pp. 224–5, 669. Schoolcraft, part i. p. 271. Dobrizhoffer, vol. ii. p. 84. Du Tertre, Hist. Gén. des Antilles, etc.; Paris, 1667, vol. II. p. 371. Turner, 'Polynesia,' p. 531.

[3] Humboldt, Vues, pl. 56.

priests, which represented the moon devouring the sun."[3]
Yet the Mexicans preserved the memory of an earlier state of
astronomical knowledge, by calling eclipses of the sun and
moon *tonatiuh qualo, metztli qualo*, that is, "the sun's being
eaten," "the moon's being eaten," just as the Finns say, *kuu
syödää*, "the moon is eaten," and the Tahitians that she is *na-
tua*, that is, "bitten" or "pinched."[1] In the Mexican celebra-
tion of the *Netonatiuh-qualo*, or eclipse of the sun, two of the
captives sacrificed appeared as likenesses of the sun and moon.[2]

When a thing or an art is named in one country by a word
belonging to the language of another, as *maize*, *hammock*,
algebra, and the like, it is often good evidence that the thing
or art itself came from thence, bringing its name with it.   This
kind of evidence, bearing upon the progress of civilization, has
been much and successfully worked, but it has to be used with
great caution when the foreign language is an important medium of instruction, or spoken by a race dominant or powerful
in the country.   As instances of words good or bad as historical evidence, may be taken the Arabic words in Spanish.
While *alquimia* (alchemy), *albornóz* (bornoos), *acequia* (irrigating channel), *albaricoque* (apricot), and many more, may really
carry with them historical information of more or less value, it
must be borne in mind, that the influence of the Arabic language in Spain was so great, that it has often given words for
what was there long before Moorish times, *alacran* (scorpion),
alboroto (uproar), *alcor* (hill), and so on; not satisfied with
their own word for head, to express a head of cattle, the
Spaniards must needs call it *res*, Arabic *ras*, head.   So the New
Zealanders' use of *buka-buka* for book is good evidence as to
who taught them to read; but the name that the Tahitian
nobles are now commonly adopting, instead of the native term
arii, is bad evidence as to the origin of caste among them; they
like the title of *tavana*, which is a native attempt at *governor*.[*]

Even the etymology of a word may sometimes throw light
upon the transmission of art and knowledge from one country
to another, as where we may see how the Roman made *sub-*

<hr>

[1] Castrén, 'Finnische Mythologie;' pp. 63–5.   Ellis. Polyn. Res., vol. ii. p. 418.
[2] Nieremberg. Hist. Nat.; Antwerp, 1635, p. 143.   Humboldt, Vues, pl. 23.

stantia by translating ὑπόστασις, and the German, making himself a word for "superstition," *aberglaube*, Flemish *over-geloof*, that is "over-belief," had the *super* of *superstitio* before him when he introduced into his language a notion which it had perhaps hardly realized before. To take a more speculative case of a very different kind, the tea-urns used in Russia are well known, but where did the Russians get the invention from? They get their tea from China, where tea-urns much resembling our own have long been in use. But the apparatus is no new thing in Europe, and the specimen in the Naples Museum, if it were coloured with the conventional chocolate colour, and had a tap put in to replace the original one which is lost, would perhaps be only remarked upon at an English tea-table as being beautiful but old-fashioned. It was kept hot by charcoal burning in a tube in the middle, like the Russian urns. Now the name of a vessel just answering this description has been preserved, *authepsa* (αὐθέψης, "self-boiler"), and of this term the Russian name for their urns, *samovar*, "self-boiler," is an exact translation. The coincidence suggests that they may have received both the thing and its name through Constantinople. Moreover, there is reason to think that the Western element in Chinese art is far more important than is popularly supposed, and the tea-urn is so peculiar an apparatus, and so strikingly alike in ancient Italy and in China, that it is scarcely possible that the two should be the results of separate invention. Imperfect as the evidence is, there is at least some ground for the view that the hot water urn originated very early in Europe, and travelled east as far as China.

It often happens that an old art or custom, which has been superseded for general purposes by some more convenient arrangement, is kept up long afterwards in solemn ceremonies and other matters under the control of priests and officials, who are commonly averse to change; as inventions have often to wait long after they have come into general use before they are officially recognized. Wooden tallies were given for receipts by our Exchequer up to the time of George IV., as if to keep up, as long as might be, the remembrance of the time when "our forefathers had no other books but the score and the tally." It is true that the notched Exchequer tally had long had a Latin inscription on it, and at last there was given into the bargain a fair English receipt, written on a separate paper. The tally survives still, not only in the broken sixpence, and in the bargains of peasants in outlying districts,[1] but in the counterfoil of the banker's cheque. Some evidence of this ceremonial keeping up of arts superseded in private life, will be given in the chapters on the Stone Age and Firemaking.

Such helps as these in working out the problem of the Origin and Progress of Culture grow scarcer as we descend among the lower races, and those of which we have little or no historical knowledge. Mere observation of arts in use, and of objects belonging to tribes living or dead, forms at present the bulk of the evidence of the history of their culture accessible to us. Of these records an immense mass has been collected, but they are very hard to read.

Sometimes, indeed, an object carries its history written in its form, as some of the Esquimaux knives brought to England which are carved out of a single piece of bone, in imitation of European knives with handles, and show that the maker was acquainted with those higher instruments, though he had not the iron to make a blade of, or even a few scraps to fix along the edge of the bone blade, as they so often do.

The keeping up in stone architecture of designs belonging to wooden buildings, furnishes conclusive proofs of the growth, in several countries, of the art of building in stone from the art of building in wood,—an argument which is used with extraordinary clearness and power in Mr. Fergusson's Handbook. In Central America and Asia Minor there are still to be seen stone buildings more or less entirely copied from wooden constructions, while in Egypt a like phenomenon may be traced in structures belonging to the remote age of the pyramids. The student may see, almost as if he had been standing by when they were built, how the architect, while adopting the new material, began by copying from the wooden structures to which he had been accustomed. Speaking of the Lycian tombs

---

[1] Pictet, 'Origines,' part ii. p. 125.

which still remain with their beams, planks, and panels, as it were turned from wood into stone, Mr. Fergusson remarks upon the value of such monuments as records of the beginning of stone architecture among the people who built them. " . . . wherever the process can be detected, it is in vain to look for earlier buildings. It is only in the infancy of stone architecture that men adhere to wooden forms, and as soon as habit gives them familiarity with the new material, they abandon the incongruities of the style, and we lose all trace of the original form, which never reappears at an after age."[1]

There could hardly be a better illustration of an ethnological argument derived from the mere presence of an art, than in Marsden's remark about the iron-smelters of Madagascar. It is well known that the Madagascans are connected by language with the great Malayo-Polynesian family which extends half round the globe; but the art of smelting iron has only been found in the islands of this vast district near Eastern Asia, and in Madagascar itself. Even in New Zealand, where there is good iron ore, there was no knowledge of iron. Now at the time of our becoming acquainted with the races of Africa, in central latitudes and far down into the south, they were iron-smelters, and had been so for we know not how long, and Africa is only three or four hundred miles from Madagascar, whereas Sumatra is three or four thousand. Nevertheless, Marsden's observation connects the art in Madagascar with the distant Eastern Archipelago, and not with the neighbouring African continent. The process of smelting in small furnaces or pits is much the same in these two districts, but the bellows are different. The African bellows consist of two skins with valves worked alternately by hand, so as to give a continuous draught, much the same as those of modern India. These were not only in use among the ancient Greeks and Romans, but are still to be found in Southern Europe; I saw a wandering tinker at work at Pæstum with a pair of goatskins with the hair on, which he compressed alternately to drive a current of air into his fire, opening and shutting with his hands the

<hr>

[1] Fergusson, 'Illustrated Handbook of Architecture,' London, 1855, vol. i. pp. 118, 208, 220, etc.

slits which served as valves. Several of these skin-bellows are often used at once in Africa, and there are to be found improved forms which approach more nearly to our bellows with boards, but the principle is always the same.[1] But the Malay blowing apparatus is something very different; it is a double-barreled air forcing-pump. It consists of two bamboos, four inches in diameter and five feet long, which are set upright, forming the cylinders, which are open above, and closed below except by two small bamboo tubes which converge and meet at the fire. Each piston consists of a bunch of feathers or other soft substance, which expands and fits tightly in the cylinder while it is being forcibly driven down, and collapses to let the air pass as it is drawn up; and a boy perched on a high seat or stand works the two pistons alternately by the piston-rods, which are sticks. (It is likely that each cylinder may have a valve to prevent the return draught.) Similar contrivances have been described elsewhere in the Eastern Archipelago, in Java, Mindanao, Borneo, and New Guinea, and in Siam, the cylinders being sometimes bamboos and sometimes hollowed trunks of trees. Marsden called attention to the fact that the apparatus used in Madagascar is similar to that of Sumatra. There is a description and drawing in Ellis's 'Madagascar,' which need not be quoted in detail, as it does not differ in principle from that of the Eastern Archipelago. A single cylinder is sometimes used in Madagascar, and perhaps also in Borneo, but as a rule the far more advantageous plan of working two or several at once is adopted. The Chinese tinkers, who practise the art, quite unknown in Europe, of patching a cast-iron vessel with a clot of melted iron, perform this extraordinary feat with an air forcing-pump, which has indeed but a single trunk and a piston packed with feathers, but is improved by valves and a passage which give it what is known as a "double action," so that the single barrel does the work of two in the ruder construction of the islands.[2]

---

[1] Petherick, pp. 293, 295. Andersson, p. 301. Backhouse, Narr. of a Visit to the Mauritius and S. Africa; London, 1844, p. 377. Du Chaillu, 'Equatorial Africa;' p. 91, etc. etc.

[2] Marsden, p. 181. Raffles, Hist. of Java, vol. i. pp. 168, 173. Dampier,

It seems from the appearance of this remarkable apparatus in Madagascar and in the Eastern Archipelago, that the art of iron-smelting in these distant districts has had a common origin. Very likely the art may have gone from Sumatra or Java to Madagascar, but if so, this must have happened when they were in the Iron Age, to which we have no reason to suppose they had come in the time of their connexion with the ironless Maoris and Tahitians. Language throws no light on the matter; iron is called in Malay, *bäsi*, and in Malagasy, *vi*.

It is but seldom that the transmission of an art to distant regions can be traced, except among comparatively high races, by such a beautiful piece of evidence as this. The state of things among the lower tribes which presents itself to the student, is a substantial similarity in knowledge, arts, and customs, running through the whole world. Not that the whole culture of all tribes is alike,—far from it; but if any art or custom belonging to a low tribe is selected at random, it is twenty to one that something substantially like it may be found in at least one place thousands of miles off, though it very frequently happens that there are large portions of the earth's surface lying between, where it has not been observed. Indeed, there are few things in cookery, clothing, arms, vessels, boats, ornaments, found in one place, that cannot be matched more or less nearly somewhere else, unless we go into small details, or rise to the level of the Peruvians and Mexicans, or at least of the highest South Sea Islanders. A few illustrations may serve to give an idea of the kind of similarity which prevails so largely among the simpler arts of mankind.

The most rudimentary bird-trap is that in which the hunter is his own trap, as in Australia, where Collins thus describes it :—
" A native will stretch himself upon a rock as if asleep in the sun, holding a piece of fish in his open hand; the bird, be it hawk or crow, seeing the prey, and not observing any motion in the native, pounces on the fish, and, in the instant of seizing

'Voyages,' London, 1703–9, 5th ed. vol. i. p. 332. Bishop of Labuan, in Tr. Eth. Soc.; London, 1863, p. 29. G. W. Earl, 'Papuans;' London, 1853, p. 78. Mouhot, 'Travels in Indo-China,' etc.; London, 1864, vol. ii. p. 133. Ellis, 'Madagascar;' vol. i. p. 307. Percy, 'Metallurgy;' London, 1864, pp. 255, 273–6, 740.

it, is caught by the native, who soon throws him on the fire and makes a meal of him." Ward, the missionary, declares that a tame monkey in India, whose food the crows used to plunder while he sat on the top of his pole, did something very near this, by shamming dead within reach of the food, and seizing the first crow that came close enough. When he had caught it, the story says, he put it between his knees, deliberately plucked it, and threw it up into the air. The other crows set upon their disabled companion and pecked it to death, but they let the monkey's store alone ever after. The Esquimaux so far improves upon the Australian form of the art as to build himself a little snow-hut to sit in, with a hole large enough for him to put his hand through to clutch the bird that comes down upon the bait.[1]

There is a curious little art, practised in various countries, that of climbing trees by the aid of hoops, fetters, or ropes. Father Gilij thus describes it among the Indians of South America:—"They are all extremely active in climbing trees, and even the weaker women may be not uncommonly seen plucking the fruit at their tops. If the bark is so smooth and slippery that they cannot go up by clinging, they use another means. They make a hoop of wild vines, and putting their feet inside, they use it as a support in climbing."[2] This is what the toddy-drawer of Ceylon uses to climb the palm with,[3] but the negro of the West Coast of Africa makes a larger hoop round the tree and gets inside it, resting the lower part of his back against it, and jerks it up the trunk with his hands, a little at a time, drawing his legs up after it.[4] Ellis describes the Tahitian boys tying their feet together, four or five inches apart, with a piece of palm-bark, and with the aid of this fetter going up the cocoa-palms to gather the nuts;[5] and Backhouse mentions a different plan in use in opossum-catching in Van Diemen's Land. The native women who climbed the tall,

<hr>

[1] Collins, vol. i. p. 648. Ward, 'Hindoos,' p. 43. Klemm, C. G., vol i. p. 314; vol. ii. p. 292.

[2] Gilij, 'Saggio di Storia Americana,' Rome, 1780–4, vol. ii. p. 40. See Bates, The Naturalist on the R. Amazons,' London, 1863, vol. ii. p. 191.

[3] Tennent, 'Ceylon,' vol. ii. p. 523. See Plin., xiii. 7.

[4] Klemm, C. G., vol. iii. p. 236.   [5] Ellis, vol. i. p. 371.

smooth gum-trees did not cut notches after the Australian plan, except where the bark was rough and loose near the ground. Having got over this part by the notches, they threw round the tree a rope twice as long as was necessary to encompass it, put their hatchets on their bare, cropped heads, and placing their feet against the tree and grasping the rope with their hands, they hitched it up by jerks, and pulled themselves up the enormous trunks almost as fast as a man would mount a ladder.[1]

The ancient Mexican art of turning the waters of their lakes to account by constructing floating gardens upon them, has been abandoned, apparently on account of the sinking of the waters, which are now shallow enough to allow the mud gardens to rest upon the bottom. At the time of Humboldt's visit to Mexico, however, there were still some to be seen, though their number was fast decreasing. The floating gardens, or *chinampas*, which the Spaniards found in great numbers, and several of which still existed in his time on the lake of Chalco, were rafts formed of reeds, roots, and branches of underwood. The Indians laid on the tangled mass quantities of the black mould, which is naturally impregnated with salt, but by washing with lake water is made more fertile. "The chinampas," he continues, "sometimes even carry the hut of the Indian who serves as guard for a group of floating gardens. They are towed, or propelled with long poles, to move them at will from shore to shore."[2] Though floating gardens are no longer to be met with in Mexico, they are still in full use in the shallow waters of Cashmere. They are made of mould heaped on masses of the stalks of aquatic plants, and will mostly bear a man's weight, though the fruit is generally picked from the banks. They differ from the ancient Mexican chinampas in not being towed from one place to another, but impaled on fixed stakes, which keep them to their moorings, but allow them to rise and fall with the level of the water.[3]

The floating islands of the Chinese lakes are far more arti-

[1] Backhouse, 'Australia,' p. 172.
[2] Humboldt, 'Essai Politique;' Paris, 1811, vol. ii. p. 185, etc.
[3] Torrens, 'Travels in Ladakh,' etc.; London, 1862, p. 271.

ficial structures than those of Mexico or Cashmere. The missionary Huc thus describes those he saw on the lake of Pinghou:—" We passed beside several *floating islands*, quaint and ingenious productions of Chinese industry which have perhaps occurred to no other people. These floating islands are enormous rafts, constructed generally of large bamboos, which long resist the dissolving action of water. Upon these rafts there is placed a tolerably thick bed of good vegetable mould, and thanks to the patient labour of some families of aquatic agriculturists, the astonished eye sees rising from the surface of the waters smiling habitations, fields, gardens, and plantations of great variety. The peasants on these farms seem to live in happy abundance. During the moments of rest left them from the tillage of the rice plots, fishing is at once their lucrative and agreeable pastime. Often when they have gathered in their crop upon the lake, they throw their net and draw it on board their island loaded with fish. . . . Many birds, especially pigeons and sparrows, stay by their own choice in these floating fields to share the peaceable and solitary happiness of these poetical islanders. Towards the middle of the lake, we met with one of these farms attempting a voyage. It moved with extreme slowness, though it had the wind aft. Not that sails were wanting; there was a very large one above the house, and several others at the corners of the island; moreover, all the islanders, men, women, and children, provided with long sweeps, were working with might and main, though without putting much speed into their farm. But it is likely that the fear of delay does not much trouble these agricultural mariners, who are always sure to arrive in time to sleep on land. They are often seen to move from place to place without a motive, like the Mongols in the midst of their vast prairies; though, happier than those wanderers, they have learnt to make for themselves as it were a desert in the midst of civilization, and to ally the charms and pleasures of a nomade with the advantages of a sedentary life."[1]

Such coincidences as these, when found in distant regions between whose inhabitants no intercourse is known to have

---

[1] Huc, ' L'Empire Chinois,' Paris, 1854, 2nd ed. p. 114.

taken place, are not to be lightly used as historical evidence of
connexion. It is safest to ascribe them to independent invention, unless the coincidence passes the limits of ordinary probability. Ancient as the art of putting in false teeth is in the
Old World, it would scarcely be thought to affect the originality
of the same practice in Quito, where a skeleton has been found
with false teeth secured to the cheek-bone by a gold wire,[1] nor
does the discovery in Egypt of mummies with teeth stopped
with gold, appear to have any historical connexion with the
same contrivance among ourselves.[2] Thus, too, the Australians were in the habit of cooking fish and pieces of meat in hot
sand, each tied up in a sheet of bark, and this is called *yudarn
dookoon*, or "tying-up cooking,"[3] but it does not follow that
they had learnt from Europe the art of dressing fish *en papil-
lotte*.

Perhaps the occurrence of that very civilized instrument, the
fork for eating meat with, in the Fiji Islands, is to be accounted for by considering it to have been independently invented there. The Greeks and Romans do not appear to have
used forks in eating, and they are said not to have been introduced in England from the South of Europe, till the beginning
of the seventeenth century.[4] At any rate, Hakluyt thus trans-
lates, in 1598, a remark made by Galeotto Perera, concerning
the use of chopsticks in China;—"they feede with two sticks,
refraining from touching their meate with their hands, even as
we do with forkes," but he finds it necessary to put a note in
the margin, "We, that is the Italians and Spaniards."[5] How
long forks had been used in the South of Europe, and where
they originally came from, does not seem clear, but there is a
remark to the purpose in William of Ruysbruck's description
of the manners of the Tutars, through whose country he travelled about 1253. "They cut up (the meat) into little bits in a
dish with salt and water, for they make no other sauce, and then

[1] Bollaert, Res. in New Granada, etc.; London, 1860, p. 63.
[2] Wilkinson, Pop. Acc., vol. ii. p. 350   [3] Grey, Journals, vol. ii. p. 278.
[4] Wright, 'Domestic Manners,' p. 457.
[5] Hakluyt, 'The Principal Navigations, Voyages,' etc.; London, 1598, vol. ii.
part ii. p. 68.

with the point of a knife or with a little fork (*furricula*), which they make for the purpose, like those we use for eating pears and apples stewed in wine, they give each of the guests standing round one mouthful or two, according to their numbers."[1]

The circumstances under which the fork makes its appearance in the Fiji Islands, are remarkable. If it is known elsewhere in Polynesia (except of course as distinctly adopted with other European fashions), it is certainly not commonly so, and its use appears to be connected with the extraordinary development of the art of cooking there, as contrasted with most of the Pacific islands, where, generally speaking, there were no vessels in which liquid was boiled over the fire, and boiling, if done at all, was done by a ruder process. But the Fijians were accomplished potters, and continue to use their earthen vessels for the preparation of their various soups and stews, for fishing the hot morsels out of which the forks are used, perhaps exclusively. Those we hear of particularly are the "cannibal forks" for eating man's flesh, which are of wood, artistically shaped and sometimes ornamented, and were handed down as family heirlooms. Each had its individual name; for instance, one which belonged to a chief celebrated for his enormous cannibalism was called *undroundro,* "a word used to denote a small person or thing carrying a great burden."[2] It would be a remarkable point if, as Dr. Seemann thinks, the fork were only used for this purpose,[3] and we might be inclined to theorize on its invention as connected with the tabu, so common in Polynesia, which restricts the tabued person from touching his food with his hands, and compels him to be fed by some one else, or in default, to grovel on the ground and take up his food with his mouth. But a description by Williams of the furniture of a Fijian household, seems to imply its use for ordinary purposes as well. "On the hearth, each set on three stones, are several pots, capable of holding from a quart to five gallons. Near these are a cord for binding fuel, a skewer for trying cooked food, and, in the better houses, a wooden fork—a luxury which, probably, the Fijian enjoyed

[1] Gul. de Rubruquis, in Hakluyt, vol. i. p. 75.   See Ayton, in Purchas, vol. iii. p. 212.   [2] Williams, 'Fiji,' vol. i. pp. 212–3.   [3] Seemann, 'Viti,' p. 170.

when our worthy ancestors were wont to take hot food in their
practised fingers."[1]   But whether the use of the fork in eating
came about in Fiji as a consequence of the common use of
stewed food, or from some more occult cause, it seems probable that their use of it and ours may spring from two independent inventions.   That they got the art of pottery from
Asia is indeed likely enough, but there seems very little ground
for thinking that the eating-fork came to them from Asia, or
from anywhere else.

If an art can be found existing in one limited district of the
world, and nowhere else, there seems to be ground for assum-
ing that it was invented by the people among whom it is found,
with much greater confidence than if it appears in several
distant places.   Any one, however, who thinks this an unfair
inference, may console himself with the knowledge that Ethnologists seldom get a chance of using it at present, except for
very trifling arts or for unimportant modifications.   Indeed,
any one who claims a particular place as the source of even the
smallest art, from the mere fact of finding it there, must feel
that he may be using his own ignorance as evidence, as though
it were knowledge.   It is certainly playing against the bank,
for a student to set up a claim to isolation for any art or custom, not knowing what evidence there may be against him,
buried in the ground, hidden among remote tribes, or contained
even in ordinary books, to say nothing of the thousands of
volumes of forgotten histories and travels.

Among the inventions which it seems possible to trace to
their original districts, is the hammock, which is found, as it
were, native in a great part of South America, and the West
Indies, and is known to have spread thence far and wide over
the world, carrying with it its Haitian name, *hamac*.

The boomerang is a peculiar weapon, and moreover there
are found beside it in its country, Australia, intermediate forms
between it and the battle-axe or pick ; so that there is ground
for considering it a native invention developed through such
stages into its most perfect form.   Various Old World missiles
have indeed been claimed as boomerangs ; a curved weapon

[1] Williams, vol. I. p. 133.

shown on the Assyrian bas-reliefs, the throwing-cudgel of the
Egyptian fowler, the African *lissán* or curved club, the iron
hungamunga of the Tibbûs, but without clear proof being
brought forward that these weapons, or the boomerang-like
iron projectiles of the Neam Nam, have either of the great
peculiarities of the boomerang, the sudden swerving from the
apparent line of flight, or the returning to the thrower. Mr.
Samuel Ferguson has written a very learned and curious paper[1]
on supposed European analogues of the boomerang, in concluding which he remarks, not untruly, that "many of the
foregoing inferences will, doubtless, appear in a high degree
speculative." As might be expected, he makes the most of
the obscure description of the *catcia*, set down about the beginning of the seventh century by Bishop Isidore of Seville.[2]
But what is far more to the purpose, Mr. Ferguson seems to
have made trial of a curved club of ancient shape, and some
hammer- and cross-shaped weapons, such as may have been
used in Europe, and to have made them fly with something of
the returning flight of the boomerang. On the whole, it would
be rash to assert that the principle of the boomerang was quite
unknown in the Old World. Another remarkable weapon, the
bolas, seems to be isolated in the particular region of South
America where it was found in use, and was therefore very
likely invented there; but its principle is known also among
the Esquimaux, whose thin thongs, weighted with bunches of
ivory knobs, are arranged to wind themselves round the bird
they are thrown at, in much the same way as the much stouter
cords, weighted at the ends with two or three heavy stone balls,
which form the *bolas* of the Southern continent.

A few more instances may be given, rather for their quaint-
ness than for their importance. The Australians practise an
ingenious art in bee-hunting, which I have not met with anywhere else. The hunter catches a bee, and gums a piece of

---

[1] S. Ferguson, in Trans. R. I. A.; Dublin, 1843, vol. xix.

[2] "Est enim genus Gallici teli ex materia quàm maximè lenta, quae jacta qui-
dem non longe propter gravitatem evolat: sed quò pervenit, vi nimia perfrin-
git: quòd si ab artifice mittatur: rursum redit ad eum, qui misit," etc. (Isid.
Orig. xviii. 7.)

down to it, so that it can fly but slowly, and he can easily follow it home to the hive, and get the honey.[1] The North American bee-hunters do not appear to know this contrivance. Again, there is the curious art of changing the colour of a live macaw's feathers from blue or green to brilliant orange or yellow, by plucking them and rubbing some liquid into the skin (it is said the milky secretion from a small frog or toad), which causes the new feathers to grow with a changed colour.[2] This is done in South America, but, so far as I know, not elsewhere; and it seems reasonable to suppose that it was invented there.

The pellet-bow, which is a bow strung with a broad strap, or with a double string and net, and has been found in use for shooting clay-pellets or stones at small game, and even as a weapon in war, is a modification of the bow, used in South America but perhaps not elsewhere.[3] And the natives of the Malayan peninsula have very likely a monopoly of the device of perforating growing bamboos, so as to convert them into living Æolian flutes.[4]

When an art is practised upon some material which belongs exclusively, or in a large degree, to the place where the art is found, the probability that it was invented on the spot becomes almost a certainty. No one would dispute the claim of the Peruvians or Chilians to have discovered the use, for manure, of the *huanu*, or, as we call it, "guano," which their exceptionally rainless climate has allowed to accumulate on their coasts, nor the claim of the dwellers in the hot regions near the Gulf of Mexico to have found out how to make their *chocollatl* from a native plant.

On the other hand, when tribes are found living among the very materials which are turned to account by simple arts elsewhere, and yet are ignorant of those arts, we have good ethnological evidence as to their condition when they first settled in

<hr>

[1] Lang, p. 328. Backhouse, Austr., p. 880.

[2] Wallace, 'Travels on the Amazon and Rio Negro,' London, 1853, p. 291. De la Condamine, in Pinkerton, vol. xiv. p. 218.

[3] Dobrizhoffer, vol. ii. p. 370. Klemm, C. G., vol. ii. p. 17. Southey, vol. ii. p. 369; vol. iii. p. 663.   [4] Tennent, 'Ceylon,' vol. i. p. 82.

the place where we become acquainted with them. In investigating the difficult problem of Polynesian civilization, this state of things often presents itself, not uniformly, but in a partial, various way, that gives us a glimpse here and there of the trains of events that must have taken place, in different times and places, to produce the complex result we have before us. It is clear that a Malayo-Polynesian culture, proved by the combined evidence of language, mythology, arts, and customs, has spread itself over a great part of the Southern Islands, from the Philippines down to New Zealand, and from Easter Island to Madagascar, though the pure Malayo-Polynesian race only forms a part of the population of the district in which its language and civilization more or less predominate. The original condition of the Malayo-Polynesian family, as determined by the state of its lower members, presents us with few arts not found at least in a rudimentary state in Australia, though these arts were developed with immensely greater skill and industry. In most of the South Sea Islands there was no knowledge of pottery, nor of the art of boiling food in vessels over a fire. Great part of the race was strictly in the stone age, knowing nothing of metals. The sugar-cane grew in Tahiti, but the natives only chewed it, knowing nothing of the art of sugar-making ;[1] nor did they make any use of the cotton-plant, though it grew there.[2] The art of weaving was unknown in most of the islands away from Asia. Though the cocoa-nut palm was common, they did not tap it for toddy ; and Dr. Seemann taught the Fijians the art of extracting sago from their native sago-palms.[3]

In other districts, however, a very different state of things was found. In Sumatra and other islands near Asia, and in Madagascar, iron was smelted and worked with much skill. The simplest kind of loom had appeared in the Eastern Archipelago, only, as the evidence seems to show, to be supplanted

---

[1] Cook, First Voy. H., vol. ii. p. 166. In the Fiji Islands, Williams, vol. i. pp. 63, 71, says that the sugar-cane is cultivated, and sugar made ; but he gives no opinion as to the age of these arts.

[2] J. R. Forster, Observations (Cook's Second Voy.), London, 1778, p. 384.

[3] Seemann, pp. 291, 429.

by a higher kind.[1] Pottery was made there, and even far into Polynesia, as in the Fiji Islands. All those things were probably introduced from Asia, to which country so very large a part of the present Malay culture is due, but there are local arts found cropping up in different groups of islands, which may be considered as native inventions peculiar to Polynesia. Thus, in some of the islands, it was customary to keep bread-fruit by fermenting it into a sour paste, in which state it could be stored away for use out of season, an art of considerable value. This paste was called *mahi* in Tahiti, where Captain Cook first saw it prepared, but it would seem to have been invented at a period since the part of the race which went to the Sandwich Islands were separated from the Tahitians, for the Sandwich Islanders knew nothing of it till the English brought it to them from Tahiti.[2] The use of the intoxicating liquor known as *ava*, *kava*, or *yangona*, appears to be peculiar to Polynesia, and therefore probably to have been invented there. It is true that the usual, though not universal practice of preparing it by chewing, gives it some resemblance to liquors so prepared on the American continent, but these latter are of an entirely different character, being fermented liquors of the nature of beer, made from vegetables rich in starch, while the *ava* is not fermented at all, the juice of the plant it is made from being intoxicating in its fresh state.[3]

[1] Marsden, p. 163.

[2] Cook's First Voy. II., vol. ii. p. 198 ; Third Voy., vol. iii. p. 141.

[3] The etymology of *kava* or *ava* is of interest. Its original meaning may have been that of bitterness or pungency ; *kawa*, N. Z. = pungent, bitter, strong (as spirits, etc.) ; *'ava*, Tah. = a bitter, disagreeable taste ; *kava*, Rar. Mang. Nuk., *'a'ava*, Sam., *awa awa*, Haw. = sour, bitter, pungent. Thence the name may have been given, not only to the plant of which the intoxicating drink is made, the *Macropiper methysticum*, *kava*, Tong. Rar. Nuk. ; *'ava*, Sam. Tah. Haw. ; but also in N. Z. to the *Macropiper excelsum*, or *kawa kawa*, and in Tahiti to tobacco, *'ava 'ava*. Lastly, the drink is named in Tahiti and in other islands from the plant it is expressed from. But Mariner's Tongan vocabulary seems to go the other way ; *cava* = the pepper plant ; also the root of this plant, of which is made a peculiar kind of beverage, etc. ; *cavaca* = bitter, brackish, also intoxicated with cava, or anything else. This looks as though the name of the plant gave a name to the quality of bitterness, as we say "peppery" in the sense of hot. (See the Vocabularies of Mariner, Hale, Buschmann, and the Church Miss. Soc., N. Z.) Southey (Hist. of Brazil, vol. i. p. 246) compares the word *kava* with

The miscellaneous pieces of evidence given in this chapter
have been selected less as giving grounds for arguments safe
from attack, than as examples of the sort of material with
which the Ethnologist has to deal.   The uncertainty of many
of the inferences he makes must be counterbalanced by their
number, and by the concurrence of independent lines of reasoning in favour of the same view.   But in the arguments given
here in illustration of the general method, only one side of
history has been kept in view, and the facts have been treated
generally as evidence of movement only in a forward direction,
or (to define more closely what is here treated as Progress) of
the appearance and growth of new arts and new knowledge,
whether of a profitable or hurtful nature, developed at home
or imported from abroad.   Yet we know by what has taken
place within the range of history, that Decline as well as Progress in art and knowledge really goes on in the world.   Is
there not then evidence forthcoming to prove that degradation
as well as development has happened to the lower races beyond
the range of direct history?   The known facts bearing on this
subject are scanty and obscure, but by examining some direct
evidence of Decline, it may be perhaps possible to form an
opinion as to what indirect evidence there may probably be,
and how it is to be treated; though actually to find this and
use it, is a very different matter.

There are developments of Culture which belong to a particular climate or a particular state of society, which require a
despotic government, a democratic government, an agricultural
life, a life in cities, a state of continued peace or of continued
war, an accumulation of wealth which exceeds what is wanted
for necessaries and is accordingly devoted to luxury and refinement, and so forth.   Such things are all more or less local and

the South American word *caou-in* or *kaawy*, a liquor made from maize or the
mandioc root by chewing, boiling with water, and fermenting; but the idea of
bitterness or pungency is unsuitable to this liquor. Diaz (Dic. da Lingua Tupy)
gives perhaps a more accurate form, caulm = viubo, a derivative perhaps from
cad = beber (vinho). To show how easily such accidental coincidences as that
of *kawa* and *caulm* may be found, a German root may be pointed out for both,
looking as suitable as though it were a real one, *kauen*, to chew. '

unstable. The Chinese do not make now the magnificent cloisonné enamels and the high-class porcelain of their ancestors; we do not build churches, or even cast church-bells, as our forefathers did. In Egypt the extraordinary development of masonry, goldsmiths' work, weaving, and other arts which rose to such a pitch of excellence there thousands of years ago, have died out under the influence of foreign civilizations which contented themselves with a lower level of excellence in those things, and there seems to be hardly a characteristic native art of any importance practised there, unless it be the artificial hatching of eggs, and even this is found in China. As Sir Thomas Browne writes in his 'Fragment on Mummies,' "Egypt itself is now become the land of obliviousness and doteth. Her ancient civility is gone, and her glory hath vanished as a phantasma. Her youthful days are over, and her face hath become wrinkled and tetrick. She poreth not upon the heavens, astronomy is dead unto her, and knowledge maketh other cycles."

The history of Central America presents a case somewhat like that of Egypt. The not uncommon idea that the deserted cities, Copan, Palenque, and the rest, are the work of an extinct and quite unknown race, does not agree with the published evidence, which proves that the descendants of the old builders are living there now, speaking the old languages that were spoken before the Spanish Conquest. The ancient cities, with their wonders of masonry and sculpture, are deserted, the special native culture has in great measure disappeared, and the people have been brought to a sort of low European civilization; but a mass of records, corroborated in other ways, show us the Central Americans before the Conquest, building their great cities and living in them, cultivating, warring, sacrificing, much like their neighbours of Mexico, with whose civilization their own was intimately allied. An epitome of the fate of the ruined cities may be given in the words which conclude a remarkable native document published in Quiché and French by the Abbé Brasseur,—"Ainsi donc c'en est fait de tous ceux du Quiché, qui s'appelle *Santa-Cruz*." The ruins of the great city of Quiché are still to be seen; Santa Cruz, its ancecessor, is a poor village of two thousand souls, a league or so away.[1]

Among the lower races, degeneration is seen to take place as a result of war, of oppression by other tribes, of expulsion into less favourable situations, and of various other causes. But arts which belong to the daily life of the man or the family, and cannot be entirely suppressed by violent interference, do not readily disappear unless superseded by some better contrivance, or made unnecessary or very difficult by a change of life and manners. When the use of metals, of pottery, of the flint and steel, of higher tools and weapons, once fairly establishes itself, a falling back appears to be uncommon. The Metal Age does not degenerate into the Stone Age except under very peculiar circumstances. The history of a higher weapon is generally that it supplants those that are less serviceable, to be itself supplanted by something better. We read of the Indian orator who exhorted his brethren to cast away the flint and steel of the white man, and to return to the fire-sticks of their ancestors, but such things are rather talked of than done.

Cases of savage arts being superseded by a higher state of civilization are common enough. An African guide, or an Australian, will know a man by his footmark, while we hardly know what a footmark is like; at least, nine Englishmen out of ten of the shoe-wearing classes will not know that the footprints in the Mexican picture-writings, as copied in Fig. 16,

Fig. 16.

are true to nature, till they have looked at the print of a wet foot on a board or a flagstone. Captain Burton remarked, on

<hr>

[1] Brasseur, 'Popol Vuh,' pp. 315–7. See also Diego de Landa, Rel.

his road to the great Salt Lake, that bones and skulls of cattle were lying scattered about,[1] though travellers are often put to great straits for fuel. The Gauchos of South America know better, for when they kill a beast on a journey, they use the bones as fuel to cook the flesh,[2] as the Scythians did in the time of Herodotus; living in a country wanting wood, they made a fire of the bones of the beasts sacrificed, and boiled the flesh over it in a kettle, or if that were not forthcoming, in the paunch of the animal itself, "and thus the ox boils himself, and the other victims each the like."[3]

It sometimes happens that degeneration is caused by conquest, when the conquering race is in anything at a lower level than the conquered. There is one art whose history gives some extraordinary cases of this kind of decline, the art of irrigation by watercourses. Within a few years one people, the Spaniards, conquered two nations, the Moors and the Peruvians, who were skilful irrigators, and had constructed great works to bring water from a distance to fertilize the land. These works were for the most part allowed to go to rack and ruin, and in Peru, as in Andalusia, great tracts of land which had been fruitful gardens fell back into parched deserts; while in Mexico the ruins of the great native aqueduct of Tetzcotzinco tell the same tale. Here, as in the irrigation of British India under our own rule, the results of higher culture in the conquered race declined in the face of a lower culture of the conquerors, but the sequel is still more curious. The Spaniards in America became themselves great builders of watercourses, and their works of this kind in Mexico are very extensive, and of great benefit to the drier regions where they have been constructed. But when a portion of territory that had been under Spanish rule was transferred to the United States, what the Spaniards had done to the irrigating works of the Moors and Peruvians, the new settlers did to theirs. In Froebel's time they were letting the old works go to ruin; thus history repeats itself.[4]

The disappearance of savage arts in presence of a higher

[1] Burton, 'City of the Saints,' p. 60.   [2] Darwin, Journal, p. 194.
[3] Herod., iv. 61. See Ezekiel xxiv. 5 in LXX. Klemm, C. G., vol. ii. p. 229 (bones rubbed with fat burnt by Esquimaux).   [4] Tylor, 'Mexico,' pp. 157–161.

civilization is however mostly caused by their being superseded by something higher, and this can hardly be called a decline of culture, which must not be confounded with the physical and moral decline of so many tribes under the oppression and temptation of civilized men. Real decline often takes place when a rude but strong race overcomes a cultivated but weak race, and of this we have good information; but neither this change, nor that which takes place in the savage in presence of the civilized invader, gives the student of the low races all the information he needs. What he wants besides is to put the high races out of the question altogether, and to find out how far a low race can lose its comparatively simple arts and knowledge, without these being superseded by something higher; in fact, how far such a race can suffer pure decline in culture. This information is, however, very hard to get.

Livingstone's remarks on the Bakalahari of South Africa show us a race which has fallen in civilization, but this fall has happened, partly or wholly, through causes acting from without. The great Kalahari desert is inhabited by two races, the Bushmen, who were perhaps the first human inhabitants of the country, and who never cultivate the soil, or rear any domestic animals but dogs, and the Ba-Kalahari, who are degraded Bechuanas. These latter are traditionally reported to have once possessed herds of cattle like the other Bechuanas, and though their hard fate has forced them to live a life much like that of the Bushmen, they have never forgotten their old ways. They hoe their gardens annually, though often all they can hope for is a supply of melons and pompkins. And they carefully rear small herds of goats, though Livingstone has seen them obliged to lift water for them out of small wells with a bit of ostrich egg-shell, or by spoonfuls.[1] This remarkable account brings out strongly the manful struggle of a race which has been brought down by adverse circumstances, to keep up their former civilization, while the Bushmen, who, for all we know, may never have been in a higher condition than they are now, make no such effort. If we may judge these two races by the same standard, the Bushmen are either no lower than

---

[1] Livingstone, p. 49.

they have ever been, or if they have come down from a condition approaching that of the Bechuanas, the process of degradation must indeed have been a long one.

Tribes who are known to have once been higher in the scale of culture than they are now, are to be met with in Asia. Some of the coast Tunguz live by fishing, though they are still called Orochi, which is equivalent to the term " Reindeer Tunguz." No doubt the tradition is true of the Goldi that, though they have no reindeer now, they once had, like the Tunguz tribes north of the Amur.[1]   There are Kalmucks north of the Caspian who have lost their herds of cattle and degenerated into fishermen. The richest of them has still a couple of cows. They look upon horses, camels, and sheep as strange and wondrous creatures when foreigners bring them into their country. They listen with wonder to their old men's stories of life in the steppes, of the great herds and the ceaseless wanderings over the vast plains, while they themselves dwell in huts of reeds, and carry their household goods on their backs when they have to move to a new fishing-place.[2]   The miserable " Digger Indians " of North America are in part Shoshonees or Snake Indians, who were brought down to their present state by their enemies the Blackfeet, who got guns from the Hudson's Bay Company, and thus conquered the Snakes, and took away their hunting-grounds.   They lead a wandering life, lurking among hills and crags, slinking from the sight of whites and Indians, and subsisting chiefly on wild roots and fish, and such game as so helpless a race is able to get.   They are lean and abject-looking creatures, deserving the name of *gens de pitié* given them by the French trappers, and they have been driven to abandon arts which they possessed in their more fortunate days, such as riding, and apparently even hut-building; but how far their degradation has brought with it decline in other parts of their former culture, it is not easy to say.[3]

Here, then, we have cases of material evidence which, as we happen to have other means of knowing, ought to be treated

---

[1] Ravenstein, p. 318.   [2] Klemm, C. G., vol. iii. p. 4.

[3] Buschmann, 'Spuren der Aztekischen Sprache im nördlichen Mexico,' etc. etc. (Abh. der K. A. v. W., 1854); Berlin, 1859, p. 633, etc.

as recording decline. The sculptures and temples of Central America are the work of the ancestors of the present Indians, though if history, tradition, and transitional work had all perished, it would hardly be thought so. The gardening of the Bakalahari, if the account of their origin is to be received, is a proof, not of an art gained, but of a higher level of civilization for the most part lost.

It thus appears that, in the abstract, when there is found among a low tribe an art or a piece of knowledge which seems above their average level, three ways are open by which its occurrence may be explained. It may have been invented at home, it may have been imported from abroad, or it may be a relic of a higher condition which has mostly suffered degradation, like the column of earth which the excavator leaves to measure the depth of the ground he has cleared away.

Ethnologists have sometimes taken arts which appeared to them too advanced to fit with the general condition of their possessors, and have treated them as belonging to this latter class. But where such arguments have had no aid from direct history, but have gone on mere inspection of the arts of the lower races, all that I can call to mind, at least, seem open to grave exception.

Thus the boomerang has been adduced as proof that the Australians were once in a far higher state of civilization.[1] It is true that the author who argued thus confounded the boomerang with the throwing-cudgel, or, as a Hampshire man would call it, the *squoyle*, of the Egyptian fowler, so that he had at least an imaginary high civilization in view, of which the boomerang was an element. But, as has been mentioned, intermediate forms between the boomerang and the war-club or pick, are known in Australia, a state of things which fits rather with growth than with degeneration.[2]

In South America, Humboldt was so struck with the cylinders of very hard stone, perforated and sculptured into the forms of animals and fruits, that he founded upon them the argument that they were relics of an ancient civilization from

[1] W. Cooke Taylor, The Nat. Hist. of Society; London, 1840, vol. i. p. 205.
[2] See Eyre, vol. ii. p. 308; Klemm, C. G., vol. i. p. 316, pl. vii.

which their possessors had fallen. "But it is not," he says,
"the Indians of our own day, the dwellers on the Oronoko and
the Amazons whom we see in the last degree of brutalization,
who have perforated substances of such hardness, giving them
the shapes of animals and fruits. Such pieces of work, like
the pierced and sculptured emeralds found in the Cordilleras
of New Granada and Quito, indicate a previous civilization. At
present the inhabitants of these districts, especially of the hot
regions, have so little idea of the possibility of cutting hard
stones (emerald, jade, compact felspar, and rock crystal), that
they have imagined the green stone to be naturally soft when
taken out of the ground, and to harden after it has been
fashioned by hand."[1]   But while mentioning Humboldt's argument, it must also be said that he had not had an opportunity
of learning how these ornaments were made. Mr. Wallace has
since found that at least plain cylinders of imperfect rock crystal, four to eight inches long, and one inch in diameter, are
made and perforated by very low tribes on the Rio Negro.
They are not, as Humboldt seems to have supposed, the result
of high mechanical skill, but merely of the most simple and
savage processes, carried on with that utter disregard of time
that lets the Indian spend a month in making an arrow. They
are merely ground down into shape by rubbing, and the perforating of the cylinders, crosswise or even lengthwise, is said
to be done thus :—a pointed flexible leaf-shoot of wild plantain
is twirled with the hands against the hard stone, till, with the
aid of fine sand and water, it bores into and through it, and
this is said to take years to do. Such cylinders as the chiefs
wear are said sometimes to take two men's lives to perforate.[2]
The stone is brought from a great distance up the river, and is
very highly valued. It is, of course, not necessary to suppose
that these rude Indians came of themselves to making such
ornaments; they may have imitated things made by races in a
higher state of culture; but the evidence, as it now stands,
does not go for much in proving that the tribes of the Rio
Negro have themselves fallen from a higher level.

[1] Humboldt & Bonpland, vol. ii. p. 481, etc.
[2] Wallace, p. 278.

On the other hand, it is much easier to go on pointing out arts practised by the less civilized races, which seem to have their fitting place rather in a history of progress than of degeneration. This remark applies to the case just mentioned, of the intermediate forms between the boomerang and the war-club being found in Australia, as though to mark the stages through which the perfect instrument had been developed. Several such cases occur among the arts of fire-making and cooking described in the following chapters. To glance for a moment at the history of Textile Fabrics (into which I hope to go more fully at a future time), it may be noticed that the spindle for twisting thread has been found in use in Asia, Africa, and North and South America, among people whose ruder neighbours had no better means of making their finest thread or cord than by twisting it with the hand, by rolling the fibres with the palm, on the thigh or some other part of the body. Again, though every known tribe appears to twist cord, and to make matting or wicker-work, the combination of these two arts, weaving, which consists in matting twisted threads, is very far from being general among the lower races. The step seems from our point of view a very simple one, but a large proportion of mankind had never made it. Now there is a curious art, which is neither matting nor weaving, found among tribes to whom real weaving was unknown. It consists in laying bundles of fibres, not twisted into real cord, side by side, and tying or fastening them together with transverse cords or bands; varieties of fabrics made in this way are well known in New Zealand and among the Indians of North-Western America; and Mr. Henry Christy pointed out to me a sack-like basket made in this way, which he found in use in 1856 among an Indian tribe N.W. of Lake Huron, a very good example of this interesting transition-work. Nor do we look in vain for such a fabric in Europe; it is found in the Lake Habitations of Switzerland. M. Troyon's work shows a specimen from Wangen, which belongs to the Stone Age.[1] Mr. John Evans has three specimens of fabrics from the Swiss Lakes, which form a series of great in-

---

[1] Troyon, 'Habitations Lacustres;' Lausanne, 1860, pl. vii. fig. 24, pp. 43, 429, 403.

terest. The first (Fig. 17) is also from Wangen, and, to use the description accompanying the sketches he has kindly given me, "the warp consists of strands of un-twisted fibre (hemp?) bound to-gether at intervals of about an inch apart by nearly similar strands 'wat-tled in' among them." The next specimen (Fig. 18), from Nieder Wyl, shows a great advance, for "the warp consists of twisted string, and the woof of a finer thread also twisted." The third specimen is a piece of ordinary plain weaving. Now all these things, European, Polynesian, and American, seem to be in their natural and rea-sonable places in a progress upward, but it is hard to imagine a people, under any combination of circum-stances, dropping down from the art of weaving, to adopt a more tedious and less profitable way of working up the fibre which it had cost them so much trouble to prepare; knowing the better art, and deliberately devoting their material and

Fig. 17.

time to practising the worse. So it is a very reasonable and natural thing, that tribes who had been used to twist their thread by hand, should sometimes over-come their dislike to change, and adopt the spindle when they saw it in use; or such a tribe might be supposed capable of inventing it; but the going back from the spindle to hand-twisting is a thing scarcely conceivable. A spindle is made too easily by any one who has once caught the idea of it; a stick and a bit of some-

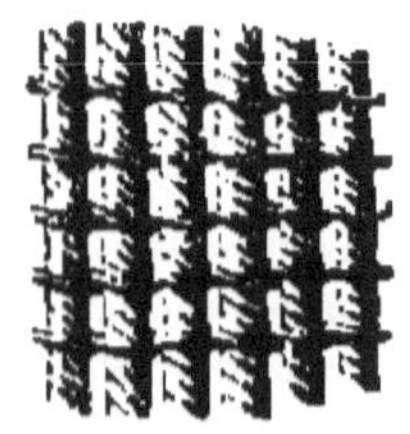

Fig. 18.

thing heavy for a whorl is the whole machine. Not many months ago, an old lady was seen in the isle of Islay, comfortably spinning her flax with a spindle, which spindle was simply a bit of stick with a potato stuck on the end of it.

To conclude, the want of evidence leaves us as yet much in the dark as to the share which decline in civilization may have had in bringing the lower races into the state in which we find them. But perhaps this difficulty rather affects the history of particular tribes, than the history of Culture as a whole. To judge from experience, it would seem that the world, when it has once got a firm grasp of new knowledge or a new art, is very loth to lose it altogether, especially when it relates to matters important to man in general, for the conduct of his daily life, and the satisfaction of his daily wants, things that come home to men's "business and bosoms." An inspection of the geographical distribution of art and knowledge among mankind, seems to give some grounds for the belief that the history of the lower races, as of the higher, is not the history of a course of degeneration, or even of equal oscillations to and fro, but of a movement which, in spite of frequent stops and relapses, has on the whole been forward; that there has been from age to age a growth in Man's power over Nature, which no degrading influences have been able permanently to check.

CHAPTER VIII.

THE STONE AGE—PAST AND PRESENT.

THE Stone Age is that period in the history of mankind during which stone is habitually used as a material for weapons and tools.   Antiquaries find it convenient to make the Stone Age cease whenever metal implements come into common use, and the Bronze Age, or the Iron Age, supervenes.   But the last traces of a Stone Age are hardly known to disappear anywhere, in spite of the general use of metals; and in studying this phase of the world's history for itself, it may be considered as still existing, not only among savages who have not fairly come to the use of iron, but even among civilized nations.   Wherever the use of stone instruments, as they were used in the Stone Age proper, is to be found, there the Stone Age has not entirely passed away.   The stone hammers with which tinkers might be found at work till lately in remote districts in Ireland,[1] the huge stone mallets with wooden handles which are still used in Iceland for driving posts and other heavy hammering,[2] and the lancets of obsidian with which the Indians of Mexico still bleed themselves, as their fathers used to do before the Spanish Conquest,[3] are stone implements which have survived for centuries the general introduction of iron.

Mere natural stones, picked up and used without any artificial shaping at all, are implements of a very low order.   Such

[1] Wilde, Cat. of Mus. of R. I. Acad. ; Dublin, 1857, p. 50.

[2] Klemm, 'Allgemeine Culturwissenschaft ;' Leipzig & Sondershausen, 1855–8, part ii. p. 68.   [3] Brasseur, 'Mexique,' vol. iii. p. 640.

natural tools are often found in use, being for the most part
slabs, water-worn pebbles, and other stones suited for hammers
and anvils, and their employment is no necessary proof of a
very low state of culture. Among the lower races, Dr. Milligan
gives a good instance of their use, in describing the shell-
mounds left by the natives on the shores of Van Diemen's
Land. In places where the shells found are univalves, round
stones of different sizes are met with ; one, the larger, on which
they broke the shells ; the other, and smaller, having served as
the hammer to break them with. But where the refuse-mounds
consist of oysters, mussels, cockles, and other bivalves, there
flint-knives, used to open them with, are generally found.[1] Sir
George Grey's description of the sites of native encampments,
so frequently met with in Australia, will serve as another example. The remains of such an encampment consist of a circle
of large flat stones arranged round the place where the fire has
been ; on each of the flat stones a smaller stone for breaking
shell-fish ; beside each pair of stones a large shell used for a
cup, and, scattered all around, broken shells and bones of
kangaroos.[2]

Nor are cases hard to find of the use of these very low repre-
sentatives of the Stone Age carried up into higher levels of
civilization. Thus the tribes of Central and Southern Africa,
though often skilful in smith's work, have not come thoroughly
to the use of the iron hammer and anvil. Travellers describe
them as forging their weapons and tools with a stone of handy
shape and size, on a lump of rock which serves as an anvil ;
while sometimes an iron hammer is used to give the last finish.[3]
The quantities of smooth rolled pebbles found in our ancient
English hill-forts were probably collected for sling-stones ; but
larger pebbles, very likely used as cracking-stones, are found
in early European graves.[4] At the present day, the inhabitants
of Heligoland and Rügen not only turn to account the natural
net-sinkers formed by chalk-flints, out of which the remains of a

[1] Milligan, in Tr. Eth. Soc. ; London, 1863, vol. ii. p. 129.
[2] Grey, Journals, vol. i. pp. 71, 100.
[3] Casalis, p. 131 ; Petherick, p. 395 ; Burton, Central Africa, vol. ii. p. 312 ;
Backhouse, Africa, p. 877.   [4] Klemm, C. W., part ii. p. 87.

sponge, or such thing, has been washed, leaving a convenient hole through the flint to tie it by; but they have been known to turn such a perforated flint into a hammer, by fixing a handle in the hole.[1]   And lastly, the women who shell almonds in the south of France still use a smooth water-worn pebble (*couède, couèdou*), as their implement for breaking the shells.

The distinction between natural and artificial implements is of no practical value in estimating the state of culture of a Stone-Age tribe. A natural chip or fragment of stone may have been now and then used as an edged or pointed tool; but we have not the least knowledge of any tribe too low habitually to shape such instruments for themselves. There is, however, a well-marked line of distinction in the Stone Age which divides it into a lower and a higher section. We have no historical knowledge of any tribe who have used stone instruments, and have not been in the habit of grinding or polishing some of them. But there are remains which clearly prove the existence of such tribes, and thus the Stone Age falls into two divisions, the Unground Stone Age and the Ground Stone Age.[2]

To the former and ruder of these two classes belong the instruments of the Drift or Quaternary deposits, and of the early bone caves, and, in great part at least, those of the Scandinavian shell-heaps or kjökkenmöddings. Even should a few ground instruments prove to belong to these deposits, the case would not be much altered, for the finding of hundreds of unground implements unmixed with ground ones would still show a vast predominance of chipping over grinding, which would justify their being classed in an Unground Stone Age, quite distinct from the Ground Stone Age in which modern tribes have been found living.

The rude flint implements found in the drift gravels of the Quaternary (*i. e.* Post-Tertiary) series of strata, belong to the earliest known productions of human art. Since the long unappreciated labours of M. Boucher de Perthes showed the historical importance of these relics, the date of the first appearance of man on the earth has been much debated. I have no purpose of attempting to discuss the collection of geological and

---

[1] Klemm, C. W., part ii. p. 12.   [2] See Mr. Lubbock's Lectures, etc.

antiquarian fact and argument brought forward in Sir Charles
Lyell's 'Antiquity of Man,' not only with reference to the men
of the drift period, but to those of the bone caves, and of the
early shell-heaps and peat-bogs. But it may be remarked that
geological evidence, though capable of showing the lapse of vast
periods of time, has scarcely admitted of these periods being
brought into definite chronological terms; yet it is only geological evidence that has given any basis for determining the
absolute date at which the makers of the drift implements lived
in France and England. In an elaborate paper lately published, Mr. Prestwich infers, from the time it must have taken
to excavate the river-valleys, even under conditions much more
favourable than now to such action, and to bore into the underlying strata the deep pipes or funnels now found lined with
sand and gravel, that a very long period must have elapsed
since the implement-bearing beds began to be laid down. But
his opinion is against extreme estimates, and favours the view
that the now undoubted contemporaneity of man with the mammoth, the *Rhinoceros tichorhinus*, etc., is rather to be accounted
for by considering that the great animals continued to live to a
later period than had been supposed, than that the age of man
on earth is to be stretched to fit with an enormous hypothetical
date. Mr. Prestwich thus sums up his view of the subject,
"That we must greatly extend our present chronology with
respect to the first existence of man appears inevitable; but
that we should count by hundreds of thousands of years is, I am
convinced, in the present state of the inquiry, unsafe and premature."[1]

A set of characteristic drift implements[2] would consist of
certain tapering instruments like huge lance-heads, shaped,
edged, and pointed, by taking off a large number of facets, in
a way which shows a good deal of skill and feeling for symmetry; smaller leaf-shaped instruments; flints partly shaped
and edged, but with one end left unwrought, evidently for holding in the hand; scrapers with curvilinear edges; rude flake-

[1] Prestwich, On the Geological Position and Age of the Flint-Implement-Bear-
ing Beds, etc. (from Phil. Trans.); London, 1864.
[2] See Evans, 'Flint Implements in the Drift;' London, 1862.

knives, etc. Taken as a whole, such a set of types would be very unlike, for instance, to a set of chipped instruments belonging to the comparatively late period of the cromlechs in France and England. But a comparison of particular types with what is found elsewhere, breaks down any imaginary line of severance between the men of the Drift and the rest of the human species. The flake knives are very rude, but they are like what are found elsewhere, and there is no break in the series which ends in the beautiful specimens from Mexico and Scandinavia. The Tasmanians sometimes used for cutting or notching wood a very rude instrument. Eye-witnesses describe how they would pick up a suitable flat stone, knock off chips from one side, partly or all round the edge, and use it without more ado; and there is a specimen corresponding exactly to this description in the Taunton Museum. An implement found in the Drift near Clermont would seem to be much like this. The drift tools with a chipped curvilinear edge at one end, which were probably used for dressing leather and other scraping, are a good deal like specimens from America. The leaf-shaped instruments of the Drift differ principally from those of the Scandinavian shell-heaps, and of America, in being made less neatly and by chipping off larger flakes; and there are leaf-shaped instruments which were used by the Mound-Builders of North America, perhaps for fixing as teeth in a war-club in Mexican fashion,[1] which differ rather in finish than in shape from the Drift specimens. Even the most special type of the Drift, namely, the pointed tapering implement like a great spear-head, differs from some American implements only in being much rougher and heavier. There have been found in Asia stone implements resembling most closely the best marked of the Drift types. Mr. J. E. Taylor, British Consul at Bassrah, obtained some years ago from the sun-dried brick mound of Abu Shahrein in Southern Babylonia, two taper pointed instru ments[2] of chipped flint, which, to judge from a cast of one of them, would be passed without hesitation as drift implements. As to the date to which these remarkable specimens belong,

[1] Squier & Davis, p. 211.
[2] Vaux, in Proc. Soc. Ant., Jan. 19, 1860.

there is no sufficient evidence. Again, a stone instrument, found in a cave at Bethlehem, does not differ specifically from the Drift type.

With the Unground Stone Age of the Drift, that of the Bone Caves is intimately connected. In the Drift, geological evidence shows that a long period of time must have been required for the accumulation of the beds which overlie the flint implements, for the cutting out of the valleys to their present state, and so on, since the time when the makers of these rude tools and weapons inhabited France and England in company with the *Rhinoceros tichorhinus*, the mammoth, and other great animals now extinct. In the Bone Caves this natural calendar of strata accumulated and removed is absent, but their animal remains border on the fauna of the Drift, and the Drift series of stone implements passes into the Cave series,[1] so that the men of the Drift may very well be the makers of some Cave implements contemporaneous with the great quaternary mammals.

The explorations made with such eminent skill and success in the caverns of M. Périgord by Mr. Lartet and Christy,[2] bring into view a wonderfully distinct picture of rude tribes inhabiting the south of France, at a remote period characterized by a fauna strangely different from that at present belonging to the district, the reindeer, the aurochs, the chamois, and so forth. They seem to have been hunters and fishers, having no domesticated animals, not even the dog; but they made themselves rude ornaments, they sewed with needles with eyes, and they decorated their works in bone, not only with hatched and waved patterns, but with carvings of animals done with considerable skill and taste. Yet their stone implements were very rude, to a great extent belonging to absolute Drift types, and destitute of grinding, with one curious set of exceptions, certain granite pebbles with a smooth hollowed cavity, some of which resemble stones used by the Australians for grinding some-

---

[1] See, for instance, W. Boyd Dawkins, in Proc. Somersetshire Archæological Soc., 1861-2, p. 197.

[2] Lartet & Christy, 'Cavernes du Périgord;' Paris, 1804 (from 'Revue Archéologique').

thing in, perhaps paint to adorn themselves with. It is very curious to find these French tribes going so far in the art of shaping tools by grinding, and yet, so far as we know, never catching the idea of grinding a celt.

The stone implements of the Scandinavian shell-heaps are a good deal like those of the Drift and the Caves, as regards their flint-flakes and leaf-shaped instruments, but they are characterized by the frequent occurrence of a kind of celt which is not a Drift type. It is rudely shaped from the flint, the natural fracture of which gives it a curved form which may be roughly compared to that of a man's front tooth, if it tapered from root to edge.[1] Here, also, the Unground Stone Age prevails, though a very few specimens of higher types have been found. I may quote Mr. Christy's opinion that the thousands of characteristic implements are to be taken as the standard of what was made and used, while, as has very often happened in old deposits lying in accessible situations, a few things may have got in in comparatively modern times.

Beside the want of grinding, the average quality of the instruments of the Unground Stone Age is very low, notwithstanding that its best specimens are far above the level of the worst of the later period. These combined characters of rudeness and the absence of grinding give the remains of the Unground Stone Age an extremely important bearing on the history of Civilization, from the way in which they bring together evidence of great rudeness and great antiquity. The antiquity of the Drift implements is, as has been said, proved by direct geological evidence. The Cave implements, even of the reindeer period, are proved by their fauna to be earlier, as they are seen at a glance to be ruder, than those of the cromlech period, and of the earliest lake-dwellings of Switzerland, both belonging to the Ground Stone Age. To the student who views Human Civilization as in the main an upward development, a more fit starting-point could scarcely be offered than this wide and well-marked progress from an earlier and lower, to a later and higher, stage of the history of human art.

[1] Lubbock in Nat. Hist. Review, Oct. 1861. Merlot in Soc. Vaudoise des Sc. Nat., 1859.

To turn now to the productions of the higher or Ground Stone Age, grinding is found rather to supplement chipping than to supersede it. Implements are very commonly chipped into shape before they are ground, and unfinished articles of this kind are often found. Moreover, such things as flake-knives, and heads for spears and arrows, have seldom or never been ground in any period, early or late, for the obvious reason that the labour of grinding them would have been wasted, or worse. Flake-knives of obsidian appear to have been sometimes finished by grinding in Mexico,[1] but most stone knives of the kind seem to have been used as they were flaked off. This question of grinding or not grinding stone implements is brought out clearly by some remarks of Captain Cook's, on his first voyage to the South Seas. He noticed that the natives of Tahiti used basalt to make their adzes of, and there it was necessary to sharpen almost every minute, for which purpose a stone and a cocoa-nut shell full of water were kept always at hand. When he saw the New Zealanders using, for the finishing of their nicest work, small tools of jasper, chipped off from a block in sharp angular pieces like a gunflint, and throwing them away as soon as they were blunted, he concluded they did not grind them afresh because they could not.[2] This, however, was not the true reason, as their grinding jade and other hard stones clearly shows; but it was simply easier to make new ones than to grind the old. A good set of implements of the Ground Stone Age will consist partly of instruments made by mere chipping, such as varieties of spear-heads, arrow-heads, and flake-knives, and partly of ground implements, the principal classes of which are celts, axes, and hammers.

The word celt (Latin *celtis*, a chisel) is a convenient term for including the immense mass of instruments which have the simple shape of chisels, and might have been used as such. No doubt many or most of them were really for mounting on handles, and using as adzes or axes; but in the absence of a handle, or a place for one, or a mark where one has been, it is often impossible to set down any particular specimen as certainly

---

[1] Torquemada, 'Monarquia Indiana;' Seville, 1615, vol. ii. p. 627.
[2] Cook, First Voy. H., vol. ii. p. 220; vol. iii. p. 60.

a chisel, an axe, or an adze. When, however, the cutting edge is hollowed as in a gouge, it is no longer possible to use it as an axe, though it retains the other two possible uses of chisel and adze. The water-worn pebble, in which a natural edge has been made straighter and sharper by grinding, may be taken as the original and typical form of the celt. Rude South American tribes select suitable water-worn stones and rub down their edges, sometimes merely grasping them in the hand to use them, and sometimes mounting them in a wooden handle; and axes made in this way, by grinding the edge of a suitable pebble, and fixing it in a withe handle, are known in Australia. Moreover, the class to which this almost natural instrument belongs, that, namely, which has a double-convex cross section, is far more numerous and universally distributed than the double-flat, concavo-convex, triangular, or other forms.

Where artificially-shaped celts are found only chipped over, in high Stone Age deposits, as in Scandinavia, they are generally to be considered as unfinished; but when celts of hard stone are found only ground near the edge, and otherwise left rough from chipping, they may be taken as denoting a rude state of art. Thus flint celts ground only near the edge are found in Northern Europe, and even in Denmark; but in general celts of the hardest stone are found, during the Ground-Stone Age, conscientiously ground and polished all over, and every large celt of hard stone which is finished to this degree represents weeks or months of labour, done not so much for any technical advantage, as for the sake of beauty and artistic completeness.

The primitive hammer, still used in some places, is an oval pebble, held in the hand. Above this comes the natural pebble, or the artificially-shaped stone, which is grooved or notched to have a bent withe fastened round it as a handle, as our smiths mount heavy chisels. Above this again is the highest kind, the stone hammer with a hole through it for the handle. This is not found out of the Old World, perhaps not out of Europe; and even the Mexicans, who in many things rivalled or excelled the stone-workers of ancient Europe, do not seem to have got beyond grooving their hammers. The stone axe proper, as distinguished from the mere celt by its more complex shape, and by its being bored or otherwise fitted for a handle, is best represented in the highest European Stone Age, and in the transition to the Bronze Age.

Special instruments and varieties are of great interest to the Ethnographer, as giving individuality to the productions of the Stone Age of different times and places. Thus, the rude triangular flakes of obsidian with which the Papuans head their spears are very characteristic of their race. These spears were probably what they were using in Schouten's time; "long staves with very long sharpe things at the ends thereof, which (as we thought) were finnes of black fishes."[1] Among celts, the Polynesian adze blade, to be seen in almost any museum, is a well-marked type; as is the American double hatchet,[2] and an elaborately-formed American knife.[3] The Pech's knives or Pict's knives, of Shetland, made from a rock with a slaty cleavage, seem peculiar. They appear to be efficient instruments, as an old woman was seen cutting cabbage with one not long since.

As there are a good many special instruments like these in different parts of the world, the idea naturally suggests itself of trying to use them as ethnological evidence, to prove connexion or intercourse between two districts where a similar thing is found. For instance, among the most curious phenomena in the history of stone implements is the occurrence of one of the highest types of the Stone Age, the polished celt of green jade, of all places in the world, in Australia, where the general character of the native stone implements is so extremely low. There is a quarry of this very hard and beautiful stone in Victoria, and the natives on the river Glenelg grind it into double-convex hatchet blades, a process which must require great labour, and these blades they fix with native thread into cleft sticks, and use them as battle-axes. Two of the blades in question are in the Museum of the Society of Antiquaries in Edinburgh, presented by Dr. Mackay, who got them near

---

[1] Purchas, vol. i. p. 95.   [2] Schoolcraft, part ii. pl. 18, figs. 1 and 2.
[3] Id., part ii. pl. 45, figs. 1-3. Another specimen in the Edinburgh Antiquaries' Museum, presented by Dr. Daniel Wilson.

the place where they were made. They are only inferior
to the finest celts of the same material from New Zealand,
in wanting the accuracy of outline which the Maori would have
given, and the conscientious labour with which he would have
ground down the whole surface till every inequality or flaw
had disappeared, whereas the Australian has been content
with polishing into the hollow places, instead of grinding them
out. Were we obliged to infer, from the presence of these
high-class celts in Australia, that the natives in one part of the
country had themselves developed the making of stone implements so immensely beyond the rest of their race, while they
remained in other respects in the same low state of civilization,
the quality of stone implements would have to be pretty much
given up as a test of culture anywhere. Fortunately there is
an easier way out of the difficulty. Polished instruments of
this green jade have been, long ago or recently, one of the
most important items of manufacture in the islands of the
Indian Ocean and the Pacific, and the South Australians may
have learnt from some Malay or Polynesian source the art of
shaping these high-class weapons. The likelihood of this being
their real history is strengthened by proofs we have of intercourse between Australia and the surrounding islands. Besides
the known yearly visits of the trepang-fishers of Macassar to
the Gulf of Carpentaria, and the appearance of the outrigger-
canoe in East Australia in Captain Cook's time, there is mythological evidence which seems to carry proof of connexion far
down the east coast.

Another coincidence of this kind may be mentioned here,
though in the absence of collateral evidence it would be un-
wise to draw any conclusion from it. There is a well-known
New Zealand weapon, the *mére*, or *pátu-pátu*. It is an edged
club of bone or stone, which has been compared to a beaver's
tail, or is still more like a soda-water bottle with the bulb
flattened, and it is a very effective weapon in a hand-to-hand
fight, being so sharp that a man's skull may be split at one
blow with it. Through the neck it has a hole for a wrist-cord.
The *mére* is made of the bone of a whale, or of stone, and the
finest, which are of green jade and worked with immense

labour, were among the most precious heirlooms of the Maori Chiefs.   One would think that such a peculiar weapon was hardly likely to be made independently by two races; but Klemm gives a drawing of a sharp-edged Peruvian weapon, of dark brown jasper,[1] which is so exactly like the New Zealand *mére*, even to the wrist-cord, that a single drawing of one of the latter, shown in front and profile in Fig. 19, will serve for both. There can hardly be a mistake about this weapon being really Peruvian, for another from Cuzco, of a greenish amphibolic stone, is figured by Rivero and Tschudi,[2] curiously enough, in company with a wooden war-club,

Fig. 19.   from Tanga in Colombia which is hardly distinguishable from a common Polynesian form.   If we knew of any connexion between the civilizations of Peru and the South Sea Islands, those extraordinary resemblances might be accounted for without hesitation, as caused by direct transmission.

When, however, their full value has been given to the differences in the productions of the Ground Stone Age, there remains a residue of a most remarkable kind.   In the first place, a very small number of classes, flake-knives, scrapers, spear and arrow-heads, celts and hammers, take in the great mass of specimens in museums; and in the second place, the prevailing character of these implements, whether modern or thousands of years old, whether found on this side of the world or the other, is a marked uniformity.   The Ethnographer who has studied the stone implements of Europe, Asia, North or South America, or Polynesia, may consider the specimens from the district he has studied, as types from which those of other districts differ, as a class, by the presence or absence of a few peculiar instruments, and individually in more or less important details of shape and finish, unless, as sometimes happens, they do not perceptibly differ at all.   So great is this uniformity in the stone implements of different places and times,

<hr>

[1] Klemm, C. W., part ii. p. 26.
[2] Rivero & Tschudi, Ant. Per. Plates, pl. xxiii.

that it goes far to neutralize their value as distinctive of different races.   It is clear that no great help in tracing the minute history of the growth and migration of tribes, is to be got from an arrow-head which might have come from Patagonia, or Siberia, or the Isle of Man, or from a celt which might be, for all its appearance shows, Mexican, Irish, or Tahitian.   If an observer, tolerably acquainted with stone implements, had an unticketed collection placed before him, the largeness of the number of specimens which he would not confidently assign, by mere inspection, to their proper countries, would serve as a fair measure of their general uniformity. Even when aided by mineralogical knowledge, often a great help, he would have to leave a large fraction of the whole in an unclassed heap, confessing that he did not know within thousands of miles or thousands of years, where and when they were made.

How, then, is this remarkable uniformity to be explained ? The principle that man does the same thing under the same circumstances will account for much, but it is very doubtful whether it can be stretched far enough to account for even the greater proportion of the facts in question.   The other side of the argument is, of course, that resemblance is due to connexion, and the truth is made up of the two, though in what proportions we do not know.   It may be that, though the problem is too obscure to be worked out alone, the uniformity of development in different regions of the Stone Age may some day be successfully brought in with other lines of argument, based on deep-lying agreements in culture, which tend to centralize the early history of races of very unlike appearance, and living in widely distant ages and countries.

To turn to an easier branch of the subject, I have brought together here, as a contribution to the history of the Stone Age, a body of evidence which shows that it has prevailed in ancient or up to modern times, in every great district of the inhabited world.   By the aid of this, it may be possible to sketch at least some rude outline of the history of its gradual decline and fall, which followed on the introduction of metal in later periods, up to our own times, when the universal use of iron has left nothing of the ancient state of things, except a few remnants of interest to ethnologists and antiquaries, but of no practical importance to the world at large.

In the first place, there are parts of the world whose inhabitants, when they were discovered in modern times by more advanced races, were found not possessed of metals, but using stone, shell, bone, split canes, and so forth, for purposes in making tools and weapons to which we apply metals. Now as we have no evidence that the inhabitants of Australia, the South Sea Islands, and a considerable part of North and South America, had ever been possessed of metals, it seems reasonable to consider those districts as countries where original Stone Age conditions had never been interfered with, until they came within the range of European discovery.

But in other parts of North and South America, such interference had already taken place before the time of Columbus. The native copper of North America had been largely used by the race known to us as the " Mound Builders," who have left as memorials of their existence the enormous mounds and fortifications of the Mississippi Valley.[1] They do not seem to have understood the art of melting copper, or even of forging it hot, but to have treated it as a kind of malleable stone, which they got in pieces out of the ground, or knocked off from the great natural blocks, and hammered into knives, chisels, axes, and ornaments. The use of native copper was by no means confined to the Mound Builders, for the European explorers found it in use for knives, ice-chisels, ornaments, etc., in the northern part of the continent, especially among the Esquimaux and the Canadian Indians.[2] The copper which Captain Cook found in abundance among the Indians of Prince William's Sound, was no doubt native.[3] Even meteoric iron has been found in use among the Esquimaux. There is a harpoon-point of walrus tusk in the British Museum, headed

with a blade of meteoric iron, and a knife, also of tusk, which
is edged by fixing in a row of chips of meteoric iron along a
groove. But these instruments do not appear old; they are
just like those in which the Esquimaux at present mount
morsels of European iron, and there is no evidence that they
used their native meteoric iron, until their intercourse with
Europeans in modern times had taught them the nature and
use of the metal. It is indeed very strange that there should
be no traces found among them of knowledge of metal-work,
and of other arts, which one would expect a race so receptive
of foreign knowledge to have got from contact with the
Northmen, in the tenth and following centuries; but I have
not succeeded in finding any distinct evidence of the kind.

In the lower part of the Northern Continent, in Peru and
some other districts of the Southern, the Stone Age was not
extinct at the time of Columbus; it was indeed in a state of
development hardly surpassed anywhere in the world, but at
the same time several metals were in common use. Gold and
silver were worked with wonderful skill, but chiefly for ornamental purposes. Though almost all the gold and silver work
of Mexico has long ago gone to the melting-pot, there are still
a few specimens which show that the Spanish conquerors were
not romancing in the wonderful stories they told of the skill
of the native goldsmiths. I have seen a pair of gold eagle ornaments in the Berlin Museum, which will compare almost with
the Etruscan work for design and delicacy of finish. But what
is still more important is that bronze, made of well-judged proportions of copper and tin, was in use on both continents.
The Peruvians used bronze, and perhaps copper also, for tools
and weapons. The Mexican bronze axe-blades are to be seen
in collections, and we know by the picture-writings that both
the Mexicans[1] and the builders of the ruined cities of Central
America,[2] mounted them by simply sticking them into a
wooden club, as the modern African mounts his iron axe-blade.
The little bronze bells of Mexico[3] and South America are cored
castings, which are by no means novice's work, and other

<hr>

[1] Mendoza Codex, in Kingsborough, vol. I.   [2] Dresden Codex, Id.
[3] Tylor, 'Mexico,' p. 230.

bronze castings from the latter country are even more remarkable.[1]

How the arts of working gold, silver, copper, and bronze came into America, we do not know, nor can we even tell whether their appearance on the Northern and Southern Continent was independent or not. It is possible to trace Mexican connexion down to Nicaragua, and perhaps even to the Isthmus of Panama, while on the other hand the northern inhabitants of South America were not unacquainted with the nations farther down the continent. But no certain proof of connexion or intercourse of any kind between Mexico and Peru seems as yet to have been made out. All that we know certainly is that gold, silver, copper, tin, and bronze had there intruded themselves among the implements and ornaments of worked stone, though they had scarcely made an approach to driving them out of use, and that the traditions of both continents ascribed their higher culture to certain foreigners who were looked upon as supernatural beings. If we reason upon the supposition that these remarkably unanimous legends may perhaps contain historical, in combination with mythical elements, the question suggests itself, where, for a thousand or fifteen hundred years before the Spanish discovery, were men to be found who could teach the Mexicans and Peruvians to make bronze, and could not teach them to smelt and work iron? The people of Asia seem the only men on whose behalf such a claim can be sustained at all. The Massagetæ of Central Asia were in the Bronze Age in the time of Herodotus, who, describing their use of bronze for spear and arrow-heads, battle-axes, and other things, and of gold rather for ornamental purposes, remarks that they make no use of iron or silver, for they have none in their country, while gold and bronze abound.[2] Four centuries later, Strabo modifies this remark, saying that they have no silver, little iron, but abundance of gold and bronze.[3] The Tatars were in the Iron Age when visited by mediæval travellers, and the history of the transition from bronze to iron in Central Asia, of which we seem to have here

[1] Ewbank, 'Brasil;' New York. 1856, pp. 454-463.
[2] Herod., i. 215.   [3] Strabo, xi. 8, 6.

a glimpse, is for the most part obscure. The matter is, however, the more worthy of remark from its bearing on the argument for the connexion of the culture of Mexico and that of Asia, grounded by Humboldt on the similarities in the mythology and the calendar of the two districts.

If we now turn to the history of the Stone Age in Asia, Africa, and Europe, we shall indeed find almost everywhere evidence of a Stone Period, which preceded a Bronze or Iron Period, but this is only to be had in small part from the direct inspection of races living without metal implements. The Kamchadals of north-eastern Asia, a race as yet ethnologically isolated, were found by the Kosak invaders using cutting-tools of stone and bone. It is recorded that with these instruments it took them three years to hollow out a canoe, and one year to scoop out one of the wooden troughs in which they cooked their food;[1] but probably a large allowance for exaggeration must be made in this story. It is curious to notice that, thirty or forty years ago, Erman got in Kamchatka one of the Stone Age relics found in such enormous numbers in Mexico, a fluted prism of obsidian, off which a succession of stone blades had been flaked; but though one would have thought that the comparatively recent use of stone instruments in the country would have been still fresh in the memory of the people, the natives who dug it up had no idea what it was.[2] Stone knives, moreover, have been found in the high north-east of Siberia, on the site of deserted yourts of modern date, said to have been occupied by the settled Chukchi, or Shalags.[3]

In China, the following curious passage seems to record a comparatively modern use of stone implements. Referring to Nan-hiu-fu, in the province of Kwan-tong, in Southern China, it is stated, " They find, in the mountains and among the rocks which surround it, a heavy stone, so hard that hatchets and other cutting instruments are made from it."[4] It is to be remembered that China is not inhabited only by the race usually known to us as the Chinese, but by another, or several

[1] Kracheninnikow, p. 29.   [2] Erman, 'Reise,' vol. iii. p. 452.
[3] Sarytschew, in Coll. of Mod. etc., Voy. and Tr.; London, 1807, vol. v. p. 35.
[4] Grosier, ' De la Chine ;' Paris, 1818, vol. i. p. 191.

other far less cultured races ; the mountains of Kwan-tong and
the other southern provinces being especially inhabited by such
rude and seemingly aboriginal tribes.   There is, besides, a Chinese tradition speaking of the use of stone for weapons among
themselves in early times, which implies at least the knowledge
that this is a state of things characterizing a race at a low stage
of culture, and may really embody a recollection of their own
early history ; Fu-hi, they say, made weapons.   These were of
wood, those of Shin-nung were of stone, and Chi-yu made
metal ones.[1]

Among the great Tatar race to which the Turks and Mongols, and our Hungarians, Lapps, and Finns belong, accounts
of a Stone Age may be found, in the most remarkable of which
the widely prevailing idea that stone instruments found buried
in the ground are thunderbolts, is very well brought into view.
In the Chinese Encyclopædia of the emperor Kang-hi, who
began to reign in 1662, the following passage occurs :—

" ' Lightning-stones.'—The shape and substance of lightning-
stones vary according to place.   The wandering Mongols,
whether of the coasts of the eastern sea, or the neighbourhood
of the Sha-mo, use them in the manner of copper and steel.
There are some of these stones which have the shape of a
hatchet, others that of a knife, some are made like mallets.
These lightning-stones are of different colours; there are
blackish ones, others are greenish.   A romance of the time of
the Tang, says that there was at Yu-men-si a great Miao de-
dicated to the Thunder, and that the people of the country
used to make offerings there of different things, to get some of
these stones. This fable is ridiculous. The lightning-stones are
metals, stones, pebbles, which the fire of the thunder has meta-
morphosed by splitting them suddenly and uniting inseparably
different substances.   There are some of these stones in which
a kind of vitrification is distinctly to be observed."[2]

Moreover, within the last century the Tunguz of North-
Eastern Siberia, belonging to the same Tatar race, were using

[1] Goguet, vol. iii. p. 231.
[2] ' Mémoires concernant l'Histoire, etc., des Chinois, par les Missionaires de
Pékin ;' Paris, 1776, etc., vol. iv. p. 474   Klemm, C. G., vol. vi. p. 467.

stone arrow-heads,[1] while Tacitus long before made a similar remark as to their relatives the Finns, whose "only hope is in their arrows, which, from want of iron, they make sharp with bones." "Sola in sagittis spes, quas, inopia ferri, ossibus asperant."[2] But the Tunguz have been expert iron-workers as long as we have any distinct knowledge of them, and arrow-heads of stone and bone may survive, for an indefinite number of centuries, the main part of the Stone Age to which they properly belong. Even the Egyptians, in the height of their civilization, used stone arrow-heads in hunting, notwithstanding their vast wealth of bronze and iron. The peculiar arrows which are being shot at wild oxen in the bas-reliefs of Beni Hassan[3] are still to be seen in collections; they are special as to their wedge-shaped flint heads, fixed with the broad edge foremost, a shape like that of the wooden-headed bird-bolts of the Middle Ages. The stone arrow-heads found on the battle-field of Marathon are often described, but they may have all been shot by the barbarian troops, and most others found in Greece are probably pre-Aryan. It is clear that metal must be very common and cheap to be used in so wasteful a way as in heading an arrow, perhaps only for a single shot.

If we go back eighteen hundred years, an account may be found of a people living under Stone Age conditions in a part of Asia much less remote than Tartary and China. Strabo gives the following description of the fish-eaters inhabiting the coast of the present Beloochistan, on the Arabian Sea, and, like the Aleutian Islanders of modern times, building their huts of the bones of whales, with their jaws for doorways:—"The country of the Ichthyophagi is a low coast, for the most part without trees, except palms, a sort of acanthus, and tamarisks; of water and cultivated food there is a dearth. Both the people and their cattle eat fish, and drink rain- and well-water, and the flesh of the cattle tastes of fish. In making their dwellings, they mostly use the bones of whales, and oyster-shells, the ribs serving for beams and props, and the jaw-bones for

[1] Ravenstein, p. 4.
[2] Tac. Germ. xlvi.; and see Grimm, G. D. S., vol. I. p. 173.
[3] Wilkinson, Pop. Acc., vol. I. pp. 222, 353.

doorways; the vertebrae they use form ortars, in which they pound their sun-dried fish, and of this, with the mixture of a little corn, they make bread, for, though they have no iron, they have mills. And this is the less wonderful, seeing that they can get the mills from elsewhere, but how can they dress the millstones when worn down? with the stones, they say, with which they sharpen their arrows and darts [of wood, with points] hardened in the fire. Of the fish, part they cook in ovens, but most they eat raw, and they catch them in nets of palm-bark."[1]

Though direct history gives but partial means of proving the existence of a Stone Age over Asia and Europe, the finding of ancient stone tools and weapons, in almost every district of these two continents, proves that they were in former times inhabited by Stone Age races, though whether in any particular spot the tribes we first find living there are their descendants as well as their successors, this evidence cannot tell us. How, for instance, are we to tell what race made and used the obsidian flakes which were found with polished agate and carnelian beads under the chief corner-stone of the great temple of Khorsabad? All through Western Asia, and north of the Himalaya, stone implements are scattered broadcast through the land. Further east, the account of the lightning-stones, just quoted from the Encyclopædia of Kang-hi, goes to prove that stone implements are found in China, and therefore that the inhabitants once made and used them; and this inference especially makes it probable that the legend of stone weapons having been once in use may be a piece of genuine traditional history.

Japan abounds in Stone Age relics, of which Van Siebold has given drawings and descriptions in his great work;[2] and his own collection at Leyden is very rich in specimens. The arrow-heads of obsidian, flint, chert, etc., are of types like those found elsewhere. Their presence is sometimes accounted for by stories that they were rained from the sky, or that every

<hr>

[1] Strabo, xv. 2, 2.

[2] Ph. Fr. v. Siebold, Nippon, Archiv zur Beschreibung von Japan; Leyden, 1832, etc., part ii. plates xi. to xiii. pp. 45, etc.

year an army of spirits fly through the air with rain and storm; when the sky clears, people go out and hunt in the sand for the stone arrows they have dropped. The arrow-heads are found most abundantly in the north of the great island of Nippon, in the so-called land of the Wild Men, a population who were only late and with difficulty brought under the Mikado dynasty, and who belong to the same Aino race as the present inhabitants of the island of Jesso and the southern Kuriles. In Japan, stone celts are frequently to be found in the collections of minerals of native amateurs, and they are still sometimes dug up with other objects of stone. They seem only of average symmetry and finish. Here, again, the natives call such a stone celt a " thunderbolt," *Rai fu seki*, or *Tengu no masakari*, "battleaxe of Tengu," Tengu being the guardian of heaven. The notion is also current that they are implements of the Evil Spirit, whose symbol is the fox, whence the names of "Fox-hatchet," "Fox-plane." As a fox-plane, a double-flat celt is shown in Siebold's plates, which may have served the purpose of a plane, or, if it was fixed to a handle, that of an adze. Regularly shaped stone knives (not mere flakes) are represented; some are like the stone knives of Egypt, but rougher; the Japanese recognise them as "stone-knives." Some which have been dug up are kept in the temples as relics of the time of the Kami, the spirits or divinities from whom the Japanese hold themselves to be descended, and whose worship is the old religion of the Japanese, the way or doctrine of the Kami, more commonly known by the Chinese term, Sin-tu. Some stone knives, drawn by Siebold on Japanese authority, seem to be of a slaty rock, which has admitted of their being very neatly made in curious shapes. One very highly finished specimen is called the stone knife of the " Green Dragon," a term which may be explained by the fact that the conventional dragon of Japan has a sword at the end of his tail.

Again, Java abounds in very high-class stone implements, and such things are found on the Malay peninsula, though in both these districts the natives, unlike the Polynesians, whose language is so closely connected with theirs, do not even know what stone celts are, and hold with so many other nations that they are thunderbolts.[1]

In India, an account of the discovery by Mr. H. P. Le Mesurier of a great number of ancient stone celts was published in 1861. He found them stored up in villages of the Jubbulpore district, near the Mahadeos, and in other sacred places; and since then many more have been met with by other observers.[2] Mr. Christy's specimens are ordinary stone celts of indifferent quality.

In Europe, ancient stone implements are found from east to west, and from north to south, the relics perhaps of races now extinct, or absorbed in others, or of the Tatar population of Finland and Lapland, or of that unclassed race which survives in the Basque population about the Pyrenees, who, unlike the Finns and Lapps, cannot as yet claim relationship with a surviving parent stock.

As to our own Aryan or Indo-European race, our first knowledge of it, at the remote period of which a picture has been reconstructed by the study of the Vedas, and a comparison of the Sanskrit with other Aryan tongues, shows a Bronze Age prevailing among them when they set out on their migrations from Central Asia to found the Aryan nations, the Indians, Persians, Greeks, Germans, and the rest.[3] A general view of the succession of metal to stone all over the world, justifies a belief that the Aryans were no exception to the general rule, and that they, too, used stone instruments before they had metal ones; but there is little known evidence bearing on the matter beyond that of a few Aryan words, which are worth mentioning, though they will not carry much weight of argument.

The nature of this evidence may be made clear, by noticing how it comes into existence in places where the introduction of metal is matter of history. In these places it sometimes hap-

<hr>

[1] Yates, in 'Archæological Journal,' No. 12. Earl, 'Papuans,' pp. 175–6.

[2] Le Mesurier, in Journ. As. Soc. Bengal, 1861, No. 1, p. 81. Theobald, As. Soc., Apr. 1864, etc. etc.

[3] Weber, 'Indische Skizzen,' Berlin, 1857, p. 9. Max Müller, Lectures second series, p. 230, etc.

pens that old words, referring to stone and stone instruments,
are transferred to metal and metal instruments, and these
words take their place as relics of the Stone Age preserved in
language. Thus, in North America the Algonquin names for
copper and brass are *miskwaubik* and *ozauraubik*, that is to say,
"red-stone" and "yellow-stone;" while the name *e-reck*, that
is, "stone," is used by some Indian tribes of California for all
metals indiscriminately. In the Delaware language, *opeek* is
"white," and *assuun* is "stone;" so that it is evident that the
name of silver, *opsssuun*, means "white-stone," while the ter-
mination "stone" is discernible in *wisauaasuu*, "gold." In the
Mandan language, the words *maki*, "knife," and *makitshuke*,
"flint," are clearly connected.[1] Having thus examples of the
way in which the Stone Age has left its mark in language, in
races among whom it has been superseded within our knowledge, it is natural that we should expect to find words marking
the same change, in the speech of men who made the same
transition in times not clearly known to history. What has
been done in this way as yet comes to very little, but Jacob
Grimm has set an example by citing two words, *hammer*, Old
Norse *hamarr*, meaning both "hammer" and "rock," and Latin
saxum, a name possibly belonging to a time when instruments
to cut with, *secure*, were still of stone, and which still keeps
close to Old German *sahs*, Anglo-Saxon *seax*, a knife.[2] There
may possibly be some connexion between *sagitta*, arrow, and
saxum, stone, and in like manner between Sanskrit *çili*, arrow,
çila, stone, while in the Semitic family of languages, Hebrow
חֵץ, *chetz*, arrow, חָצָץ, *châtzâtz*, gravel-stone, are both related
to the verb חָצַץ, *châtzatz*, to cut. But against the inference
from these words, that their connexion belongs to a time when
stone was the usual material for sharp instruments, there lies
this strong objection, that knife and stone might get from the
same root names expressing sharpness, or any other quality
they have in common, without having anything directly to do
with one another, while the same word, *hamar*, may have been
found an equally suitable name for "hammer" and "rock,"

<hr>

[1] Schoolcraft, part ii. pp. 389, 397, 483, 506; part iii. pp. 426, 448.
[2] Grimm, D. M., p. 105; G.D.S., p. 610.

without the hammer being so called because all hammers were originally stones.[1]

Among the Semitic race, however, it seems possible to bring forward better evidence than this of an early Stone Age. If we follow one way of translating, we find in two passages of the Old Testament an account of the use of sharp stones or stone knives for circumcision; Exodus iv. 25, "And Zipporah took a stone" (צֹר, *tzor*), and Joshua v. 2, "At that time Jehovah said to Joshua, Make thee knives of stone" (חַרְבוֹת צֻרִים, *charvoth tzurim*). As they stand, however, these passages are not sufficient to prove the case, for there is much the same ambiguity as to the original meaning of *tzor, tzūr*, as in the etymologies of some of the words just mentioned. Gesenius refers them to צוּר *tzūr*, to cut, and the readings "an edge, a knife," and "knives of edges, *i.e.* sharp knives," have so far at least an equal claim. It remains to be seen which view is supported by further evidence.

In the first place, the Septuagint altogether favours the opinion that the knives in question were of stone, by reading in the first place ψῆφον, a stone, or pebble, and in the second, μαχαίρας πετρίνας ἐκ πέτρας ἀκροτόμου, stone knives of sharp-cut stone. These are mentioned again in the remarkable passage which follows the account of the death and burial of Joshua (Joshua xxiv. 29–30), "And it came to pass after these things, that Joshua the son of Nun, the servant of Jehovah, died, being a hundred and ten years old, and they buried him in the border of his inheritance in Timnath Serah, which is in Mount Ephraim, on the north side of the hill of Gaash." Here follows in the LXX. a passage not in the Hebrew text which has come down to us. "Καὶ ἐκεῖ ἔθηκαν μετ' αὐτοῦ εἰς τὸ μνημεῖον ἐν ᾧ ἔθαψαν αὐτὸν ἐκεῖ, τὰς μαχαίρας τὰς πετρίνας, ἐν αἷς περιέτεμε τοὺς υἱοὺς Ἰσραὴλ ἐν Γαλγάλοις, ὅτε ἐξήγαγεν αὐτοὺς ἐξ Αἰγύπτου καθὰ συνέταξε Κύριος· καὶ ἐκεῖ εἰσὶν ἕως τῆς σήμερον ἡμέρας."[2] "And there they laid with him in the

---

[1] In this connexion are the meanings of *armas* in Boehtlingk & Roth, and Benfey, O. W. L., part i. p. 156.

[2] LXX., Ed. Field, Oxford, 1859. Elsewhere Gilead instead of Gaash, and other differences.

tomb wherein they buried him there, the stone knives, wherewith he circumcised the children of Israel at the Gilgals, when he led them out of Egypt, as the Lord commanded. And they are there unto this day." Any one who is disposed to see in this statement a late interpolation, may imagine an origin for it. The opening of a tumulus containing, as they so commonly do, a quantity of sharp instruments of stone, might suggest to a Jew who only knew such things as circumcising knives, the idea that he saw before him the tomb of Joshua, and, buried with his body, the stone knives wherewith he circumcised the children of Israel.

How far the modern Jews follow the translation "stone," "knives of stone," I cannot entirely say, but two modern Jewish translations of the Pentateuch which I have consulted read "stone" in Exodus iv. 25. It is to be remarked that the Rabbinical law admits such a use; it stands thus:—

" בכל מלין , ואפילו בצור ובזכוכית ובכל דבר הכורת ,
חוץ מבקרומית של קנה לפי שקוסמים נחוים כמנה ויבא
לידי סכנה , ומצוה מן המובחר למול בברזל בין בסכין בין
במספרים ונהגו למול בסכין "

"We may circumcise with anything, even with a flint, with crystal (glass) or with anything that cuts, except with the sharp edge of a reed, because enchanters make use of that, or it may bring on a disease, and it is a precept of the wise men to circumcise with iron, whether in the form of a knife or of scissors, but it is customary to use a knife." Now as Professor Lazarus, a most competent judge in such matters, remarked to me with reference to this question, the mere mention of a practice in the Rabbinical books is not good evidence that it ever really existed, seeing that their writers habitually exercise their fertile imaginations in devising cases which might possibly occur, and then argue upon them as seriously as though they were real matters of practical importance. But there are observed facts, which tend to bring these particular ordinances out of the region of fancy, and into that of fact. As to the prohibition of the use of the reed knife, it is to be no-

ticed that this (in the form of a sharp splinter of bamboo) was
the regular instrument with which circumcision was performed
in the Fiji islands.[1]   And as to the use of the stone circumcising knife, it is stated by Leutholf, who is looked upon as a
good authority, that it was in use in Æthiopia in his time,—
" The Alnajah, an Æthiopian race, perform circumcision with
stone knives."   " Alnajah gens Æthiopum cultris lapideis cir-
cumcisionem peragit."[2]   This would be in the sixteenth century.   And though the modern Jews generally use a steel
knife, there appears to be a remarkable exception to this custom ; that when a male child dies before the eighth day, it is
nevertheless circumcised before burial, but this is done, not
with the ordinary instrument, but with a fragment of flint or
glass.[3]

Under the reservation just stated, a recognition among the
Jewish ordinances of the practice of slaughtering a beast with
a [sharp] stone, may here be cited from the Mishna :—

השוחט במגל יד , בצור , ובקנה , שחיטתו כשרה [4]

" If a person has slaughtered [a beast] with a hand-sickle, a
[sharp] stone, or a reed, it is *cusher*," *i.e.* clean, or fit to be
eaten.   Here not only the context, but the necessity of shed-
ding the animal's blood, proves that a proper cutting instrument
of stone, or at least a sharp-edged piece, is meant.

Before drawing any inference from these pieces of evidence,
it will be well to bring together other accounts of the use of
cutting instruments of stone, glass, etc., by people who, though
in possession of iron knives, for some reason or other did not
choose to apply them to certain purposes.   Thus the practice
of sacrificing a beast, not with a knife or an axe, but with a
sharp stone, has been observed on the West Coast of Africa
during the last century, as will be more fully detailed in page
222.

[1] Mariner, vol. i. p. 329 ; vol. ii. p. 253 ; Vocab. s. vv. " camo," " tcfe."
Williams, ' Fiji,' vol. i. p. 166.
[2] Ludolf ' Historia Æthiopica ;' Frankfort-on-Maine, 1581, lib. 1. 21.
[3] My authority for this statement is Mr. Philip Abraham, Secretary of the
Reformed Synagogue in Margaret Street, Cavendish Square.
[4] Mishna, Treatise Cholin, ch. i. 2.

An often quoted instance of the use of a stone knife for a
ceremonial purpose, where iron would have been much more
convenient, is the passage in Herodotus which relates that, in
Egypt, the mummy-embalmers made the incision in the side of
the corpse with a sharp Æthiopic stone.[1] The account given
by Diodorus Siculus is fuller :—" And first, the body being laid
on the ground, he who is called the scribe marks on its left side
how far the incision is to be made. Then the so-called slitter
(paraschistes), having an Æthiopic stone, and cutting the flesh
as far as the law allows, instantly runs off, the bystanders pur-
suing him and pelting him with stones, cursing him, and as it
were, turning the horror of the deed upon him," for he who
hurts a citizen is held worthy of abhorrence.[2] There are two
kinds of stone knives found in excavations and tombs in Egypt,
both of chipped flint, and very neatly made ; one kind is like
a very small cleaver, the other has more of the character of a
lancet, and would seem the more suitable of the two for the
embalmer's purpose.

A story related by Pliny, of the way in which the balsam of
Judea, or " balm of Gilead," was extracted, comes under the
same category. The incisions, he says, had to be made in the
tree with knives of glass, stone, or bone, for it hurts it to
wound its vital parts with iron, and it dies forthwith.[3]

With regard to the reason of such practices as these, it has
been suggested that there was a practical advantage in the use
of the stone knife for circumcision, as less liable to cause inflammation than a knife of bronze or iron. From this point of
view Pliny's statement has been quoted, that the mutilation of
the priests of Cybele was done with a sherd of Samian ware
(Samiâ testâ), as thus avoiding danger.[4] But as regards iron,
at least, the ordinary Jewish practice shows that there is not
much in this, while a dead body is not liable to inflammation,
and yet the ancient Egyptians used, and the modern Jews use,
the stone knife in operating upon it. I heard the reason
assigned, in the latter case, that it is undesirable to use on the
living subject an instrument which has been applied to such a

<hr>

[1] Herod., ii. 86.   [2] Diod. Sic., i. 91.   [3] Plin., xli. 54.
[4] Plin., xxxv. 40. xi. 109.

purpose; but if this were all, it would be far less troublesome
to have a second knife than to use so miserable a substitute;
and the argument does not touch the Egyptian case of the
embalmers.   I cannot but think that most, if not all, of the
series are to be explained as being, to use the word in no
harsh sense, but according to what seems its proper etymology, cases of *superstition*, of the "standing over" of old
habits into the midst of a new and changed state of things, of
the retention of ancient practices for ceremonial purposes, long
after they had been superseded for the commonplace uses of
ordinary life.   Such a view takes in every instance which has
been mentioned, though the reason of iron not being adopted
by the modern Jews in one case as well as in another is not
clear.   As to Pliny's story of the balm of Gilead, I am told,
on competent authority, that the use of stone and such things
instead of iron for making incisions in the tree, if ever it
really existed, could be nothing but a superstition without any
foundation in reason.   It may perhaps tell in favour of the story
being true, that it is only one of a number of cases mentioned
by Pliny, of plants as to which the similar notion prevailed,
that they would be spoiled by being touched with an iron instrument.[1]   There seems, on the whole, to be a fair case for believing that among the Israelites, as in Ethiopia and Egypt, a
a ceremonial use of stone instruments long survived the general adoption of metal, and that such observances are to be
interpreted as relics of an earlier Stone Age; while incidentally
the same argument makes it probable that the rite of circumcision belonged to the Stone Age among the ancient Israelites,
as we know it does among the modern Australians.[2]

With regard to the foregoing accounts, there is a point which
requires further remark.   Glass has been mentioned by the
side of stone, as a material for making sharp instruments of;
and it may seem at first sight an unreasonable thing to make
the use of a production which belongs to so advanced a state
of civilization as glass, evidence of a Stone Age.   But savages
have so unanimously settled it, that glass is a kind of stone

<hr>

[1] Plin., xix. 57, xxiii. 81, xxiv. 6, 02.
[2] G. F. Angas, 'South Australia Illustrated;' London, 1847, pl. v.

peculiarly suitable for such purposes, that where a knife of
glass, or a weapon armed with it, is found, it may be confidently set down as the immediate successor of a stone one.
The Fuegians and the Andaman Islanders are found to have
used in this manner the bits of broken glass that came in their
way; the New Zealanders have been observed to take a piece
of glass in place of the sharp stone with which they cut their
bodies in mourning for the dead; and the North American
Indians to fix one in a wooden handle, in place of the sharp
stone with which the native phleme used to be armed.[1]   The
Australians substituted such pieces, when they could get them,
for the angular pieces of stone with which their lances and
jagged knives were mounted. Mr. Christy has some interesting
specimens of these Australian instruments, which date themselves in a curious way as belonging to the time of contact
with Europeans. They were originally set with stone teeth;
but where these have been knocked out, their places have been
filled by new ones of broken glass.

To complete the survey of the Stone Age and its traces in
the world, Africa has now to be more fully examined. This
great continent is now entirely in the Iron Age. The tribes
who do not smelt their own iron, as the Bushmen, get their sup-
plies from others; and in the immense central and western
tracts above the Equator, there appears to be no record of
tribes living without it. In South Africa, however, the case
is different; and the accounts of the English voyages round
the Cape of Good Hope about the beginning of the seventeenth
century, collected in Purchas's 'Pilgrimes,' give quite a clear
history of the transition from the Stone to the Iron Age, which
was then taking place.

Then as now, the inhabitants of Madagascar had their iron
knives and spear-heads; and they would have silver in payment for their cattle, 1s. for a sheep, and 3s. 6d. for a cow.
But on the West African coast, north of the Cape, there were
pastoral tribes, probably Hottentots, who evidently did not
know then, as they do now, how to work the abundant iron

[1] Fitz Roy, Voy. of H.M.S. Adventure and Beagle; London, 1839, vol. ii.
p. 184. Moual, p. 305. Yate, p. 243. Loskiel, p. 114.

ore of their country. At Saldanha Bay, in 1508, John Davis could get fat-tailed sheep and bullocks for bits of old iron and nails, and in 1604 a great bullock was still to be bought for a piece of an old iron hoop. But only seven years later, Nicholas Dounton, "Captaine of the Pepper-Corne," begins to write ruefully of the change in this delightful state of things. "Saldania having in former time been comfortable to all our nation travelling this way, both outwards and homewards, yeolding them abundance of flesh, as sheepe and beeves brought downe by the salunge inhabitants, and sold for trifles, as a beife for a piece of an iron hoope of fourteene inches long, and a sheepe for a lesser piece;" but now this is at an end, spoilt perhaps by the Dutchmen, "who use to spoyle all places where they come (onely respecting their owne present occasions) by their ouer much liberalitie," etc. etc.[1]

Specimens of stone implements from South Africa have been brought to Europe. A double-flat stone adze mounted in a very peculiar way in a withe handle, brought from Little Fish Bay, about 15° S. Lat., has been described and figured,[2] and Mr. Christy has an ordinary small spear- or large arrow-head found among the Hottentots, and ticketed "poisoned," and a lance-head from Fish River. Lastly, a native Dámara story clearly preserves a recollection of the time, possibly several generations ago, when stone axes were used to cut down trees. The tale is a sort of "House that Jack built," in which a little girl's mother gives her a needle, and she goes and finds her father sewing thongs with thorns, so she gives him the needle and he breaks it and gives her an axe. "Going farther on she met the lads who were in charge of the cattle. They were busy taking out honey, and in order to get at it they were obliged to cut down the trees with stones." She addressed them :—"Our sons, how is it that you use stones in order to get at the honey? Why do you not say, Our first-born, give us the axe?" and so on.[3]

[1] Purchas, vol. i. pp. 116, 133, 275, 417.

[2] G. V. du Noyer, in 'Archæological Journal,' 1847. A drawing in Klemm, C. W., part ii. p. 71, would seem to be from this, or one almost absolutely like it.

[3] Bleek, 'Reynard in Africa,' p. 90.

Going back two thousand years or so, record is to be found at least of a partial Stone Age condition in North-Eastern Africa. It appears from Herodotus that the African Ethiopians in the army of Xerxes not only headed their arrows with sharp stone, but had spears armed with sharpened horns of antelopes, while the Libyans had wooden javelins hardened at the point by fire.[1] Strabo mentions in Ethiopia a tribe who pointed their reed arrows in this way, and another who used as weapons the horns of antelopes.[2] It is interesting to observe that in South Africa the spear headed in this way has survived up to our own time; Mr. Andersson saw the natives at Walfisch Bay spearing the fish left at low water, with a gemsbock's horn attached to a slender stick.[3]

Traces of a Stone Age in Egypt, in the use of the stone arrow-head, and of the stone knife for ceremonial purposes, have been already spoken of. No account of the finding of stone implements in North Africa seems to have been published, but Mr. Christy, in a journey made in Algeria in 1863, found them there, as elsewhere.[4] He met with flint flake-knives, arrow-heads, and polished celts, at Constantine; flakes, arrow-heads, and a beautifully chipped lance-head of quartzite, at Dellys on the coast; and flakes and a large pick-shaped instrument, from the desert south-east of Oran, on the confines of Morocco. At Bou-Merzoug, on the plateau of the Atlas, south of Constantine, he found, in a bare, deserted, stony place among the mountains, a collection of tombs, 1000 or 1500 in number, made of the rude limestone slabs, set up with one slab to form a roof, so as to make, not mere cromlechs, but closed chambers where the bodies were packed in. Tradition says that a wicked people lived there, and for their sins stones were rained upon them from heaven, so they built these chambers to creep into. Near this remarkable necropolis, Mr. Christy found flint-flakes and arrow-heads.

[1] Herod., vii. 69, 71. [2] Strabo, xvi. 4, 9, 11. [3] Andersson, p. 15.
[4] A paper by Mr. Christy, embodying some account of his discoveries in the reindeer caves of Central France, and mentioning his finding stone implements in North Africa, and the distribution of such in different parts of the world, was read before the Ethnological Society in June, 1864.

If we go westward as far as the Canary Islands, we find a race, considered to be of African origin, living in the fourteenth century under purely Stone Age conditions, making hatchets, knives, lancets, and spear-heads of obsidian, and axes of green jasper, and pointing their spears and digging-sticks with horns.[1] It is possible that they might have once had the use of iron, and have lost it on removing to the islands, where there is no ore, but no evidence of this having been the case seems to have been found.

In Western Africa, when the god Gimawong came down to his temple at Labode on the Gold Coast once a year, with a sound like a flight of wild geese in spring, his worshippers sacrificed an ox to him, killing it not with a knife, but with a sharp stone.[2] Klemm looks upon this as a sign of the high antiquity of the ceremony, and, taking into consideration the evidence as to the keeping up of the use of stone for ceremonial purposes into the Iron Age, the inference seems a highly probable one, although there is another side to this argument. In order to bring this into view, and to adduce some other facts bearing on evidence of the Stone Age, it will be necessary to say here something more of the Myth of the Thunderbolt.

For ages it has been commonly thought that, with the flash of lightning, there falls, sometimes at least, a solid body which is known as the thunder-bolt, thunder-stone, etc., as in the dirge in 'Cymbeline,'—

> "Fear no more the lightning-flash,
>   Nor the all-dreaded thunder-stone."

The actual falling of meteoric stones may have had to do with the growth of this theory, but whatever its origin, it is one of the most widely spread beliefs in the world. The thing considered to be the thunderbolt is not always defined in accounts given. It is described as a stone,[3] or it may be a bit of iron-

---

[1] Barker-Webb & Berthelot, 'Histoire Naturelle des Iles Canaries ;' Paris, 1842, etc., vol. i. part i. pp. 62, 107, 138. Bory de St. Vincent, 'Essai sur les Isles Fortunées ;' Paris, An XI. (1803–4), pp. 68, 75–6, 150.

[2] Römer, p. 54. Klemm, C. G., vol. iii. p. 378.

Bosman, 'Beschryving van de Guinese Goud-Kust,' etc.; Utrecht, 1704, p. 109.

ore, or perhaps iron,[1] or a belemnite, βελεμνίτης, so called from βέλεμνον, a dart, apparently with the idea of its being a thunder-bolt ; for this spear-like fossil is still called in England a " thunder-stone." Dr. Falconer mentions the name of " lightning-bones" or " thunder-bones," given to fossil bones brought down as charms from the plateau of Chanthan in the Himalayas,[2] where, of course, frequent thunderstorms are seen to account for their presence. But it is also believed that the stone celts and hammers found buried in the ground are thunderbolts. The country folks of the west of England still hold that the " thunder-axes" they find, once fell from the sky. In Brittany, the itinerant umbrella-mender of Carnac inquires on his rounds for *pierres de tonnerre*, and takes them in payment for repairs; and these are fair examples of what may be found in other countries in Europe, and not in those inhabited by our Aryan race alone, for the Finns have the same belief.[3] The remarkable Chinese account of the thunder-stones has been already quoted, and it has been noticed that stone celts are held to be thunderbolts in Japan and the Eastern Archipelago. Even in a country where the use of stone axes by the Indians is matter of modern history, and in some places actually survives to this day, the Brazilians use, for such a stone axe-blade, their Portuguese word *corisco*,[4] that is, " lightning," " thunderbolt" (Latin *coruscare*).

As the stone axes and hammers are but one of several classes of objects thought to be thunderbolts, it is probable that the Myth took them to itself at a time when their real use and nature had been forgotten, and the reason of their being found buried underground was of course unknown. This view is supported by the fact of the existence of such instruments being also accounted for by taking them up into mythology in other ways. Thus in Japan the stone arrow-heads are rained from heaven, or dropped by the flying spirits who shoot them, while in Europe they are fairy weapons, *albschosse, elf-bolts,*

---

[1] Speke, Journal of Disc. ; Edin. and London, 1863, p. 223.
Proc. R. Geog. Soc., Feb. 25, 1861, p. 41.
Klemm, C. W., part ii. p. 65 ; and see Castrén, ' Finnische Mythologie,' p. 43.
Pr. Max. v. Wied, ' Reise nach Brasilien ;' Frankfort, 1820-1, vol. ii. p. 35.

shot by fairies or magicians, and in the North of Ireland the wizards still draw them out from the bodies of "overlooked" cattle.[1]   Dr. Daniel Wilson mentions an interesting post-Christian myth, which prevailed in Scotland till the close of the last century, that the stone hammers found buried in the ground were Purgatory Hammers for the dead to knock with at the gates.[2]

The inability of the world to understand the nature of the stone implements found buried in the ground, is not more conspicuously shown in the myths of thunderbolts, elfin arrows, and purgatory hammers, than in the sham science that has been brought to bear upon them in Europe, as well as in China. It is instructive to see Adrianus Tollius, in his 1649 edition of 'Boethius on Gems,' struggling against the philosophers.   He gives drawings of some ordinary stone axes and hammers, and tells how the naturalists say that they are generated in the sky by a fulgureous exhalation conglobed in a cloud by the circumfixed humour, and are as it were baked hard by intense heat, and the weapon becomes pointed by the damp mixed with it flying from the dry part, and leaving the other end denser, but the exhalations press it so hard that it breaks out through the cloud, and makes thunder and lightning.   But, he says, if this be really the way in which they are generated, it is odd that they are not round, and that they have holes through them, and those holes not equal through, but widest at the ends. It is hardly to be believed, he thinks.[3]   Speculation on the natural origin of high-class stone weapons and tools has now long since died out in Europe, but some faint echoes of the Chinese emperor's philosophy were heard among us but lately, in the arguments on the natural formation of the flint implements in the Drift.

With regard, then, to the use of thunderbolts as furnishing evidence of an early Stone Age, it may be laid down that such a myth, when we can be sure that it refers to artificial stone

[1] Wilde, Cat. R. I. A., p. 19.

[2] Wilson, Archaeology, etc., of Scotland ; Edinburgh, 1851, pp. 124, 184, etc.

[3] Boethius, 'Gemmarum & Lapidum Historia,' recensuit etc. Adrianus Tollius ; Leyden, 1649, p. 482.

implements, proves that such things were found by a people who, being possessed of metal, had forgotten the nature and use of these rude instruments of earlier times. Kang-hi's remarks that some of the so-called "lightning-stones" were like hatchets, knives, and mallets, and Pliny's mention of some of the *cerauniæ* or thunder-stones being like axes,[1] are cases in point. But the more mention of the belief in thunderbolts falling, as for example in Madagascar[2] and Arracan,[3] only gives a case for further inquiry on the suspicion that the thunderbolts in these regions may turn out to be stone implements, as they have so often done elsewhere.

The thunderbolt is thought to have a magical power, and there is especially one notion, in connexion with which it comes into use. This is that it preserves the place where it is kept from lightning, the idea being apparently here, as in the belief about the "wildfire" which will be presently mentioned, that where the lightning has struck, it will not strike again, so that the place where a thunderbolt is put is made safe by having been already struck once, though harmlessly. In Germany, the house in which it is kept is safe from the storm; when a tempest is approaching, it begins to sweat, and again it is said of it, that "he who chastely beareth this, shall not be struck by lightning, nor the house or town where that stone is,"[4] while nearly the same idea comes out in Pliny's account of the *brontia*, which is "like the heads of tortoises, and falling, as they think, with thunder, puts out, if you will believe it, what has been struck by lightning."[5] These notions suggest an interpretation of the curious account given by Sir James Emerson Tennent of the *wajira-chumbatan*, placed on the top of Singhalese dagobas or shrines, to protect them from lightning.[6] As *wajira* is Sanskrit *vajra*, the thunderbolt, the virtue of the device may have lain, as in the preceding cases, in some object supposed to be the thunderbolt, or at least to represent it, as a stone celt, a diamond, or some other precious stone.

In the mythology of our race, the bolt of the Thunder-god

---

[1] Plin. xxxvii. 51.   [2] Ellis, 'Madagascar,' vol. i. pp. 30, 309.
[3] Coleman, Myth. of Hindoos, p. 327.   [4] Grimm, D. M., pp. 164, 1170.
[5] Plin., xxxvii. 55.   Tennent, 'Ceylon,' vol. i. p. 509.

4

holds a prominent place. To him, be he Indra or Zeus the
Heaven-god, or the very thunder itself in person, Thunor or
Thor, the Aryans give as an attribute the bolt which he hurls
with lightning from the clouds. Now it is clear that this was
the meaning of the Roman Jupiter Lapis. The sacred flint
was kept in the temple of Jupiter Feretrius, and brought out to
be sworn by, and with it the pater patratus smote the victim
slain to consecrate the solemn treaties of the Roman people.
" 'If by public counsel,' he said, 'or by wicked fraud, they
swerve first, in that day, O Jove, smite thou the Roman people, as I here to-day shall smite this hog; and smite them so
much more, as thou art abler and stronger.' And having said
this, he struck the hog with a flint stone."[1]

To those who read this, it is evident that the flint of Jupiter
was held either to be a thunderbolt or to represent one, and
the practice cannot be taken as having of necessity come down
from an early Stone Age, seeing that it might quite as well
have sprung up among a race possessed of metals. The sacred
instrument is commonly spoken of indefinitely, as *lapis silex*,
saxum silex, but it may have been a flint implement found
buried in the ground, for already in the ancient song of the
' Arval Brethren,' the thunderbolt is spoken of as a celt (*cu-
neus*) " quom tibei cunei decatumum tonarunt,"[2] and, as has
been shown, at least this development of the myth of the thunderbolt belongs to an age when the nature of the buried stone
implement has been forgotten. Yet if all we know about the
matter was that victims were sacrificed with a flint on certain
occasions, and that the Fetiales carried these flints with them
into foreign countries where a treaty was to be solemnized, it
might be quite plausibly argued that we had here before us a
practice which had come down, unchanged, from the time when
the fathers of the Roman race used stone implements for the
ordinary purposes of life. This is the other side of the argument, which must not be kept out of sight in interpreting,
as a relic of the Stone Age, the West African ceremony of

<hr>

[1] Liv., i. 24; xxx. 43. Grimm, D. M., p. 1171.
[2] Kuhn, ' Herabkunft des Feuers,' p. 228.

slaughtering the beast on the yearly sacrifice to Gimawong, not with a knife, but with a sharp stone.[1]

The examination of the evidence bearing on the Stone Age thus brings into view two leading facts. In the first place, within the limits of the Stone Age itself, an unmistakable upward development in the course of ages is to be discerned, in the traces of an early period when stone implements were only used in their rude chipped state, and were never ground or polished, followed by a later period when grinding came to be applied to improve such stone instruments as required it. And in the second place, a body of evidence from every great district of the habitable globe uniformly tends to prove, that where man is found using metal for his tools and weapons, either his ancestors or the former occupants of the soil, if there were any, once made shift with stone. It would be well to have the evidence fuller from some parts of the world, as from Southern Asia and Central Africa, but we need not expect from thence anything but confirmation of what is already known.

[1] A passage in Klemm, C. G., vol. iv. p. 81, relating to a Circassian practice of sacrificing with a "thunderbolt," arises from a misunderstanding. See J. S. Bell, 'Circassia,' vol. ii. pp. 98, 108.

CHAPTER IX.

FIRE, COOKING, AND VESSELS.

THERE are a number of stories, old and new, of tribes of mankind living in ignorance of the art of fire-making. Such a state of things is indeed usually presupposed by the widespread legends of first fire-makers or fire-bringers, and Plutarch, in his essay on the question "Whether water or fire is the more useful?", gives a typical view of the matter. Fire was invented, as they say, by Prometheus, and our life shows that this was not a poetic fiction. For there are some races of men who live without fire, houseless, hearthless, and dwelling in the open air.[1] The modern point of view is, however, very different from Plutarch's, and when the mention of a fireless race appears in company with a Prometheus, mythology, not history, claims it. The mere assertion that in a certain place a race is, or was, to be found living without fire is more difficult to deal with. In examining a collection of such statements, it is well to pay particular attention to the modern ones, on which collateral evidence may be brought to bear.

What is known of the native civilization of the Canary Islands, the making of pottery, the cooking in underground ovens, the use of the fire-drill, leaves no doubt that the Guanches knew how to produce and use fire at the time of the European expeditions in the 14th and 15th centuries. Yet Antonio Galvano, writing his treatise about the middle of the sixteenth cen-

[1] Plut., 'Aqua an Ignis utilior?'

tury, declares that "in times past they ate raw meat, for want of fire." Farther on in the same book he has another story of a fireless people. In 1529, Alvaro de Saavedra, returning from the Moluccas toward the Pacific coast of Mexico, sailed eastward along the north coast of New Guinea, and having gone four or five degrees south of the Line, crossed again to the north, and discovered an island of tattooed people, which he called Isla de los Pintados, or the isle of painted men. Beyond this island, in 10° or 12° N., they found many small smooth ones together, full of palms and grass, and these they called Los Jardines, "The Gardens." The natives had no domestic animals, they were dressed in a white cloth of grass, ate cocoa-nuts for bread, and raw fish, which they took in the praus which they made out of drift pine-wood with their tools of shell. They stood in terror of fire, for they had never seen it (espan-taram se do fogo, porque nunca o viram).[1] I am not aware that these islands have been identified, but they would seem to be somewhere about the Radak or Chatham group. The account of the natives, to judge by its general consistency with what is known of the common eating of raw vegetables and fish in other coral islands in the Pacific, seems to have come mostly or altogether from an eye-witness, and the statement that they had no fire is not to be summarily set down as a mere fiction, like that about the Canary Islands. It has fortunately happened, however, that a very similar story has come up in our own time about another coral island, under circumstances which allow of its accuracy being tested. When the United States' Exploring Expedition, under Commodore Wilkes, visited Fakaafo or Bowditch Island in 1841, they made the following remarks:—"There was no sign of places for cooking, nor any appearance of fire, and it is believed that all their provisions are eaten raw. What strengthened this opinion, was the alarm the natives felt when they saw the sparks emanating from the flint and steel, and the emission of smoke from the mouths of those who were smoking cigars."[2]

[1] Galvano, 'Discoveries of the World;' Hakluyt Soc., London, 1862, pp. 66, 174-9, 238.

[2] Wilkes, Narr. of U. S. Exploring Exp., 1838–42; London, 1845, vol. v. p. 18.

Curiously enough, within the very work which contains these remarks, particulars are given which show that fire was in reality a familiar thing in the island. Mr. Hale, the ethnographer to the expedition, not only mentions the appearance of smoke on the neighbouring Duke of York's Island as being evidence of natives being there, but he gives the name for fire in the language of Fakaafo, *afi*,[1] a most widely-spread Malayo-Polynesian word, corresponding to the Malay form *apī*. Some years later, the Rev. George Turner again mentions this word *afi*, and gives besides a native story about fire, which is an interesting example of the way in which a mere myth may nevertheless be a piece of historical evidence. The account which the inhabitants of Fakaafo give of the introduction of fire among themselves is thus related. "The origin of fire they trace to Mafuike, but, unlike the Mafuike of the mythology of some other islands, this was an old blind *lady*. Talangi went down to her in her lower regions, and asked her to give him some of her fire. She obstinately refused until he threatened to kill her, and then she yielded. With the fire he made her say what fish were to be cooked with it, and what were still to be eaten raw, and then began the time of cooking food." Utter myth as this story is, it yet joins with the evidence of language in bringing the history of the islanders who tell it into connexion with the history of the distant New Zealanders. It belongs to the great Polynesian myth of Maui, who, the New Zealand story says, went away to the dwelling of his great ancestress Mahuika, and got fire from her.[2] And it proves that, even in the past time when these two versions of the story branched off, one to be found in Fakaafo, and the other in New Zealand, the origin of fire must have been already a thing of the forgotten past, or a myth would not have been applied to explain it.

In his account of the natives of Fakaafo, Mr. Turner speaks of their recollection of the time when they used fire in felling trees, and he mentions, moreover, some curious native ordi-

---

[1] Hale, Ethnography, etc., of U. S. Exp. ; Philadelphia ed. vol. vi. 1846, pp. 140, 363.

[2] Sir G. Grey, 'Polynesian Mythology ;' London, 1855, pp. 46–9.

nances respecting fire. "No fire is allowed to be kindled at night in the houses of the people all the year round. It is sacred to the god, and so, after sundown, they sit and chat in the dark. There are only two exceptions to the rule: first, fire to cook fish caught in the night, but then it must not be taken to their houses, only to the cooking-house; and second, a light is allowed at night in a house where there happens to be a confinement."[1] It is likely that the American explorers may have misinterpreted the surprise of the natives at seeing cigars smoked, and fire produced from the flint and steel, as well as the eating of raw fish and the absence of signs of cooking in the dwellings. If the similar story of the islanders of Los Jardines really came from an eye-witness, it may have arisen in much the same way. In Kotzebue's time, the people of the Radack group (which may be perhaps the very Jardines in question) were just as much astonished at the smith's forge, though fire was a well-known thing to them.[2]

The circumstances of Magalhaens' discovery of the Ladrones or Marian Islands, and the Philippines, in 1521, are known to us from the narrative of his companion Antonio Pigafetta, who describes the manners and customs of the natives, but without a hint that fire was anything strange to them. This preposterous addition must be sought in later authors. In 1652, Horn, not content with quoting Galvano's stories of the Canaries and Los Jardines, adds the natives of the Philippines as a race destitute of fire.[3] But the story of the Ladrone Islanders is even more remarkable than this.

The arts of these people are described by Pigafetta with some detail. He mentions the slight clothing of bark worn by the women, the mats and baskets, the wooden houses, the canoes with outriggers, and he notices that the natives had no weapons but lances pointed with fish bones, and had no notion of what arrows were. They stole everything they could lay hands on, and at last Magalhaens went on shore with forty men, burnt

<hr>

[1] Turner, 'Polynesia,' pp. 627-8, and Vocab.

[2] Otto v. Kotzebue, 'Entdeckungs-Reise;' Weimar, 1821, vol. ii. p. 67.

[3] Hornius, 'De Originibus Americanis;' The Hague, 1652, pp. 204, 51. See Goguet, vol. i. p. 69.

forty or fifty of their houses, and killed seven of the people.
A hundred and eighty years afterwards the Jesuit Father Le
Gobien brought out a new feature in the story. "What is
most astonishing, and what people will find it hard to believe,
is that they had never seen fire. This so necessary element
was entirely unknown to them. They neither knew its use nor
its qualities; and they were never more surprised than when
they saw it for the first time on the descent that Magellan
made on one of their islands, where he burnt some fifty of their
houses, to punish these islanders for the trouble they had given
him. They at first regarded the fire as a kind of animal which
attached itself to the wood on which it fed. The first who
came too near it having burnt themselves frightened the rest,
and only dared look at it from afar; for fear, they said, of being bitten by it, and lest this terrible animal should wound
them by its violent breath," etc. etc. He goes on to tell how
they soon got accustomed to it and learnt to use it.[1]

It is a curious illustration of the change in historical criticism
that has come since 1700, that the Jesuit historian should have
expected so singular a story, not mentioned by the eye-witness
who described the discovery, to be received without the production of the slightest evidence, a hundred and eighty years
after date, and that the public should have justified his confidence in their credulity by believing and quoting his account.
Whether he took it directly from any other book or not I cannot tell; but it is to be observed, that if we add Galvano's
story about Los Jardines to Pigafetta's mention of Magalhaens
burning the houses of the Ladrone Islanders, we may account
for the appearance of all Father Le Gobien's story, except the
idea of the fire being an animal, which may be supplied out of
Herodotus. "By the Egyptians also it hath been held that
fire is a living beast, and that it devours everything it can seize,
and when filled with food it perishes with what it has devoured."[2]

There are stories of fireless men in America, to which I can
only refer. Father Lafitau speaks indefinitely of there being

<hr>

[1] Le Gobien, 'Histoire des Isles Marianes;' Paris, 1700, p. 44.
[2] Herod., iii. 16.

such.[1] Father Lombard, of the Company of Jesus, writing in 1730 from Kourou, in French Guyana, gives an account of the tribe of Amikouanes on the river Oyapok, who are also called "long-eared Indians," their ears being stretched to their shoulders. This nation, he says, which has been hitherto unknown, is extremely savage; they have no knowledge of fire.[2]

It is a very curious thing that one of the oldest stories of a race of fireless men is also the newest. In Ethiopia, says the geographer Pomponius Mela, "there are people to whom fire was so totally unknown before the coming of Eudoxus, and so wondrously were they pleased with it when they saw it, that they had the greatest delight in embracing the flames and hiding burning things in their bosoms till they were hurt."[3] Pliny places these fireless men in his catalogue of monstrous Ethiopian tribes, between the dumb men and the pygmies. To some, he says, the use of fire was unknown before the time of Ptolemy Lathyrus, king of Egypt.[4] His mention of the name of Ptolemy Lathyrus shows that he, too, is quoting the voyages of Eudoxus of Cyzicus. Whether there was such a person as Eudoxus, and whether he really made the voyages attributed to him or not, is not very clear; but his story, like that of Sindbad, embodies notions current at the time it was written. And with such tenacity does the popular mind hold on to old stories, that now, after a lapse of some two thousand years, the fireless men and the pygmies are brought by the modern Ethiopians into even closer contact than in the pages of Pliny. Dr. Krapf was told that the Dokos, men four feet high, living south of Kaffa and Susa, subsisted on roots and serpents, and were not acquainted with fire.[5] As far as the pygmies are concerned, there appears to be a foundation for the story, in a race of small men really living there. Krapf was shown a slave four feet high, who, they told him, was a Doko. But between four feet and three spans, the height assigned by Pliny to pygmy races elsewhere,[6] there is a difference. Nor is this

[1] Lafitau, 'Mœurs des Sauvages Américains;' Paris, 1724, vol. i. p. 40.
[2] 'Lettres Édifiantes et Curieuses;' Paris, 1731, vol. xx. p. 222. Goguet, l. c.
[3] Mela, iii. c. 9.　　　　　[4] Plin., vi. 35, and see ii. 67.
[5] Krapf, Travels, etc., in East Africa; London, 1860, p. 61, etc. See Perty, 'Grundzüge der Ethnographie;' Leipzig, 1859, p. 218.　　　[6] Plin., vii. 2.

the only instance of the wonderful permanence of old stories in
this part of the world, quite irrespectively of their being true.
Within no great distance, an old negro gave Mr. Petherick an
account of the monstrous men he had met with in his travels,
the men with four eyes, the men with eyes under their armpits, the men with long tails, and the men whose ears were so
big that they covered their bodies;[1] so nearly has the modern
African kept to the wonder-tales that were current in the time
of Pliny.[2]

An unquestionable account of a fireless tribe would be of the
highest interest to the ethnographer, proving, as it would do,
a great step forward made by the races who can produce fire,
for this is an art which, once learnt, could hardly be lost.   But
when we see that stories of such tribes have been set up again
and again without any sound basis, while further information,
when brought to bear on a series of such stories, tells against
them so far as it goes, we are hardly warranted in trusting
others of the same kind just because we have no means of testing them.   A cause is required for the appearance of such
stories in the world, but it does not follow that this cause must
be the real existence of fireless tribes; a mere belief in their
existence will answer the purpose, and this belief is known to
have been current for ages, especially coming out in the Pro-
methens-legends of various regions of the world.   Experience
shows how such an idea, when once fairly afloat, will assert itself from time to time in stories furnished with place, date, and
circumstance.   It must be remembered, too, that the fireless
men form only one of a number of races mentioned by writers,
old and new, as being distinguished by the want of something
which man usually possesses, who have no language, no names,
no idea of spiritual beings, no dreams, no mouths, no heads,
or no noses, but whose real existence more accurate knowledge
has by no means tended to confirm.

In connexion with the stories of fireless tribes, some accounts
of a kind of transitional state may be mentioned here.   Mr.
Backhouse was told by a native of Van Diemen's Land, that
his ancestors had no means of making fire before their ac-

<hr>

[1] Petherick, p. 367.   [2] Plin., vi. 35, vii. 2.

quaintance with Europeans. They got it first from the sky,
and preserved it by carrying firebrands about with them, and
if these went out, they looked for the smoke of the fire of some
other party, or for smouldering remains of a lately-abandoned
fire of their own.[1] This curious account fits with the Tas-
manian myth recorded by Mr. Milligan, which tells how fire
was thrown down like a star by two black-fellows, who are
now in the sky, the twin stars Castor and Pollux.[2] Moreover,
Mr. Milligan himself, on the question being put to him, has
answered it in a way very much corresponding to Mr. Backhouse's account, to the effect that the Tasmanians never produced fire by artificial means at all, but always carried it with
them from one camping place to another. Again, a statement
of the same kind is reported to have been made by Mr. Mac
Douall Stuart at the 1864 Meeting of the British Association,
that fire was obtained by the natives of the southern part of
Australia by the friction of two pieces of wood over a bunch
of dry grass; but that in the north this mode is unknown, firebrands being constantly carried about and renewed, and if, by
any accident, they become extinguished, a journey of great
length has to be undertaken in order to obtain fire from other
natives.[3] Now if it is hard to believe that the Tasmanians
used fire, but knew of no means of producing it, it is ten times
harder to imagine that among a population like that of Australia, so given to travelling and to intercourse among neighbouring tribes, and who, as we know, have had for generations
one of the commonest contrivances for making fire, this contrivance should not have reached districts in the north. It
may be over-scepticism, but I think it will be safer to wait for
more evidence before deciding positively that any known race
of fire-users have not also been fire-makers, especially as the
carrying about of burning brands, so as to be able to make a
fire wherever they went at a moment's notice, was the habitual
practice in parts of Australia where the natives were perfectly
able to make new fire, if they chose, with their fire-drill. They
simply found it more convenient to carry it about.

[1] Backhouse, 'Australia,' p. 99.   [2] See Chapter XII.
[3] 'Athenæum,' Oct. 15, 1864, p. 503.

The accounts, then, of the finding of fireless tribes are of a highly doubtful character; possibly true to some extent, but not probably so. Of the existence of others who are possessed of fire, but cannot produce it for themselves, there is more considerable evidence. But, on the other hand, both the possession of fire, and the art of making it, belong certainly to the vast majority of mankind, and have done so as far back as we can trace. The methods, however, which have been found in use for making fire are very various. A survey of the condition of the art in different parts of the world, as known to us by direct evidence, is enough to make it probable that nearly all the different processes found in use are the successors of ruder ones; and, beside this, there is a mass of indirect evidence which fills up some of the shortcomings of history, as it does in the investigation of the Stone Age. Among some of the highest races of mankind, the lower methods of fire-making are still to be seen cropping out through the higher processes by which, for so many ages, they have been overlaid. The friction of two pieces of wood may perhaps be the original means of fire-making used by man; but, between the rudest and the most artificial way in which this may be done, there is a considerable range of progress.

One of the simplest machines for producing fire is that which may be called the "stick-and-groove." A blunt-pointed stick

Fig. 20.

is run along a groove of its own making in a piece of wood lying on the ground, somewhat as shown in the imaginary drawing, Fig. 20. Mr. Darwin says that the very light wood of the *Hibiscus tiliaceus* was alone used for the purpose in Tahiti. A native would produce fire with it in a few seconds; he himself found it very hard work, but at length succeeded. This stick-and-groove process has been repeatedly described in the South Sea Islands, namely, in Tahiti, New Zealand, the Sandwich, Tonga, Samoa, and

Radack groups ;[1] but I have never found it distinctly mentioned
out of this region of the world. Even should it be known
elsewhere, its isolation in a particular district round which
other processes prevail would still be an ethnographical fact
of some importance. It is to be noticed also, that it comes
much nearer than "fire-drilling" to the yet simpler process of
striking fire with two pieces of split bamboo. The silicious coating of this cane makes it possible to strike fire with it ; and this
is done in Eastern Asia, and also in the great Malay islands of
Borneo and Sumatra,[2] at or near the source whence the higher
Polynesian race is supposed to have spread over the Pacific
Islands. But it would appear that the striking fire with bamboo, simple as it seems, is for some reason not so convenient
as the use of the more complex friction-apparatus; for Marsden
seems to consider the fire-drill as the regular native instrument
in Sumatra, though he says he has also seen the same effect
produced more simply by rubbing one bit of bamboo, with a
sharp edge, across another.

By a change in the way of working, the " stick-and-groove " becomes the "fire-drill." I have
been obliged to coin both these
terms, no suitable ones being
forthcoming. The fire-drill, in
its simplest form, is represented
in Fig. 21 ; and Captain Cook's
remarks on it and its use, among
the native tribes of Australia,
may serve also as a general description of it all over the world,
setting aside minor details. "They

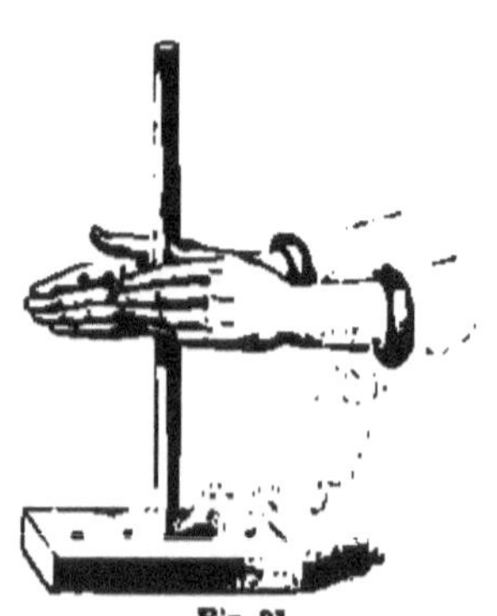

Fig. 21.

produce fire with great facility, and spread it in a wonderful

<hr>

[1] Darwin, in Narr., vol. iii. p. 488. Polack, vol. i. p. 165. Tyerman and Bennet,
vol. i. p. 141. Buschmann, 'Die Marquizes,' etc.; Berlin, 1843, pp. 140–1.
Mariner, Tomb., s. vv. tofe-afi, tolongu, rowuatoo. S. S. Farmer, 'Tonga,' etc.;
London, 1858, p. 128. Walpole, 'Four Years in the Pacific;' London, 1849,
vol. ii. p. 377. Kotzebue, vol. iii. p. 154.

[2] Bowring, vol. i. p. 806. St. John, vol. i. p. 137. Marsden, p. 60. See
Tennent, 'Ceylon,' vol. i. p. 105.

manner. To produce it they take two pieces of dry soft wood; one is a stick about eight or nine inches long, the other piece is flat: the stick they shape into an obtuse point at one end, and pressing it upon the other, turn it nimbly by holding it between both their hands, as we do a chocolate mill, often shifting their hands up, and then moving them down upon it, to increase the pressure as much as possible. By this method they get fire in less than two minutes, and from the smallest spark they increase it with great speed and dexterity."[1] It appears usual both in Australia and elsewhere to lay the lower piece on the ground, holding it firm with feet or knees. A good deal may depend on the kind of wood used, and its dryness, etc., for in some countries it seems to take much more time and labour, two men often working it, one beginning at the top of the stick when his companion's hands have come down nearly to the bottom, and so on till the fire comes.

Contrasting with the isolation of the stick-and-groove in a single district, the geographical range of the simple fire-drill is immense. Its use among the Australians forms one of the characters which distinguish their culture from that of the Polynesians; while it appears again among the Malays in Sumatra[2] and the Carolines.[3] It was found by Cook in Unalashka,[4] and by the Russians in Kamchatka; where, for many years, flint and steel could not drive it out of use among the natives, who went on carrying every man his fire-sticks.[5] There is reason to suppose that it prevailed in India before the Aryans invaded the country, bringing with them an improved apparatus, for at this day it is used by the wild Veddahs of Ceylon, a race so capable of resisting foreign innovation that they have not learnt to smoke tobacco.[6] It prevails, or has done so within modern times, through great part of South Africa,[7] and it was in use among the Guanches of the Canary Islands in the seventeenth

[1] Cook, First Voy. II., vol. iii. p. 234. Angas, S. Australia, pl. 27.
[2] Marsden, p. 60.   [3] Kotzebue, vol. iii. p. 154.
[4] Cook, Third Voy., vol. ii. p. 518.   [5] Krasheninnikow, p. 80.
[6] Tennent, 'Ceylon,' vol. ii. p. 451. Bailey in Tr. Eth. Soc., 1863, p. 291.
[7] Casalis, p. 189. Klemm, C. W., part i. p. 67.

century.[1] In North America it is described among Esquimaux and Indian tribes.[2] It was in use in Mexico,[3] and Fig. 22, taken from an ancient Mexican picture-writing, shows the drill being twirled; while fire, drawn in the usual conventional manner, comes out from the hole where the point revolves. It was in use in Central America,[4] in the West Indies,[5] and in South America, down as far as the Straits of Magellan.[6]

Fig. 22.

The name of "fire-drill" has not, however, been adopted merely with reference to this simplest form. This rude instrument is, as may well be supposed, very wasteful of time and power, and it has been improved by several contrivances which so closely correspond to those applied to boring-tools, that the most convenient plan is to classify them together. Even the clumsy plan of the simple fire-drill has been found in use for boring holes. It has been mentioned at page 187, as in use for drilling hard stone among rude Indians of South America, and, what is much more surprising, the natives of Madagascar bored holes by working their drill between the palms of their hands,[7] though they were so far advanced in the arts as to make and use iron tools, and of course the very drills worked in this primitive way were pointed with iron.

The principle of the common carpenter's brace, with which

[1] Glas, 'Canary Islands,' London, 1764, p. 8.

[2] Klemm, C. G., vol. ii. p. 239. Schoolcraft, part i. p. 214. Loskiel, p. 70. Lafitau, 'Mœurs des Sauvages Américains;' Paris, 1724, vol. ii. p. 242.

[3] Kingsborough, Selden MS., Vatican MS.

[4] Brasseur, 'Popol-Vuh,' pp. 64, 218, 243.

[5] Oviedo, 'Hystoria General de las Indias;' Salamanca, 1547, vi. 5.

[6] Spix and Martius, vol. ii. p. 387, and plates. Purchas, vol. iii. p. 863; vol. iv. p. 1345. Molina, vol. ii. p. 122. Dobrishoffer, vol. ii. p. 118. Garcilaso de la Vega, 'Comentarios Reales' (2nd ed.); Madrid, 1723, p. 198.

[7] Ellis, 'Madagascar,' vol. i. p. 317.

he works his centre-bit, is applied to fire-making by a very simple device represented in Fig. 29, which is drawn according

Fig. 29.

to Mr. Darwin's description of the plan used by the Gauchos of the Pampas; "taking an elastic stick about eighteen inches long, he presses one end on his breast, and the other (which is pointed) in a hole in a piece of wood, and then rapidly turns the curved part, like a carpenter's centre-bit."[1]   The Gauchos, it should be observed, are not savages, but half-wild herdsmen of mixed European, Indian, and African blood, who would probably only use such a means of kindling fire when the flint and steel were for the moment not at hand, and their fire-drill is not only like the carpenter's brace, but most likely suggested by it.

To wind a cord or thong round the drill, so as, by pulling the two ends alternately, to make it revolve very rapidly, is a great improvement on mere hand-twirling.   As Kuhn has pointed out, this contrivance was in use for boring in Europe in remote times; Odysseus describes it in telling how he and his companions put out the eye of the Cyclops :—

> οἱ μὲν μοχλὸν ἑλόντες ἐλάϊνον, ὀξὺν ἐπ' ἄκρῳ,
> ὀφθαλμῷ ἐνέρεισαν· ἐγὼ δ' ἐφύπερθεν ἀερθείς,
> δίνεον, ὡς ὅτε τις τρυπῷ δόρυ νήϊον ἀνὴρ
> τρυπάνῳ, οἱ δέ τ' ἔνερθεν ὑποσσείουσιν ἱμάντι
> ἁψάμενοι ἑκάτερθε, τὸ δὲ τρέχει ἐμμενὲς αἰεί.[2]

"They then seizing the sharp-cut stake of the wood of the olive
  Thrust it into his eye, the while I standing above them,
  Bored it into the hole :—as a shipwright boreth a timber,
  Guiding the drill that his men below drive backward and forward,
  Pulling the ends of the thong while the point runs round without
      ceasing."

In modern India, butter-churns are worked with a cord in

[1] Darwin, in Narr., vol. iii. p. 468.
[2] Kuhn, 'Herabkunft des Feuers,' p. 39.   Hom. Od., ix. 382.

this way, and the Brahmans still use a cord-drill in producing
the sacred fire, as will be more fully stated presently.   Halfway round the world, the same thing is found among the Esquimaux.   Davis (after whom Davis's Straits are named) describes in 1586 how a Greenlander "beginne to kindle a fire
in this mauer: he tooke a piece of a board wherein was a
hole halfe thorow: into that hole he puts the end of a round
stick like unto a bedstaffe, wetting the end thereof in Tmne,
and in fashion of a turner with a piece of lether, by his violent
motion doeth very speedily produce fire."[1]   The cut, Fig. 24,
is taken from a drawing of the last century, representing two
Esquimaux making fire, one holding a cross-piece to keep the
spindle steady and force it well down to its bearing, while the
other pulls the thong.[2]   This form of the apparatus takes two

Fig. 24.

men to work it, but the Esquimaux have devised a modification of it which a man can work alone.   Sir E. Belcher thus
describes its use for drilling holes by means of a point of green
jade:—"The thong ... being passed twice round the drill,
the upper end is steadied by a mouthpiece of wood, having a

[1] Hakluyt, vol. iii. p. 104.
[2] Henry Ellis, 'Voyage to Hudson's Bay;' London, 1748, pp. 132, 234.

R

piece of the same stone imbedded, with a countersunk cavity.
This held firmly between the teeth directs the tool. Any work-
man would be astonished at the performance of this tool on
ivory; but having once tried it myself, I found the jar or vi-
bration on the jaws, head, and brain, quite enough to prevent
my repeating it."[1]　There is a set of Esquimaux apparatus for
making fire in the same manner, in the Edinburgh Industrial

Fig. 25.

Museum, and Fig. 25 is intended to show the way in which
it is worked. The thong-drill with the mouthpiece has been
found in use in the Aleutian Islands, both for boring holes and
for making fire.[2]　Lastly, there is a kind of cord-drill used by
the New Zealanders in boring holes through hard greenstone,
etc., in which the spindle itself is weighted. It is described as
a "sharp wooden stick ten inches long, to the centre of which
two stones are attached, so as to exert pressure and perform
the office of a fly-wheel. The requisite rotatory motion is
given to the stick by two strings pulled alternately."[3]　There
must of course be some means of keeping the spindle upright.
The New Zealanders do not seem to have used their drill for
fire-making as well as for boring, but to have kept to their
stick-and-groove.

[1] Sir E. Belcher, in Tr. Eth. Soc., 1861, p. 140.
[2] Kotzebue, vol. iii. p. 155.
[3] Thomson, 'New Zealand,' vol. i. p. 203.

To substitute for the mere thoug or cord a bow with a loose string, is a still further improvement, for one hand now does the work of two in driving the spindle. The centre, in which its end turns, may be held down with the other hand, or (as is very usual) act against the breast of the operator. The bow-drill, thus formed, is a most ancient and well-known boring instrument, familiar to the artisan in modern Europe as it was in ancient Egypt. The only place where I have found any notice of its use for fire-making is among the North American Indians. The plate from which Fig. 26 is taken is marked by Schoolcraft as representing the apparatus used by the Sioux, or Dacotahs.[1] If they really used it, they may possibly have caught the idea from the European bow-drill.

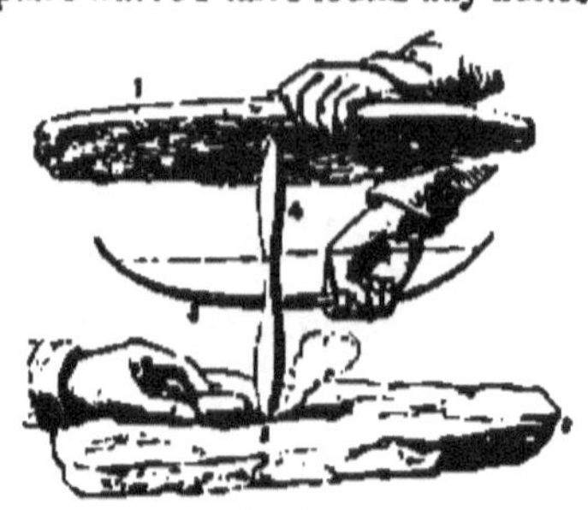

Fig. 26.

Lastly, there is a curious little contrivance, known to English toolmakers as the "pump-drill," from its being worked up and down like a pump. That kept in the London tool-shops is all of metal, expanding into a bulb instead of the disk shown in Fig. 27, which represents the kind used in Switzerland, consisting of a wooden spindle, armed with a steel point, and weighted with a wooden disk. A string is made fast to the ends of the cross-piece, and in the middle to the top of the spindle. As the hand brings the cross-piece down it unwinds the cord, driving the spindle round; as the hand is lifted again, the disk, acting as a fly-wheel, runs on and re-winds the cord, and so on. Holtzappfel says that the pump-drill is as well known among the Oriental nations as the breast-drill, though it is little used in England except by china and glass menders.[2] Perhaps it may have found its way over from Asia

---

[1] Schoolcraft, part iii. pl. 28. But the description, p. 278, does not correspond, being that of the simple hand fire-drill, and the accompanying figure, under which "Iroquois" is written, is wrongly drawn.

[2] Holtzappfel, 'Turning and Mechanical Manipulation,' London, 1856, vol. ii. p. 557.

to the South Sea Islands ; at any rate it is found there. Fig. 28
shows it as used in Fakaafo or Bowditch Island, differing from
the Swiss form only in being armed with a stone instead of a
steel point, and in having no hole through the cross-piece.[1]

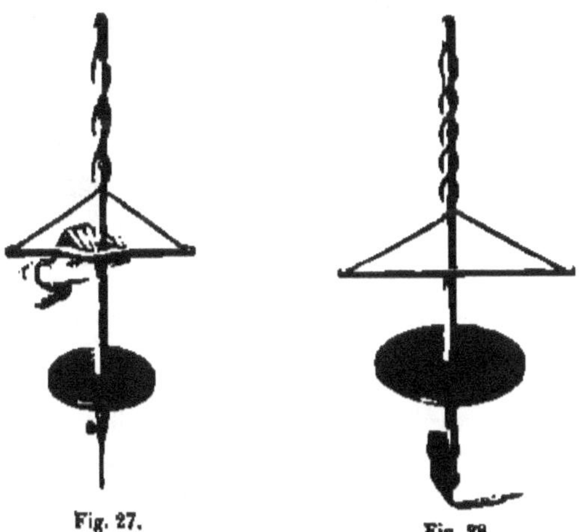

Fig. 27.   Fig. 28.

Mr. Turner describes it in the neighbouring Samoan or Navi-
gators' Islands, as pointed with a nail or a sail needle, got from
the foreigners,[2] but the specimen presented by him to the
Hunterian Museum at Glasgow has a stone point. The natives
use it for drilling their fish-hooks made of shell ; for which purpose, as for drilling holes in china, it is peculiarly adapted, the
lightness and evenness of its pressure lessening the danger of
cracking these brittle materials. One would think that this
quality would make the pump-drill particularly unsuitable for
fire-making ; but, nevertheless, by making it very large and
heavy, it has been turned to this service in North America,
among the Iroquois Indians. Fig. 29 (drawn to a small scale) represents their apparatus, which is thus described by Mr. Lewis
H. Morgan :—"This is an Indian invention, and of great antiquity. . . . It consisted of an upright shaft, about four feet in
length, and an inch in diameter, with a small wheel set upon

[1] Wilkes, U. S. Exp., vol. v. p. 17.   [2] Turner, p. 273.

the lower part, to give it momentum. In a notch at the top of the shaft was set a string, attached to a bow about three feet in length. The lower point rested upon a block of dry wood, near which are placed small pieces of punk. When ready to use, the string is first coiled around the shaft, by turning it with the hand. The bow is then pulled downwards, thus uncoiling the string, and revolving the shaft towards the left. By the momentum given to the wheel, the string is again coiled up in a reverse manner, and the bow again drawn up. The

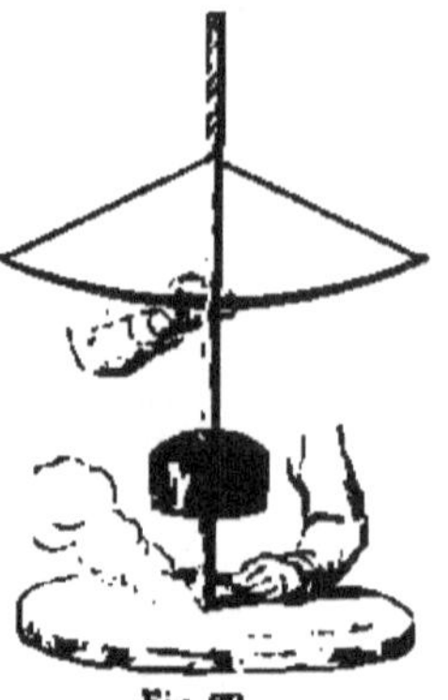

Fig. 29.

bow is again pulled downwards, and the revolution of the shaft reversed, uncoiling the string, and recoiling it as before. This alternate revolution of the shaft is continued, until sparks are emitted from the point where it rests upon the piece of dry wood below. Sparks are produced in a few moments by the intensity of the friction, and ignite the punk, which speedily furnishes a fire."[1]

. It is now necessary to notice other methods of producing fire which have been found in use in various parts of the world.

The natives of Tierra del Fuego are notably distinguished from their northern neighbours by their way of fire-making. In 1520, Magalhaens on his famous voyage visited the gigantic Patagonians, who thought the Spaniards had come down from heaven, and who, explaining to the European visitors the native theology, told them of their chief god, Setebos. The savages who thus helped to furnish the picture of the "servant-monster," Caliban,[2] showed their manner of making fire, which was by the friction of two pieces of wood.[3] But the Fuegians have

<hr>

[1] L. H. Morgan, 'League of the Iroquois;' Rochester, U. S., 1851, p. 381.

[2] Cal.—"Hast thou not dropped from heaven?" ('Tempest,' act ii. scene 2.)
Cal.—. . . . .
  "It would control my dam's god, Setebos." (Id. act i. scene 2).

[3] Pigafetta, in Pinkerton, vol. xi.

for centuries used a higher method, striking sparks with a flint from a piece of iron pyrites upon their tinder.   This process is described as still in use,[1] and is evidently what Captain Wallis meant by saying (in 1767), that "To kindle a fire they strike a pebble against a piece of mundic."[2]   A much earlier account of the same thing appears in the voyage of Sarmiento de Gamboa, in 1579–80.[3]   Iron pyrites answers extremely well instead of the steel, and was found in regular use in high northern latitudes in America, among the Slave and Dog Rib Indians.[4]   It is probably the "iron-stone" which the Esquimaux call *njarak-nariminilik*, and from which they strike fire with a fragment of flint,[5] and is perhaps referred to in Father Le Jeune's statement that the Algonquin Indians strike fire with two minerals (*pierres de mine*).[6]   The use of iron pyrites for striking fire was known to the Greeks and Romans, and it shared with flint the name of *fire-stone*, πυρίτης, *pyrites*, which it and some other metallic sulphurets have since taken entire possession of.

Two accounts of a process of fire-making in and about North-West America are unfortunately indefinite.   Captain Cook remarked that in Unalashka the natives produced fire by striking two stones, one with a good deal of brimstone rubbed on it.[7] Their neighbours, the Aloutian Islanders, Kotzebue says, make fire by striking together two stones with sulphur rubbed in, over dry moss also strewed with sulphur.[8]   It does not seem an easy thing to light tinder in this way with two flints, though particles of the sulphur easily ignite, and I have been told by a gun-flint maker that gunpowder may be lighted by throwing a quantity of flint chips violently down upon it on a flagstone.

[1] W. P. Snow, 'Tierra del Fuego,' etc.; London, 1857, vol. ii. p. 360.

[2] Wallis, in Hawkesworth, vol. i. p. 171.

[3] Sarmiento de Gamboa, 'Viage al Estrecho de Magallanes;' Madrid, 1768, p. 229. "Y unos pedazos de pedernal, pasados, y pintados de margarita de oro y plata: y preguntándoles que para qué era aquello? dixeron por señas, que para sacar fuego; y luego uno de ellos tomó unas plumas de las que trahía, y sirviéndole de yesca, sacó fuego con el pedernal.   Paréceme que es (essea?) de metal de plata d oro de veta, porque es al natural como el cariqairo de porro en el Pirú."

[4] Mackenzie, 'Voyages;' London, 1801, p. 39.   Klemm, C. G., vol. ii. p. 26.

[5] Hayes, 'Arctic Boat Journey;' London, 1860, p. 217.

[6] Le Jeune, 'Relation,' etc. (1634); Paris, 1635, p. 91.   Lafitau, vol. ii. p. 212.

[7] Cook, Third Voy., vol. ii. p. 513.   [8] Kotzebue, vol. iii. p. 155.

Father Zucchelli, who was a missionary in West Africa about the beginning of last century, gives the following account of the way in which, he. says, the negroes made fire on their journeys :—" When they found a fire-stone (Feuerstein) on the road, they lay down by it on their knees, took a little piece of wood in their hands, and threw sand between the stone and the wood, rubbing them so long against one another till the wood began to burn, and herewith they all lighted their pipes, and so went speedily forth again smoking on their journey."[1]   It is possible that not flint (as is usual), but pyrites, may here be meant by *feuerstein.*

The flint and steel may have come into use at any time after the beginning of the Iron age, but history fails to tell us the date of its introduction in Greece and Rome, China, and most other districts of the Old World. In modern times it has made its way with iron into many new places, though it has not always been able to supersede the fire-sticks at once ; sometimes, it seems, from a difficulty in getting flints. For instance, it was necessary in Sumatra to import the flints from abroad, and thus they did not come immediately into general use among the natives ; and there may perhaps be a similar reason for the fire-drill having held its ground to this day among some of the iron-using races of Southern Africa.

The Greeks were, familiar with the use of the burning-lens in the time of Aristophanes, who mentions it in the ' Clouds,' in a dialogue between Socrates and Strepsiades :—

" *Socrates.* Very good : now I'll set you another smart question. If some one entered an action against you to recover five talents, tell me, how would you cancel it ?

. . . .

Strepsiades. I have found a very clever way to cancel the suit, as you will agree yourself.

Socrates. What kind of a way ?

Strepsiades. Have you ever seen that stone in the druggists' shops, that pretty, transparent one, that they light fire with?

Socrates. The crystal, you mean ?

Strepsiades. I do.

Socrates. Well, what then ?

[1] Zucchelli, ' Merckwürdige Missions- and Reise-Beschreibung nach Congo ;' Frankfort, 1715, p. 344.

Strepsiades. Suppose I take this, and when the clerk enters the suit, I stand thus, a long way off, towards the sun, and melt out the letters!

Socrates. Very clever, by the Graces!"[1]

At a much later period Pliny mentions that glass balls with water put into them, when set opposite to the sun, get so hot as to set clothes on fire; and that he finds surgeons consider the best means of cautery to be a crystal ball placed opposite to the sun's rays.[2] The Chinese commonly use the burning-lens to light fire with, as well as the flint and steel.[3]

The fact that fire may be produced by reflecting the sun's rays with mirrors was known as early as Pliny's time (A.D. 23–79), as he remarks, "seeing that concave mirrors placed opposite to the sun's rays ignite things more easily than any other fire."[4] There is some reason to suppose that the knowledge of this phenomenon worked backwards into history, attaching itself to two famous names of old times, Archimedes and Numa Pompilius. The story of Archimedes setting the fleet on fire at Syracuse with burning mirrors, probably unknown as it was to historians for centuries after his time, need not be further remarked on here; but the story of Numa reappears on the other side of the world, under circumstances which make its discussion a matter of importance to ethnography.

It is related by Plutarch in his life of Numa, written in the first century, that among the ordinances made for the Vestal Virgins when they were established in Rome, there was the following. If the sacred fire which it was their duty to keep continually burning should happen to go out, it was not to be lighted again from another fire, but new fire was to be made by lighting from the sun a pure and undefiled flame. "And they kindle it especially with vessels which are shaped hollow from the side of an isosceles triangle with a (vertical) right angle, and converge from the circumference to a single centre. When such an instrument is set opposite to the sun, so that the impinging rays from all sides crowd and fold together round the centre, it divides the rarefied air, and quickly kindles

<hr>

[1] Aristoph., Nubes, 757, etc.

[2] Pliny, xxxvi. 67, xxxvii. 10.

[3] Davis, vol. iii. p. 61.

[4] Pliny, ii. 111.

the lightest and driest matters applied to it, the beams acquiring by the repulsion a body and fiery stroke."[1] Stories of Numa's ordinances will hardly be claimed as sober history, though it is possible that such a process as this may have been used, at least in late times, to rekindle the fire of Vesta. But there is in Festus another account of the way in which this was done, having in its favour every analogy from the practices of kindling the sacred fire among our Indo-European race, both in Asia and in Europe. "If the fire of Vesta were extinguished, the virgins were scourged by the priests, whose practice it was to drill into a board of auspicious wood till the fire came, which was received and carried to the temple by the virgin, in a brazen colander."[2]

The parallel passage to that in the life of Numa is to be found in the account of the feast of Raymi, or the Sun, celebrated in ancient Peru, according to Garcilaso de la Vega, whose 'Commentaries' were first published in 1609-16, the Spanish discovery having taken place in 1527. He says this festival was celebrated at the summer solstice. "The fire for this sacrifice had to be new, given, as they said, by the hand of the sun. For which purpose they took a great bracelet, which they call *Chipana* (like the others which the Incas commonly wore on the left wrist), which bracelet the high priest kept; it was larger than the common ones, and had as its medallion a concave cup like a half orange, highly polished, they set it against the sun, and at a certain point where the rays issuing from the cup came together, they put a little finely-carded cotton, as they did not know how to make tinder, which shortly took fire, as it naturally does. With this fire, thus given by the hand of the Sun, the sacrifice was burnt, and all the meat of that day was roasted. And they carried some of the fire to the Temple of the Sun, and to the House of the Virgins, where they kept it up all the year, and it was a bad

---

[1] Plutarch, 'Vita Numæ,' in. 7.

[2] Festus. "Ignis Vestæ si quando interstinctus esset, virgines verberibus afficiebantur a pontificibus, quibus mos erat tabulam felicis materiæ tamdiu terebrare, quousque exceptum ignem cribro æneo virgo in ædem ferret." See Val. Max., I. i. 0.

omen if they let it out in any way.   If, on the eve of the festival, which was when the necessary preparations for the following day were made, there was no sun to light the new fire, they made it with two thin smooth sticks as big as one's little finger, and half a yard long, boring one against the other (*barresando uno con otro*); these little sticks are cinnamon coloured, and they call both the sticks themselves and the fire-making *V-yaca*, one and the same term serving for noun and verb.   The Indians use them instead of flint and steel, and carry them on their journeys to get fire when they have to pass the night in uninhabited places," etc. etc.[1]

If circumstantiality of detail were enough to make a story credible, we might be obliged to receive this one, and even to argue on the wonderful agreement of the manner of kindling the sacred fire in Rome and in Peru.   But the coincidences between Garcilaso's Virgins of the Sun and Plutarch's Vestal Virgins go farther than this.   We are not only expected to believe that there were Virgins of the Sun, that they kept up a sacred fire whose extinction was an evil omen, and that this fire was lighted by the sun's rays concentrated in a concave mirror.   We are also told that in Cuzco, as in Rome, the virgin found unfaithful was to be punished by the special punishment of being buried alive.[2]   This is really too much.   Whatever may be the real basis of fact in the accounts of the Virgins of the Sun and the feast of Raymi, the inference seems, to me at least, most probable, that part or all of the accessory detail is not history, but the realization of an idea of which Garcilaso himself strikes the key-note when he says of this same feast of Raymi, that it was celebrated by the Incas "in the city of Cuzco, *which was another Rome*" (*que fue otra Roma*).[3]   Those who happen to have experience of the old chroniclers of Spanish America know how the whole race was possessed by a passion for bringing out the Old World stories in a new guise, with a local habitation and a name in America.   Garcilaso's story of

---

[1] Garcilaso de la Vega, p. 198.

[2] Id., p. 109.   Compare Diego Fernandez, Hist. del Peru, Seville, 1571, "y nadie podia tratar, ni conversar con estas Mamaconas.   Y si alguno lo intentaua, luego le enterrauan biuo."   [3] Id., p. 195.

the burning-mirror, supposing it to be an adaptation from
Plutarch, would not even be the best illustration of this modern phase of Mythology; that distinction must be reserved for
the reproduction by another chronicler of another of Plutarch's
stories, that of the shout that was raised when the Roman
herald proclaimed the liberty of the Greeks,—such a shout that
it brought the crows tumbling down into the race-course from
the sky above.[1]   The Incas, says Sarmiento, "were so feared,
that if they went out through the kingdom, and allowed a
curtain of their litters to be lifted that their vassals might see
them, they raised so great an acclamation that they made the
birds fall from where they were flying above, so that the people
could catch them in their hands."[2]

Against the abstract possibility of Garcilaso's story of the
lighting of the sacred fire with concave mirrors, there is no
more to be said than against Plutarch's.   With a good para-
bolic mirror only two inches in diameter, I have lighted brown
paper under an English sun of no extraordinary power, and
other surfaces which will make a good caustic will answer,
though of course they have less burning power than a parabo-
loid of revolution of equal size.   There is even a material basis
out of which the Peruvian story may have grown.   In the ancient tombs of Peru, mirrors both of pyrites and obsidian have
been found.   Some, three or four inches in diameter, were
probably mere broken nodules of pyrites, polished on the flat
side, but one is mentioned measuring about a foot and a half
(probably in circumference), which had a beautifully-polished
concave surface, so as to magnify objects considerably,[3] and
such a mirror may have been used for making fire.   Indeed,
the objection to the story of the Virgins of the Sun is not that
any of the details I have mentioned must of necessity be un-
true, but that the apparent traces of absorption from Plutarch
invalidate whatever rests on Garcilaso de la Vega's unsup-
ported testimony.

To conclude the notice of the art of fire-making in general,

[1] Plut., T. Quinct. Flaminius, x.
[2] Sarmiento, MS. cited in Prescott, Peru, vol. i. p. 25.
[3] Juan & Ulloa, 'Relacion Historica,' Madrid, 1748, p. 619.

its last phase, the invention of lucifer matches in our own day, is fast spreading over the world, and bringing most other fire-making instruments down to the condition of curious relics of a past time.

But though some of the higher methods date far back in the history of the Old World, the employment of the wooden friction-apparatus in Europe, even for the practical purposes of ordinary life, has come up through the classical and mediæval times into the last century, and for all we know it may still exist. Pliny speaks of its finding a use among the outposts of armies and among shepherds, a stone to strike fire with not being always to be had;[1] and in a remarkable account dating from 1768, which will be quoted presently, its use by Russian peasants for making fire in the woods is spoken of as an existing custom, just as, at a much more recent date, it is mentioned that the Portuguese Brazilians still have recourse to the fire-drill, when no other means of getting a light are forthcoming.[2] For the most part, however, the early use of the instrument in the Old World is only to be traced in ancient myths, in certain ceremonial practices which have been brought down unchanged into a new state of culture, and in descriptions by Greek and Roman writers of the art. It had lost, even then, its practical importance in everyday life, though lingering on, as it still does in our own day, in rites for which it was necessary to use pure *wild fire*, not the tame fire that lay like a domestic animal upon the hearth.

The traditions of inventors of the art of fire-making by the friction of wood have in so far an historical value, that they bring clearly into view a period when this was the usual practice. There is a Chinese myth that points to such a state of things, and which moreover presents, in the story of the " fire-bird," an analogy with a set of myths belonging to our own race, which may well be due to a deep-lying ethnological connexion. " A great sage went to walk beyond the bounds of the moon and the sun; he saw a tree, and on this tree a bird, which pecked at it and made fire come forth. The sage was struck

[1] Pliny, xvi. 77.
[2] Pr. Max. v. Wied, 'Reise nach Brasilien' (1815–7), vol. ii. p. 19.

with this, took a branch of the tree and produced fire from it, and thence this great personage was called Suy-jin."[1]   The friction-apparatus itself, apparently of the kind spoken of here as the fire-drill, is mentioned in Morrison's Chinese Dictionary.   "*Suy*, an instrument to obtain fire.   A speculum for obtaining fire from the sun is called *suy* or *kin-suy*. *Mŭh-suy*, an utensil to procure fire from wood by rotatory friction. *Suy-jin-she*, the first person who procured fire for the use of man." The very existence of a Chinese name for the fire-drill shows that it is, or has been, in use in the country.

The absence of evidence relating to fire-making in the Bible is remarkable.   If, indeed, the following passage from the cosmogony of Sanchoniathon be founded on a Phœnician legend, it preserves a record of the use of the fire-stick among the Semitic race.   "They say that from the wind Kolpia, and his wife Baau, which is interpreted Night, there were born mortal men, called Æon and Protogonos; and Æon found how to get food from trees.   And those born from them were called Genos and Genea, and they inhabited Phœnicia. . . . Moreover, they say that, again, from Genos, son of Æon and Protogonos, there were born mortal children, whose names were Phos, Pur, and Phlox (Light, Fire, and Flame).   These, they say, found out how to make fire from the friction of pieces of wood, and taught its use."[2]

Thus, too, though direct history does not tell us that the Finns and Lapps used the fire-drill before they had the flint and steel, there is a passage safely preserving the memory of its use in a Finnish poem, whose native metre is familiar to our ears from its imitation in 'Hiawatha;'

> " Panu parka, Tuonen poika,
> kirnasi tulisen kirnun,
> säkeisin säihytteli,
> pukemissa puhtaissa,
> walkehissa waatteissa."
>
> " Panu, the poor son of Tuoni,
> Churning fiercely at the fire-churn,

<hr>

[1] Goguet, vol. iii. p. 321. See Kuhn, p. 28, etc.
[2] Euseb., Præp. Evang. i. x.

> Scattering fiery sparks around him,
> Clothèd in a pure white garment,
> In a white and shining garment."[1]

It is, however, by our own race that the most remarkable body of evidence of the ancient use of the fire-drill has been preserved. The very instrument still used in India for kindling the sacrificial fire seems never to have changed since the time when our ancestors left their eastern home to invade Europe. It is thus described:—"The process by which fire is obtained from wood is called churning, as it resembles that by which butter in India is separated from milk. . . . It consists in drilling one piece of arani-wood into another by pulling a string tied to it with a jerk with the one hand, while the other is slackened, and so alternately till the wood takes fire. The fire is received on cotton or flax held in the hand of an assistant Brahman."[2] By this description it would seem that the Indian instrument is the same in principle as the Esquimaux thong-drill, shown in Fig. 24. It is driven by a three-stranded cord of cowhair and hemp; and there is probably a piece of wood pressed down upon the upper end of the spindle, to keep it down to its bearing.[3] In the name of Prometheus the fire-maker, the close connection with the Sanskrit name of this spindle, *pramantha*, has never been broken. Possibly both he and the Chinese Suy-jin may be nothing more than personifications of the fire-drill.

Professor Kuhn, in his mythological treatise on 'Fire and Ambrosia,' has collected a quantity of evidence from Greek and Latin authors, which makes it appear that the fire-making instrument, whose use was kept up in Europe, was not the stick-and-groove, but the fire-drill. The operation is distinctly described as boring or drilling; and it seems, moreover, that the fire-drill was worked in ancient Europe, as in India and among the Esquimaux, with a cord or thong, for the spindle is

---

[1] Kuhn, p. 110.   [2] Stevenson, in Kuhn, p. 13.

[3] If so, the upper and lower blocks may be the *upper and lower arani*, and the spindle the *pramantha*, or *ddtra*. See Kuhn, pp. 13, 16, 78; also Boehtlingk and Roth, s. v. *arani*, *ddtra*. The anointing with butter (Kuhn, p. 78), corresponds to the use of train oil by the Esquimaux.

compared to, or spoken of as, a τρύπανον, which instrument, as appears in the passage quoted from the Odyssey at page 240, was a drill driven by a thong.[1]

The traces of the old fire-making in modern Europe lie, for the most part, in close connexion with the ancient and wide-spread rite of the New Fire, which belongs to the Aryans among other branches of the human race, and especially with one variety of this rite, which has held its own even in Germany and England into quite late times, in spite of all the efforts of the Church to put it down. This is what the Germans call *nothfeuer*, and we *needfire*; though whether the term is to be understood literally, or whether it has dropped a guttural, and stands for fire made by *kneading* or rubbing, is not clear.

What the nature and object of the needfire is, may be seen in Reiske's account of the practice in Germany in the seventeenth century:—"When a murrain has broken out among the great and small cattle, and the herds have suffered much harm, the farmers determine to make a needfire. On an appointed day there must be no single flame of fire in any house or on any hearth. From each house straw, and water, and brushwood must be fetched, and a stout oak-post driven fast into the ground, and a hole bored through it; in this a wooden wind-lass is stuck, well smeared with cart-pitch and tar, and turned round so long that, with the fierce heat and force, it gives forth fire. This is caught in proper materials, increased with straw, heath, and brushwood, till it breaks out into a full needfire; and this must be somewhat spread out lengthways between walls or fences, and the cattle and horses hunted with sticks and whips two or three times through it," etc.[2] Various ways of arranging the apparatus are mentioned by Reiske and other authorities quoted by Grimm, such as fixing the spindle between two posts, etc. How the spindle is turned is some-times doubtful; but in several places the Indian practice of driving it with a rope wound round it, and pulled backwards and forwards, comes clearly into view; while sometimes a cart wheel is spun round upon an axle; or a spindle is worked round

[1] Kuhn, 'Herabkunft des Feuers,' etc., pp. 36–40, citing Theophrastus, Hesychius, Simplicius, Festus, etc. [2] Grimm, D. M., p. 570.

with levers, or two planks are rubbed violently together, till the fire comes.[1]

The last two recorded accounts of the needfire known to Kuhn are from Hanover in 1828, and from England in 1826.[2] The 'Mirror' of June 24th of that year takes from the 'Perth Courier' a description of the rite, as performed not far from Perth, by a farmer who had lost several cattle by some disease:—"A few stones were piled together in the barn-yard, and wood-coals having been laid thereon, the fuel was ignited by *will-fire*, that is, fire obtained by friction: the neighbours having been called in to witness the solemnity, the cattle were made to pass through the flames, in the order of their dignity and age, commencing with the horses and ending with the swine."

Some varieties of the rite of the New Fire, connected with the Sun-worship so deeply rooted in the popular mind from before the time of the Vedas, were countenanced, or at least tolerated, by the Church. Such are the bonfires at Easter, Midsummer Eve, and some other times; and, in one case, there is ground for supposing that the old rite was taken up into the Roman Church, in the practice of putting out the church candles on Easter Eve, and lighting them again with consecrated new-made fire,—

> "On Easter Eve the fire all is quencht in every place,
> And fresh againe from out the flint is fetcht with solemne grace :
> The priest doth blow this against great daungers many one,
> A brande whereof doth every man with greedie mind take home,
> That, when the fearefull storme appeares, or tempest blacke arise,
> By lighting this he safe may be from stroke of hurtful skies."[3]

Here the traces of the Indian mythology come out with beautiful clearness. The lightning is the fire that flies from the heavenly fire-churn, as the gods whirl it in the clouds. The New Fire is its representative on earth; and, like the thunderbolt, preserves from the lightning-flash the house in which it is, for the lightning strikes no place twice.

But in this ceremony the flint and steel has superseded the

[1] Grimm, D. M., pp. 570-9.   [2] Kuhn, p. 45.
[3] Brand, 'Popular Antiquities;' London, 1853, vol. i. p. 157.

ancient friction-fire; and, indeed, the Western clergy, as a
rule, discountenanced it as heathenish. In the Capitularies of
Carloman, in the eighth century, there is a prohibition of " illos
sacrilegos ignes quos *niedfyr* vocant."[1] The result of this opposition by the Church was, in great measure, to break the connexion between the old festivals of the Sun, which the Church
allowed, and the lighting of the needfire, which is so closely
connected with the Sun-worship in our ancient Aryan mythology. Still, even in Germany, there are documents that bring
the two together. A glossary to the Capitularies says, " the
rustic folks in many places in Germany, and indeed on the
feast of St. John the Baptist, pull a stake from a hedge and
bind a rope round it, which they pull hither and thither till it
takes fire," etc.; and a Low German book of 1593 speaks of
the " *nodfürr*, that they sawed out of wood" to light the
St. John's bonfire, and through which the people leapt and
ran, and drove their cattle.[2]

It appears, however, that the Eastern and Western churches
differed widely in their treatment of the old rite. The Western
clergy discountenanced, and, as far as they could, put down the
needfire; but in Russia it was not only allowed, but was (and
very likely may be still) practised under ecclesiastical sanction,
the priest being the chief actor in the ceremony. This interesting fact seems not to have been known to Grimm and
Kuhn, and the following passage, which proves it, is still further remarkable as asserting that the ancient fire-making by
friction was still used in Russia for practical as well as ceremonial purposes in the last century. It is contained in an account of the adventures of four Russian sailors, who were
driven by a storm upon the desert island of East-Spitzbergen.[3]
" They knew, however, that if one rubs violently together two
pieces of dry wood, one hard and the other soft, the latter will
catch fire. Besides this being the way in which the Russian
peasants obtain fire when they are in the woods, there is also

<hr>

[1] Cap. Carlomanni in Grimm, D. M., p. 570.

[2] Grimm, D. M., pp. 570, 579. See also Migne, Lex. s. v. " Nedifri."

[3] .P. L. le Roy, 'Erzählung der Begebenheiten,' etc.; Riga, 1760. (An E. Tr. in
Pinkerton, vol. I.)

a religious ceremony, performed in every village where there is
a church, which could not have been unknown to them. Perhaps
it will be not disagreeable for me here to give an account of
this ceremony, though it does not belong to the story. The
18th of August, Old Style, is called by the Russians *Frol i
Lavior*, these being the names of two martyrs, called Florus
and Laurus in the Roman Kalendar; they fall, according to
this latter, on the 20th of the said month, when the Festival of
the Beheading of John is celebrated. On this day the Russian
peasants bring their horses to the village church, at the side of
which they have dug the evening before a pit with two outlets.
Each horse has his bridle, which is made of lime-tree bark.
They let the horses, one after the other, go into this pit, at the
opposite outlet of which the priest stands with an asperging-
brush in his hand, with which he sprinkles them with holy
water. As soon as the horses are come out, their bridles are
taken off, and they are made to go between two fires, which
are kindled with what the Russians call *Giroy agon*, that is,
' living fire,' of which I will give the explanation, after remark-
ing that the peasants throw the bridles of the horses into one of
these fires to burn them up. Here is the manner of kindling
this *Giroy agon*, or living fire. Some men take hold of the
ends of a maple staff, very dry, and about a fathom long. This
staff they hold fast over a piece of birch-wood, which must also
be very dry, and whilst they vigorously rub the staff upon the
last wood, which is much softer than the first, it inflames in a
short time, and serves to kindle the pair of fires, of which I
have just made mention."

To sum up now, in a few words, the history of the art of
making fire, it appears that the common notion that the friction of two pieces of wood was the original method used, has
strong and wide-lying evidence in its favour, and very little
that can be alleged against it. It has been seen that in many
districts where higher methods have long prevailed, its former
existence as a household art is proved by traces that have come
down to us in several different ways. Where the use of pyrites
for striking fire is found existing in company with it in North
America, it is at least likely that the fire-stick is the older in-

strument. Perhaps the most notable fact bearing on this question is the use of pyrites by the miserable inhabitants of Tierra
del Fuego. I do not know that the fire-sticks have ever been
seen among them, but it seems more reasonable to suppose that
they were used till they were supplanted by the discovery of the
fire-making property of pyrites, than to make so insignificant a
people an exception to a world-wide rule. This art of striking
fire, instead of laboriously producing it with the drill, is not,
indeed, the only thing in which the culture of this race stands
above that of their northern neighbours, for, as has been mentioned, these last were found using no navigable craft but rafts,
while the Fuegians had bark canoes, and those by no means of
the lowest quality. It is worthy of note that the Peruvians,
though they had pyrites, and broke the nodules to polish the
faces into mirrors, do not seem to have used it to strike fire
with. If they did not, their civilization stood in this matter
below that of the much-despised Fuegians. The ancient Mexicans also made mirrors of polished pyrites, and perhaps they
may have used it to strike fire ;[1] but the wooden friction-apparatus was certainly common among them. Even the fire-drills
of Peru and Mexico were of the simplest kind, twirled between
the hands without any contrivance to lessen the labour, so that
even the rude Esquimaux and Indian tribes have reached, in
this respect, a higher stage of art than these comparatively
civilized peoples.

To turn now from the art of making fire to one of its principal uses to mankind. The art of Cooking is as universal as
Fire itself among the human race ; but there are found, even
among savages, several different processes that come under the
general term, and a view of the distribution of these processes
over the world may throw some light on the early development
of Human Culture.

Roasting or broiling by direct exposure to the fire seems the
one method universally known to mankind, but the use of some
kind of oven is also very general. The Andaman Islanders

---

[1] It seems by a passage in Boturini (p. 18), that he had some reason to think
they used flint to strike fire with, and if so, as they had no iron, they probably
used pyrites.

keep fire continually smouldering in hollow trees, so that they
have only to clear away the ashes at any time to cook their
little pigs and fish.[1] In Africa, the natives take possession of
a great ant-hill, destroy the ants, and clear out the inside, leaving only the clay walls standing, which they make red hot with
a fire, so as to and bake joints of rhinoceros within.[2] But these
are unusual expedients, and a much commoner form of savage
oven is a mere pit in the ground. In the most elaborate kind
of this cooking in underground ovens, hot stones are put in
with the food, as in the familiar South-Sea Island practice,
which is too well known to need description. The Malagasy
plan seems to be the same;[3] but the Polynesians and their
connexions have by no means a monopoly of the art, which is
practised with little or no difference in other parts of the world.
The Guanches of the Canary Islands buried meat in a hole in
the ground, and lighted a fire over it;[4] and a similar practice
is still sometimes found in the island of Sardinia,[5] while among
the Beduins, and in places in North and South America, the process comes even closer to that used in the South Seas.[6] It is
this wide diffusion of the art which makes it somewhat doubtful whether Klemm is right in considering its occurrence in
Australia as one of the results of intercourse with more civilized islands. The natives cook in underground ovens on
very distant parts of the coast; sometimes hot stones are used,
and sometimes not.[7]

When meat or vegetables are kept for many hours on a
grating above a slow fire, the combination of roasting and
smoking brings the food into a state in which it will keep for a
long while, even in the tropics. Jean de Lery, in the account
of his adventures among the Indians of Brazil, about 1557, de-

<hr>

[1] Moust, p. 308.
[2] Klemm, C. G., vol. iii. p. 222. Moffat, Missionary Labours, etc., in S. Africa;
London, 1842, p. 521.
[3] Ellis, Madagascar, vol. i. p. 72.
[4] Barker-Webb and Berthelot, vol. i. part i. p. 134.
[5] Maury, 'La Terre & l'Homme;' Paris, 1857, p. 572.
[6] Klemm, C. G., vol. ii. p. 28; vol. iv. p. 120. FitzRoy, in Tr. Eth. Soc.,
1861, p. 4.
[7] Cook, 1st Voy. II., vol. iii. p. 233. Lang, p. 347. Grey, Journals, vol. i.
p. 178; vol. ii. p. 274. Klemm, C. G., vol. i. p. 307. Eyre, vol. ii. p. 249.

scribes the wooden grating set up on four forked posts, "which in their language they call a *boucan;*" on this they cooked food with a slow fire underneath, and as they did not salt their meat this process served them as a means of keeping their game and fish.[1] To the word *boucan* belongs the term *bou-canier, buccaneer,* given to the French hunters of St. Domingo, from their preparing the flesh of the wild oxen and boars in this way, and applied less appropriately to the rovers of the Spanish Main. The process has been found elsewhere in South America,[2] and perhaps as far North as Florida.[3] The Haitian name for a framework of sticks set upon posts, *barbacoa,* was adopted into Spanish and English; for instance, the Peruvian air-bridges, made over difficult ground by setting up on piles a wattled flooring covered with earth, are called *barbacoas;*[4] and Dampier speaks of having "a Barbacue of split Bamboos to sleep on."[5] The American mode of roasting on such a frame-work is the origin of our term to *barbecue,* though its meaning has changed to that of roasting an animal whole. The art of bucaning or barbecuing, as practised by the Americans, is found in Africa, in Kamchatka, the Eastern Archipelago, and the Pelew Islands;[6] and it merges into the very common process of smoking meat to make it keep.

The mere inspection of these simple and wide-spread varieties of cooking gives the ethnographer very little evidence of the way in which they have been invented and spread over the world. But from the more complex art of Boiling there is something to be learnt. There are races of mankind, such as the Australians, the Fuegians and some other South American tribes, and the Bushmen, who do not seem to have known how to boil food when they first came into the view of Europe,

[1] Lery, Hist. d'un Voy., etc., 1600, p. 153. Southey, Brazil, vol. i. p. 216; vol. iii. pp. 337, 381. The word *boucan* seems connected with that now commonly used in Brazil. "*Mocaem,* donde fizemos *moyaens, assar na labareda.*" Dias, Dic. da Lingua Tupy.

[2] Wallace, p. 220. Humboldt and Bonpland, vol. ii. p. 550. Purchas, vol. v. p. 809.   [3] Hakluyt, vol. iii. p. 307.

[4] Tschudi, 'Peru,' vol. ii. p. 202.   [5] Dampier, vol. ii. part i. p. 90.

[6] Burton, 'Central Africa,' vol. ii. p. 282. Krascheninnikow, p. 46. Dampier, vol. iii. part ii. p. 24. Keate, p. 203. See Earl, 'Papuans,' p. 165.

while the higher peoples of the world, and a great proportion
of the lower ones, have had, so long as we know anything of
them, vessels of pottery or metal which they put liquids into,
and set over the fire to boil. Between these two conditions,
however, there lies a process which has been superseded by
the higher method within modern times over a large fraction
of the earth's surface, and which there is some reason to believe once extended much further. It is even likely that the
art of Boiling, as commonly known to us, may have been developed through this intermediate process, which I propose to
call *Stone-Boiling*.

There is a North American tribe who received from their
neighbours the Ojibwas, the name of Assinaboins, or "Stone-
Boilers," from their mode of boiling their meat, of which Catlin gives a particular account. They dig a hole in the ground,
take a piece of the animal's raw hide, and press it down with
their hands close to the sides of the hole, which thus becomes
a sort of pot or basin. This they fill with water, and they
make a number of stones red-hot in a fire close by. The meat
is put into the water, and the stones dropped in till the meat
is boiled. Catlin describes the process as awkward and tedious,
and says that since the Assinaboine had learnt from the Mandans to make pottery, and had been supplied with vessels by
the traders, they had entirely done away the custom, "except-
ing at public festivals; where they seem, like all others of the
human family, to take pleasure in cherishing and perpetuating
their ancient customs."[1] Elsewhere among the Sioux or Dacotas, to whom the Assinaboine belong, the tradition has been
preserved that their fathers used to cook the game in its own
skin, which they set up on four sticks planted in the ground,
and put water, meat, and hot stones into it.[2] The Sioux had the
art of stone-boiling in common with the mass of the northern
tribes. Father Charlevoix, writing above a century ago, speaks
of the Indians of the North as using wooden kettles and boiling the water in them by throwing in red-hot stones, but even
then iron pots were superseding both these vessels and the
pottery of other tribes.[3] To specify more particularly, the

<hr>
[1] Catlin, vol. I. p. 51.   [2] Schoolcraft, part ii. p. 176.   [3] Charlevoix, vol. vi. p. 47

Micmacs and Souriquois,[1] the Blackfeet and the Crees,[2] are known to have been stone-boilers; the Shoshonees or Snake Indians, like the far more northerly tribes of Slaves, Dog-Ribs, etc.,[3] still make, or lately made, their pots of roots plaited or rather twined so closely that they will hold water, boiling their food in them with hot stones;[4] while, west of the Rocky Mountains, the Indians used similar baskets to boil salmon, acorn porridge, and other food in,[5] or wooden vessels such as Captain Cook found at Nootka Sound, and La Pérouse at Port Français.[6] Lastly, Sir Edward Belcher met with the practice of stone-boiling in 1826 among the Esquimaux of Icy Cape.[7]

So instantly is the art of stone-boiling supplanted by the kettles of the white trader, that, unless perhaps in the north-west, it might be hard to find it in existence now. But the state of things in North America, as known to us in earlier times, is somewhat as follows. The Mexicans, and the races between them and the Isthmus of Panama, were potters at the time of the Spanish discovery, and the art extended northward over an immense district, lying mostly between the Rocky Mountains and the Atlantic, and stretching up into Canada. In Eastern North America the first European discoverers found the art of earthenware-making in full operation, and forming a regular part of the women's work, and on this side of the continent, as high at least as New England, the site of an Indian village may be traced, like so many of the ancient settlements in the Old World, by innumerable fragments of pottery. But the Stone-Boilers extended far south on the Pacific side, and also occupied what may be roughly called the northern half of North America.

In that north-eastern corner of Asia which is of such extreme interest to the ethnographer, as preserving the lower human culture so near the high Asiatic civilization, and yet so little influenced by it, the art of Stone-boiling was found in full force.

<hr>

[1] Schoolcraft, part i. p. 81.
[3] Mackenzie, p. 37, and see p. 207.
[5] Schoolcraft, part iii. pp. 107, 146.
[6] Cook, Third Voy., vol. ii. p. 321.   Klemm, C. G., vol. ii. pp. 26, 69.
[7] Belcher, in Tr. Eth. Soc., vol. i. 1861, p. 133.

[2] Harmon, p. 323.
[4] Schoolcraft, part i. p. 211.

The Kamchadals, like some American tribes, used hollowed wooden troughs for the purpose, and long resisted the use of the iron cooking pots of the Russians, considering that the food only kept its flavour properly when dressed in the old-fashioned way.[1]

Thus the existence of a great district of Stone-Boilers in Northern Asia and America is made out by direct evidence, but beside this we know of the practice in a southern district of the world.

Captain Cook made a remark concerning the New Zealanders, that "having no vessel in which water can be boiled, their cooking consists wholly of baking and roasting.[2] The inference that people who have no vessel that will stand the fire must therefore be unable to boil food, may, for anything I know, be true when he makes it in Tierra del Fuego and in Australia,[3] but in New Zealand it breaks down, for there is evidence that the Maoris knew the art of stone-boiling, though they used it but little. It is found among them under circumstances which give no ground for supposing that it was introduced after Captain Cook's visit. The curious dried human heads of New Zealand, which excel any mummies that have ever been made in the preservation of the features of the dead, were first brought over to England by Cook's party. From a careful description of the process of preparing them, made since, it appears that one thing done to them is to throw them "into boiling water, into which red-hot stones are continually cast, to keep up the heat;"[4] and a remark made by another writer places the existence of stone-boiling as a native New Zealand art beyond question. "The New Zealanders, although destitute of vessels in which to boil water, had an ingenious way of heating water to the boiling point, for the purpose of making shell-fish open. This was done by putting red-hot stones into wooden vessels full of water."[5] When, therefore, we find them boiling and eating the berries of the *Laurus tawa*, which are harmless when boiled, but poisonous in their raw state, it is

[1] Kracheninnikow, p. 30.   Erman, Reise, vol. iii. p. 423.
[2] Cook, First Voy. II., vol. iii. p. 51; also Third Voy., vol. i. p. 158.
[3] First Voy. II., vol. ii. p. 59; vol. iii. p. 233.
[4] Yate, 'New Zealand,' p. 132.   [5] Thomson, 'New Zealand,' vol. i. p. 160.

not necessary to suppose this to have been found out since
Captain Cook's time, as the boiling was probably done before
with hot stones.[1]

In several other Polynesian islands, it appears from Cook's
journals that stone-boiling was in ordinary use in cookery.
The making of a native pudding in Tahiti is thus described.
Bread-fruit, ripe plantains, taro, and palm or pandanus nuts,
were rasped, scraped, or beaten up fine, and baked separately.
A quantity of juice, expressed from cocoa-nut kernels, was put
into a large tray or wooden vessel. The other articles, hot
from the oven, were deposited in this vessel, and a few hot
stones were also put in to make the contents simmer. Few
puddings in England, he says, equal these. In the island of
Anamooka, they brought him a mess of fish, soup, and yams
stewed in cocoa-nut liquor, "probably in a wooden vessel, with
hot stones." The practice seems to have existed in the Marquesas, and in Huaheine he describes the preparation of a dish
of *poi* in a wooden trough with hot stones.[2] What the Polynesian notion of a pudding is, as to size, may be gathered from
the account of two missionaries who arrived at the island of
Rurutu, and were received by a native who paddled out to
meet them through a rough sea, in a wooden *poi*-dish, seven
feet long and two and a half wide.[3]

I fear that the Tahitian recipe for making *poi* must spoil the
good old story of Captain Wallis's tea-urn. A native who was
breakfasting on board the Dolphin saw the tea-pot filled from
the urn, and presently turned the cock again and put his hand
underneath, with such effects as may be imagined. Captain
Wallis, knowing that the natives had no earthen vessels, and
that boiling in a pot over the fire was a novelty to them, and
putting all these things together in telling the story, interpreted the howls of the scalded native as he danced about the
cabin, and the astonishment of the rest of the visitors, as
proving that the Tahitians "having no vessel in which water
could be subjected to the action of fire, ... had no more idea

[1] Yate, p. 43.

[2] Cook, Third Voy., vol. ii. p. 49 ; vol. i. p. 233. Second Voy., vol. i. p. 310. First
Voy. II., vol. ii. p. 251.   [3] Tyerman & Bennet, vol. i. p. 493.

that it could be made hot, than that it could be made solid."[1] No doubt the natives were surprised at hot water coming out of so unlikely a place, but the world seems to have accepted both the story and the inference without stopping to consider that hot water could not be much of a novelty among people to whom boiled pudding was an article of daily food. Captain Wallis's story (as is so commonly the case with accounts of savages) may be matched elsewhere. "And we went now," says Kotzebue, in the account of his visit to the Radack islands, "to Rarick's dwelling, where the kettle had already been set on the fire, and the natives were assembled round it, looking at the boiling water, which seemed to them alive." Yet on another island of the same chain it is remarked that the *mogomuk* is made by drying the root of a plant, and pressing the meal into lumps; when it is to be eaten, some of this is broken off, stirred with water in a cocoa-nut shell, and boiled till it swells up into a thick porridge ("und kocht ihn, bis er zu einem dicken Brei aufquillt,"), etc.[2]

Though the natives of the islands mentioned, and no doubt of many others, were still stone-boilers in Cook's time, pottery had already made its appearance in Polynesia, in districts so situated that the art may reasonably be supposed to have travelled from island to island from the Eastern Archipelago, where perhaps the Malays received it from Asia. By Cook and later explorers earthen vessels were found in the Pelew, Fiji, and Tonga groups, and in New Caledonia.[3] By this time it is likely that these and European vessels may have put an end to stone-boiling in Polynesia, so that its displacement by the introduction of pottery and metal will have taken place by the same combination of the influence of neighbouring tribes and of Europeans which have produced a similar effect in North America.

This is what history tells us of the art, but there is some slight evidence which may, perhaps, lead us to infer that the

<hr>

[1] Wallis, H., vol. i. pp. 240, 264.   [2] Kotzebue, vol. ii. pp. 47, 65.
[3] Cook, Second Voy., vol. i. p. 214; vol. ii. p. 105. Third Voy., vol. L p. 375. Klemm, C. G., vol. iv. p. 272. Williams, 'Fiji,' vol. i. p. 60. Turner, p. 424. Mariner, vol. ii. p. 272. Keate, p. 336.

Stone-boilers once occupied districts in Europe. In spite of
ages of contact with the Indo-European race, a branch of the
great Tatar family, the Finns, have kept up into modern times
a relic of the practice.   Linnæus, on his famous Lapland Tour,
in 1732, recorded the fact that in East Bothland "The Finnish
liquor called Lura is prepared like other beer, except not being
boiled, instead of which red-hot stones are thrown into it."[1]
Moreover, the quantities of stones, evidently calcined, which
are found buried in our own country, sometimes in the sites of
ancient dwellings, give great probability to the inference which
has been drawn from them, that they were used in cooking.
It is true that their use may have been for baking in underground ovens, a practice found among races who are Stone-
boilers, and others who are not.

In Asia, I have met with no positive evidence of the existence of stone-boiling beyond Kamchatka, but some extremely rude boiling-vessels have been observed among Sibe.ian
tribes, the use of which is either to be explained by the absence
or scarcity of earthenware or metal pots, or by the keeping up
of old habits belonging to a time of such absence or scarcity.
The Dutch envoy, Ysbrants Ides, remarks of the Ostyaks, " I
have also seen a copper kettle among them, and some other
kettles of bark sewed together, in which they can boil food
over the hot coals, but not in the flame of the fire."[2]   Now
just such bark-kettles as these have been seen in use among a
North American tribe on the Unijah, or Peace River, near the
Rocky Mountains. They were stone-boilers, using for this
purpose the regular *watape* pots, or rather baskets, of woven
roots of spruce fir, but they had also kettles, " made of spruce-
bark, which they hang over the fire, but at such a distance as
to receive the heat without being within reach of the blaze ;
a very tedious operation."[3] In Siberia, among the Ostyaks, the
practice has been observed of using the paunch of the slaughtered beast as a vessel to cook the blood in over the fire,[4] and

<hr>

[1] Linnæus, Tour, vol. ii. p. 231.
[2] E. Ysbrants Ides, ' Reiss naar China ;' Amsterdam, 1710, p. 27.
[3] Mackenzie, p. 207.
[4] Erman (E. Tr.), vol. ii. pp. 456, 457.

the same thing has been noticed among the Reindeer Koriaks.[1]
Thus the story told by Herodotus of the Scythians, who, when
they had not a suitable cauldron, used to boil the flesh of the
sacrificed beast in its own paunch,[2] seems to give a glimpse of
a state of things in the centre of Asia, resembling that which
has continued into modern times in the remote North-East. It
is thus not unlikely that the use of stone-boiling, to meet the
want of suitable vessels for direct boiling over the fire, may
once have had a range in Asia far beyond the Kamchatkan
promontory.[3]

It may be that the more convenient boiling, in vessels set
over the fire, was generally preceded in the world by the
clumsier stone-boiling, of which the history, so far as I have
been able to make it out from evidence within my reach, has
thus been sketched.   Of vessels used for the higher kind
of boiling, as commonly known to us, something may now be
said.

It is not absolutely necessary that vessels of earthenware,
metal, etc., should be used for this purpose.   Potstone, lapis
ollaris, has been used by the Esquimaux, and by various Old
World peoples, to make vessels which will stand the fire.[4]
The Asiatic paunch-kettles have just been mentioned, and
kettles of skins have been described among the Esquimaux,[5]
and even among the inhabitants of the Hebrides, of whose way
of life George Buchanan gives the following curious account :
—"In food, clothing, and all domestic matters, they use the
ancient parsimony.   Their meat is supplied by hunting and
fishing.   The flesh they boil with water in the paunch or hide
of the slaughtered beast ; out hunting they sometimes eat it
raw, when the blood has been pressed out.   For drink they
have the broth of the meat.   Whey that has been kept for
years, they also drink greedily at their feasts.   This kind of

<hr>

[1] Krachenlennikow, p. 142.

[2] Herod., iv. 61.

[3] The frequent use of wicker baskets for holding liquids, in Africa, may have a
bearing on the history of stone-boiling.   See mention of hot stones for melting or
boiling fat, in Bleek, ' Reynard in Africa,' pp. 8-10.

[4] Crantz, p. 78 ; Linnæus, vol. i. p. 356 : Klemm, C. G., vol. ii. p. 266, etc. etc.

[5] Martin Frobisher, in ' Hakluyt,' vol. iii. pp. 68, 95.

liquor they call bland."[1] Beside these animal materials, parts of several plants will answer the purpose, as the bark used for kettles in Asia and America, the spathes of palms, in which food is often boiled in South America,[2] the split bamboos in which the Dyaks, the Sumatrans, and the Stiéns of Cambodia, boil their rice, and cocoa-nut shells, as just mentioned in the Radack group; Captain Cook saw a cocoa-nut shell used in Tahiti, to dry up the blood of a native dog in, over the fire.[3] These facts should be borne in mind in considering the following theory of the Origin of the Art of Pottery.

It was, I believe, Goguet who first propounded, in the last century, the notion that the way in which pottery came to be made, was that people daubed such combustible vessels as these with clay, to protect them from the fire, till they found that the clay alone would answer the purpose, and thus the art of pottery came into the world. The idea was not a mere effort of his imagination, for he had met with a description of the plastering of wooden vessels with clay in the Southern Hemisphere. It is related that a certain Captain Gonneville sailed from Honfleur in 1503, doubled the Cape of Good Hope, and came to the Southern Indies. There he found a gentle and joyous people, living by hunting and fishing, and a little agriculture, and he speaks of cloaks of mats and skins, feather work, bows and arrows, beds of mats, villages of thirty to eighty huts of stakes and wattles, etc., " and their household utensils of wood, even their boiling-pots, but plastered with a kind of clay, a good finger thick, which prevents the fire from burning them."[4] What to make of this curious story I do not know, but as to the theory of the origin of pottery which Goguet founded upon it, a quantity of evidence has made its appearance since his time, which all goes in its favour.

[1] 'Rerum Scoticarum Historia, anctore Georgio Buchanano Scoto;' (ad ea.) Edinburgh, 1528, p. 7.

[2] Spix and Martius, vol. ii. p. 688. Wallace, p. 508.

[3] St. John, vol. i. p. 137. Marsden, p. 60. Mouhot, vol. ii. p. 245. Cook, Third Voy., vol. ii. p. 35. See Coleman, p. 318; Mariner, vol. ii. p. 272.

[4] Goguet, vol. i. p. 77. 'Mémoires touchant l'Établissement d'une Mission Chrestienne dans le troisième monde, autrement appellé la Terre Australe,' etc.; Paris, 1663, pp. 10–16.

The comparison of two accounts of vessels found, one among the Esquimaux, the other among their neighbours the Unalashkans (whose language contains proofs of intimate contact with them[1]), may serve to give an idea of the way in which clay may come to supersede less convenient materials, and a gradual approach be made towards the potter's art. When James Hall was in Greenland, in 1605, he found the natives boiling food over their lamps, in vessels with stone bottoms, and sides of whale's fins.[2] In Unalashka, Captain Cook found that some of the natives had got brass kettles from the Russians, but those who had not, made their own "of a flat stone, with sides of clay, not unlike a standing pye."[3] He thought it likely that they had learnt to boil from the Russians, but the Russians could hardly have taught them to make such vessels as these, and the appearance of a kettle with a stone bottom (no doubt potstone), and sides of another material, at the two opposite sides of America, gives ground for supposing it to have been in common use in high latitudes.

From the examination of an earthen vessel from the Fiji Islands, Dr. D. S. Price considers that it was very likely made by moulding clay on the outside of the shell or rind of some fruit. The vessel in question is made watertight after the South American manner by a varnish of resin. The evident and frequent adoption of gourd-shapes in the earthenware of distant parts of the world does not prove much, but as far as it goes it tells in favour of the opinion that such gourd-like vessels may be the successors of real gourds, made into pottery by a plastering of clay. Some details given in 1841 by Squier and Davis, in their account of the monuments in the Mississippi Valley, are much more to the purpose. "In some of the Southern States, it is said, the kilns, in which the ancient pottery was baked, are now occasionally to be met with. Some are represented still to contain the ware, partially burned, and retaining the rinds of the gourds, etc., over which they were modelled, and which had not been entirely removed by the

[1] Buschmann, Azt. Spr., p. 702.   [2] Purchas, vol. iii p. 817.
[3] Cook, Third Voy., vol. ii. p. 510.

fire."   " Among the Indians along the Gulf, a greater degree
of skill was displayed than with those on the upper waters of
the Mississippi and on the lakes. Their vessels were generally
larger and more symmetrical, and of a superior finish. They
moulded them over gourds and other models and baked them
in ovens. In the construction of those of large size, it was
customary to model them in baskets of willow or splints, which,
at the proper period, were burned off, leaving the vessel perfect in form, and retaining the somewhat ornamental markings
of their moulds. Some of those found on the Ohio seem to
have been modelled in bags or nettings of coarse thread or
twisted bark. These practices are still retained by some of the
remote western tribes. Of this description of pottery many
specimens are found with the recent deposits in the mounds."[1]
Prince Maximilian of Wied makes the following remark on
some earthen vessels found in Indian mounds near Harmony,
on the Wabash River:—"They were made of a sort of grey
clay, marked outside with rings, and seemed to have been
moulded in a cloth or basket, being marked with impressions
or figures of this kind."[2]

It has been thought, too, that the early pottery of Europe
retains in its ornamentation traces of having once passed
through a stage in which the clay was surrounded by basket-
work or netting, either as a backing to support the finished
vessel, or as a mould to form it in. Dr. Klemm advanced this
view twenty years ago. "The imitation (of natural vessels) in
clay presupposes numerous trials. In the Friendly Islands, we
find vessels which are still in an early stage; they are made of
clay, slightly burnt, and enclosed in plaited work; so also the
oldest German vessels seem to have been, for we observe on
those which remain an ornamentation in which plaiting is imitated by incised lines. What was no longer wanted as a necessity was kept up as an ornament."[3]

Dr. Daniel Wilson made a similar remark, some years later,
on early British urns which, he says, " may have been strength-

<hr>

[1] Squier & Davis, pp. 105, 187.
[2] Pr. Max. Voyage, vol. i. p. 108. Klemm, C. G., vol. ii. p. 68.
[3] Klemm, C. G., vol. i. p. 189.

ened by being surrounded with a platting of cords or rushes. . . . It is certain that very many of the indented patterns on British pottery have been produced by the impress of twisted cords on the wet clay,—the intentional imitation, it may be, of undesigned indentations originally made by the platted network on ruder urns," etc.[1]   Mr. G. J. French mentions experiments made by him in support of his views on the derivation of the interlaced or guilloche ornaments on early Scottish crosses, etc., from imitation of earlier structures of wickerwork.   He coated baskets with clay, and found the wicker patterns came out on all, but better on the sun-dried ones than in those burnt in the kiln, in which the markings were injured by the shrinkage, and he even seems to think that some ancient urns still preserved were actually moulded in this way, judging from the lip being marked as if the wicker-work had been turned in over the clay coating inside.[2]

Taken all together, the evidence of so many imperfect and seemingly transitional forms of pottery makes it probable that it was through such stages that the art grew up into the more perfect form in which we usually find it, and in which it has come to be clearly understood that clay, alone or with some mixture of sand or such matters to prevent cracking, is capable of being used without any extraneous support.

Such is the evidence by means of which I have attempted to trace the progress of mankind in three important arts, whose early history lies for the most part out of the range of direct record.   Its examination brings into view a gradual improvement in methods of producing fire; the supplanting of a rude means of boiling food by a higher one; and a progress from the vessels of gourds, bark, or shell of the lower races to the pottery and metal of the higher.   On the whole, progress in these useful arts appears to be the rule, and whether its steps be slow or rapid, a step once made does not seem often to be retraced.

<hr>

[1] Wilson, Archæology, etc., of Scotland, p. 289.
[2] G. J. French, An Attempt, etc.; Manchester (printed), 1858.

CHAPTER X.

SOME REMARKABLE CUSTOMS.

It has long been an accepted doctrine that among the similar customs found prevailing in distant countries, there are some which are evidence of worth to the ethnologist. But in dealing with these things he has to answer, time after time, a new form of the hard question that stands in his way in so many departments of his work. He must have derived from observation of many cases a general notion of what Man does and does not do, before he can say of any particular custom which he finds in two distant places, either that it is likely that a similar state of things may have produced it more than once, or that it is unlikely—that it is even so unlikely as to approach the limit of impossibility, that such a thing should have grown up independently in the two, or three, or twenty places where he finds it. In the first case it is worth little or nothing to him as evidence bearing on the early history of mankind, but in the latter it goes with more or less force to prove that the people who possess it are allied by blood, or have been in contact, or have been influenced indirectly one from the other or both from a common source, or that some combination of these things has happened; in a word, that there has been historical connexion between them.

I give some selected cases of the Argument from Similar Customs, both where it seems sound and where it seems unsound, before proceeding to the main object of this chapter, which is to select and bring into view, from the enormous mass

of raw material that lies before the student, four groups of
world-wide customs which seem to have their roots deep in the
early history of mankind.

It is a remarkable thing to find in Africa the practice which
we associate exclusively with Siam and the neighbouring countries, of paying divine honours to the pale-coloured, or as it
is called, the "white" elephant. A native of Enarea (in East
Africa, south of Abyssinia) told Dr. Krapf that white ele-
phants, whose hide was like the skin of a leper, were found in
his country, but such an animal must not be killed, for it is
considered an Adbar or protector of man and has religious
honours paid to it, and any one who killed it would be put to
death.[1] There may be a historical connexion between the veneration of the white elephant in Asia and Africa, but the
habit of man to regard unusual animals, or plants, or stones,
with superstitious feelings of reverence or horror is so general,
that no prudent ethnologist would base an argument upon it,
and still less when he finds that in Africa the albino buffalo
shares the sanctity of the elephant.

On the other hand, a custom prevalent in two districts comparatively near these may be quoted as an example of sound
evidence of the kind in question. In his account of the Sulu
Islands, north-east of Borneo, Mr. Spenser St. John speaks of
a superstition in those countries, that if gold or pearls are put
in a packet by themselves they will decrease and disappear,
but if a few grains of rice are added, they will keep. Pearls
they believe will actually increase by this, and the natives always put grains of rice in the packets both of gold and precious
stones.[2] Now Dr. Livingstone mentions the same thing at the
gold diggings of Manica in East Africa, south of the Zambesi,
where the natives " bring the dust in quills, and even put in a
few seeds of a certain plant as a charm to prevent their losing
any of it in the way."[3] The custom was probably transmitted
through the Mahometans, who form a known channel of connexion between Africa and the Malay Islands, but its very existence alone would prove that there must have been a connecting link somewhere.

[1] Krapf, p. 67.   [2] St. John, vol. ii. p. 235.   [3] Livingstone, p. 638.

Intercourse between Asia and America in early times is not brought to our knowledge by the direct historical information by which, for instance, distant parts of Asia and Africa are brought into contact; still there is indirect evidence tending to prove Asiatic influence far in the interior of North America, and the following may, perhaps, be held in some degree to confirm and supplement it. Johannes de Plano Carpini, describing in 1246 the manners and customs of the Tatars, says that one of their superstitious traditions concerns "sticking a knife into the fire, or in any way touching the fire with a knife, or even taking meat out of the kettle with a knife, or cutting near the fire with an axe; for they believe that so the head of the fire would be cut off."[1] The prohibition was no doubt connected with the Asiatic fire-worship, and it seems to have long been known in Europe, for it stands among the Pythagorean maxims, "πῦρ μαχαίρᾳ μὴ σκαλεύειν," "not to stir the fire with a sword," or, as it is given elsewhere, σιδήρῳ, "with an iron."[2] In the far north-east of Asia it may be found in the remarkable catalogue of ceremonial sins of the Kamchadals, among whom "it is a sin to take up a burning ember with the knife-point, and light tobacco, but it must be taken hold of with the bare hands."[3] How is it possible to separate from these the following statement, taken out of a list of superstitions of the Sioux Indians of North America? "They must not stick an awl or needle into. . . .a stick of wood on the fire. No person must chop on it with an axe or knife, or stick an awl into it. . . . Neither are they allowed to take a coal from the fire with a knife, or any other sharp instrument."[4]

The first of the four groups of customs, selected as examples of an argument taking a yet wider range, is based upon the idea that disease is commonly caused by bits of wood, stone, hair, or other foreign substances, having got inside the body of the patient. Accordingly, the malady is to be cured by the medicine-man extracting the hurtful things, usually by sucking

[1] Vincentius Belluacensis, 'Speculum Historiale,' 1473, book xxxii. c. vii.
[2] Diog. Laert. viii. 1, 17. Plut. 'De Educatione Puerorum,' xvii.
[3] G. W. Steller, 'Beschreibung von dem Lande Kamtschatka;' Frankfort, 1774, p. 274. [4] Schoolcraft, part iii. p. 230.

the affected part till they come out. Mr. Backhouse describes
the proceedings of a native doctress in South Africa, which will
serve as a typical case. A man was taken ill with a pain in his
side, and a Fingo witch was sent for. As she was quite naked,
except a rope round her waist, the missionary who lived in the
place declined to assist at the ceremony himself, but sent his
wife. The doctress sucked at the man's side, and produced
some grains of Indian corn, which she said she had drawn from
inside him, and which had caused the disease. The missionary's
wife looked in her mouth, and there was nothing there; but
when she sucked again and again, there came more grains of
corn. At last a piece of tobacco-leaf made its appearance with
the corn, and showed how the trick was done. The woman
swallowed the tobacco first to produce nausea, and then a
quantity of Indian corn, and by the help of the rope round her
waist, she was able so to control her stomach as only to produce a few grains at a time.[1] In North and South America,
in Borneo, and in Australia, the same cure is part of the doctor's work, with the difference only that bones, bits of wood,
stones, lizards, fragments of knife-blades, balls of hair, and
other miscellaneous articles are produced, and that the tricks
by which he keeps up the pretence of sucking them out are
perhaps seldom so clever as the African one.[2] In Australia the
business is profitably worked by one sorcerer charming bits of
quartz into the victim's body, so that another has to be sent for
to get them out.[3] It has been already mentioned that in the
North of Ireland the wizards still extract elf-bolts, that is, stone
arrow-heads, from the bodies of bewitched cattle.[4] Southey,
who knew a great deal about savages, goes so far as to say of
this cure by sucking out extraneous objects, as practised by
the native sorcerers of Brazil, that "their mode of quackery
was that which is common to all savage conjurors;"[5] at any
rate, its similarity in so many and distant regions is highly re-

[1] Backhouse, 'Africa,' p. 231.
[2] Long's Exp., vol. I. p. 261.   Klemm, C. G., vol. II. pp. 169, 385.   St. John,
vol. I. pp. 62, 201.   Lang, 'Queensland,' p. 342.   Eyre, vol. ii. p. 360.
[3] Grey, Journals, vol. ii. p. 337.
[4] Wilde, Cat. R. I. A., p. 19.   [5] Southey, 'Brazil,' vol. I. p. 239.

markable. It is to be noticed that, in this special imposture, we have not only the belief that a disease is caused by some extraneous substance inside the body, but we have also this belief turned to account in remote parts of the world by the same knavish trick. It is hard even to see a reason for the belief, and much harder to imagine the sucking-cure to have grown independently out of it in several places.

In the civilized world, the prohibition from marrying kindred has usually stopped short of forbidding the marriage of cousins german. It is true that the Roman Ecclesiastical Law is, at least in theory, very different from this. Hallam says, "Gregory I. pronounces matrimony to be unlawful as far as the seventh degree, and even, if I understand his meaning, as long as any relationship could be traced, which seems to have been the maxim of strict theologians, though not absolutely enforced."[1] But this disability may be reduced by the dispensing power to the ordinary limits; and in practice the Society of Friends go farther than the Canon Law, for they really prohibit the marriage of first cousins. If, however, we examine the law of marriage among certain of the middle and lower races scattered far and wide over the world, a variety of such prohibitions will be found, which overstep the practice, and sometimes even approach the theory of the Roman Church. The matter belongs properly to that interesting, but difficult and almost unworked subject, the Comparative Jurisprudence of the lower races, and no one not versed in Civil Law could do it justice; but it may be possible for me to give a rough idea of its various modifications, as found among races widely separated from one another in place, and, so far as we know, in history.

In India, it is unlawful for a Brahman to marry a wife whose clan-name or *gotra* (literally, "cow-stall") is the same as his own, a prohibition which bars marriage among relatives in the male line indefinitely. This law appears in the Code of Manu as applying to the three first castes, and connexions on the female side are also forbidden to marry within certain wide limits. The Abbé Dubois, nevertheless, noticed among the Hindoos a tendency to form marriages between families already connected

[1] Hallam, 'Middle Ages,' ch. vii. part ii. See Du Cange, s. v. "generatio."

by blood; but inasmuch as, according to his account, relatives
in the male line go on calling one another brother and sister,
and do not marry, as far as relationship can be traced, were it
to the tenth generation, and the same in the female line, the
very natural wish to draw closer the family tie can only be accomplished by crossing the male and female line, the brother's
child marrying the sister's, and so on.[1]

The Chinese people is divided into a number of clans, each
distinguished by a name, which is borne by all its members,
and corresponds to a surname, or better to a clan-name, among
ourselves, for the wife adopts her husband's, and the sons and
daughters inherit it. The number of these clan-names is limited; Davis thinks there are not much above a hundred, but
other writers talk of three hundred, and even of a thousand.
Now, the Chinese law is that a man may not marry a woman
of his own surname, so that relationship by the male side, however distant, is an absolute bar to marriage. This stringent
prohibition of marriage between descendants of the male
branch would seem to be very old, for the Chinese refer its
origin to the mythic times of the Emperor Fu-hi, whose reign
is placed before the Hea dynasty, which began, according to
Chinese annals, in 2207 B.C. Fu-hi, it is related, divided the
people into 100 clans, giving each a name, " and did not allow
a man to marry a woman of the same name, whether a relative
or not, a law which is still actually in force." There appear to
be also prohibitions applying within a narrower range to relation on the female side, and to certain kinds of affinity. Du
Halde says, that " persons who are of the same family, or who
bear the same name, however distant their degree of affinity
may be, cannot marry together. Thus, the laws do not allow
two brothers to marry two sisters, nor a widower to marry his
son to the daughter of a widow whom he marries."[2]

In Siam, the seventh degree of blood-affinity is the limit
within which marriage is prohibited, with the exception that

<hr>

[1] Dubois, vol. i. p. 10. Manu, iii. 5. See Coleman, p. 201.
[2] Davis, vol. i. p. 204. Purchas, vol. iii. pp. 367, 394. Goguet, vol. iii. p. 328.
Du Halde, Descr. de la Chine; The Hague, 1736, vol. ii. p. 145. De Mailla,
vol. i. p. 0.

the king may marry his sister, as among the Incas, the Lagide dynasty, etc., and even his daughter.[1] Among the Land Dayaks of Borneo the marriage of first cousins is said to be prohibited, and a fine of a jar (which represents a considerable value) imposed on second cousins who marry.[2] In Sumatra, Marsden says that first cousins, the children of two brothers, may not marry, while the sister's son may marry the brother's daughter, but not *vice versâ*.[3] In the same island, it is stated, upon the authority of Sir Stamford Raffles, that the Battas hold intermarriage in the same tribe to be a heinous crime, and that they punish the delinquents after their ordinary manner by cutting them up alive, and eating them grilled or raw with salt and red pepper. It is stated distinctly that their reason for considering such marriages as criminal is that the man and woman had ancestors in common.[4]

Among the Tatar race in Asia and Europe, similar restrictions are to be found. The Ostyaks hold it a sin for two persons of the same family name to marry, so that a man must not take a wife of his own tribe.[5] The Tunguz do not marry second cousins; the Samoieds "avoid all degrees of consanguinity in marrying to such a degree, that a man never marries a girl descended from the same family with himself, however distant the affinity;" and the Lapps have a similar custom.[6] Even among the Semitic race, who, generally speaking, rival the Caribs in the practice of marrying "in and in," something of the kind is found; the tribe Hebua always marries into the tribe Modjar, and *vice versâ*.[7]

In Africa, the marriage of cousins is looked upon as illegal in some tribes, and the practice of a man not marrying in his own clan is found in various places.[8] Munzinger, the Swiss

<hr>

[1] Bowring, vol. i. p. 185. [2] St. John, vol. i. p. 192. [3] Marsden, p. 228.

[4] Letter of Raffles to Marsden, in Dr. W. Cooke Taylor, The Nat. Hist. of Society, vol. i. pp. 122–6.

[5] Bastian, vol. iii. p. 299.

[6] Klemm, C. G., vol. iii. p. 68. Acc. of Samoiedia, in Pinkerton, vol. ii. p. 532. Richardson, 'Polar Regions,' p. 345.

[7] Bastian, *l. c.*

[8] Casalis, p. 191. Backhouse, 'Africa,' p. 182. Burton in Tr. Eth. Soc., 1861, p. 321. Du Chaillu, p. 388.

traveller in East Africa, suggests Christian influence as having
operated in this direction. The Beni Amer, north of Abyssinia,
follow the rules of Islam, cousins often marrying; "the Beit
Hidel and the Allabje, on the other hand, mindful of their
Christian origin, observe blood-relationship to seven degrees."[1]
In Madagascar, Ellis says that "certain ranks are not permitted under any circumstances to intermarry, and affinity to
the sixth generation also forbids intermarriage, yet the principal restrictions against intermarriages respect descendants
on the female side. Collateral branches on the male side are
permitted in most cases to intermarry, on the observance of a
slight but proscribed ceremony, which is supposed to remove
the impediment or disqualification arising out of consanguinity."[2]

Among the natives of Australia, prohibitory marriage laws
have been found, but they are very far from being uniform, and
may sometimes have been misunderstood. Sir George Grey's
account is that the Australians, so far as he is acquainted with
them, are divided into great clans, and use the clan-name as a
sort of surname beside the individual name. Children take the
family name of the mother, and a man cannot marry a woman
of his own name, so that here it would seem that only relationship by the female side is taken into account. One effect of
the division of clans in this way, is that the children of the
same father by different wives, having different names, may be
obliged to take opposite sides in a quarrel.[3] Mr. Eyre's experience in South Australia does not, however, correspond with
Sir George Grey's in the West and North-West.[4] Collins believed the custom to be for a native to steal a wife from a tribe
at enmity with his own, and to drag her, stunned with blows,
home through the woods; her relations not avenging the
affront, but taking an opportunity of retaliating in kind. It
appears from Nind's account, that in some districts the population is divided into two clans, and a man of one clan can
only marry a woman of another.[5] In East Australia, Lang describes a curious and complex system. Through a large ex-

---

[1] Munsinger, p. 310.
[2] Ellis, 'Madagascar,' vol. i. p. 161.
[3] Grey, 'Journals,' vol. ii. pp. 225-30.
[4] Eyre, vol. ii. p. 330.
[5] Collins, vol. i. p. 550.   Klemm C. G., vol. i. pp. 288, 310.

tent of the interior, among tribes speaking different dialects, there are four names for men, and four for women, Ippai and Ippata, Kubbi and Kapota, Kumbo and Buta, Murri and Mata. If we call these four sets A, B, C, D, then the rule is that a man or woman of the tribe A must marry into B, and a member of the tribe C into D, and *vice versâ*, but the child whose father is A, takes the name of D, and so on; A's = D; B's = C; C's = B; D's = A; and the mother's name answers equally well to give the name of the child, if the mother is of the tribe B, her child will belong to the tribe D, and so on.

This ingenious arrangement, it will be seen, has much the same effect as the Hindoo regulations in preventing intermarriage in the male or female line, but allowing the male and female line to cross; the children of two brothers or two sisters cannot marry, but the brother's child may marry the sister's. Lang, however, mentions a further regulation, probably made to meet some incidental circumstances, as, so far as it goes, it stultifies the whole system; A may also marry into his or her own tribe, and the children take the name of C.[1]

In America, the custom of marrying out of the clan is frequent and well marked. More than twenty years ago, Sir George Grey called attention to the division of the Australians into families, each distinguished by the name of some animal or vegetable, which served as their crest or *kobong*; the practice of reckoning clanship from the mother; and the prohibition of marriage within the clan, as all bearing a striking resemblance to similar usages found among the natives of North America. The Indian tribes are usually divided into clans, each distinguished by a *totem* (Algonquin, *do-daim*, that is "town-mark"), which is commonly some animal, as a bear, wolf, deer, etc., and may be compared on the one hand to a crest, and on the other to a surname. The totem appears to be held as proof of descent from a common ancestor, and therefore the prohibition from marriage of two persons of the same totem must act as a bar on the side the totem descends on, which is generally, if not always, on the female side. Such a prohibition is often mentioned by writers on the North American

Indians.[1] Morgan's account of the Iroquois' rules is particularly remarkable. The father and child can never be of the same clan, descent going in all cases by the female line. Each nation had eight tribes, in two sets of four each.

1. Wolf,   Bear,   Beaver,   Turtle.
2. Deer,   Snipe,   Heron,   Hawk.

Originally a Wolf might not marry a Bear, Beaver, or Turtle, reckoning himself their brother, but he might marry into the second set, Deer, etc., whom he considered his cousins, and so on with the rest. But in later times a man is allowed to marry into any tribe but his own.[2] A recent account from North-West America describes the custom among the Indians of Nootka Sound; "a Whale, therefore, may not marry a Whale, nor a Frog a Frog. A child, again, always takes the crest of the mother, so that if the mother be a Wolf, all her children will be Wolves. As a rule, also, descent is traced from the mother, not from the father."[3]

The analogy of the North American Indian custom is therefore with that of the Australians in making clanship on the female side a bar to marriage, but if we go down further south into Central America, the reverse custom, as in China, makes its appearance. Diego de Landa says of the people of Yucatan, that no one took a wife of his name, on the father's side, for this was a very vile thing among them; but they might marry cousins german on the mother's side.[4] Further south, below the Isthmus, both the clanship and the prohibition reappear on the female side. Bernau says that among the Arrawaks of British Guiana, "Caste is derived from the mother, and children are allowed to marry into their father's family, but not into that of their mother."[5] Lastly, Father Martin Dobrizhoffer says that the Guaranis avoided, as highly criminal, marriage with the most distant relatives, and, speaking of the Abipones, he makes the following statement:—"Though the paternal indulgence of the Roman Pontiffs makes the first and

---

[1] Grey, l. c. Schoolcraft, part i. p. 53; part ii. p. 49. Loskiel, p. 72. Talbot, Disc. of Ledyard, p. 4.

[2] L. H. Morgan, p. 79.   [3] Mayne, Brit. Columbia, p. 257.

[4] Landa, p. 140.   [5] Bernau, p. 29.

second degrees of relationship alone a bar to the marriage of
the Indians, yet the Abipones, instructed by nature and the
example of their ancestors, abhor the very thought of marrying
any one related to them by the most distant tie of relationship.
Long experience has convinced me, that the respect to consanguinity, by which they are deterred from marrying into
their own families, is implanted by nature in the minds of most
of the people of Paraguay," etc.[1]

It is likely that experience of the evils of marrying near relatives may be the main ground of this series of restrictions in
different parts of the world. Professor Lazarus, whose opinion
I asked about the matter, expressed this view, with the just
remarks that the observation and reasoning of savages are
often very accurate in practical matters requiring no instrument
for their observation, and that old people with a personal experience ranging through five or six generations would have a
fair ground for judging on such a question. If this physiolo-
gical objection, often exaggerated beyond reasonable limits, be
the principal basis of the series of restrictions, their various,
anomalous, and inconsistent forms may be connected with in-
terfering causes, and this one in particular, that the especial
means of tracing kindred is by a system of surnames, clan-
names, totems, etc. But this system is necessarily one-sided,
and though it will keep up the record of descent either on the
male or female side perfectly and for ever, it cannot record
both at once. In practice, the races of the world who keep
such a record at all have had to elect which of the two lines,
male or female, they will keep up by the family name or sign,
while the other line, having no such easy means of record, is
more or less neglected, and soon falls out of sight. Under
these circumstances, it would be quite natural that the sign
should come to be considered rather than the reality, the name
rather than the relationship it records, and that a series of one-
sided restrictions should come into force, now bearing upon the
male side rather than the female, and now upon the female side
rather than the male, roughly matching the one-sided way in

<hr>

[1] Dobrizhoffer, vol. i. p. 63; vol. ii. p. 212. See Gumilla, Hist. Nat., etc., de
l'Orenoque; Avignon, 1758, vol. iii. p. 200.

which the record of kindred is kept up. In any full discussion, other points would have to be considered, such as the wish to bind different tribes together in friendship by intermarriage, and the opinion that a wife is a slave to be stolen from the stranger, not taken from a man's own people. There is a good deal in this last consideration, as we may see by the practice of the Spartan marriage, in which, though the bride's guardians had really sanctioned the union, the pretence of carrying her off by force was kept up as a time-honoured ceremony. The Spartan marriage is no isolated custom, it is to be found among the Circassians,[1] and in South America.[2] Williams says that on the large islands of the Fiji group, the custom is often found of seizing upon a woman by apparent or actual force, in order to make her a wife. If she does not approve the proceeding, she runs off when she reaches the man's house, but if she is satisfied, she stays.[3] In these cases the abduction is a mere pretence, but it is kept up seemingly as a relic of a ruder time when, as among the modern Australians, it was done by no means as a matter of form, but in grim earnest.

Lastly, restrictions from marriage are occasionally found applied to cases where the relationship is more or less imaginary, as in ancient Rome, where adoption had in some measure the effect of consanguinity in barring marriage; or among the Moslems, where relation to a foster-family operates more fully in the same way; or in the Roman Church, where sponsorship creates a restriction from marriage, even among the co-sponsors, which it requires a dispensation to remove. Again, two members of a Circassian brotherhood, though no relationship is to be traced between them, may not marry,[4] and even among the savage Tupinambas of Brazil, two men who adopted one another as brothers were prohibited from marrying each other's sisters and daughters.[5] But such practices as these may reasonably be set down as mere consequences of the transfer both of the rights and the obligations of consanguinity to

---

[1] Klemm, C. G., vol. iv. p. 26.   [2] Wallace, p. 497. See Perty, p. 270.
[3] Williams, vol. i. p. 174.   [4] Klemm, C. G., vol. iv. p. 24.
[5] Southey, vol. i. p. 250.

other kinds of connexion, and so do not touch the general question.

To consider now the third group of customs, it is natural enough that there should be found even among savage tribes rules concerning respect, authority, precedence, and so forth, between fathers- and mothers-in-law and their sons- and daughters-in-law. But with these there are found, in the most distant regions of the world, regulations which to a great extent coincide, but which lie so far out of the ordinary course of social life as understood by the civilized world, that it is hard even to guess what state of things can have brought them into existence.

Among the Arawaks of South America, it was not lawful for the son-in-law to see the face of his mother-in-law. If they lived in the same house, a partition must be set up between them. If they went in the same boat, she had to get in first, so as to keep her back turned towards him. Among the Caribs, Rochefort says, " all the women talk with whom they will, but the husband dares not converse with his wife's relatives, except on extraordinary occasions."[1] Further north, in the account of the Floridan expedition of Alvar Nuñez, commonly known as Cabeça de Vaca, or Cow's Head, it is mentioned that the parents-in-law did not enter the son-in-law's house, nor he theirs, nor his brothers'-in-law, and if they met by chance, they went a bowshot out of their way, with their heads down and eyes fixed on the ground, for they held it a bad thing to see or speak to one another ; but the women were free to communicate and converse with their parents-in-law and relatives.[2] Higher up on the North American continent, customs of this kind have often been described. In the account of Major Long's Expedition to the Rocky Mountains, it is observed that among the Omahas the father- and mother-in-law do not speak to their son-in-law, nor mention his name, nor look in his face, and *vice versâ*.[3] Among the Sioux or Dacotas, Mr. Philander

---

[1] Klemm, C. G., vol. ii. p. 77. Rochefort, Hist. Nat., etc., des Iles Antilles; Rotterdam, 1665, p. 545.

[2] Alvar Nuñez, in vol. i. of ' Historiadores Primitivos de Indias ;' Madrid, 1852, etc., chap. xxv.   [3] Long's Exp., vol. i. p. 252.

Prescott remarks on the fear of uttering certain names. The father- or mother-in-law must not call their son-in-law by name, and *vice versâ*, and there are other relationships to which the prohibition applies. He has known an infringement of it punished by cutting the offender's clothes off his back and throwing them away.[1] Harmon says that among the Indians east of the Rocky Mountains, it is indecent for the father- or mother-in-law to look at, or speak to, the son- or daughter-in-law.[2] Among the Crees, it is observed by Richardson that while an Indian lives with his wife's family his mother-in-law must not speak to or look at him, and it is also an old custom for a man not to eat or to sit down in the presence of his father-in-law.[3]

In some parts of Australia, the names of a father- or mother-in-law and of a son-in-law are set down among the personal names which must not be spoken,[4] and in the Fiji Islands prohibition of speech between parents-in-law and children-in-law has been recorded.[5] Among the Dayaks of Borneo, a man must not pronounce the name of his father-in-law, which custom Mr. St. John, who mentions it, interprets as a sign of respect.[6] On the continent of Asia, among the Mongols and Calmucks, the young wife may not speak to her father-in-law nor sit in his presence,[7] but farther north, among the Yakuts, Adolph Erman noticed a much more peculiar custom. As in other northern regions, the custom of wearing but little clothing in the hot, stifling interior of the huts is common there, and the women often go about their domestic work stripped to the waist, nor do they object to do so in the presence of strangers, but there are two persons before whom a Yakut woman must not appear in this guise, her father-in-law, and her husband's elder brother.[8] In Africa, among the Beni Amer, the wife "hides herself, as does the husband also, from the mother-in-law;" while among the Darca the wife "hides herself from

---

[1] Schoolcraft, part ii. p. 198.

[2] Franklin, 'Journey to the Shores of the Polar Sea;' London, 1823, pp. 70-1.

[3] Eyre, vol. ii. p. 339.

[4] St. John, vol. i. p. 61.

[5] Erman, E. Tr. vol. ii. p. 420.

[6] Harmon, p. 341.

[7] Williams, vol. i. p. 136.

[8] Klemm, C. G., vol. iii. p. 169.

her father-in-law, according to custom, which herein agrees
with that of the aristocratic peoples."[1] The Basuto custom
forbids a wife to look in the face of her father-in-law till the
birth of her first child,[2] and among the Banyai a man must sit
with his knees bent in presence of his mother-in-law, and must
not put out his foot towards her.[3]

Of this curious series of customs, I have met with no interpretation which can be put forward with confidence. Their
object seems to be in general the avoidance of intercourse or
connexion between parents-in-law and children-in-law, sometimes to such an extent that one person may not look at the
other, or even pronounce his or her name. But the reasons
for this avoidance are not clear.[4] It is possible that a fuller
study of the law of *tabu* may throw some light on the matter.
The extraordinary summary of Fijian customs given by the
Rev. Thomas Williams, may be here quoted in full; it is probably to be understood as taking in occasional or local practices. " A free flow of the affections between members of the
same family is further prevented by the strict observance of
national or religious customs, imposing a most unnatural re-
straint. Brothers and sisters, first cousins, fathers- and sons-
in-law, mothers- and daughters-in-law, and brothers- and sis-
ters-in-law, are thus severally forbidden to speak to each
other, or to eat from the same dish. The latter embargo extends to husbands and wives,—an arrangement not likely to
foster domestic joy." Elsewhere the same author says, " in
some parts, the father may not speak to his son after his fifteenth year."[5]

The fourth and last group of customs has long been under
notice, and lists have even been made of countries where practices belonging to it have been found.[6] One of those prac-

---

[1] Munzinger, pp. 325, 589.   [2] Casalis, p. 201.   [3] Livingstone, p. 612.
[4] See St. John, Harmon, and Franklin, *loris citatis*. Prof. Lazarus pertinently
suggests exaggeration of ordinary restrictions, and excessive reaction against the
patria potestas.
[5] Williams, ' Fiji,' vol. i. pp. 136, 165. See Mariner, vol. ii. p. 147.
[6] M'Culloh, Researches ; Baltimore, 1829, p. 99. Waitz, Anthropology, vol. i.
p. 257. Humboldt & Bonpland, E. Tr., vol. vi. p. 333. Lafitau, vol. i. p. 49.

tices has an existing European name, the *couvade*, or "hatching," and this term it may be convenient to use for the whole
set.　By working up the old information with the aid of some
new facts, I have endeavoured to give an account, not only of
the geographical distribution of the couvado, but of its nature and meaning.　The most convenient way of discussing
it is first to examine the forms it takes in South America and
the West Indies, the district where it is not only developed to
the highest degree, but is also practised with a clear notion of
what it means; and afterwards to trace its more scattered and
obscure appearances in other quarters of the world.

The following account is given by Du Tertre of the Carib
couvado in the West Indies.　When a child is born, the mother
goes presently to her work, but the father begins to complain,
and takes to his hammock, and there he is visited as though
he were sick, and undergoes a course of dieting which would
cure of the gout "the most repleto of Frenchmen.　How they
can fast so much and not die of it," continues the narrator,
"is amazing to me, for they sometimes pass the five first days
without eating or drinking anything; then up to the tenth
they drink *ouycou*, which has about as much nourishment in it
as beer. These ten days passed, they begin to eat cassava only,
drinking *ouycou*, and abstaining from everything else for the
space of a whole month.　During this time, however, they
only eat the inside of the cassava, so that what is left is like
the rim of a hat when the block has been taken out, and all
these cassava rims they keep for the feast at the end of forty
days, hanging them up in the house with a cord.　When the
forty days are up they invite their relations and best friends,
who being arrived, before they set to eating, hack the skin of
this poor wretch with agouti-teeth, and draw blood from all
parts of his body, in such sort that from being sick by pure
imagination they often make a real patient of him.　This is,
however, so to speak, only the fish, for now comes the sauce
they prepare for him; they take sixty or eighty large grains
of pimento or Indian pepper, the strongest they can get, and
after well mashing it in water, they wash with this peppery
infusion the wounds and scars of the poor fellow, who I be-

lieve suffers no less than if he were burnt alive; however, he must not utter a single word if he will not pass for a coward and a wretch. This ceremony finished, they bring him back to his bed, where he remains some days more, and the rest go and make good cheer in the house at his expense. Nor is this all, for through the space of six whole months he eats neither birds nor fish, firmly believing that this would injure the child's stomach, and that it would participate in the natural faults of the animals on which its father had fed; for example, if the father ate turtle, the child would be deaf and have no brains like this animal, if he ate manati, the child would have little round eyes like this creature, and so on with the rest."[1]

The Abate Gilij, after mentioning the wide prevalence of the fasting of the father on the birth of the child, among the tribes of the east side of South America, goes on as follows :—"But I know not if the cause is equally well known, why the Indians fast in such manner. I in the very beginning of my stay among them had the opportunity of discovering it, and this was how it happened. A fortified house having to be built for the soldiers to live in, as was usual for the defence not of the missionaries alone, but also of the reduced Indians, the Tamanacs, they being still gentiles, were summoned by the corporal Ermengildo Lealo to work at it, and it was noticed that a certain Marscajùri, when the work was done, went away fasting, without even tasting a mouthful. 'What, has he no appetite?' asked Lealo in surprise. 'To be sure he has,' rejoined the other Indians, 'but his wife has had a child to-day, so he must not make use of these victuals, for the little boy would die.' 'But when our wives are brought to bed,' said the corporal, 'we eat more abundantly and more joyously than usual, and our children do not die of it.' 'But you are Spaniards,' the fools replied, 'and if your eating does no harm to your babies, you may be sure, nevertheless, that it is most hurtful to ours.' It may be easily imagined what laughter

[1] Du Tertre, Hist. Gén. des Antilles habitées par les Français; Paris, 1667, vol. ii. p. 371, etc. See Rochefort, Hist. Nat. et Mor. des Iles des Antilles; Rotterdam, 1665, 2nd ed. p. 550. It seems from his account that the very severe fasting was only for the first child, that for the others being slight.

there was at this absurd notion. 'But not only the father's food,' the Tamanacs went on to say, 'but even killing fish or any other animal on such days, would do harm to the children.' When I knew of this nonsense, I set myself to work to seek out the motive of it, and taking aside one of the most reasonable of the savages: 'tell me,' I said, 'as the Spaniards do not fast at the birth of their children, for what reason do you fast at such a joyful moment?' 'The child is ours, and proceeds from us,' replied the savage, 'and the cooked food used by grown folks, which is profitable for us at other times, would now do the little children harm, if we ate it.' So I observed a sort of identity which he supposed to exist between father and son," etc. The missionary goes on to relate how he cured the Indian of the delusion, by showing that to give him a thrashing would have no effect on his child.[1]

Among the Arawaks of Surinam, for some time after the birth of his child, the father must fell no tree, fire no gun, hunt no large game; he may stay near home, shoot little birds with a bow and arrow, and angle for little fish; but his time hanging heavy on his hands, the most comfortable thing he can do is to lounge in his hammock.[2] Of the couvade among the fierce equestrian tribe of the Abipones, whose home lay south of the centre of the continent, the Jesuit missionary Dobrizhoffer gives a full account. "No sooner do you hear that the wife has borne a child, than you will see the Abipone husband lying in bed, huddled up with mats and skins lest some ruder breath of air should touch him, fasting, kept in private, and for a number of days abstaining religiously from certain viands; you would swear it was he who had had the child. . . . I had read about this in old times, and laughed at it, never thinking I could believe such madness, and I used to suspect that this barbarian custom was related more in jest than in earnest; but at last I saw it with my own eyes in use among the Abipones. And in truth they observe this ancestral custom, troublesome as it is, the more willingly and diligently from their being altogether persuaded that the sobriety and quiet of the fathers

[1] Gilij, 'Saggio di Storia Americana,' vol. ii. p. 133, etc.
[2] Quandt, in Klemm C. G., vol. ii. p. 83.

is effectual for the well-being of the new-born offspring, and is even necessary. Hear, I pray, a confirmation of this matter. Francisco Barreda, Deputy of the Royal Governor of Tucuman, came to visit the new colony of Concoiçum in the territory of Santiago. To him, as he was walking with me in the courtyard, the Cacique Malakin came up to pay his respects, having just left his bed, to which he had been confined in consequence of his wife's recent delivery. As I stood by, Barreda offered the Cacique a pinch of Spanish snuff, but seeing the savage refuse it contrary to custom, he thought he must be out of his mind, for he knew him at other times to be greedy of this nasal delicacy; so he asked me aside to inquire the cause of his abstinence. I asked him in the Abiponian tongue (for this Barreda was ignorant of, as the Cacique was of Spanish), why he refused his snuff to-day? 'Don't you know?' he answered, 'that my wife has just been confined? Must not I therefore abstain from stimulating my nostrils? What a danger my sneezing would bring upon my child!' No more, but he went back to his hut to lie down again directly, lest the tender little infant should take some harm if he stayed any longer with us in the open air. For they believe that the father's carelessness influences the new-born offspring, from a natural bond and sympathy of both. Hence if the child comes to a premature end, its death is attributed by the women to the father's intemperance, this or that cause being assigned; he did not abstain from mead; he had loaded his stomach with water-hog; he had swum across the river when the air was chilly; he had neglected to shave off his long eyebrows; he had devoured underground honey, stamping on the bees with his feet; he had ridden till he was tired and sweated. With raving like this the crowd of women accuse the father with impunity of causing the child's death, and are accustomed to pour curses on the unoffending husband."[1]

We have laid open to us in these accounts a notably distinct

Dobrizhoffer, 'Historia de Abiponibus;' Vienna, 1784, vol. ii. p. 231, etc. For other South American accounts of the couvade, see Dirt, Voy. de la France Equinox., p. 389. Fermin, Descr. de Surinam; Amsterdam, 1769, p. 81. Tschudi, 'Peru,' vol. ii. p. 235. Purchas, vol. iv. p. 1291. Spix & Martius, pp. 1186, 1339.

view, among the lower races, of a mental state hard to trace among those high in the scale of civilization. The Couvade implicitly denies that physical separation of "individuals," which a civilized man would probably set down as a first principle, common by nature to all mankind, till experience of the psychology of the savage showed him that he was mistaking education for intuition. It shows us a number of distinct and distant tribes deliberately holding the opinion that the connexion between father and child is not only, as we think, a mere relation of parentage, affection, duty, but that their very bodies are joined by a physical bond, so that what is done to the one acts directly upon the other. The couvade is not the only result of the opinion which thus repudiates the physical severance that seems to come so natural to us; and this opinion again belongs, like Sorcery and Divination, to the mental state in which man does not separate the subjective mental connexion from the objective physical connexion, the connexion which is inside his mind from the connexion which is outside it, in the same way in which most educated men of the higher races make this separation. A few more cases will further illustrate the effects of such a condition of mind. Not only is it held that the actions of the father, and the food that he eats, influence his child both before and after its birth, but that the actions and food of survivors affect the spirits of the dead on their journey to their home in the after life. Among the Land Dyaks of Borneo, the husband, before the birth of his child, may do no work with a sharp instrument except what is necessary for the farm; nor may he fire guns, nor strike animals, nor do any violent work, lest bad influences should affect the child; and after it is born the father is kept in seclusion indoors for several days, and dieted on rice and salt, to prevent not his own but the child's stomach from swelling.[1] In Kamchatka, the husband must not do such things as bend sledge-staves across his knee before his child is born, for such actions do harm to his wife.[2] In Greenland, beside the strict

[1] St. John, vol. i. p. 100. Tr. Eth. Soc., 1863, p. 233. Compare the eight days' fast in Madagascar of the fathers whose children were to be circumcised. Voy. of François Cauche, p. 51, in Rel. de Madagascar, etc.; Paris, 1651.

[2] Klemm, C. G., vol. ii. p. 207. Steller, 'Kamtschatka,' p. 351.

regulations imposed upon women after the birth of a child, the husband must for some weeks do no work and follow no occupation, except the procuring of necessary food, and this in order that the child may not die. When a Greenlander dies, his soul starts to travel into the land of Torngarsuk, where reigns perpetual summer, all sunshine and no night, where there is good water, and birds, fish, seals, and reindeer without end, that are to be caught without trouble, or are found cooking alive in a huge kettle. But the journey to this blessed land is difficult, the souls have to slide five days or more down a precipice all stained with the blood of those who have gone down before. And it is especially grievous for the poor souls when the journey must be made in winter or in tempest, for then a soul may come to harm, and suffer the other death, as they call it, when it perishes utterly, and nothing is left. And this is to them the most wretched fate; and therefore the survivors, for these five days or more, must abstain from certain food, and all noisy work except their necessary fishing, that the soul on its dangerous journey may not be disturbed or come to harm.[1] But perhaps no story on record so clearly shows how deeply the idea of these imaginary ties is rooted in the savage mind, as one told by Mr. Wallace in his South American tour :—"An Indian, who was one of my hunters, caught a fine cock of the rock, and gave it to his wife to feed; but the poor woman was obliged to live herself on cassava-bread and fruits, and abstain entirely from all animal food, pepper, and salt, which it was believed would cause the bird to die." The bird died after all, and the woman was beaten by her husband for having killed it by some violation of the rule of abstinence.[2]

But the explanation of the practices of the couvade, from the confusion of imaginary and real relations, sound as it may be so far it goes, is incomplete. They almost all involve giving over the parentage to the father, and leaving the mother out of the question.[3] This was an ancient Egyptian opinion, as Southey points out when mentioning its most startling deve-

---

[1] Crantz, pp. 275, 258.

[2] Wallace, p. 502. For other connected practices, see Id. p. 501. Spix and Martius, p. 381.   [3] But see Spix and Martius, p. 1180.

lopment in the practice of the Tupinambas of Brazil, who would give their own women as wives to their male captives, and then, without scruple, eat the children when they grew up, holding them simply to be of the flesh and blood of their enemies. It is strange that writers who have spoken of the couvade during the half-century since Southey wrote, and have even quoted him, should have so neglected the contribution he made to the psychology of the lower races in bringing forward as the source of this remarkable practice at once the Egyptian and American theory of parentage, and the belief in bodily union between father and child.[1]

To trace now the geographical distribution of the couvade in other parts of the world. The fasting observed in South America and the West Indies seems to extend no further; repose, careful nursing, and nourishing food being the treatment usual for the imaginary invalid. Venegas mentions this kind of couvade among the Indians of California;[2] Zuccholli, in West Africa;[3] Captain Van der Hart, in Bouro, in the Eastern Archipelago.[4] The country of Eastern Asia where Marco Polo met with the practice of the couvade in the thirteenth century, appears to be the Chinese province of West Yunnan,[5] so that the widow's remark to Sir Hudibras is true in a geographical sense,—

> " For though Chinese go to bed,
> And lie-in in their ladies' stead."

But it does not at all follow from this that the couvade was practised among the race ethnologically known to us as the Chinese. The people among whom Marco Polo found it were probably one of the distinct and less cultured races within the vast Chinese frontier, for it has been noticed among the mountain tribes known as the Mian-tsze, or " Children of the soil," who differ from the Chinese proper in body, language, and civilization, and are supposed to be, like the Sontals and Gonds of India,

---

[1] Southey, vol. i. pp. 227, 248. Compare Spix and Martius, p. 1339.
[2] Venegas, vol. i. p. 94.   [3] Zuccholli, p. 166.
[4] C. v. der Hart, 'Reise rondom bet eiland Celebes;' 'Sgravenhage, 1853, p. 107.
[5] Marco Polo, Latin ed., 1671, lib. ii. c. xli. Marsden's Tr., London, 1818, p. 431.

remnants of a race driven into the mountains by the present dwellers in the plains. A Chinese traveller among the Miau-tazo, giving an account of their manners and customs, notices, as though the idea were quite strange to him, that "In one tribe it is the custom for the father of a new-born child, as soon as its mother has become strong enough to leave her couch, to get into bed himself, and there receive the congratulations of his acquaintances, as he exhibits his offspring.[1] Another Asiatic people recorded to have practised the couvade are the Tibareni of Pontus, at the south of the Black Sea, among whom, when the child was born, the father lay groaning in bed with his head tied up, while the mother tended him with food, and prepared his baths.[2] In Europe, the couvade may be traced up from ancient into modern times in the neighbourhood of the Pyrenees. Above eighteen hundred years ago, Strabo mentions the story that among the Iberians of the North of Spain the women, "after the birth of a child, tend their husbands, putting them to bed instead of going themselves;"[3] and this account is confirmed by the existence of the practice among the modern Basques. "In Biscay," says Michel, "in vallies whose population recalls in its usages the infancy of society, the women rise immediately after child-birth, and attend to the duties of the household, while the husband goes to bed, taking the baby with him, and thus receives the neighbours' compliments."[4] It has been found also in Navarre,[5] and on the French side of the Pyrenees. Legrand d'Aussy mentions that in an old French fabliau the King of Toreloro is "au lit et en couche" when Aucassin arrives and takes a stick to him, and makes him promise to abolish the custom in his realm. And the same author goes on to

<hr>

[1] W. Lockhart, in Tr. Eth. Soc. 1861, p. 181. Rochefort (p. 550) sets down the Japanese as practising the couvade; and the same bare mention appears in later writers, who, perhaps, merely followed him. Is his statement based on proper evidence, or simply a mistake?

[2] Apoll. Rhod. Argonautica, ii. 1009. C. Val. Flacc. Argon., v. 148.

[3] Strabo, iii. 4, 17.

[4] Michel, 'Le Pays Basque,' Paris, 1857, p. 201. A. de Quatrefages, in Rev des Deux Mondes, 1850, vol. v.

[5] Laborde, 'Itinéraire de l'Espagne,' Paris, 1834, vol. I. p. 273.

say that the practice is said still to exist in some cantons of Béarn, where it is called *faire la couvade*.[1] Lastly, Diodorus Siculus notices the same habit of the wife being neglected, and the husband put to bed and treated as the patient, among the natives of Corsica about the beginning of the Christian era.[2]

The ethnological value of the four groups of customs now described is not to be weighed with much nicety. The prohibitions of marriage among distant kindred go for least in proving connexion by blood or intercourse between the distant races who practise them, as it is easy to suppose them to have grown up again and again from like grounds. But it is hard to suppose that the curiously similar restrictions in the intercourse between parents-in-law and their children-in-law can be of independent growth in each of the remote districts where they prevail, and still more difficult to suppose the quaint trick of the cure by the pretended extraction of objects from the patient's body to have made its appearance independently in Africa, in America, in Australia, in Europe. In such cases as these there is considerable force in the supposition of there being often, if not always, a historical connexion between their origin in different regions. Thus, the isolated occurrences of a custom among particular races surrounded by other races who ignore it, may be sometimes to the ethnologist like those outlying patches of strata from which the geologist infers that the formation they belong to once spread over intervening districts, from which it has been removed by denudation; or like the geographical distribution of plants, from which the botanist argues that they have travelled from a distant home. The way in which the couvade appears in the New and Old Worlds is especially interesting from this point of view. Among the savage tribes of South America it is, as it were, at home in a mental atmosphere at least not so different from that in which it came into being as to make it a mere meaningless, absurd superstition. If the culture of the

<hr>

[1] Legrand d'Aussy, 'Fabliaux du xiie et xiiie Siècle,' 3rd ed., Paris, 1829, vol. iii. " Aucassiu et Nicolette." Rochefort, l. c. [*Faire la couvade*, to sit cowring, or shonking within doors; to lurke in the campe when Gallants are at the Battell; (any way) to play least in sight (Cotgrave).]   [2] Diod. Sic., v. 14.

Caribs and Brazilians, even before they came under our knowledge, had advanced too far to allow the couvade to grow up
fresh among them, they at least practised it with some consciousness of its meaning; it had not fallen out of unison with
their mental state. Here, then, we find covering a vast compact area of country, the mental stratum, so to speak, to which
the couvade most nearly belongs. But if we look at its appearances across from China to Corsica, the state of things is
widely different; no theory of its origin can be drawn from the
Asiatic and European accounts to compete for a moment with
that which flows naturally from the observations of the missionaries, who found it not a mere dead custom, but a live
growth of savage psychology. The peoples, too, who have
kept it up in Asia and Europe seem to have been not the great
progressive, spreading, conquering, civilizing nations of the
Aryan, Semitic, and Chinese stocks. It cannot be ascribed
even to the Tatars, for the Lapps, Finns, and Hungarians
appear to know nothing of it. It would seem rather to have
belonged to that ruder population, or series of populations,
whose fate it has been to be driven by the great races out of
their fruitful lands, to take refuge in mountains and deserts.
The retainers of the couvade in Asia are the Miau-tsze of China,
and the savage Tibareni of Pontus. In Europe, they are the
Basque race of the Pyrenees, whose peculiar manners, appearance, and language, coupled with their geographical position,
favour the view that they are the remains of a people driven
westward and westward by the pressure of more powerful
tribes, till they came to these last mountains with nothing but
the Atlantic beyond. Of what stock were the original barbarian inhabitants of Corsica, we do not know; but their position, and the fact that they, too, had the couvade, would suggest their having been a branch of the same family, who escaped their persecutors by putting out to sea, and settling in
their mountainous island.

CHAPTER XI.

HISTORICAL TRADITIONS AND MYTHS OF OBSERVATION.

THE traditions current among mankind are partly historical and partly mythical. To the ethnologist they are of value in two very different ways, sometimes as preserving the memory of past events, sometimes as showing by their occurrence in different districts of the world that between the inhabitants of these districts there has been in some way a historical connexion. His great difficulty in dealing with them is to separate the fact and the fiction, which are both so valuable in their different ways; and this difficulty is aggravated by the circumstance that these two elements are often mixed up in a most complex manner, myths presenting themselves in the dress of historical narrative, and historical facts growing into the wildest myths.

Between the traditions of real events, which are History, and the pure myths, whose origin and development are being brought more and more clearly into view in our own times by the labours of Adalbert Kuhn and Max Müller, and their school, there lie a mass of stories which may be called "Myths of Observation." They are inferences from observed facts, which take the form of positive assertions, and they differ principally from the inductions of modern science in being much more generally crude and erroneous, and in taking to themselves names of persons, and more or less of purely subjective detail, which enables them to assume the appearance of real history. When a savage builds upon the discovery of great bones buried in the earth a story of a combat of the giants and monsters whose remains they are, he constructs a Myth of Observation which may shape itself into the form of a historical tradition, and be all the more puzzling for the portion of scientific truth which it really contains. The object of the present chapter is to collect a quantity of evidence, bearing on the problem how to separate Historical Traditions and Myths of Observation from pure Myths, and from one another.

Though it may not be possible to lay down any general canon of criticism by which the historical and mythical elements of tradition may be separated, it is to some extent possible to judge by internal evidence whether or not a particular legend or episode has a claim to be considered as history. It happens sometimes that a legend contains statements which are hardly likely to have come into the minds of the original narrators of the story, except by actual experience. The Chinese legend which tells us the name of the ancient sage who taught his people to make fire by the friction of wood cannot be taken as it stands for real history, seeing that so many nations ascribe this and other arts to mythic heroes, yet it embodies a recollection of a time when this was the ordinary way of producing fire. So, when the same people tell us that they once used knotted cords like the Peruvian quipus, as records of events, and that the art of writing superseded this ruder expedient, we are in no way called upon to receive the names and dates of the inventors to whom they ascribe these arts; but, at the same time, it is hard to imagine what could have put such an idea into their heads, unless there had been a foundation of fact for the story, in the actual use of quipus in the country before writing became general.

In the traditions which the Polynesians have preserved of their migrations in past times, it is likely that some historic truth may be preserved, and with their help, aided by a closer study of the languages and myths of the district, it may be some day possible for ethnologists to sketch out, at least roughly, the history of the race for ages before the European discovery. Much of the historical value of the South Sea tra-

ditions is due to their being commonly preserved in verses
kept alive by frequent repetition, and in which even small
events are placed on record with an accuracy and permanence
that yields only to written history. Thus a question that arose
when Ellis was in Tahiti, about a certain buoy that was stolen
from the 'Bounty' nearly thirty years before, was settled at
once by a couple of lines from a native song.

> "O mea eiá o Tareu eiá
> Eiá te paito a Bligh."
> " Such a one a thief, and Tareu a thief,
> Stole the buoy of Bligh."[1]

Among the mass of Central American traditions which have
become known through the labours of the Abbé Brasseur,
there occur certain passages in the story of an early migration
of the Quiché race, which have much the appearance of vague
and broken stories derived in some way from high northern
latitudes. The Quiché manuscript describes the ancestors of
the race as travelling away from the rising of the sun, and
goes on thus :—" But it is not clear how they crossed the sea,
they passed as though there had been no sea, for they passed
over scattered rocks, and these rocks were rolled on the sands.
This is why they called the place ' ranged stones and torn-up
sands,' the name which they gave it on their passage within
the sea, the water being divided when they passed." Then
the people collected on a mountain called Chi Pixab, and there
they fasted in darkness and night. Afterwards it is related
that they removed, and waited for the dawn which was approaching, and the manuscript says :—" Now, behold, our
ancients and our fathers were made lords and had their dawn ;
behold, we will relate also the rising of the dawn and the ap-
parition of the sun, the moon, and the stars." Great was their
joy when they saw the morning star, which came out first with
its resplendent face before the sun. At last the sun itself
began to come forth ; the animals, small and great, were in joy ;
they rose from the watercourses and ravines, and stood on the
mountain tops with their heads towards where the sun was

---

[1] Ellis, Polyn. Res., vol. I. p. 287.

coming. An innumerable crowd of people were there, and
the dawn cast light on all these nations at once. "At last the
face of the ground was dried by the sun : like a man the sun
showed himself, and his presence warmed and dried the surface of the ground. Before the sun appeared, muddy and wet
was the surface of the ground, and it was before the sun appeared, and then only the sun rose like a man. But his heat
had no strength, and he did but show himself when he rose,
he only remained like (an image in) a mirror, and it is not indeed the same sun that appears now, they say in the stories."[1]

Obscure as much of this is, there are things in it which
agree very curiously with the phenomena of the Arctic regions.
The cold and darkness, the sea not like a sea but like rocks
rolled on the sand, the long waiting for the sun, and its appearance at last with little strength, and but just rising above
the horizon, form a picture which corresponds with the nature
of the high north, as much as it differs from that of the tropical
regions where the tradition is found. We read of Arctic voy-
agers going out to watch for the reappearance of the sun towards the close of the long dismal winter,[2] and the judgment
that it was not indeed the sun of Central America that appeared
so strangely, may be placed by the side of a remark made by
a savage in another country. Sir George Grey, travelling in
Australia, was once telling stories of distant countries to a
party of natives round the camp fire; "I now spoke to them
of still more northern latitudes; and went so far as to describe
those countries in which the sun never sets at a certain period
of the year. Their astonishment now knew no bounds : 'Ah !
that must be another sun, not the same as the one we see
here,' said an old man ; and in spite of all my arguments to
the contrary, the others adopted this opinion."[3]

The legend of the introduction of rice in Borneo relates how
a Dayak climbed up a tree which grew downward from the
sky, and so got up to the Pleiades, and there he found a personage who took him to his house and gave him boiled rice to
eat. He had never seen rice before, and the story says that

<hr>

[1] Brasseur, 'Popol Vuh,' pp. 231–43 ; 'Mexique,' vol. I. pp. 169–76.
[2] Purchas, vol. iii. p. 499.   [3] Grey, Journals, vol. i. p. 293.

when he saw the grains, he thought they were maggots.[1] Now
there is a tradition of recent date, among the Kœthratlah Indians of British Columbia, which tells in the most graphic way
the story of the first appearance of the white men among them;
how an Indian canoe was out catching halibut, when the noise
of a huge sea-monster was heard, plunging along through the
thick mist; the Indians drew up their lines and paddled to
shore, when the monster proved to be a boat full of strange-
looking men. "The strangers landed, and beckoned the Indians to come to them and bring them some fish. One of
them had over his shoulder what was supposed to be a stick:
presently he pointed it to a bird that was flying past—a violent
poo went forth—down came the bird to the ground. The Indians died! as they revived, they questioned each other as to
their state, whether any were dead, and what each had felt.
The whites then made signs for a fire to be lighted; the Indians proceeded at once, according to their usual tedious practice, of rubbing two sticks together. The strangers laughed,
and one of them, snatching up a handful of dry grass, struck a
spark into a little powder placed under it. Instantly another
poo!—and a blaze. The Indians died! After this the new-
comers wanted some fish boiled : the Indians, therefore, put
the fish and water into one of their square wooden buckets,
and set some stones on the fire; intending, when they were
hot, to cast them into the vessel, and thus boil the food. The
whites were not satisfied with this way : one of them fetched
a tin kettle out of the boat, put the fish and some water into
it, and then, strange to say, set it on the fire. The Indians
looked on with astonishment. However, the kettle did not
consume; the water did not run into the fire. Then, again,
the Indians died! When the fish was eaten, the strangers
put a kettle of rice on the fire; the Indians looked at each
other, and whispered *Akshahn, akshahn !*, or 'Maggots, maggots !' "[2]

Again, the Australians have had the same idea of what rice
was, for in the Moorundo dialect it is called "yeeliloe," or

[1] St. John, vol. i. p. 202, and see under, Chap. XII.
[2] Mayne, 'British Columbia,' p. 279.

"maggots,"[1] a name which, of course, dates from the recent time when foreigners brought it to the country. When, therefore, we are told in the Borneo tale that the first Dayak who saw grains of rice took them for maggots, we are, I think, justified in believing this notion to be in Borneo, as elsewhere, a real reminiscence of the introduction of rice into the country, though this piece of actual history comes to us woven into the texture of an ancient myth. There is reason to suppose that rice was introduced into the Malay islands from Asia; in Marsden's time it had not been adopted even in Engano and Batu, which are islands close to Sumatra.[2]

When a tradition is once firmly planted among the legendary lore of a tribe, there seems scarcely any limit to the time through which it may be kept up by continual repetition from one generation to the next; unless such an event as the coming of a stronger and more highly cultivated race entirely upsets the old state of society, and destroys the old landmarks. The traditions of the Polynesians, for instance, seem often to be of great age, for they occur among the natives of distant islands whose languages have had time to diverge widely from a common origin; but even the most long-lived stories are fast disappearing, under European influence, from the memory of the people. The historical value of a tradition does not of necessity vary inversely with its age, and indeed this rule-of-three test goes for very little, for some very old stories are, beyond a doubt, of greater historical value than other very new ones current in the same tribe.

There is even a certain amount of evidence which tends to prove that the memory of the huge animals of the quaternary period has been preserved up to modern times in popular tradition. It is but quite lately that the fact of man having lived on the earth at the same time with the mammoth has become a generally received opinion, though its probability has been seen by a few far-sighted thinkers for many years past, and it had been suggested long before the late discoveries in the Drift-beds, that several traditions, found in different parts of

[1] Eyre, vol. ii. p. 393.
[2] Marsden, pp. 467, 474. See Ellis, 'Madagascar,' vol. L p. 89.

the world, were derived from actual memory of the remote time when various great animals, generally thought to have died out before the appearance of man upon the earth, were still alive. The subject is hardly in a state to express a decided opinion upon, but the evidence is worthy of the most careful attention.

Father Charlevoix, whose ' History of New France ' was published in 1744, records a North American legend of a great elk. " There is current also among these barbarians a pleasant enough tradition of a great Elk, beside whom others seem like ants. He has, they say, legs so high that eight feet of snow do not embarrass him: his skin is proof against all sorts of weapons, and he has a sort of arm which comes out of his shoulder, and which he uses as we do ours." [1] It is hard to imagine that anything but the actual sight of a live elephant can have given rise to this tradition. The suggestion that it might have been founded on the sight of a mammoth frozen with his flesh and skin, as they are found in Siberia, is not tenable, for the trunks and tails of these animals perish first, and are not preserved like the more solid parts, so that the Asiatic myths which have grown out of the finding of these frozen beasts, know nothing of such appendages. Moreover,

Fig. 30.

no savage who had never heard of the use of an elephant's trunk would imagine from a sight of the dead animal, even if its trunk were perfect, that its use was to be compared with that of a man's arm.

The notion that the Indian story of the Great Elk was a real reminiscence of a living proboscidian, is strengthened by a remarkable drawing, Fig. 30, from one of

the Mexican picture-writings. It represents a masked priest
sacrificing a human victim, and Humboldt copies it in the
' Vues des Cordillères' with the following remarks :—" I should
not have had this hideous scene engraved, were it not that the
disguise of the sacrificing priest presents some remarkable and
apparently not accidental resemblances with the Hindoo Ganesa
[the elephant-headed god of wisdom]. The Mexicans used
masks imitating the shape of the heads of the serpent, the
crocodile, or the jaguar. One seems to recognize in the sacri-
ficer's mask the trunk of an elephant or some pachyderm resembling it in the shape of the head, but with an upper jaw
furnished with incisive teeth. The snout of the tapir no doubt
protrudes a little more than that of our pigs, but it is a long
way from the tapir's snout to the trunk figured in the ' Codex
Borgianus.' Had the peoples of Aztlan, derived from Asia,
some vague notions of the elephant, or, as seems to me much
less probable, did their traditions reach back to the time when
America was still inhabited by those gigantic animals, whose
petrified skeletons are found buried in the marly ground on
the very ridge of the Mexican Cordilleras ?"[1] It may be worth
while to notice in connection with Humboldt's remarks, that
when Mr. Bates showed a picture of an elephant to some South
American Indians, they settled it that the creature must be a
large kind of tapir.[2]

Attempts have been made by other writers to connect the
memory of animals now extinct, with mythological tales current in the regions to which they belong. Dr. Falconer is disposed to connect the huge elephant-fighting and world-bearing
tortoises of the Hindoo mythology with a recollection of the time
when his monstrous Himalayan tortoise, the *Colossochelys Atlas*,
the restoration of which forms so striking an object in the British
Museum, was still alive.[3] The savage tribes of Brazil have
traditions about a being whom they call the Curupira. "Sometimes he is described as a kind of orang-otang, being covered
with long, shaggy hair, and living in trees. At others he is

---

[1] Humboldt, Vues des Cord., pl. xv.; Borgia MS. in Kingsborough, vol. iii.
[2] Bates, ' Amazons,' vol. ii. p. 128.
[3] Falconer, in Proc. Zool. Soc., part xii., 1844, p. 86.

said to have cloven feet, and a bright red face.   He has a wife and children, and sometimes comes down to the roças to steal the mandioca."   Similar to, or the same as this being, is the Caypór, whom the Indians, in their masquerades, represent as a bulky, misshapen monster, with red skin and long shaggy red hair, hanging halfway down his back.[1]   With reference to these Brazilian stories, Mr. Carter Blake remarks—" In Brazil the Indians had a tradition of a gigantic anthropoid ape, the cayporé, which represented the African gorilla.   No such ape exists in the present day ; but in the post-pliocene in Brazil, remains have been preserved of an extinct ape (*Protopithecus antiquus*) four feet high, which might possibly have lived down to the human period, and formed the subject of the tradition."[2] Lastly, Colonel Hamilton Smith has collected a quantity of evidence, thought by him to bear on the preservation of the memory of extinct creatures, adding to Father Charlevoix's great Elk, and the Père aux Bœufs from Buffon, a North American " Naked Bear," and an East Indian " Elephant-Horse," etc., and endeavouring to identify them in nature.[3]

To proceed now from the traditions which have, or may set up some sort of claim to have, a historical foundation, to the Myths of Observation, which are so often liable to be confounded with them : it is to be noticed that if the inference from facts, which forms the basis of such a myth, should happen to be a correct one, and if the story should also happen to have fairly dropped out of sight the evidence out of which it grew, its separation from a real tradition of events may be hardly possible.   Fortunately for the Ethnologist, it is very common for such stories to betray their unhistoric origin in one or both of these ways, either by recording things which seemed indeed probable when the myths arose, but which modern knowledge repudiates, or by having embodied with them the facts which have been appealed to for ages as confirmation of their truth, but which we are now in a position to recognize at once as the very basis on which their mythical structure was raised.

[1] Bates, ' Amazons,' vol. I. p. 73 ; vol. ii. p. 204.
[2] C. Carter Blake in Tr. Eth. Soc. 1863, p. 160.
[3] C. Hamilton Smith, Nat. Hist. of Human Sp., pp. 104–6.

A good example of a Myth of Observation is a story current in Egypt in Strabo's time, but which he, having indeed a considerable knowledge of geology, declines to believe. "But one of the wondrous things," he says, "which we saw about the pyramids, must not be passed over. There lie in front of the pyramids certain heaps of the masons' rubbish, and among these there are found pieces in shape and size like lentils, and in some, as it were, half-peeled grains. They say, the leavings of the workmen's food have been turned into stone, but this is not likely, for at home among us there is a longish ridge of hill in a plain, and this is full of lentil-like stones of tufa, etc."[1]

To men whose country has the open sea to its west it seems that the sun plunges at night into its waters. Now the sun is evidently a mass of matter at a distance, and very hot, and when red-hot bodies come in contact with water there follows a hissing noise; and thus the inference is easy and straightforward, that when the sun dips into the waves such a sound ought to be heard. From the inference that the hissing might be heard, to the assertion that it has actually been heard, is the easy step by which the crude argument of early science passes into the full-grown Myth of Observation. In two distant countries where the world seems to end westward in the boundless ocean, the story is to be found. The Sacred Promontory, that is Cape St. Vincent, Strabo says, is the westernmost point, not of Europe alone, but of the whole habitable earth, and there Posidonius tells how the vulgar say the sun goes down larger on the ocean-coast, and with a noise almost as it were the sea hissing as the sun plunges into its depths and is quenched; but this is false, as well as that the night follows instantly upon its setting.[2] So in the Pacific, in some of the Society Islands, the name for sunset means the falling of the sun into the sea, and the sun itself is thought to be a substance resembling fire. Mr. Ellis asked them how they knew it fell into the sea, and they said they had not seen it, but some people of Borabora or Maupiti, the most western islands, had once heard the hissing occasioned by its plunging into the ocean.[3]

[1] Strabo, xvii. 1, 34.   [2] Strabo, iii. 1, 5.   [3] Ellis, Polyn. Res., vol. ii. p. 414.

From the incredulous geographer who records the stories of the fossil lentils and the hissing sun, yet another Myth of Observation may be taken, which shows well the easy transition from "it may have been," to "it was," which lies at their root. Mr. Catlin, in one of his journeys, says that he came to a place where he saw rocks "looking as if they had actually dropped from the clouds in such a confused mass, and all lay where they had fallen." So in old times, a round plain between Marseilles and the mouths of the Rhone was called the "stony" plain, from its being covered with stones as big as a man's fist. You would think, says Pomponius Mela, that the stones had rained there, so many are they, and so far and wide do they lie.[1] Now Æschylus, says Strabo, having perceived the difficulty of accounting for these stones, or having heard about it from some one else, has wrested the whole matter into a myth. In some lines of his, preserved to us by Strabo's quotation of them, Prometheus, explaining to Hercules his way from the Caucasus to the Hesperides, tells him how when his missiles fail him in his fight with the Ligurians, and the soft earth will not even afford him a stone, Jove, pitying his defenceless state, will rain down a shower of round pebbles over the ground, hurling which he will easily rout his foes.[2]

Fossil remains have for ages been objects of curious speculation to mankind. In the most distant regions where huge bones have been found, they have been explained, truly enough, as being the bones of monstrous beasts, and as plausibly, though, as later investigations have shown within the last century, not so correctly, as bones of giants. Given the belief that the earth was formerly inhabited by monsters and giants, the myth-making power of the human mind gave "a local habitation and a name" wherever it was required, and the battles of these monsters with each other, and with man, were worked into the general mass of popular tradition, with gradually increasing fulness and accuracy of detail. The Asiatic sagas which have grown out of the finding of the frozen mammoths, and the fossil remains of these and other great extinct animals, are excellent cases in point. Many of them have been

____
[1] Catlin, vol. ii. p. 70.   Mela, ii. c. 5.   [2] Strabo, iv. 1, 7.

collected and criticized in an admirable paper published more than twenty years ago by Von Olfers, of Berlin.[1]

The Siberians are constantly finding bones and teeth of mammoths imbedded in the faces of cliffs or river banks at some depth below the surface. Often a mass of earth or gravel falls away from such a cliff, and exposes such remains. How could they have got there? A plausible explanation suggested itself, that the creature was a huge burrowing animal, and lived underground. Not only the skeleton, but the body in tolerable preservation with flesh and skin being found in a frozen state in high Northern latitudes, the notion grew up that it was a monstrous kind of burrowing rat, and it is described in Chinese books under such names as *fen-shu*, or " digging rat," *yen-men*, or " burrowing ox," *shu-mu*, " mother of mice," and so on. A difficulty which suggested itself to the native Siberian geologists was met in a characteristic manner. It was strange that whenever they came upon a mammoth imbedded in a cliff, it was always dead. It must be a creature unable to bear the air or the light, and when in the course of its subterranean wanderings it breaks through to the outer air, it dies immediately. With so much knowledge of the natural history of the creature to start from, other details grow round it in the usual way. Yakuts and Tunguz have seen the earth heave and sink, as a mammoth walked beneath. It frequents marshes, and travels underground, never appearing above the surface of the earth or water during the day, but has been seen at dawn in lakes and rivers, just as it dived below. The account of it given in the Chinese Encyclopædia of Kang-hi is as follows:—

" *Fen-shu.*—The cold is extreme and almost continual on the coast of the Northern Sea, beyond the Tai-tong-Kiang; on this coast is found the animal *Fen-shu*, which resembles a rat in shape, but is as big as an elephant; it dwells in dark caverns, and ever shuns the light. There is got from it an ivory as white as that of the elephant, but easier to work, and not liable to split. Its flesh is very cold, and excellent for refresh-

---

[1] J. F. M. v. Olfers, ' Die Ueberreste vorweltlicher Riesenthiere in Beziehung an Ostasiatischen Sagen und Chinesischen Schriften ' (Berlin Acad., 1839); Berlin, 1840.

ing the blood.   The ancient book *Shin-y-King*, speaks of this animal in the following terms :—There is in the extreme north, among the snows and ice which cover this region, a *shu* (rat), which weighs up to a thousand pounds, its flesh is very good for those who are heated.   The *Tse-shu* calls it *fen-shu*, and speaks of another kind which is of less size ; it is only, says this authority, as large as a buffalo, it burrows like the moles, shuns the light, and almost always stays in its underground caves.   It is said that it would die if it saw the light of the sun, or even of the moon."[1]

The story of the mammoth being a burrowing animal, which has arisen from the finding its remains exposed in cliffs or banks deep below the surface, becomes the more valuable as evidence of the growth of myths, from the fact that on the other side of the world a like story has developed itself from a like origin. When Darwin visited certain cliffs of the River Parana, between Buenos Ayres and Santa Fé, where many bones of Mastodons are found, he says, " The men who took me in the canoe, said they had long known of these skeletons, and had often wondered how they had got there : the necessity of a theory being felt, they came to the conclusion that, like the bizcacha, the mastodon was formerly a burrowing animal."[2]   The bizcacha is a small rabbit-like rodent, common on the Pampas.

Other fossil remains beside those of the mammoth have given rise to myths of observation in Siberia.   The curved tusks of the *Rhinoceros tichorhinus* are something like the claws of a monstrous bird, and when both tusks are found united by part of the skull, the whole might very well be taken by a man totally ignorant of anatomy, for the bird's foot with two claws. The Siberians not only believe the horns of the rhinoceros to be the claws of an enormous bird, and call them " bird's claws " accordingly, but a family of myths has developed itself out of this belief, how these winged monsters lived in the country in the time of the ancestors of the present inhabitants, who fought with them for the possession of the land.   One story tells how the country was wasted by one of them, till a wise man fixed a

[1] Mém. conc. les Chinois, vol. iv. p. 481.   Klemm, C. G., vol. vi. p. 471.
[2] Darwin, p. 127.

pointed iron spear on the top of a pine-tree, and the bird alighted there, and skewered itself upon the lance.

Adolf Erman connects, with much plausibility, the well-known *rukh* of the Arabian Nights, and the *griffin* (γρύψ) of Herodotus, with the tales of monstrous birds current in the gold-producing regions of Siberia; and he even suggests the remark that gold-bearing sand really underlies the beds which contain these fossil "bird's claws" as an explanation of the passage, "it is said that the Arimaspi, one-eyed men, seize (the gold) from underneath the griffins (λέγεται δὲ ὑπὲκ τῶν γρυπῶν ἁρπάζειν Ἀριμασποὺς ἄνδρας μουνοφθάλμους).[1] At about the same time as Herodotus, Ctesias brings out more fully the familiar figure of the griffin. "There is also gold," he says, "in the Indian country, not found in the streams and washed, as in the river Pactolus; but there are many and great mountains, wherein dwell the griffins, four-footed birds of the greatness of the wolf, but with legs and claws like lions. The feathers on the rest of their bodies are black, but red on the breast. Through them it is that the gold in the mountains, though plentiful, is most difficult to get."[2] That the Siberian myths of monstrous birds have passed into the mediæval notions of the griffins admits of no question whatever. Albertus Magnus describes them as quadrupeds, with birds' beaks and wings; they dwell in Scythia, and possess the gold, and silver, and precious stones. The Arimaspi fight with them. In its nest the griffin lays the agate for its help and medicine. It is hostile to men and horses; it has long claws, which are made into goblets; they are as big as ox-horns, as indeed the creature itself is bigger than eight lions; of its feathers are made strong bows, arrows, and lances.[3] With regard to this description, it is to be observed that the horns, cut in slices, are really used for plating bows;[4] but the bird's quills, as they are still considered to be in the country where they are found, are the leg-bones of other animals.[5] The rhinoceros horns, supposed

---

[1] Herod., iii. 116.   Erman, Reise, vol. i. pp. 711-2.
[2] Ctesias, 'De Rebus Indicis,' 12.
[3] Klemm, C. G., vol. i. p. 155, and see p. 101.
[4] Olfers, p. 13.   [5] Erman, vol. i. p. 711.

to be griffins' claws, were mounted in gold and silver in Europe in the middle ages, and preserved as relics in churches. There is or was one in Corpus Christi College, Cambridge, mounted on little gilt claws, which sufficiently show what it was thought to be.

The Chinese idea that the mammoth was a huge rat, and the very name of " Mother of Mice" given to it, fit curiously with a set of North American stories, which may have a like origin in the finding of fossil remains of enormous size. The name of the " Père aux Bœufs," probably the translation of a native Indian name, was given to an extinct animal whose huge bones were found on the banks of the Ohio.[1] The Indians of New France, Father Paul le Jeune relates in 1635, " say besides, that all the animals of each species have an elder brother, who is as the beginning and origin of all the race, and this elder brother is marvellously great and powerful. The elder brother of the beavers, they told me, is perhaps as big as our hut."[2] There are current among the Iroquois, says Morgan, fables of a buffalo of such huge dimensions as to thresh down the forest in his march.[3] And lastly, in one of the North American tales of the Sun-Catcher, we find a creature to which the name of " Mother of Mice" may well belong. When the Sun was to be set free from the snare, the animals debated who should go up and sever the cord, and the dormouse went, " for at this time the dormouse was the largest animal in the world; when it stood up it looked like a mountain." The whole story, which goes on to tell how it has come to pass that the dormice are but small creatures now, is given here in the next chapter.

The native tribes of the lower end of South America explained the reason why they, unlike the Spaniards, had no herds of cattle in their country, by an interesting story, which has the air of a myth of observation founded upon the examination of caves containing fossil bones. They had a multiplicity of inferior deities below the two great powers of Good and Evil, who, there as elsewhere on the American continent, are

---

[1] Buffon, Hist. Nat. (ed. Sonnini), vol. xxviii. p. 264.
[2] Le Jeune, Relations (1634), vol. i. p. 46.
[3] Morgan, p. 166.

above all.   Each of the lower deities presides over one particular caste or family of Indians, of which he is supposed to have been the creator. "Some make themselves of the caste of the tiger, some of the lion, some of the guanaco, and others of the ostrich, etc.   They imagine that these deities have each their separate habitations, in vast caverns under the earth, beneath some lake, hill, etc.; and that when an Indian dies, his soul goes to live with the deity who presides over his particular family, there to enjoy the happiness of being eternally drunk. They believe that their good deities made the world, and that they first created the Indians in their caves, gave them the lance, the bow and arrows, and the stone-bowls, to fight and hunt with, and then turned them out to shift for themselves. They imagine that the deities of the Spaniards did the same by them; but that, instead of lances, bows, etc., they gave them guns and swords.   They suppose that when the beasts, birds, and lesser animals were created, those of the more nimble kind came immediately out of their caves; but that the bulls and cows being the last, the Indians were so frightened at the sight of their horns, that they stopped up the entrance of their caves with great stones.   This is the reason they give why they had no black cattle in their country till the Spaniards brought them over, who more wisely had let them out of the caves." [1]

The possibility that the Brazilian belief in the caypor or wild ape-like being of the woods may be derived from a recollection of a great extinct ape has been already mentioned, but there is a circumstance which rather favours the idea of its being a myth, founded on the examination of fossil bones. Like the mammoth, and the mastodon, and the creators of the beasts and birds, he is thought to live underground.   "They believe he has subterranean campos and hunting grounds in the forest, well stocked with pacas and deer." [2]   It is possible, too, that the notion of subterranean animals, who die if they see the daylight, like the mammoths of Siberia, may be traced in various stories.   Thus, the Fijians tell a tale of two rocks,

[1] Thos. Falkner, 'A Description of Patagonia,' etc.; Hereford, 1774, p. 114.
[2] Bates, vol. ii. p. 204.

malo and female Lado, which are two deities who were turned by the sight of daylight into stone;[1] and in the West Indies there were men who dwelt in Cimmerian darkness in their caves, and coming out were turned into stones and trees by the sight of the sun.[2]

Tales of giants and monsters, which stand in direct connexion with the finding of great fossil bones, are scattered broadcast over the mythology of the world. Huge bones, found at Punto Santa Elena, in the north of Guayaquil, have served as a foundation for the story of a colony of giants who dwelt there.[3] The whole area of the Pampas is a great sepulchre of enormous extinct animals; no wonder that one great plain should be called the "Field of the Giants," and that such names as "the hill of the giant," "the stream of the animal," should be guides to the geologist in his search for fossil bones.[4]

In North America it is the same. The fossil bones of Mexico are referred to the giants who dwelt in the land in early times, and were found living in the plains of Tlascala by the Olmecs, who came there before the Toltecs. At the time of the conquest, Bernal Diaz was told of their huge stature and their crimes; and, to show him how big they were, the people brought him a bone of one of them, which he measured himself against, and it was as tall as he, who was a man of reasonable stature. He and his companions were astonished to see those bones, and held it for certain that there had been giants in that land.[5] The Indians of North America tell how their mythic hero, Manabozho, "killed the ancient monsters whose bones we now see under the earth." They use pieces of the bones of these monsters as charms, and most likely the pieces of bone drawn in their pictures as instruments of magic power are such. They tell of giants who could stride over the

---

[1] Seemann, 'Viti,' p. 60.   [2] Oviedo, in Purchas, vol. v. p. 959.

[3] Humboldt, Vues des Cord., pl. 26.   Rivero and Tschudi, Ant. Per. p. 51.

[4] Darwin, in Narr., vol. iii. p. 155.

[5] Bernal Diaz, Conq. de la Nueva España, Madrid, 1795, vol. i. p. 350. Tylor, 'Mexico,' p. 248. Clavigero, vol. i. p. 125. Humboldt, Vues des Cord., pl. 26.

largest rivers, and the tallest pine-trees. The Winnebagos say
their monstrous medicine animal still exists, and they have
pieces of the bones which belong to them, which they use as
charms. The Dacotas use such bones for "medicine," and say
they belong to the great horned water-beast, the Unk-a-ta-he.
Hiawatha helped the Indians to subdue the great monsters that
overran the country. The "Tom Thumb" of the Chippewas
killed the giants, and hacked them into little pieces, saying,
"Henceforth let no man be larger than you are now," and so
men became of their present size.[1] There are plenty more
such stories. One mentioned by Dr. Wilson has the interesting feature that monsters and giants both perished by the
thunderbolts of the Great Spirit, and in another all the monsters were thus slain except the Big Bull, who went off to the
Great Lakes.[2] It must be borne in mind, however, that in spe-
culating on the origin of tales such as these, possible recollections of contests of men with huge animals now extinct must
be taken into consideration, as well as inferences from the
finding of large bones, and sometimes even both causes may
have worked together.

In the Old World, myths both old and new connected with
huge bones, fossil or recent, are common enough.[3] Marcus
Scaurus brought to Rome, from Joppa, the bones of the monster who was to have devoured Andromeda, while the vestiges
of the chains which bound her were to be seen there on the
rock;[4] and the sepulchre of Antæus, containing his skeleton,
60 cubits long, was found in Mauritania.[5]

Don Quixote was beforehand with Dr. Falconer in reasoning
on the huge fossil bones so common in Sicily as remains of
ancient inhabitants, as appears from his answer to the barber's
question, how big he thought the giant Morgante might have
been? " . . . Moreover, in the island of Sicily there have
been found long-bones and shoulder-bones so huge, that their
size manifests their owners to have been giants, and as big as

[1] Schoolcraft, part i. pp. 310, 390; part ii. pp. 175, 224; part iii. pp. 232, 315,
319.   [2] Wilson, 'Prehistoric Man,' vol. i. p. 112.
[3] In Polynesia, see Mariner, vol. i. p. 313.
[4] Plin., ix. 4; v. 14.   [5] Strabo, xvii. 3, 8.

great towers, for this truth geometry sets beyond doubt."
Again, the fossil bones so plentifully strewed over the Sewalik,
or lowest ranges of the Himalayas, belonged to the slain Ra-
kis,[1] the gigantic Rakshasas of the Indian mythology. The
remains of the Dun Cow that Guy Earl of Warwick slew are
or were to be seen in England, in the shape of a whale's rib
in the church of St. Mary Redcliffe, and some great fossil bone
kept, I believe, in Warwick Castle. "The giant sixteen feet
high, whose bones were found in 1577 near Reyden under an
uprooted oak, and examined and celebrated in song by Felix
Plater, the renowned physician of Basle, has been long ago
banished by later naturalists into a very distant department of
zoology; but the giant has from that time forth got a firm
standing-ground beside the arms of Lucerne, and will keep it,
all critics to the contrary notwithstanding."[2]

It would be tedious to enumerate more instances in which
traditions of giants and huge beasts have been formed both in
ancient and modern times from the finding of great fossil
bones. But the remarks of St. Augustine on a great fossil
tooth he saw are worthy of attention, as throwing some light
on the connexion of such bones with the belief that man was
once both enormously larger and longer-lived than he is now,
and that his stature has diminished in the course of ages to its
present dimensions; as it is held by the Moslems that Adam
was sixty feet high, of the measure of a tall palm-tree, and
that the true believers will be restored in Paradise to this original stature of the human race, and that the houris who will
attend them will be of proportionate dimensions. It seems as
if Linnæus may have held such an opinion, at least his editor
gives the following as his reading of a passage in the notes of
his northern tour, where unfortunately the original is obscure.
"I have a notion that Adam and Eve were giants, and that
mankind from one generation to another, owing to poverty and
other causes, have diminished in size. Hence perhaps the di-
minutive stature of the Laplanders."[3]

St. Augustine's observations are contained in his chapter

[1] Torrens, 'Ladák,' etc., p. 87.   [2] Olfers, p. 3.
[3] Linnæus, 'Tour,' vol. i. p. 28.

"Concerning the long life of men before the flood, and the greater size of their bodies." He makes these remarks, he says, in case any infidel should raise a doubt about men having lived to so great an age. "So some indeed do not believe that men's bodies were formerly much greater than now." Virgil, he continues, expresses the huge size of the men of former times, how much more then in the younger periods of the world, before the celebrated deluge. "But concerning the magnitude of their bodies, the graves laid bare by age or the force of rivers and various accidents especially convict the incredulous, where they have come to light, or where bones of the dead of incredible magnitude have fallen. I have seen, and not I alone, on the shore by Utica, so huge a molar tooth of a man, that were it cut up into small models of teeth like ours, it would seem enough to make a hundred of them. But this I should think had belonge to some giant; for beside that the bodies of all men were then much larger than ours, the giants again far exceeded the rest."[1]

Among the traditions preserved from remote ages by the human race, there are perhaps none more important to the ethnologist than those which relate, in every great district of the world, and with so much unity combined with so much variety, the occurrence of a great Deluge in long past time. In studying these Diluvial Traditions it is of the highest consequence that he should be able to separate the results of the memory of real events from those of observation of natural phenomena and of purely mythological development. Humboldt in part states the problem in his remarks on the four devastations of the earth, by famine, fire, hurricane, and deluge, as represented in the Mexican picture-writing. "Whatever may be their true origin, it does not appear less certain that they are fictions of astronomical mythology, modified either by a dim remembrance of some great revolution which our planet has undergone, or in accordance with the physical and geological hypotheses to which the appearance of marine petrifactions and fossil bones give rise, even among peoples at the greatest distance from civilization."[2]

[1] Aug., 'De Civitate Dei,' xv. 9.   [2] Humboldt, Vues des Cord., pl. 28.

That the observation of shells and corals in places above the level of the sea, and even on high mountains, should have given rise to legends of great floods which deposited them there, is natural enough, and quite consistent with the growth of myths of monsters and giants from the observation of fossil bones. Marine productions being found at heights of many hundred feet above the sea, the question would evidently occur to the men who speculated so ingeniously about the fossil bones, how did these productions of the sea get upon the mountains? As to fossil crustaceans, the Arabian geographer Abu-Zeyd explains their appearance in Ceylon by setting them down as sea-animals like craw-fish, which, when they come out of the sea, are converted into stone,[1] but the appearance of sea-shells on mountains could hardly be so accounted for. Two alternatives suggest themselves to explain the occurrence of shells in such situations; either the sea may have been up to the mountain, or the mountain may have been down in the sea. Modern geologists have in most cases to adopt the latter alternative, but till recent times the former was oftener than not held to be the more probable. Water is the type of all that is movable, fluctuating, unstable, while the firm earth is immovable, permanent, solid, and it is not to the purpose to argue that modern knowledge has reversed this older view, with so many other doctrines which seemed to rest on the plain evidence of the senses, and only failed, as many of our own theories have no doubt to fail, from the narrowness of their range of observation.

The fossils imbedded in high ground have been appealed to, both in ancient and modern times, both by savages and civilized men, as evidence in support of their traditions of a flood, and moreover the argument, apparently unconnected with any tradition, is to be found, that because there are marine fossils in places away from the sea, therefore the sea must once have been there. In the Society Islands, tradition tells how a flood that rose over the tops of the mountains, was raised by the sea-god Ruahatu. A fisherman caught his hooks in the hair of the god as he lay sleeping among his coral groves, and woke

[1] Tennent, 'Ceylon,' vol. i. p. 14.

him, but, strange to say, though in his anger he drowned the rest of the inhabitants of the land in the deluge, he allowed the fisherman himself to find safe refuge with his wife and child on a small, low, coral island close to Raiatea, and they repeopled the earth. How the little island was preserved they give no account, but they appeal to the *farero*, coral, and shells, found at the tops of the highest mountains, as proof of the inundation.[1] In Samoa it is the universal belief that of old the fish swam where the land now is, and tradition adds that when the waters abated, many of the fish of the sea were left on the land, and afterwards were changed into stones. Hence, they say, there are stones in abundance in the bush and among the mountains, which were once sharks, and other inhabitants of the deep.[2] In the North the Moravian missionary Cranz records that, "The first missionaries found among the Greenlanders a tolerably distinct tradition of the Deluge, of which almost all heathen nations still know something, namely, that the world was once tilted over (umgekantert) and all men were drowned, but some became fire-spirits. The only man who remained alive, smote afterwards with his stick upon the ground, and there came out a woman, with whom he peopled the earth again. They tell, moreover, that far up in the country, where men could never have dwelt, there are found all sorts of remains of fishes, and even bones of whales on a high mountain; wherefrom they make it clear that the earth was once flooded."[3] It is interesting to compare this argument with the explanation the Kamchadals give of the bones of whales, which in their country also are found on high mountains. They fear all high mountains, says Steller, especially volcanos, and also hot springs, and believe that some mountains are the abodes of spirits. "When one asks them what the devils do up there, they reply, 'they cook whales.' I asked, where they got them? The answer was, they go down to the sea at night and catch so many, that one brings home five to ten of them, one hanging to each finger. When I asked, how do you know this? they said their *Stariki* or old people

[1] Ellis, Polyn. Res., vol. ii. p. 58.   [2] Turner, 'Polynesia,' p. 242.
[3] Cranz, p. 262.

had always said so and believed it themselves. Withal they appealed to the observation, that there were many bones of whales found on all burning mountains. I asked whence come the flames there sometimes, and they answered, when the spirits have heated up their mountains as we do our *yurts*, they fling the rest of the brands out up the chimney, so as to be able to shut up. They said moreover, God in heaven sometimes does so too at the time when it is our summer and his winter, and he warms up his yurt; whereby they explain the veneration of the lightning."[1]

In the geological theories of classical times, the inference from fossil shells found inland, high or low above the sea level, was commonly that the sea had once been there, though it need not always follow that it was the sea which had since changed its level. Herodotus argues from the shells on the mountains in Egypt,[2] and Xanthus from the fossil shells, like cockles and scallops, which he had seen far from the sea, that there had been sea in old times where the land had since been left dry. Eratosthenes notices the existence of quantities of oyster-shells and bits of wreck of seagoing ships near the temple of Ammon, far inland in Libya, while Strato expresses the opinion that this temple was once close to the sea, though since thrown inland by the retiring of the waters.[3] Describing the region of Numidia farther west, Pomponius Mela relates that, " Inland and far enough from the coast (if the thing be credible) they tell that in a wondrous way the spines of fish, and fragments of murex and oyster-shells, stones worn in the ordinary manner by the waves and not differing from those of the sea, anchors fixed in the rocks, and other similar signs and vestiges of the sea that once spread to those places, exist and are found on the barren plains."[4] So Ovid says in his remarkable statement of the Pythagorean doctrines,—

> " Et procul a pelago conchæ jacuere marinæ
>   Et vetus inventa est in montibus anchora summis,"

and argues thence that sea has been converted into land.[5]

<hr>

[1] Steller, p. 47.   [2] Herod., ii. 12.   [3] Strabo, i. 3, 4.
[4] Mela, i. c. 6.   [5] Ov. Met., xv. 264.

In the Chinese Encyclopædia from which I have already quoted two remarkable passages, an account is to be found bearing on the present subject. "*Eastern Tartary.*—In travelling from the shore of the Eastern Sea toward Che-lu, neither brooks nor ponds are met with in the country, although it is intersected by mountains and valleys. Nevertheless there are found in the sand, very far away from the sea, oyster-shells and the shields of crabs. The tradition of the Mongols who inhabit the country is that it has been said from time immemorial that in remote antiquity the waters of the deluge flooded the district, and when they retired, the places where they had been made their appearance covered with sand. . . . However it may have happened, to follow the great geographer Ti-chi, a part of this country is in great plains, where several hundred leagues are found to have been covered by the waters and since abandoned; this is why these deserts are called the Sandy Sea, which indicates that they were not originally covered with sand and gravel."[1]

Again, the presence of fossil shells on high mountains has long been adduced as evidence of the Noachic flood. Thus Tertullian connects the sea-shells on mountains with the reappearance of the earth from below the waters,[2] and the argument may be followed up through later times, and was current in England till quite recently. In the ninth edition of Horne's 'Introduction to the Scriptures,' published in 1846, the evidence of fossils is confidently held to prove the universality of the Deluge; but the argument disappears from the next edition, published ten years later.

To the statements of classical writers as to anchors and pieces of wreck being found inland, some more modern accounts must be added. From time to time, whether from upheaval of the earth's surface or other geological changes, ships and things belonging to them have been found far inland, in places for ages out of reach of navigable waters. Buffon speaks of fragments of vessels being found in a mountain lake in Portugal, far from the sea, and mentions a statement of Sabinus,

<hr>

[1] Mém. conc. les Chinois, vol. iv. p. 474.   Klemm, C. G., vol. vi. p. 467.
[2] Tert., 'De Pallio,' ii.   H. F. Link, 'Die Urwelt,' etc.; Berlin, 1821, p. 4.

Y

in his commentary on the lines just quoted from Ovid, that in
the year 1460 a vessel was found with its anchors, in a mine in
the Alps.[1]   This is, no doubt, the same story that Antonio
Galvano refers to, when he says, "Thus they tell of finding
hulls of ships and iron anchors in the mountains of Switzerland
very far inland, where it appears that there was never sea nor
salt water."[2]

The possible bearing of such phenomena on the formation of
diluvial traditions is clearly shown by their having been repeatedly claimed, like the fossil shells, as evidence of the former
presence of the sea, and even of the Biblical deluge.   It is
not, however, necessary, from this point of view, that the accounts in question should all be true; it is enough that they
should be believed and reasoned upon.   In the seventeenth
century, Fray Pedro Simon relates that some miners, running
an adit into a hill near Callao, "met with a ship which had on
top of it the great mass of the hill, and did not agree in its
make and appearance with our ships," whence people judged
that it had been left there by the Flood, and the fact is cited in
proof of the habitation of the country in antediluvian times.[3]
Writing in 1730, Strahlenberg gives it as his opinion that the
mammoth bones in Siberia are relics of the Deluge, and goes
on to add a like example, that some thirty years earlier the
whole lower hull of a ship with a keel was found in Barabinsk
Tartary, where nevertheless there is no ocean.[4]   Lastly, in
Scotland it is quite a common thing for ancient canoes hollowed from a single tree to be found buried in places remote
from navigable channels, while the skeletons of whales are
found in similar situations.   Sir John Clerk thus remarks upon
a canoe found near Edinburgh in 1726.   "The washings of the
river Carron discovered a boat, 13 or 14 feet underground; it
is 36 feet in length, and 4½ in breadth, all of one piece of oak.
There were several strata above it, such as loam, clay, shells,

---

[1] Buffon, 'Théorie de la Terre,' vol. iii. p. 119.

[2] Galvano, p. 50.

[3] Simon, 'Noticias Historiales,' etc.; Cuenca, 1627, p. 31.

[4] Strahlenberg, 'Das Nord- und Ostliche Theil von Europa und Asien,' Stock-
holm, 1730, p. 300.   C. Hamilton Smith, p. 45.

moss, sand, and gravel; these strata demonstrate it to have been an antediluvian boat."[1]

Both in Scotland and in South America, upheaval of land in more or less modern times is a recognized fact, and the finding of boats, as of various other productions of human art, in places where they could hardly have been placed by man, is readily accounted for between this upheaval and the effects of ordinary accumulation and degradation.

Geological evidence bearing on traditions of a Deluge is scarce. Sir Charles Lyell seems disposed to adopt the view of old writers that some of the South American deluge traditions are connected with the memory of local floods, such as are known to happen there. Dr. Szabó says that the Hungarians still preserve traditions of their plains having been once covered by a freshwater sea, the waters of which afterwards escaped through the narrows of the Iron Gate. The draining of the country in this manner is considered by Dr. Szabó as having really happened, so that this may be a case of tradition handing down the memory of a geological change from a very remote period.[2] It would require a large body of scientific evidence of this character to make possible a thorough investigation of the Diluvial traditions of the world, and any attempt to draw a distinct line between the claims of History and Mythology must in the meantime be premature.

It fortunately happens that the difficulty in analysing the Diluvial traditions into their historical and mythological elements is one which only partially affects their use to Ethnology. Were they merely stories current in various parts of the world, saying little more than that there was once a great flood, or giving details only harmonizing within limited districts, they might be explained as Myths of Observation which had not necessarily any common origin. There are some which, taken by themselves, could not stand against this argument, but the general state of things found over the world is widely different from this. The notion of men having existed before the flood, and having been all destroyed except a few who escaped and

<hr>

[1] Bibl. Topog. Brit., London, 1790, vol. iii. part 1. p. 241. Wilson, 'Archæology, etc. of Scotland,' p. 32.   [2] Geol. Journal, Feb. 1863.

re-peopled the earth, does not flow so immediately from the observation of natural phenomena that we can easily suppose it to have originated several times independently in such a way, yet this is a feature common to the great mass of flood traditions. Still more strongly does this argument apply to the occurrence f some form of raft, ark, or canoe, in which the survivors are usually saved, unless, as in some cases, they take refuge directly on the top of some mountain which the waters never cover.   The idea is indeed conceivable, if somewhat far-fetched, that from the sight of a boat found high on a mountain there might grow a story of the flood which carried it there, while the people in it escaped to found a new race.   But it lies outside all reasonable probability to suppose such circumstances to have produced the same story in several different places, nor is it very likely that the dim remembrances of a number of local floods should accord in this with the amount of consistency that is found among the flood-traditions of remote regions of the world.   The occurrence of an ark in the traditions of a deluge, found in so many distant times and places, seems to entitle them to be received as derived from a single source, and thus forming part of the mass of evidence from art, custom, and belief, which supports the theory of a deep-lying historical connexion of the mental development of the whole human race.

As to Myths of Observation in general, the line of demarcation which separates them on the one hand from traditions of real events, and on the other from more purely mythic tales, is equally hard to draw.   Even the stories which have their origin in a mere realized metaphor, or a personification of the phenomena of nature, will attach themselves to real persons, places, or objects, as strongly as though they actually belonged to them.   To the subjective mind of the myth maker, every hill and valley, every stone and tree, that strikes his attention, becomes the place where some mythic occurrence happened to gods, or heroes, or fair women, or monsters, or ethereal beings.   When once the tale is made, the rock or tree becomes evidence of its truth to future generations: " the bricks are alive at this day to testify it; therefore, deny it not."

CHAPTER XII.

GEOGRAPHICAL DISTRIBUTION OF MYTHS.

THE student of the early History of Mankind finds in Comparative Mythology the same use and the same difficulty which lie before him in so many other branches of his subject. He can sometimes show, in the mythical tales current among several peoples, coincidences so quaint, so minute, or so complex, that they could hardly have arisen independently in two places, and these coincidences he claims as proofs of historical connexion between the tribes or nations among whom they are found. But his great difficulty is how to be sure that he is not interpreting as historical evidence analogies which may be nothing more than the results of the like working of the human mind under like conditions. His ever-recurring problem is to classify the crowd of resemblances which are continually thrusting themselves upon him, so as to keep those things which are merely similar apart from those which, having at some spot of the earth's surface their common source and centre of diffusion, are really and historically united.

No attempt is made in the present chapter to lay down definite rules for the solution of this important problem, but a few illustrations are given of the more general analogies running through the Folk-lore of the world, which Ethnology, for the present at least, has to set aside; and then a few facts are stated, bearing on the diffusion of Myths by recognized channels of intercourse, with the view of introducing a group of similar episodes, which it is for the reader to reject as caused by independent growth or modern transmission, or to accept as a contribution to the early History of the New World.

Firstly, then, there are found among savage tribes myths like in their character, and therefore no doubt in their origin, to those of the great Aryan race which have in our own times been so successfully traced to the very point where they arose out of the contemplation of nature. No one has yet done for the myths of the lowest tribes what has been done for those of our more highly developed race by Kuhn and Müller, and their school in Germany and England; but Schirren, by his treatment of the gods and mythic ancestors of the South Sea Islanders as personifications of the phenomena of nature, has made an important step toward extending the modern method of interpretation to the Mythology of the World.[1] Still, a very slight acquaintance with the popular tales of America, Polynesia, even Australia and Van Diemen's Land, will show that they are the same in their nature and often in their incidents, by virtue of the like nature of the minds which conceived them.

As Zeus, the personified Heaven of our own race, drops tears on earth which mortals call rain, so does the heaven-god of Tahiti;

> "Thickly falls the small rain on the face of the sea,
> They are not drops of rain, but they are tears of Oro."[2]

In the dark patches on the face of the moon, the Singhalese sees the pious hare that offered itself to Buddha to be cooked and eaten, when he was wandering hungry in the forest. The Northman saw there the two children whom Mâni the Moon caught up, as they were taking the water from the well Byrgir, and who are carrying the bucket on the pole between them to this day. Elsewhere in Europe, Isaac has been seen carrying the bundle of wood up Mount Moriah for his own sacrifice, and Cain bringing from his field a load of thorns as his offering to Jehovah. Our own "Man in the Moon" was set up there for picking sticks on a Sunday, and he, too, carries his thorn-bush, as Caliban had seen, "I have seen thee in her, and I do

---

[1] Schirren, 'Die Wanderungen der Neuseeländer und der Mauimythos,' Riga, 1856.　　[2] Ellis, Polyn. Res., vol. i. p. 631.

adore thee; my mistress showed me thee, thy dog, and bush." In the Samoan Islands in the Central Pacific, the dweller in the moon is a woman. Her name was Sina, and she was beating out paper-cloth with a mallet. The moon was just rising, and looked like a great bread-fruit, so Sina asked her to come down and let her child have a bit of her. But the moon was very angry at the idea of being eaten, and took up Sina, child, and mallet and all, and there they are to be seen to this day.[1]

The heavenly bodies are gods and heroes, and tales of their deeds in love and arms are found among the lower as among the higher races. Apollo and Artemis, Helios and Selene, are brother and sister, and so in the Polar Regions the Sun is a maiden and the Moon her brother. The Esquimaux tale tells how, when the girl was at a festive gathering, some one declared his love for her by shaking her by the shoulders, after the manner of the country. She could not tell who it was in the dark hut, so she smeared her hand with soot, and when he came back, she blackened his face with her hand. When a light was brought, she saw it was her brother, and fled, and he rushed after her. She came to the end of the earth and sprang out into the sky, and he followed her. There they became the Sun and Moon, and this is why the moon is always chasing the sun through the heavens; and the moon is sometimes dark as he turns his blackened cheek toward the earth.[2]

The natives of Van Diemen's Land, whose dismal history is now closing in total extinction, are among the lowest tribes known to Ethnology. Yet to them, as to higher races, the idea is familiar that the stars are men, or beings of a higher order who have appeared as men on earth. Their myth of the two heroes who are now the twin stars Castor and Pollux, is thus told by Milligan, as related by a native of the Oyster Bay Tribe;

" My father, my grandfather, all of them lived a long time ago, all over the country; they had no fire. Two black-fellows came, they slept at the foot of a hill,—a hill in my own country. On the summit of a hill they were seen by my fathers,

---

[1] Grimm, D. M., pp. 679–83. Turner, p. 217. See Mariner, vol. ii. p. 127.
[2] Hayes, 'Arctic Boat Journey,' p. 253. A different version in Crantz, p. 205.

my countrymen, on the top of the hill they were seen standing : they threw fire like a star,—it fell amongst the blackmen, my countrymen. They were frightened,—they fled away, all of them ; after a while they returned, they hastened and made a fire,—a fire with wood ; no more was fire was lost in our land. The two black-fellows are in the clouds ; in the clear night you see them like two stars.[1] These are they who brought fire to my fathers.

The two blackmen staid awhile in the land of my fathers. Two women were bathing ; it was near a rocky shore, where mussels were plentiful. The women were sulky, they were sad ; their husbands were faithless, they had gone with two girls. The women were lonely ; they were swimming in the water, they were diving for cray-fish. A sting-ray lay concealed in the hollow of a rock,—a large sting-ray ! The sting-ray was large, he had a very long spear ; from his hole he spied the women, he saw them dive : he pierced them with his spear,— he killed them, he carried them away. Awhile they were gone out of sight. The sting-ray returned, he came close to the shore, he lay in still water, near the sandy beach ; with him were the women, they were fast on his spear,—they were dead !

The two blackmen fought the sting-ray ; they slew him with their spears ; they killed him ;—the women were dead ! The two blackmen made a fire,—a fire of wood. On either side they laid a woman,—the fire was between : the women were dead !

The blackmen sought some ants, some large blue ants ; they placed them on the bosoms of the women. Severely, intensely were they bitten. The women revived,—they lived once more.

Soon there came a fog, a fog dark as night. The two blackmen went away, the women disappeared : they passed through the fog, the thick dark fog ! Their place is in the clouds. Two stars you see in the clear cold night ; the two blackmen are there,—the women are with them : they are stars above."[2]

[1] Castor and Pollux.
[2] Milligan, Papers, etc., of R. Soc. of Tasmania, vol. iii. part ii. 1859, p. 274.

It is not needful to accumulate great masses of such tales as these, in order to show that the myth-making faculty belongs to mankind in general, and manifests itself in the most distant regions, where its unity of principle developes itself in endless variety of form. There may indeed be a remote historical connexion at the root of some of the analogies in myths from far distant regions, which have just been mentioned; but when resemblances in Mythology are brought forward as proofs of such historical connexion, they must be closer and deeper than these. Mythological evidence, to be used for such a purpose, requires a systematic agreement in the putting together of a number of events or ideas, which agreement must be so close as to make it in a high degree improbable that two such combinations should have occurred separately, or at least the tales or ideas found alike in distant regions must be of so quaint and fantastic a character as to make it, on the very face of the matter, unlikely that they should have been invented twice. But it is both easier and safer to appeal to the effects of known intercourse between different peoples in spreading beliefs and popular tales, as evidence of the way in which historical connexion really does record itself in Mythology, than to lay down *à priori* rules as to what the effects of such connexion ought to be.

When we consider how short the time is since the Iudians of North America have been acquainted with guns, the fact that there has been recorded, as one of their native beliefs, the notion that there are men who have charmed lives, and can only be killed with a silver bullet, may prepare us for the way in which savages can take up foreign mythology into their own. Again, it might be naturally expected that Bible stories learnt from missionaries, settlers, and travellers, should pass in a more or less altered shape into the folk-lore of savage races. Moffat gives a good instance which happened to himself. He had never succeeded in finding a deluge-tradition in South Africa, but making inquiries in a Namaqua village, he came upon a somewhat intelligent native who had one to tell, so he began with great satisfaction to take it down in writing. By the time it was finished, however, he began to suspect, for it bore the impress of the Bible, though the Hottentot declared that he had received it from his forefathers, and had never seen or heard of a missionary.   Mr. Moffat was puzzled, and suspended his judgment till, a little while afterwards, the mystery was un-ravelled by the appearance of the very missionary from whom the native story-teller had received his teaching.[1]   As another case of the same kind, may be quoted the following servile version of the story of Joseph and his brethren, found in Hawaii as the story of Waikelenuiaiku.   His father had ten sons and one daughter; he was beloved by his father, and hated by his brethren, and they threw him into a pit, but his eldest brother felt more compassion for him than the rest.   He escaped out of the pit, into the country of King Kamohoalii, and there he was confined in a dungeon with the prisoners.   He bade his companions dream, and interpreted the dreams of four of them.   One had seen a ripe banana, and his spirit ate it, the next dreamt of a banana, and the next of a hog, in the same way, but the fourth dreamt that he saw awa, that he pressed out the juice, and his spirit drank it.   The three first dreams the foreigner interpreted for evil, and the dreamers were put to death in course of time, but to the fourth he prophesied de-liverance and life, and he was saved, and told the King, who set Waikelenuiaiku at liberty, and made him a principal chief in the kingdom.[2]

There is sometimes a crudeness about these tales adopted from foreign sources, which gives us the means of positively condemning them.   But the power which myths have of tak-ing root the moment they are transplanted into a new country, often makes it impossible to tell whether they are of old date and historical value, or mere modern intruders.   There is rea-son to believe that a story carried into a distant place by civi-lized men may spread and accommodate itself to the circum-stances of the country, so that in a very few years' time it may be quite honestly collected as a genuine native tale, even by the very people who originally introduced it, like the farmer's hack that he sold in the morning, and bought back in the af-

[1] Moffat, 'Missionary Labours, etc., in S. Africa;' London, 1842, p. 126.
[2] Hopkins, 'Hawaii;' London, 1862, p. 67.

ternoon with a fresh mane and tail, as a new horse.   Of course this is the same kind of diffusion of myths which has been going on from remote ages among mankind, one of the very processes which have preserved to Ethnology aids of such high importance for the reconstruction of early history.   It is only unfortunate that its results in modern times, by confounding the evidence of early and late intercourse between different peoples, have done so much to impair its historical value.

Among the stories found in circulation among outlying races, there are many, beside those relating to a Deluge, which appear to be really united by ancient and deep-lying bonds of connexion with Biblical episodes, and the extreme difficulty, or impossibility, of separating a great part of these ancient stories from those which have grown up in modern times under Christian influences, is a very serious loss to early history.   Still it is better to submit to this, than to base Ethnological arguments on evidence that will not bear the test of criticism.   It is not only to Scriptural stories that this objection lies.   Episodes from the classics and other European sources may be carried into distant lands by colonists and missionaries, and it may be laid down as a general rule, that stories which may have been transplanted in this way in modern times, must be rejected as independent evidence of remote intercourse between distant races among whom they are found.   It is when a connexion between two peoples has been already made probable by evidence not liable to be thus impeached, that these stories can be taken into consideration as secondary evidence, which, once proved to be safe, may be of extraordinary interest and value.

Before proceeding to the comparison of a number of American myths with their analogues in the Old World, it is to be premised that the view of a connexion between the inhabitants of America and Asia by no means rests on one of those vague and misty theories, which have too often been allowed to pass current as solid Ethnological arguments.   The researches of Alexander von Humboldt brought into view, half a century ago, evidence which goes with great force to prove that the civilization of Mexico and that of Asia have, in part at least, a common origin, and that therefore the population of these regions are united, if not by the tie of common descent and relationship by blood, at least by intercourse, direct or indirect, in past times. Of this evidence, the similarity of the chronological calendars is perhaps the strongest point. Not only are series of names like our signs of the zodiac used to record periods of time, but such series are combined together, or with numbers, in both countries, in a complex, perverse, and practically purposeless manner, which, whatever its origin, can hardly by any stretch of probability be supposed to have come up independently in the minds of two different peoples. The theory of the successive destructions and renovations of the world, at the end of long cycles of years, was pointed out by Humboldt as another bond of connexion between Mexico and the Old World; and these agreements between North America and Asia can hardly be read but as indications of a deep-rooted connexion, which ought to have left many other traces beside those. Of customs, the occurrence of which in America as well as in the Old World would be well explained by such a view, something has already been said. Of the North or South American myths which closely resemble tales current in Asia, Polynesia, and elsewhere in the world, eight are discussed here, the World-Tortoise, the Man swallowed by the Fish, the Sun-Catcher, the Ascent to Heaven by the Tree, the Bridge of the Dead, the Fountain of Youth, the Tail-Fisher, and the Diable Boiteux.

In the Old World, the Tortoise Myth belongs especially to India, and the idea is developed there in a variety of forms. The Tortoise that upholds the earth is called in Sanskrit *Kúrmarája*, " King of the Tortoises," and the Hindoos believe to this day that the world rests upon its back. Sometimes the snake Sesha bears the world on its head, or an elephant carries it upon its back, and both snake and elephant are themselves supported by the great tortoise. The earth, rescued from the deluge which destroys mankind, is set up with the snake that bears it resting on the floating tortoise, and a deluge is again to pour over the face of the earth when the world-tortoise, sinking under its load, goes down into the great waters. When the Daityas and Dánavas churned the Sea of Milk to make the *emrita*, the drink of immortality, they took the mountain Mandara for the churning-stick, and the serpent Vâsuki was the thong that was wound round it, and pulled back and forwards to drive the churn. In the midst of the milky sea, Vishnu himself, in the form of a tortoise, served as a pivot for the mountain as it was whirled around.[1]

The notion of the earth being itself a great tortoise swimming in the midst of the ocean, is thus described by Reinaud:— " According to Varâha-Mihira, the Indians represented to themselves the inhabited part of the world under the form of a tortoise floating upon the water; it is in this sense that they call the World *Kûrma-chakra*, that is to say, 'the wheel of the tortoise.' "[2]   And lastly, the ancient Vedic Books of India, which so often supply the means of tracing the most florid developments of mythology back to more simple child-like views of nature, present, as really existing in very early times, the original idea out of which the whole series of myths of the World-Tortoise seems to have grown. To man in the lower levels of science, the earth is a flat plain over which the sky is placed like a dome, as the arched upper shell of the tortoise stands upon the flat plate below, and this is why the tortoise is the symbol and representative of the World. The analogy of other conceptions of heaven and earth, as formed by the two halves of the shell of Brahma's Egg, or by the two calabashes shut together in the mythology of the Yorubas of Africa,[3] is indeed sufficient to lead us to the opinion that this was the original meaning of the World-Tortoise, but the following passage from Weber will enable us to substitute fact for inference.

[1] Bœhtlingk & Roth, *s. v.* Kûrma. Wilson, *s. v.* Kûrmarâja. Coleman, p. 12. Vans Kennedy, ' Researches,' London, 1831, pp. 216, 243. Holwell, ' Historical Events,' etc., London, 1766–7, part ii. p. 109. Falconer, in Proc. Zool. Soc., 1844, p. 80. Baldæus, in Churchill's Voyages, vol. iii. p. 818. Wilson, ' Vishnu Purana,' London, 1810, p. 75. W. v. Humboldt (Kawi-Spr., vol. i. p. 240) says with reference to the Naga Padoha, the great snake on whose three horns the world rests,—" It seems to me not unlikely, that the idea of a world-bearing elephant lies at the bottom of the whole saga [of the snake, that is] and that the double meaning of Sanskrit nâga, *elephant* and *snake*, has brought confusion into the story."

[2] Reinaud, ' Mémoire sur l'Inde,' Paris, 1849, p. 116.

[3] Pott, ' Anti-Kaulen,' Lemgo, 1863, p. 68.

"The earth is conceived in the Çatapatha Bráhmana as the under shell (adharam kapálam) of the Tortoise Kûrma, which represents the Triple World. The upper shell is the sky, the body lying between the two shells is the atmosphere (nabhas, antari-ksham) which connects them."[1]

There are tales to be found in the Old World that seem remnants of the great Indian myth of the World-Tortoise, which have degenerated, as myths so often do when they come down into an age which has quite lost the consciousness of their meaning, into mere wonder-tales. It is related in the first voyage of Sindbad, that he and his companions came, as they sailed along, to an island like one of the gardens of Paradise, and there they anchored the ship, and went ashore, and lighted fires to cook food. But the island was a great fish, on whose back sand had accumulated, and trees had grown from times of old, and when it felt the fire on its back, it moved and went down to the bottom of the sea. In El-Kazwini's account of the animals of the water, there is a version of this story, which describes the creature as a huge tortoise; "The tortoise," he says, "is a sea and land animal. As to the sea-tortoise, it is very enormous, so that the people of the ship imagine that it is an island. One of the merchants hath related, saying, 'We found in the sea an island elevated above the water, having upon it green plants; and we went forth to it, and dug [holes for fire] to cook; whereupon the island moved, and the sailors said, Come ye to your place; for it is a tortoise, and the heat of the fire hath hurt it; lest it carry you away!—By reason of the enormity of its body,' saith he (i. e. the narrator above mentioned), 'it was as though it were an island; and earth collected upon its back in the length of time, so that it became like land, and produced plants.'"[2]

The striking analogy between the Tortoise-myths of North America and India is by no means a matter of new observation;

<hr>

[1] Weber, 'Indische Studien;' Berlin, 1850, etc., vol. i. p. 187. See also p. 81. I may mention having set down this conception as the probable basis of the Tortoise-myths before meeting with this direct evidence from ancient India. The coincidence defends such an interpretation of the myths from the charge of being far-fetched and fanciful.

[2] Lane, 'The Thousand and One Nights,' London, 1859, vol. iii. pp. 6, 79.

it was indeed remarked upon by Father Lafitau nearly a century and a half ago.[1]   Three great features of the Asiatic stories are found among the North American Indians, in the fullest and clearest development. The earth is supported on the back of a huge floating Tortoise, the Tortoise sinks under water and causes a deluge, and the Tortoise is conceived as being itself the Earth floating upon the face of the deep.

In the last century, Loskiel, the Moravian missionary, remarked of the North American Indians, that "Some imagine, that the earth swims in the sea, or that an enormous tortoise carries the world on its back."[2] Schoolcraft, an unrivalled authority on Indian mythology within his own district, remarks that the turtle is "an object held in great respect, in all Indian reminiscence. It is believed to be, in all cases, a symbol of the earth, and is addressed as a mother." In the Iroquois mythology, there was a woman of heaven who was called Atahentsic, and one of the six men of heaven became enamoured of her. When it was discovered, she was cast down to earth, and received on the back of a great turtle lying on the waters, and there she was delivered of twins. One was "The Good Mind," the other was "The Bad Mind," and thus the two great powers of the Indian dualism, the Good and Evil Principle, came into the world, and the tortoise expanded and became the earth,[3] or, as it is elsewhere related, the otter and the fishes disturbed the mud at the bottom of the ocean, and drawing it up round the tortoise, formed a small island, which, gradually increasing, became the earth.[4] Father Charlevoix gives two different versions of the story. In one place it is Taronyawagon, the King of Heaven, who gave his wife so mighty a kick that she flew out of the sky and down to earth, and fell upon the back of a tortoise, which, cleaving the waters of the deluge with its feet, at last uncovered the earth, and carried the woman to the foot of a tree, where she was delivered of twin sons, and the elder, who was called Tawiskaron, killed his younger brother. In another place the story is like Schoolcraft's.[5] Among the Mandans, Catlin found a legend which

[1] Lafitau, vol. i. p. 99.
[2] Loskiel, part i. p. 30.
[3] Schoolcraft, part i. pp. 300, 316.
[4] Coleman, p. 15.
[5] Charlevoix, vol. vi. pp. 146, 65.

brings in the same notion of the World-tortoise, but shows by the difference of the necessary circumstances that it was not in America a mere part of a particular story, but a mythological conception which might be worked into an unlimited variety of myths. The tale that the Mandan doctor told Catlin, was that the earth was a large tortoise, that it carried dirt upon its back, and that a tribe of people who are now dead, and whose faces were white, used to dig down very deep in this ground to catch badgers. One day they stuck a knife through the shell of the tortoise, and it sank and sank till the water ran over its back, and they were all drowned but one man.[1]

The Myth of the World-Tortoise is one of those which have this great value in the comparison of Asiatic and American Mythology, that it leaves not the least opening for the supposition of its having been carried by modern Europeans from the Old to the New World. But it is to be seen, even from the tales which have just been quoted, that it is mixed up in America with incidents and ideas more familiar to the European mind; and the stories told only with reference to the World-Tortoise may serve to give a glimpse into the vast ethnological field which lies in the Red Indian traditions, ready to be worked. The Deluge, Cain and Abel, Ahriman and Ormuzd, Romulus and Remus, all have their analogies among the legends of these wild hunters. In the story which Charlevoix tells just before that which I have quoted, there is Noah's raven and Pandora's casket.

To proceed now to the story of the Man swallowed by the Fish. It is related in the Chippewa tale of the Little Monedo, that there was once a little boy, of tiny stature, and growing no bigger with years, but of monstrous strength. He had done before various wondrous feats, and one day he waded into the lake, and called "You of the red fins, come and swallow me." Immediately that monstrous fish came and swallowed him, and he, seeing his sister standing in despair on the shore, called out to her, and she tied an old mocassin to a string, and fastened it to a tree near the water's edge. The fish said to the boy-man under water, "What is that floating?" The boy-

[1] Catlin, vol. i. p. 181.

man said to the fish, " Go take hold of it, and swallow it as fast
as you can." The fish darted towards the old shoe, and swallowed it; the boy-man laughed to himself, but said nothing
till the fish was fairly caught, and then he took hold of the line
and hauled himself to shore. When the sister began to cut
the fish open she heard her brother's voice from inside the fish,
calling to her to let him out, so she made a hole, and he crept
through, and told her to cut up the fish and dry it, for it would
last them a long while for food.[1]

In the Old World, the Hindoo story of Saktideva tells that
there was once a king's daughter who would marry no one but
the man who had seen the Golden City, and Saktideva was in
love with her; so he went travelling about the world seeking
some one who could tell him where this Golden City was. In
the course of his journeys he embarked on board a ship bound
for the island of Utsthala, where lived the King of the Fishermen, who, Saktideva hoped, would set him on his way. On
the voyage there arose a great storm and the ship went to
pieces, but a great fish swallowed Saktideva whole. Then,
driven by the force of fate, the fish went to the island of Utsthala, and there the servants of the King of the Fishermen
caught it, and the King, wondering at its size, had it cut open,
and Saktideva came out unhurt, to pass through other adventures, and at last to see the Golden City, and to marry, not the
Princess only, but her three sisters beside.[2]

The analogy of these curious tales with the leading episode
of the Book of Jonah is of course evident, and it might appear as though this very ancient story were possibly the direct
origin of one or both of them ; as regards dates, the American
story has been but recently taken down, and even the Hindoo
tale only comes out of a mediæval Sanskrit collection. But
both agree in differing from the history of Jonah, in the fish
being cut open to let the man out. Something very like this
occurs in the myth of the Polynesian Sun-god Maui. He was
born on the sea-shore, and his mother flung him into the foam
of the surf; then the seaweed wrapped its long tangles round

[1] Schoolcraft, part iii. pp. 318-20.
[2] Somadeva Bhatta, vol. ii. pp. 118-184.

him, and the soft jelly-fish rolled themselves about him to protect him as he was drifted on shore again, and his great ancestor the Sky, Tumu-nui-ki-te-Rangi, saw the flies and the
birds collected in clusters and flocks, and ran and stripped the
encircling jelly-fish off, and behold there lay within a human
being; so the old man took the child and carried it home.[1] As
the Polynesian Maui is among the clearest and completest personifications of the Sun, there is some force in Schirren's argument that this story means the Sun being set free by the Sky
at dawn, from the Earth which covers him at night;[2] for it
must be remembered here that one of the most prominent ideas
of the Polynesian Mythology is that the Earth is a huge fish,
which Maui draws up with his line from the bottom of the sea,
and that Maui's death, the sunset, is told in the story of his
creeping into the mouth of his great ancestress, Hine-nui-to-po,
whom you may see flushing, and, as it were, opening and shutting, where the horizon meets the sky; there Maui crept in,
and perished.   And not only would such an explanation of the
tale of the Red Indian 'Tom Thumb' be a fitting one, in that
he, like so many personifications of the Sun in other countries,
is a slayer of Giants, but he will appear a few pages further on
as the Sun-Catcher in a plain, open Solar myth.   In any full
discussion of the group of tales, it would be necessary to inves-
tigate their correspondence with the European stories of Tom
Thumb, who was swallowed by the cow and came out unhurt,
and of Little Red Riding-Hood, who was swallowed whole by
the wolf, and came out alive when the hunter cut him open.[3]

In the next myth, that of the Sun-Catcher, the Polynesian
Sun-god Maui again makes his appearance.   He began to
think that it was too soon after the rising of the sun that it
became night again, and that the sun again sank down below
the horizon, every day, every day; so at last he said to his
brothers, "Let us now catch the sun in a noose, so that we
may compel him to move more slowly, in order that mankind
may have long days to labour in to procure subsistence for

<hr>

[1] Grey, 'Polynesian Mythology,' pp. 18, 31.
[2] Schirren, pp. 143–44, 29.   But the legend is very erroneously given.
[3] J. & W. Grimm, 'Marchen,' vol. 1. pp. 142, 198, 29.

themselves." Then they began to spin and twist ropes to
make a noose to catch the sun in, and thus the art of rope-
making was discovered. And Maui took his enchanted weapon,
which, like Samson's, was a jawbone, the jawbone of his ancestress Muri-ranga-whenua, and he and his brothers travelled
off through the desert, till they came very far, very far, to the
eastward, to the very edge of the place out of which the sun
rises. There they set the noose, and at last the sun came up
and put his head and fore-paws through it; then the brothers
pulled the ropes tight and held him fast, and Maui rushed
at him with his magic weapon. Alas! the sun screams aloud,
he roars; Maui strikes him fiercely with many blows; they
hold him for a long time, at last they let him go, and then,
weak from wounds, the sun crept slowly along its course.[1]
Another version of the story was taken down in the Samoan
Islands. There was once a man who, like the white people,
though it was years before pipes, muskets, or priests were
heard of, never could be contented with what he had; pudding was not good enough for him, and he worried his family
out of all heart with his new ways and ideas. At last he set
to build himself a house of great stones, to last for ever; so he
rose early and toiled late, but the stones were so heavy and so
far off, and the sun went round so quickly, that he could get on
but very slowly. One evening he lay awake, and thought
and thought, and it struck him that as the sun had but one
road to come by, he might stop him and keep him till the
work was done. So he rose before the dawn, and pulling out
in his canoe as the sun rose, he threw a rope round his neck;
but no, the sun marched on and went his course unchecked.
He put nets over the place where the sun rose, he used up all
his mats to stop him, but in vain; the sun went on, and laughed
in hot winds at all his efforts. Meanwhile the house stood still,
and the builder fairly despaired. At last the great Itu, who
generally lies on his mats, and cares not at all for those he has
made, turned round and heard his cry, and, because he was a
good warrior, sent him help. He made the *fucchere* creeper
grow, and again the poor man sprang up from the ground near

<hr>

[1] Grey, 'Polynesian Mythology.' pp. 56–8.

his house, where he had lain down in despair. He took his
canoe and made a noose of the creeper. It was the bad season,
when the sun is dull and heavy; so up he came, half asleep
and tired, nor looked about him, but put his head into the
noose. He pulled and jerked, but Itu had made it too strong.
The man built his house—the sun cried and cried, till the
island of Savai was nearly drowned; but not till the last stone
was laid, was he suffered to resume his career. None can break
the *faeehore*. It is the Itu's cord.[1]

Other versions of this episode in the great Maui-myth have
been taken down in the Pacific Islands,[2] and a like variety is
found in the corresponding tales from North America. Among
the Ojibwas, the Sun-Catcher is evidently the same personage
as the Boy swallowed by the Fish in the last group of stories.
At the time when the animals reigned in the earth, they
had killed all but a girl and her little brother, and these two
were living in fear and seclusion. The boy never grew bigger
than a little child, and his sister used to take him out with her
when she went to get food for the lodge-fire, for he was too
little to leave alone; a big bird might have flown away with
him. One day she made him a bow and arrows, and told him
to hide where she had been chopping, and when the snow-
birds came to pick the worms out of the wood, he was to shoot
one. That day he tried in vain to kill one, but the next, toward nightfall, she heard his little footsteps on the snow; he
brought in a bird, and told his sister she was to take off the
skin and to put half the bird at a time into the pottage, for
till then men had not begun to eat animal food, but had lived
on vegetables alone. At last the boy had killed ten birds, and
his sister made him a little coat of the skins. "Sister," said
he one day, "are we all alone in the world? Is there nobody
else living?" Then she told him that those they feared, and
who had destroyed their relatives, lived in a certain part, and
he must by no means go that way; but this only made him
eager to go, and he took his bow and arrows and started.

[1] Walpole, 'Four Years in the Pacific,' vol. ii. p. 375.
[2] Turner, 'Polynesia,' pp. 245, 248. Tyerman & Bennet, vol. ii. p. 40; and
see vol. i. p. 483. Ellis, Polyn. Res., vol. ii. p. 415.

When he had walked a long while, he lay down on a knoll, where the sun had melted the snow, and fell fast asleep; but while he was sleeping the sun beat so hot upon him, that his bird-skin coat was all singed and shrunk. When he awoke and found his coat spoilt, he vowed vengeance against the sun, and bade his sister make him a snare. She made him one of deer's sinew, and then one of her own hair, but they would not do. At last she brought him one that was right; he pulled it between his lips, and, as he pulled, it became a red metal cord. With this he set out a little after midnight, and fixed his snare on a spot just where the sun would strike the land, as it rose above the earth's disc, and sure enough he caught the sun, so that it was held fast in the cord and did not rise. The animals who ruled the earth were immediately put into a great commotion. They had no light. They called a council to debate upon the matter, and to appoint some one to go and cut the cord, for this was a very hazardous enterprise, as the rays of the sun would burn whoever came so near. At last the dormouse undertook it, for at this time the dormouse was the largest animal in the world. When it stood up it looked like a mountain. When it got to the place where the sun was snared, its back began to smoke and burn with the intensity of the heat, and the top of its carcass was reduced to enormous heaps of ashes. It succeeded, however, in cutting the cord with its teeth, and freeing the sun; but it was reduced to a very small size, and has remained so over since.[1]

In this North American tale we have the Sun-Catcher of the South Sea Islands, combined with part of our own Jack and the Beanstalk. As Jack, in spite of his mother's prayers, goes up the ladder that is to take him to the dwelling of the Giant who killed his father, so the boy of the American tale will not heed his sister's persuasion, but goes to seek the enemies who had slain his kindred. In the next two versions, also from North America, the incident of the going up a tree to the country in the sky, as Jack goes up his beanstalk, makes its appearance. And in all three, the loosing of the imprisoned sun is

[1] Schoolcraft, 'Oneota;' New York and London, 1845, p. 75. See ante, p. 312.

told in a story of which the European fable of the Lion and the Mouse might be a mere moralized remnant.

In the story found among the Wyandots, in the seventeenth century, by the missionary Paul le Jeune, it is related that there was a child whose father was killed and eaten by a bear, and his mother by the Great Hare; a woman came and found the child, and adopted him as her little brother, calling him Chakabech. He did not grow bigger than a baby, but he was so strong that the trees served as arrows for his bow. When he had killed the destroyers of his parents, he wished to go up to heaven, and climbed up a tree; then he blew upon it, and it grew up and up till he came up to heaven, and there he found a beautiful country. So he went down to fetch his sister, building huts as he went down to lodge her in; brought her up the tree into heaven, and then broke off the tree low down: so no one can go up to heaven that way. Then Chakabech went out and set his snares for game, but when he got up at night to look at them, he found everything on fire, and went back to his sister to tell her. Then she told him he must have caught the Sun, going along by night he must have got in unawares, and when Chakabech went to see, so it was; but he dared not go near enough to let him out. But by chance he found a little Mouse, and blew upon her till she grew so big that she could set the Sun free, and he went again on his way; but while he was held in the snare, day failed down here on earth.[1]

The first and second American versions of the Sun-Catcher come from near the great lakes, but the third is found among the Dog-Rib Indians, far in the north-west, close upon the Esquimaux who fringe the northern coast. When Chapewee, after the deluge, formed the earth, and landed the animals upon it from his canoe, he " stuck up a piece of wood, which became a fir-tree, and grew with amazing rapidity, until its top reached the skies. A squirrel ran up this tree, and was pursued by Chapewee, who endeavoured to knock it down, but could not

<hr>

[1] Le Jeune (1637) in 'Relations des Jésuites dans la Nouvelle-France,' Quebec, 1858, vol. i. p. 54. Schoolcraft, part iii. p. 320. See also page 336, in the present Chapter.

overtake it. He continued the chase, however, until he reached the stars, where he found a fine plain, and a beaten road. In this road he set a snare, made of his sister's hair, and then returned to the earth. The sun appeared as usual in the heavens in the morning, but at noon it was caught by the snare which Chapewee had set for the squirrel, and the sky was instantly darkened. Chapewee's family on this said to him, you must have done something wrong when you were aloft, for we no longer enjoy the light of day. 'I have,' replied he, 'but it was unintentionally.' Chapewee then endeavoured to repair the fault he had committed, and sent a number of animals up the tree to release the sun by cutting the snare, but the intense heat of that luminary reduced them all to ashes. The efforts of the more active animals being thus frustrated, a ground mole, though such a grovelling and awkward beast, succeeded by burrowing under the road in the sky until it reached and cut asunder the snare which bound the sun. It lost its eyes, however, the instant it thrust its head into the light, and its nose and teeth have ever since been brown, as if burnt."[1]

The origin of the story of the Sun-Catcher is not yet clear, but probably some piece of unequivocal evidence will be found to explain it. It may be noticed that there are to be found in the Old World ideas of the sun being bound with a cord to hold it in check. In Reynard the Fox, the day is bound with a rope, and its bonds only let it come slowly on. In a Hungarian tale midnight and dawn are bound, so that they can get no further towards men.[2] This notion is curiously like the Peruvian story of the Inca who denied the pretension of the Sun to be the door of all things, for if he were free, he would go and visit other parts of the heavens where he had never been. He is, said the Inca, like a tied beast who goes over round and round in the same track.[3]

The legend of the Ascent to Heaven by the Tree has just

---

[1] Richardson, Narr. of Franklin's Second Exp., London, 1828, p. 201.

[2] Grimm, D. M., p. 700. See Steinthal, 'Die Sage von Simson,' in Lazarus & Steinthal's 'Zeitschrift,' Berlin, 1862, vol. ii. p. 111.

[3] Garcilaso de la Vega, part i. viii. 8. See also Acosta, Hist. del Nuevo Orbe, chap. v.

been brought forward in two of its American versions,[1] taken down at periods two centuries apart, and among tribes not only separated by long distance, but speaking languages of two distinct families, and yet in both cases embodying also the story of the Sun-Catcher. A further examination of the story of Jack and the Bean Stalk, and the analogous tales which are spread through the Malay and Polynesian districts and North America, will bring into view the vast ramifications of a mythic episode flourishing far and wide in these distant regions, though so scantily represented in the folk-lore of Europe.

Once upon a time there was a poor widow, and she had one son, and his name was Jack. One day she sent him to sell the cow, but when he saw some pretty-coloured beans that the butcher had, he was so delighted that he gave the cow for them and brought his prize home in triumph. When the poor mother saw the beans that Jack had brought home she flung them away, and they grew and grew till next morning they had grown right up into the sky. So Jack climbed up sorely against his mother's will, and saw the fairy, and went to the house of the giant who had killed his father, and stole the hen that laid the golden eggs, and did various other wonderful things, till at last the giant came running after him and followed him down the bean-stalk, but Jack was just in time to cut the ladder through, and the wicked Giant tumbled down head first into the well, and there he was drowned.

So runs the good old nursery tale of Jack and the Bean-Stalk. That it is found in England and yet is not general in the folk-lore of the rest of our race in Europe is remarkable. Mr. Campbell says it is not known in the Highlands of Scotland, while in Germany Wilhelm Grimm only compares it with two poor, dull little stories, one a version distinctly connected with our English tale, the other perhaps so, but neither worth repeating here.[2]

In another American tradition, found current among the Mandans, the ascent is not from the earth to the sky, but from the regions underground to the surface. It is thus related in

<hr>

[1] See also Schoolcraft, part iii. p. 517 ; part i. plate 52, p. 376.

[2] J. & W. Grimm, 'Märchen,' vol. ii. p. 133; vol. iii. pp. 192, 321.

the account of Lewis and Clarke's expedition. "Their belief in a future state is connected with this tradition of their origin: the whole nation resided in one large village underground near a subterraneous lake: a grape-vine extended its roots down to their habitation and gave them a view of the light: some of the most adventurous climbed up the vine and were delighted with the sight of the earth, which they found covered with buffalo and rich with every kind of fruits: returning with the grapes they had gathered, their countrymen were so pleased with the taste of them that the whole nation resolved to leave their dull residence for the charms of the upper region; men, women, and children ascended by means of the vine; but when about half the nation had reached the surface of the earth, a corpulent woman who was clambering up the vine broke it with her weight, and closed upon herself and the rest of the nation the light of the sun. Those who were left on earth made a village below where we saw the nine villages; and when the Mandans die they expect to return to the original seats of their forefathers; the good reaching the ancient village by means of the lake, which the burden of the sins of the wicked will not enable them to cross."[1]

The set of Malayo-Polynesian stories which tell of the climbing from earth to heaven by a tree or vine-like plant is, besides, a good illustration of the unity of the Island Mythology from Borneo to New Zealand. The Dayak tale of the man who went up to heaven and brought down rice has been already cited. It is thus told by Mr. St. John:—"Once upon a time, when mankind had nothing to eat but a species of edible fungus that grows upon rotting trees, and there were no cereals to gladden and strengthen man's heart, a party of Dayaks, among whom was a man named Si Jura, whose descendants live to this day in the Dayak village of Simpok, went forth to sea. They sailed on for some time, until they came to a place at which they heard the distant roar of a large whirlpool, and, to their amazement, saw before them a huge fruit-tree rooted in the sky, and thence hanging down with its branches touching the waves. At the request of his companions, Si Jura climbed among its boughs

[1] Lewis & Clarke, p. 139. Catlin, vol. i. p. 178. See Loskiel, p. 31.

to collect the fruit which was in abundance, and when he was there he found himself tempted to ascend the trunk and find out how the tree grew in that position. He did so, and at length got so high that his companions in the boat lost sight of him, and after waiting a certain time coolly sailed away loaded with fruit. Looking down from his lofty position, Si Jura saw his friends making off, so he had no other resource but to go on climbing in hopes of reaching some resting-place. He therefore persevered climbing higher and higher, till he reached the roots of the tree, and there he found himself in a new country—that of the Pleiades. There he met a being in form of a man, named Si Kira, who took him to his home, and hospitably entertained him. The food offered was a mess of soft white grains—boiled rice. 'Eat,' said Si Kira. 'What, those little maggots?' replied Si Jura. 'They are not maggots, but boiled rice;' and Si Kira forthwith explained the process of planting, weeding, and reaping, and of pounding and boiling rice. . . . So Si Jura made a hearty meal, and after eating, Si Kira gave him seed of three kinds of rice, instructed him how to cut down the forest, burn, plant, weed, and reap, take omens from birds, and celebrate harvest feasts; and then, by a long rope, let him down to earth again near his father's house.'[1]

In the Malay island of Celebes a story is found which contains the episode of the heaven-plant, but in a different connexion. It is indeed a legend of no common interest, as bringing the old European story of the Swan-coat[2] together with an equally unmistakable version of a tale found also among the natives of New Zealand. Seven heavenly nymphs came down from the sky to bathe, and they were seen by Kasimbaha, who thought first that they were white doves, but in the bath he saw that they were women. Then he stole one of the thin

---

[1] St. John, vol. i. p. 202.

[2] Among a number of instances, in the Völundarqvitha, three women sit on the shore with their swan-coats beside them, ready to turn into swans and fly away. Or three doves fly down to a fountain and become maidens when they touch the earth. Wieland takes their clothes and will not give them back till one consents to be his wife, etc. etc. Grimm, D. M., pp. 398–402.

robes that gave the nymphs their power of flying, and so he caught Utahagi, the one whose robe he had stolen, and took her for his wife, and she bore him a son. Now she was called Utahagi from a single white hair she had, which was endowed with magic power, and this hair her husband pulled out. As soon as he had done it, there arose a great storm, and Utahagi went up into heaven. The child cried for its mother, and Kasimbaha was in great grief, and cast about how he should follow Utahagi up into the sky. Then a rat gnawed the thorns off the rattans, and he clambered up by them with his son upon his back till he came to heaven. There a little bird showed him the house of Utahagi, and after various adventures he took up his abode among the gods.[1]

From Celebes to New Zealand the distance is some four thousand miles, but among the Maoris a tale is found which is beyond doubt of common origin with this. There was once a great chief called Tawhaki, and a girl of the heavenly race, whose name was Tango-tango, heard of his valour and his beauty and came down to earth to be his wife, and she bore a daughter to him. But when Tawhaki took the little girl to a spring and had washed it, he held it out at arm's length and said, "Faugh, how badly the little thing smells." When Tango-tango heard this, she was bitterly offended and began to sob and weep, and at last she took the child and flew up to heaven with it. Tawhaki tried to stop her and besought her to stay, but in vain, and as she paused for a minute with one foot resting on the carved figure at the end of the ridge-pole of the house, above the door, he called to her to leave him some remembrance of her. Then she told him that he was not to lay hold of the loose root of the creeper, which dropping from aloft sways to and fro in the air, but rather to lay fast hold on that which hanging down from on high has again struck its fibres into the earth. So she floated up into the air and vanished, and Tawhaki remained mourning: at the end of a month he could bear it no longer, so he took his younger brother with him, and two slaves, and started to look for his

<hr>

[1] Schirren, p. 126. Compare Bornean story, Bp. of Labuan in Tr. Eth. Soc., 1863, p. 27.

wife and child. At last the brothers came to the spot where
the ends of the tendrils which hung down from heaven reached
the earth, and there they found an old ancestress of theirs,
whose name was Matakerepo. She was appointed to take
care of the tendrils, and she sat at the place where they touched
the earth and held the ends of one of them in her hands. So
next day the younger brother, Karihi, started to climb up, and
the old woman warned him not to look down when he was
midway between heaven and earth, lest he should turn giddy
and fall, and also to take care not to catch hold of a loose ten-
dril. But just at that very moment he made a spring at the
tendrils, and by mistake caught hold of a loose one, and away
he swung to the very edge of the horizon, but a blast of wind
blew forth from thence and drove him back to the other side
of the skies, and then another gust swept him heavenwards,
and again he was blown down. Just as he reached the ground
this time Tawhaki shouted to him to let go, and lo, he stood
upon the earth once more, and the two brothers wept over his
narrow escape from destruction. Then Tawhaki began to
climb, and he went up and up, repeating a powerful incantation
as he climbed, till at last he reached the heavens, and there he
found his wife and their daughter, and they took her to the
water and baptized her in proper New Zealand fashion. Lightning flashed from Tawhaki's armpits, and he still dwells up
there in heaven, and when he walks, his footsteps make the
thunder and lightning that are heard and seen on earth.[1]

There are other mythological ways beside the Heaven-tree,
by which, in different parts of the world, it is possible to go

[1] Grey, 'Polynesian Mythology,' p. 66, etc. Several incidents are here omitted.
In another version Tawhaki goes up not by the creeper but upon a spider's web.
(Thomson, N. Z., vol. i. p. 111. Yate, p. 144.) Other stories connected with this
series are to be found in the Samoan group. The taro, like the rice in Borneo, is
brought down from heaven; there was a heaven-tree, where people went up and
down, and when it fell it stretched some sixty miles; two young men went up to
the moon, one by a tree, the other on the smoke of a fire as it towered into the sky
(Turner, p. 246). In the Caroline Islands, another of these anmessödras goes up to
heaven on a column of smoke to visit his celestial father (J. R. Forster, Obs.
p. 608). In the Tonga Islands, Maui makes the fou grow up to heaven, so that the
god Etumatubua can come down by it (Schirren, p. 76).

up and down between the surface of the ground and the sky
or the regions below; the rank spear-grass, a rope or thong,
a spider's web, a ladder of iron or gold, a column of smoke, or
the rainbow.   It must be remembered in discussing such tales,
that the idea of climbing, for instance, from earth to heaven
by a tree, fantastic as it may seem to a civilized man of modern times, is in a different grade of culture quite a simple and
natural idea, and too much stress must not be laid on bare
coincidences to this effect in proving a common origin for the
stories which contain them, unless closer evidence is forthcoming.   Such tales belong to a rude and primitive state of
knowledge of the earth's surface, and what lies above and below it.   The earth is a flat plain surrounded by the sea, and
the sky forms a roof on which the sun, moon, and stars travel.
The Polynesians, who thought, like so many other peoples,
ancient and modern, that the sky descended at the horizon
and enclosed the earth, still call foreigners *papalangi*, or
"heaven-bursters," as having broken in from another world
outside.   The sky is to most savages what it is called in a
South American language, *munmuke*, that is, the "earth on
high."[1]   There are holes or windows through this roof or fir-
mament, where the rain comes through, and if you climb high
enough you can get through and visit the dwellers above, who
look, and talk, and live very much in the same way as the
people upon earth.   As above the flat earth, so below it, there
are regions inhabited by men or man-like creatures, who sometimes come up to the surface, and sometimes are visited by the
inhabitants of the upper earth.   We live as it were upon the
ground floor of a great house, with upper storeys rising one
over another above us, and cellars down below.

The Bridge of the Dead is one of the well-marked myths of
the Old World.   Over the midst of the Moslem hell stretches
the bridge Es-Sirat, finer than a hair, and sharper than the
edge of a sword.   There all souls of the dead must pass along,
but while the good reach the other side in safety, the wicked
fall off into the abyss.   The Jews, too, have their bridge of
hell, narrow as a thread, but it is only the souls of the unbe-

lievers who have to pass there.   " The brig of dread, no brader
than a thread," is in an old English wake-song from the
North Country, and the bridge where the disembodied souls
of the dead pass the river Gjöll is part and parcel of the story
of Balder, in the Prose Edda.[1]   At this day, the Karens of
Burmah tie strings across the rivers to serve as bridges for the
ghosts of the dead to pass over to their graves.[2]   Unlike
the last two stories, the Heaven-Bridge does not seem to belong to Polynesia, but then the South Sea Islanders have
little to do with bridges.   In Java, however, it is found, but in
company with purely Indian matter, such as the Sapta Patala,
the seven regions of hell, so that it is likely that it is not a real
Malay belief, but came across from Asia.   Batara Guru built a
wall of stone round Suralaya, the Dwelling of the Gods, and
round it he formed the Abyss Kawah, and set a bridge over it
to reach the single opening in the Wall of Heaven.   Off this
bridge the evildoers fall into the depths below.[3]

In North America, the Bridge of the Dead forms part of the
Indian mythology.   The Minnetarees, it is recorded in the account of Major Long's expedition, which was published in 1823,
believe that, in their way to the mansions of their ancestors
after death, they have to cross a narrow footing over a rapid
river, where the good warriors and hunters pass, but the
worthless ones fall in.[4]   Catlin's account of the Choctaw belief
is as follows:—" Our people all believe that the spirit lives in
a future state; that it has a great distance to travel after death
towards the west—that it has to cross a dreadful deep and rapid
stream, which is hemmed in on both sides by high and rugged
hills—over this stream, from hill to hill, there lies a long and
slippery pine-log, with the bark peeled off, over which the dead
have to pass to the delightful hunting-grounds.   On the other
side of the stream there are six persons of the good hunting-
grounds with rocks in their hands, which they throw at them
all when they are on the middle of the log.   The good walk on
safely to the good hunting-grounds. . . . .   The wicked see the
stones coming, and try to dodge, by which they fall down from

[1] Lane, vol. i. p. 85.   Grimm, D. M., p. 704.   See Bastian, vol. ii. p. 340.
[2] Mrs. Mason, p. 73.   [3] Schirren, pp. 122, 125.   [4] Long's Exp., vol. i. p. 280.

the log, and go thousands of feet to the water, which is dashing over the rocks."[1] In the interior of South America the idea appears again among the Manacicas. Among these people, the Maponos or priests performed a kind of baptism of the dead, and were then supposed to mount into the air, and carry the soul to the Land of the Departed. After a weary journey of many days over hills and vales, through forests, and across rivers and swamps and lakes, they came to a place where many roads met, near a deep and wide river, where the god Tatusiso stood night and day upon a wooden bridge to inspect all such travellers. If he did not consider the sprinkling after death a sufficient purgation of the sins of the departed, he would stop the priest, that the soul he carried might be further cleansed, and if resistance were made, would sometimes seize the unhappy soul and throw him into the river, and when this happened some calamity would follow among the Manacicas at home.[2]

The Bridge of the Dead may possibly have its origin in the rainbow. Among the Northmen the rainbow is to be seen in the bridge Bifröst of the three colours, over which the Æsir make their daily journey, and the red in it is fire, for were it easy to pass over, the Frost-giants and the Mountain-giants would get across it into heaven. In a remark, evidently belonging to the North American story of the Sun-Catcher, the rainbow replaces the tree up which the mouse climbs, and gnaws loose a captive in the sky.[3] The Milky Way, which among the North American Indians is the road of souls to the other world, has also a claim to be considered.[4] As in the Old World, so in the New, the Bridge of the Dead is but an incident, sometimes, but not always or even mostly, introduced into a wider belief that after death the soul of man comes to a great gulf or stream, which it has to pass to reach the country that lies beyond the grave. The Mythology of Polynesia, though it wants the Bridge, developes the idea of the gulf which the souls have to pass, in canoes

<hr>

[1] Catlin, vol. ii. p. 127.

[2] Southey, 'Brasil,' vol. iii. p. 193.

[3] Schoolcraft in Pott, 'Ungleichheit der Menschlichen Rassen,' Lemgo, 1856, p. 267.   [4] Le Jeune (1634), p. 63.

or by swimming, into a long series of myths.[1] It is not needful
to enter here into details of so well-known a feature of the
Mythology of the Old World, where Charon and his boat, the
procession of the dead by water to their long home, in modern
Brittany as in ancient Egypt, the setting afloat of the Scandinavian heroes in burning ships, or burying them in boats on
shore, are all instances of its prevalence. In North America
we hear sometimes of the bridge, but sometimes the water
must be passed in canoes. The souls come to a great lake
where there is a beautiful island, toward which they have to
paddle in a canoe of white shining stone. On the way there
arises a storm, and the wicked souls are wrecked, and the
heaps of their bones are to be seen under water, but the good
reach the happy island.[2] So Charlevoix speaks of the souls
that are shipwrecked in crossing the river which they have to
pass on their long journey toward the west,[3] and with this belief the canoe-burial of the North-West and of Patagonia hangs
together. How the souls of the Ojibwas cross the deep and
rapid water to reach the land of bliss,[4] and the souls of the
Mandans travel on the lake by which the good reach their ancient village, while the wicked cannot get across for the burden of their sins,[5] I do not know; but, like the Heaven-Bridge,
the Heaven-Gulf which has to be passed on the way to the
Land of Spirits, has a claim to careful discussion in the general
argument for the proof of historical connexion from Analogy
of Myths.

The Fountain of Youth is known to the Mythology of India.
The Açvinas let the husband of Sukanyâ go into the lake,
whence the bather comes forth as old or as young as he may
choose; and elsewhere the " ageless river," *rijarâ nadi*, makes
the old young again by only seeing it, or perhaps by bathing
in its waters.[6] Perhaps it is this fountain that Sir John Maundevile hears of early in the fourteenth century somewhere about
India. " Also toward the heed of that Forest, is the Cytee of

[1] Williams, 'Fiji,' vol. i. pp. 244, 205. Schirren, pp. 93, 110, etc.
[2] Schoolcraft, part i. p. 321. Mackenzie, p. cxix.
[3] Charlevoix, vol. vi. p. 78.   [4] Schoolcraft, part ii. p. 135.
[5] Lewis & Clarke, p. 139.   [6] Kuhn, pp. 128, 12.

Polombe. And above the Cytee is a grete Mountayne, that also is clept *Polombe*; and of that Mount the Cytee hathe his name. And at the Foot of that Mount, is a fayr Welle and a gret, that hathe odour and savour of alle Spices; and at every hour of the day, he chaungethe his odour and his savour dyversely. And whoso drynkethe 3 tymes fasting of that Watre of that Welle, he is hool of alle maner sykenesse, that he hathe. And thei that dwellen there and drynken often of that Welle, thei nevere han Sekenesse, and thei semen alle ways zonge. I have dronken there of 3 or 4 sithes; and zit, methinkethe, I fare the better. Sum men clepen it the Welle of zouthe: for thei that often drynken there of, semen alle weys zongly, and lyven with outen Sykenesse. And men seyn, that that Welle comethe out of *Paradys*: and therfore it is so vertuous."[1]

When Cambyses sent the Fish-Eaters to spy out the condition of the long-lived Ethiopians, and the messengers wondered to hear that they lived a hundred and twenty years or more, the Ethiopians took them to a fountain, where, when they had bathed, their bodies shone as if they had been oiled, and smelt like the scent of violets.[2] In Europe, too, stories of miraculously healing fountains have long been current.[3] The Moslem geographer Ibn-el-Wardi places the Fountain of Life in the dark south-western regions of the earth. El-Khidr drank of it, and will live till the day of judgment; and Ilyas or Elias, whom popular belief mixes not only with El-Khidr, but also with St. George, the Dragon-slayer, has drunk of it likewise.[4] Farther east, the idea is to be found in the Malay islands. Batara Guru drinks from a poisonous spring, but saves himself and the rest of the gods by finding a well of life; and again, Nurtjaja compels the pandit Kabib, the guardian of the caverns below the earth, where flows the spring of immortality, to let him drink of its waters, and even to take some for his descendants.[5] In the Hawaiian legend, Kamapiikai, "the child who runs over the sea," goes with forty companions to

---

[1] 'The Voiage and Travaile of Sir John Maundevile, Kt.;' London, 1725, p. 204.
[2] Herod., iii. c. 23. [3] Grimm, D. M., p. 554. Perty, p. 119.
[4] Lane, 'Thousand and One Nights,' vol. L p. 20. [5] Schirren, p. 124.

Tahiti (Kahiki, that is to say, to the land *far away*), and brings back wondrous tales of Ilaupokane, " the belly of Kane," and of the *wai ora, waiola*, " water of life," or *wai ora roa*, " water of enduring life," which removes all sickness, deformity, and decrepitude from those who plunge beneath its waters.[1] It is perhaps to this story of the Sandwich Islands that Turner refers, when he says that some South Sea islanders have traditions of a river in the spirit-world called " Water of Life," which makes the old young again, and they return to earth to live another life.[2]

One easy explanation of the Fountain of Youth suggests itself at the first glance.   Every islander who can see the sun go down old, faint, and weary into the western sea, to rise young and fresh from the waters, has the Fountain of Youth before him ; and this explanation of several, at least, of the stories is strengthened by their details, as when the fountain is described as flowing in the regions below, or in the belly of Kane, where the boy who climbs over the sea goes to it ; or when, like the dying and reviving sun, Batara Guru is poisoned, but finds the reviving water and is cured ;[3] or when the Moslem associates the drinking from the fountain with Elijah of the chariot of fire and horses of fire ; or with St. George, the favourite mediaeval bearer of the great Sun-myth. But, as these stories are not brought forward for the purpose of discussing their origin, but comparing with them a corresponding myth found across the Atlantic, it may suffice here to give the particulars of the story found current in the West Indies early in the sixteenth century.   Gomara relates that Juan Ponce de Leon, having his government taken from him, and thus finding himself rich and without charge, fitted out two caravels, and went to seek for the island of Boyuca, where the Indians said there was the fountain that turned old men back into youths (a perennial spring, says Peter Martyr, so noble that the drinking of its waters made old men young again).   For six months he went

<hr>

[1] Schirren, p. 80.   Ellis, Polyn. Res., vol. ii. p. 47.   Ellis, ' Hawaii ;' London, 1827, p. 389.   [2] Turner. p. 353.

[3] For etym. etc. of Batara Guru, see W. v. Humboldt, Kawi-Spr., vol. i. p. 100; Schirren, p. 116 ; also Crawfurd, Introd., p. cxviii. and s. vv. batara, guru.

lost and famishing among many islands, but of such a fountain he found no trace. Then he came to Bimini, and discovered Florida on Pascua Florida, (Easter Sunday), wherefrom he gave the country its name.[1]

To proceed now to the story of the Tail-Fisher. Dr. Dasent, who, in his admirable Introduction to the Norse Tales, has taken the lead in the extension of the argument from Comparative Mythology beyond the limited range within which it is aided by History and Language, has brought the popular tales of Africa and Europe into close connexion by adducing, among others, the unmistakable common origin of the Norse tale of the Bear who, at the instigation of the Fox, fishes with his tail through a hole in the ice till it is frozen in, and then pulls at it till it comes off, and the story from Bornu of the Hyæna who puts his tail into the hole, that the Weasel may fasten the meat to it, but the Weasel fastens a stick to it instead, and the Hyæna pulls till his tail breaks; both stories accounting in a similar way, but with a proper difference of local colouring, for the fact that bears and hyænas are stumpy-tailed.[2]

A similar story is told in Reynard the Fox, less appositely, of the Wolf instead of the Bear,[3] and in the Celtic story recently published by Mr. Campbell, it is again the Wolf who loses his tail. In this latter story, by that kaleidoscopic arrangement of incidents which is so striking a feature of Mythology, the losing of the tail is combined with the episode of taking the reflection of the moon for a cheese, which occurs in another connexion in Reynard,[4] and is apparently the origin of our popular saying about the moon being made of green cheese.

> " He made an instrument to know
> If the moon shine at full or no ;
> That would, as soon as e'er she shone, straight
> Whether 'twere day or night demonstrate ;

---

[1] Gomara, Hist. Gen. de las Indias; Medina del Campo, 1553, part 1. fol. xxiii. Petri Martyri De Orbe Novo (1516), ed. Hakluyt; Paris, 1587, dec. II. c. 10. Galvano, p. 123.

[2] Dasent, 'Popular Tales from the Norse;' (2nd ed.) Edinburgh, 1859, pp. l. 197.   [3] Grimm, 'Reinhart Fuchs,' pp. riv. cxxii. 51.   [4] Id. p. cxxvii.

> Tell what her d'ameter to an inch is,
> And prove that she's not made of green cheese."[1]

Here, of course, "green cheese" means, like τυρὸς χλωρός, fresh, white cheese. In the Highland tale the Fox shows the Wolf the moon on the ice, and tells him it is a cheese, and he must cover it with his tail to hide it, till the Fox goes to see that the farmer is asleep. When the tail is frozen tight the Fox alarms the farmer, and the Wolf leaves his tail behind him.[2]

"The tailless condition both of the bear and the hyæna," Dr. Dasent remarks, "could scarcely fail to attract attention in a race of hunters, and we might expect that popular tradition would attempt to account for both." The reasonableness of this conjecture is well shown in the case of two other short-tailed beasts, in a mythical episode from Central America, which bears no appearance of being historically connected with the rest, but looks as though it had been devised independently to account for the facts. When the two princes Hunahpu and Xbalanqué set themselves one day to till the ground, the axe cut down the trees and the mattock cleared away the underwood, while the masters amused themselves with shooting. But next day, when they came back, they found the trees and creepers and brambles back in their places. So they cleared the ground again, and hid themselves to watch, and at midnight all the beasts came, small and great, saying in their language "Trees, arise; creepers, arise!" and they came close to the two princes. First came the Lion and the Tiger, and the princes tried to catch them, but could not. Then came the Stag and the Rabbit, and them they caught by their tails, but the tails came off, and so the Stag and the Rabbit have still but "scarce a stump" left them to this day. But the Fox and the Jackal and the Boar and the Porcupine and the other beasts passed by, and they could not catch one till the Rat came leaping along; he was the last and they got in his way and caught him in a cloth. They pinched his head

---

[1] 'Hudibras,' part ii. canto iii.

[2] Campbell, 'Popular Tales of the West Highlands;' Edinburgh, 1860, vol. i. p. 272.

and tried to choke him, and burnt his tail over the fire, and since then the rat has had a hairless tail, and his eyes are as if they had been squeezed out of his head. But he begged to be heard, and told them that it was not their business to till the ground, for the rings and gloves and the india-rubber ball, the instruments of the princely game, were hidden in their grandmother's house, and so forth.[1]

The curious mythic art of Tail-fishing only forms a part of the stories how the Bear, the Wolf, and the Hyæna came to lose their tails in Europe and Africa. But this particular idea, taken by itself, has a wide geographical range both in the Old and New Worlds. A story current in India, apparently among the Tamil population of the South, is told by the Rev. J. Roberts, who says, speaking of the jackal, "this animal is very much like the fox of England in his habits and appearance. I have been told, that they often catch the crab by putting their tail into its hole, which the creature immediately seizes, in hope of food: the jackal then drags it out and devours it."[2]

In North America, the bearer of the story is the racoon. "Lawson relates, that those which formerly lived on the salt waters in Carolina, fed on oysters, which they nimbly snatched when the shell opened; but that sometimes the paw was caught, and held till the return of the tide, in which the animal, though it swims well, was sometimes drowned. His art in catching crabs is still more extraordinary. Standing on the borders of the waters where this shell-fish abounds, he keeps the end of his tail floating on the surface, which the crab seizes, and he then leaps forward with his prey, and destroys it in a very artful manner."[4] In South America, the art is given to two other very cunning creatures, the monkey and the jaguar. I have been informed by one of the English explorers in British Guiana, that it is a current story there, that the monkey catches fish by letting them take hold of the end of his tail. Southey, quoting from a manuscript description of the district flooded by the River Paraguay, called the Lago Xarayos, says " when

[1] Brasseur, 'Popol-Vuh,' pp. 118-25.
[2] Roberts, 'Oriental Illustrations,' p. 172.
[4] D. B. Warden, Account of U. S.; Edinburgh, 1819, vol. i. p. 109.

the floods are out the fish leave the river to feed upon certain
fruits : as soon as they hear or feel the fruit strike the water,
they leap to catch it as it rises to the surface, and in their eager-
ness spring into the air.   From this habit the Ounce has learnt
a curious stratagem ; he gets upon a projecting bough, and
from time to time strikes the water with his tail, thus imitating
the sound which the fruit makes as it drops, and as the fish
spring towards it, he catches them with his paw."[1]   More
recently, the story has been told again by Mr. Wallace ; "The
jaguar, say the Indians, is the most cunning animal in the
forest : he can imitate the voice of almost every bird and animal so exactly, as to draw them towards him : he fishes in the
rivers, lashing the water with his tail to imitate falling fruit,
and when the fish approach, hooks them up with his claws."[2]
It may be objected against the use of the tail-fishing story
as mythological evidence, that there may possibly be some
foundation for it in actual fact ; and it is indeed hardly more
astonishing, for instance, than the jaguar's turning a number
of river-turtles on their backs to be eaten at his leisure, a
story which Humboldt accepts as true.   But the way in which
the tail-fishing is attributed in different countries to one animal after another, the bear, the wolf, the hyæna, the jackal, the
racoon, the monkey, and the jaguar, authorizes the opinion
that, in most cases at least, it is one of those floating ideas
which are taken up as part of the story-teller's stock in trade,
and used where it suits him, but with no particular subordina-
tion to fact.

Lastly, another Old World story which has a remarkable
analogue in South America is that of the Diable Boiteux.
This, however, in the state in which it is known to modern
Europe, is a conception a good deal modified under Christian
influences.   In the old mythology of our race, it is the Fire-
god who is lame.   The unsteady flickering of the flames may
perhaps be figured in the crooked legs and hobbling gait of
Hephæstus, and Zeus casts him down from heaven to earth
like his crooked lightnings ; while the stories which correspond
with the Vulcan-myth on German ground tell of the laming of

<hr>

[1] Southey, vol. i. p 142.   [2] Wallace, p. 455.

Wieland, our Wayland Smith, the representative of Hephæstus. The transfer of the lameness of the Fire-god to the Devil seems to belong to the mixture of the Scriptural Satan with the ideas of heathen gods, elves, giants, and demons, which go to form that strange compound, the Devil of popular mediæval belief.[1]

There is something very quaint in the notion of a lame god or devil, but it is quite a familiar one in South Africa. The deity of the Namaquas and other tribes is Tsui'kuap, whose principal attributes seem to be the causing of pain and death. This being received a wound in his knee in a great fight, and " Wounded-knee" appears to be the meaning of his name.[2] Moffat's account, which is indeed not very clear, fits with a late remark made by Livingstone among another people of South Africa, the Bakwains. He observes that near the village of Sechele there is a cave called Lepelole, which no one dared to enter, for it was the common belief that it was the habitation of the Deity, and that no one who went in ever came out again. "It is curious," he says, " that in all their pretended dreams or visions of their god he has always a crooked leg, like the Egyptian Than."[3] Even in Australia something similar is to be found. The Biam is held to be like a black, but deformed in his lower extremities, the natives say they got many of the songs sung at their dances from him, but he also causes diseases, especially one which marks the face like small-pox.[4]

The Diablo Boiteux of South America is thus described by Pöppig, in his account of the life of the forest Indians of Mainas. " A ghostly being, the Uchuella-chaqui or Lame-foot, alone troubles the source of his best pleasure and his livelihood. Where the forest is darkest, where only the light-avoiding amphibia and the nocturnal birds dwell, lives this dangerous creature, and endeavours, by putting on some friendly shape, to lure the Indian to his destruction. As the sociable hunters do,

<hr>

[1] Welcker, ' Griechische Götterlehre ;' Göttingen, 1857, etc., vol. i. pp. 601–5. Grimm, D. M., pp. 221, 351, 937–8, 011, 963. See Schirren, p. 161.

[2] Moffat, pp. 257–9.

[3] Livingstone, p. 126. He means, I presume, Pthah, or rather Pthah-Sokari Osiris.

[4] Eyre, vol. ii. p. 362.

it gives the well understood signs, and, never reached itself,
entices the deluded victim deeper and deeper into the solitude,
disappearing with a shout of mocking laughter when the path
home is lost, and the terrors of the wilderness are increasing
with the growing shadows of night. Sometimes it separates
companions who have gone hunting together, by appearing
first in one place, then in another in an altered form; but it
never can deceive the wary hunter who in distrust examines
the footsteps of his enemy. Hardly has he caught sight of the
quite unequal size of the impressions of the feet, when he
hastens back, and for long after no one dares to make an expedition into the wilderness, for the visits of the fiend are only
for a time."[1] In South America as in Africa this is not a mere
local tale, but a widely spread belief.

In conclusion, the analogies between the Mythology of
America and of the rest of the world which have been here
enumerated, when taken together with the many more which
come into view in studying a wider range of native American
traditions, and after full allowance has been made for the possibility of independent coincidences, seem to me to warrant the
expectation that it will not be long before the American Mythology will have to be treated as embodying materials common
to other districts of the world, mixed no doubt with purely
native matter. Such a view would bring the early history of
America into definite connexion with that of other regions,
over a larger geographical range than that included in Humboldt's argument, and would bear with some force, though of
course but indirectly, on the problem of the origin and diffusion
of mankind.

[1] Pöppig, 'Reise in Chile,' etc.; Leipzig, 1836, vol. ii. p. 358. Klemm, C. G.
vol. L p. 276.

CHAPTER XIII.

CONCLUDING REMARKS.

It has been intimated that the present series of Essays affords no sufficient foundation for a definite theory of the Rise and Progress of Human Civilization in early times. Nor, indeed, will any such foundation be ready for building upon, until a great deal of preparatory work has been done. Still, the evidence which has here been brought together seems to tell distinctly for or against some widely circulated Ethnological theories, and also to justify a certain amount of independent generalization, and the results of the foregoing chapters in this way may now be briefly summed up, with a few additional remarks.

In the first place, the facts collected seem to favour the view that the wide differences in the civilization and mental state of the various races of mankind are rather differences of development than of origin, rather of degree than of kind. Thus the Gesture-Language is the same in principle, and similar in its details, all over the world. The likeness in the formation both of pure myths and of those crude theories which have been described as "myths of observation," among races so dissimilar in the colour of their skins and the shape of their skulls, tells in the same direction. And wherever the occurrence of any art or knowledge in two places can be confidently ascribed to independent invention, as, for instance, when we find the dwellers in the ancient lake-habitations of Switzerland, and the modern New Zealanders, adopting a like construction in their

curious fabrics of tied bundles of fibre, the similar step thus
made in different times and places tends to prove the similarity
of the minds that made it. Moreover, to take a somewhat
weaker line of argument, the uniformity with which like stages
in the development of art and science are found among the
most unlike races, may be adduced as evidence on the same
side, in spite of the constant difficulty in deciding whether any
particular development is due to independent invention, or to
transmission from some other people to those among whom it
is found. For if the similar thing has been produced in two
places by independent invention, then, as has just been said, it
is direct evidence of similarity of mind. And on the other
hand, if it was carried from the one place to the other, or from
a third to both, by mere transmission from people to people,
then the smallness of the change it has suffered in transplant-
ing is still evidence of the like nature of the soil wherever it
is found.

Considered both from this and other points of view, this uniform development of the lower civilization is a matter of great
interest. The state of things which is found is not indeed that
one race does or knows exactly what another race does or
knows, but that similar stages of development recur in different
times and places. There is reason to suppose that our ancestors in remote times made fire with a machine much like that
of the modern Esquimaux, and at a far later date they used the
bow and arrow, as so many savage tribes do still. The foregoing chapters treating of the history of some early arts, of the
practice of sorcery, of curious customs and superstitions, are
indeed full of instances of the recurrence of like phenomena in
the remotest regions of the world. We might reasonably expect that men of like minds, when placed under widely different circumstances of country, climate, vegetable and animal
life, and so forth, should develope very various phenomena of
civilization, and we even know by evidence that they actually
do so; but nevertheless it strikingly illustrates the extent of
mental uniformity among mankind to notice that it is really
difficult to find, among a list of twenty items of art or knowledge, custom or superstition, taken at random from a descrip-

tion of any uncivilized race, a single one to which something
closely analogous may not be found elsewhere among some
other race, unlike the first in physical characters, and living
thousands of miles off. It is taking a somewhat extreme case
to put the Australians to such a test, for they are perhaps the
most peculiar of the lower varieties of Man, yet among the
arts, beliefs, and customs, found among their tribes, there are
comparatively few that cannot be matched elsewhere. They
raise scars on their bodies like African tribes; they circumcise
like the Jews and Arabs; they bar marriage in the female line
like the Iroquois; they drop out of their language the names of
plants and animals which have been used as the personal names
of dead men, and make new words to serve instead, like the
Abipones of South America; they bewitch their enemies with
locks of hair, and pretend to cure the sick by sucking out
stones through their skin, as is done in so many other regions.
It is true that among their weapons they have one of very
marked, perhaps even specific peculiarity, the boomerang, but
the rest of their armoury, the spear, the spear-thrower, the
club, the throwing-cudgel, are but varieties of instruments
common elsewhere, and the same is true of their fire-drill, their
stone hatchet, their nets and baskets, their bark canoes and
rafts. And while among the Australians there are only a very
few exceptions to modify the general rule that whatever is
found in one place in the world may be matched more or less
closely elsewhere, piecemeal or as a whole, the proportion of
such exceptions is smaller, and consequently the uniformity of
development more strikingly marked, among most of the other
races of the world who have not risen above the lower levels of
culture.

In the next place, the collections of facts relating to various
useful arts seem to justify the opinion that, in such practical
matters at least, the history of mankind has been on the whole
a history of progress. Over almost the whole world are found
traces of the former use of stone implements, now superseded
by metal; rude and laborious means of making fire have been
supplanted by easier and better processes; over large regions
of the earth the art of boiling in earthen or metal pots over the

fire has succeeded the ruder art of stone-boiling; in three distant countries the art of writing sounds is found developing itself out of mere picture-writing, and this phonetic writing has superseded in several districts the use of quipus, or knotted cords, as a means of record and communication. In the chapter particularly devoted to evidence of progress, a number of facts are stated which seem to be records of a forward development in other arts, in times and places beyond the range of history. On the other hand, though arts which flourish in times of great refinement or luxury, and complex processes which require a combination of skill or labour hard to get together and liable to be easily disarranged, may often degenerate, yet the more homely and useful the art, and the less difficult the conditions for its exercise, the less likely it is to disappear from the world, unless when superseded by some better device. Races may and do leave off building temples and monuments of sculptured stone, and fall off in the execution of masterpieces of metal-work and porcelain, but there is no evidence of any tribe giving up the use of the spindle to twist their thread by hand, or having been in the habit of working the fire-drill with a thong, and going back to the clumsier practice of working it without, and it is even hard to fancy such a thing happening. Since the Hottentots have learnt, within the last two centuries or so, to smelt the iron ore of their country, it is hard to imagine that anything short of extirpating them or driving them into a country destitute of iron, could make them go back to the Stone Age in which their ancestors lived. Some facts are quoted which bear on the possible degeneration of savage tribes when driven out into the desert, or otherwise reduced to destitution, or losing their old arts in the presence of a higher civilization, but there seems ground for thinking that such degeneration has been rather of a local than of a general character, and has rather affected the fortunes of particular tribes than the development of the world at large. I do not think I have ever met with a single fact which seems to me to justify the theory, of which Dr. von Martius is perhaps the leading advocate, that the ordinary condition of the savage is the result of degeneration from a far higher state. The chapter on "Images and Names," which explains the arts of Magic as the effects of an early mental condition petrified into a series of mystic observances carried up into the midst of a higher culture, is indeed in the strongest opposition to the view that these superstitious practices are mutilated remnants of a higher system of belief which prevailed in former times, and this latter view is one of the strong points of the theory of degeneration. So far as may be judged from the scanty and defective evidence which has as yet been brought forward, I venture to think the most reasonable opinion to be that the course of development of the lower civilization has been on the whole in a forward direction, though interfered with occasionally and locally by the results of degrading and destroying influences.

Granting the existence of this onward movement in the lower levels of art and science, the question then arises, how any particular piece of skill or knowledge has come into any particular place where it is found. Three ways are open, independent invention, inheritance from ancestors in a distant region, transmission from one race to another; but between these three ways the choice is commonly a difficult one. Sometimes, indeed, the first is evidently to be preferred. Thus, though the floating gardens of Mexico and Cashmere are very similar devices, it seems more likely that the Mexican *chinampa* was invented on the spot than that the idea of it was imported from a distant region. Though the wattled cloth of the Swiss lake-dwellings is so similar in principle to that of New Zealand, it is much easier to suppose it the result of separate invention than of historical connexion. Though both the Egyptians and Chinese came upon the expedient of making the picture of an object stand for the sound which was the name of that object, there is no reason to doubt their having done so independently.

But the more difficult it is to account for observed facts in this way, and the more necessary it becomes to have recourse to theories of inheritance or transmission to explain them, the greater is their value in the eyes of the Ethnologist. Wherever he can judge that the existence of similar phenomena in the culture of distant peoples cannot be fairly accounted for, except

by supposing that there has been a connexion by blood or by
intercourse between them, then he has before him evidence
bearing upon the history of civilization and on the history of
mankind, evidence which shows that such movements as have
introduced guns, axes, books, into America in historic times,
have also taken place in unhistoric times among tribes whose
ancestors have left them no chronicles of past ages. Thus the
appearing of the Malay smelting-furnace in Madagascar, and
of the outrigger canoe in East Australia and the Andaman Islands, may be appealed to as evidence of historical connexion.
And it is possible that the Ethnographer may some day feel
himself justified in giving to this kind of argument a far wider
range, that he may claim, for instance, for the bow and arrow
a common origin wherever it is found, that is, over the whole
world with perhaps no exception but part of Polynesia, and
part or the whole of Australia. So, noticing that the distribution of the potter's art in North America is not sporadic, as
if a tribe here and a tribe there had wanted it and invented
it, but that it rises northwards in a compact field from Mexico
among the tribes East of the Rocky Mountains, he may
argue that it spread from a single source, and is at once a result and a proof of the transmission of civilization. Indeed, it
seems as though the recurrence of similar groups in the inven-
tories of instruments and works of the lower races, so remarkable both in the presence of like things and the comparative
absence of unlike ones, might come to supply, in a more advanced state of Ethnography, the materials for an indefinite
series of arguments bearing on the early history of man.

It is not to be denied, however, that there is usually a large
element of uncertainty in inferences of this kind taken alone,
and it is only in special cases that summary generalizations
from such evidence can as yet be admitted. Indeed, its proper
place is rather as accompanying the argument from language,
mythology, and customs, than as standing by itself. Thus the
appearance, just referred to, of the Malay blast-furnace in
Madagascar has to be viewed in connexion with the affinity in
language between Madagascar and the islands of the Eastern
Archipelago. Putting the two things together, we may assume

that the connexion with Madagascar dates from a time since
the introduction of iron-smelting in a part of the great Malayo-
Polynesian district, and belongs to that particular group of islands near the Eastern coast of Asia where this immense step
in material civilization was made. Again, the philological researches of Buschmann, which have brought into view traces
of the Aztec language up into the heart of North America,
fifteen hundred miles and more north of the City of Mexico,
join with several other lines of evidence in bringing far distant
parts of the population of the continent into historical connexion, and in showing, at least, that such communication
between its different peoples as may have spread the art of
pottery from a single locality is not matter of mere speculation.
It is in this way that it will probably be found most expedient
to use fragmentary arguments from the distribution of the arts
and sciences of savage tribes, in Ethnological districts where
a way has been already opened by more certain methods.

In its bearing on the History of Mankind, the tendency of
modern research in the region of Comparative Mythology is
not to be mistaken. The number of myths recorded as found
in different countries, where it is hardly conceivable that they
should have grown independently, goes on steadily increasing
from year to year, each one furnishing a new clue by which
common descent or intercourse is to be traced. Such evidence,
as fast as it is brought before the public, is received with the
most lively interest; and not only is its value fully admitted,
but there may even be observed a tendency to use it with too
much confidence in proof of common descent, without enough
consideration of what we know of the way in which Mythology
really travels from race to race. The cause of the occurrence
of a myth, or of a whole family of myths, may be, and no doubt
often is, mere intercourse, which has as little to do with common descent as the connexion which has planted the stories
of the Arabian Nights among the Malays of Borneo, and the
legends of Buddha among the Chinese. On the other hand,
the argument from similar customs has received, as a whole,
comparatively little attention, but it is not without importance.
Two or three, at least, of the customs remarked upon in the

present volume, in the group including the cure by sucking, the convade, and others, such as the wide-spread superstitions connected with sneezing, on which Mr. Haliburton gave a lecture, in 1863, at Halifax, Nova Scotia,[1] may be adduced as facts for the occurrence of which in distant times and places it is hard to account on any other hypothesis than that of deep-lying connexion, by blood or intercourse, among races which history, and even philology, only knows as isolated sections of the population of the world.

On the whole, it does not seem to be an unreasonable, or even an over-sanguine view, that the mass of analogies in Art and Knowledge, Mythology and Custom, confused and indistinct as they at present are, may already be taken to indicate that the civilizations of many races, whose history even the evidence of Language has not succeeded in bringing into connexion, have really grown up under one another's influences, or derived common material from a common source. But that such lines of argument should ever be found to converge in the last instance towards a single point, so as to enable the student to infer from reasoning on a basis of observed facts that the civilization of the whole world has its origin in one parent stock, is, in the present state of our knowledge, rather a theoretical possibility than a state of things of which even the most dim and distant view is to be obtained.

On another subject, on which it would not be prudent to offer a definite opinion, a few words may nevertheless be said. Every attempt to trace back the early history of civilization tends, however remotely, towards an ultimate limit—the primary condition of the human race, as regards their knowledge of the laws of nature and their power of modifying the outer world for their own ends. Such lines of investigation as go back from the Bronze or Iron Ages to the time of the use of implements of stone, from the higher to the lower methods of fire-making, from the boat to the raft, from the use of the spindle to the art of hand-twisting, and so on, seem to enable the student to see back through the history of human culture to a state of art and science somewhat resembling that of the savage

---

[1] 'Anthropological Review,' Nov. 1863, p. 491.

tribes of modern times. It is useful to work back to this point, at least as a temporary resting-place in the argument, seeing that a state of things really known to exist is generally more convenient to reason upon than a purely theoretical one. But if we may judge that the present condition of savage tribes is the complex result of not only a long but an eventful history, in which development of culture may have been more or less interfered with by degradation caused by war, disease, oppression, and other mishaps, it does not seem likely that any tribe known to modern observers should be anything like a fair representative of primary conditions. Still, positive evidence of anything lower than the known state of savages is scarce in the extreme. If indeed we may feel certain that the men whose tools and weapons are found in the Drift Beds, in the Bone Caves, and in the Shell-Heaps of Denmark, were not in the habit of grinding the edges of any of their stone implements, such a state of things may be instanced as evidence of a condition of one of the useful arts lying below anything that has been observed among the lowest savage tribes. Even if it should be established that a few isolated specimens of ground implements occur among the thousands of unground ones belonging to this lowest division of the Stone Age, its general character, as consisting almost exclusively of unground implements, would remain nearly as distinct as ever from anything recorded among tribes known to travellers or historians.

To turn to a very different department of culture, some of the facts belonging to the history of custom and superstition may for the last time be referred to, as perhaps having their common root in a mental condition underlying anything to be met with now. The remarkable custom of the *Couvade*, which in several distant regions of the world appears a mere dark superstitious mystery, finds an intelligible explanation among the South American tribes who consciously believe that different persons are not necessarily separate beings, as we take them to be, but that there is such a physical connexion between father and son, that the diet of the one affects the health of the other. The early fusion of objective and subjective relations in the mind, of the effects of which in superstitious practices handed down from age to age so much has been said in this book, may perhaps not be fully or exactly represented in the mental state of any living tribe of men.

There have been indeed few more important movements in the course of the history of mankind, than this change of opinion as to the nature and relations of what is in the mind and what is out of it. To say nothing of its vast effects upon Ethics and Religion, the whole course of Science, and of Art, of which Science is a principal element, have been deeply influenced by this mental change. Man's views of the difference between imagination and reality, of the nature of cause and effect, of the connexion between himself and the external world, and of the parts of the external world among themselves, have been entirely altered by it. To the times before this movement had gone too far, belong the developments of Mythology, so puzzling to later ages which had risen to a higher mental state, and had then thrown down the ladder they had climbed by. The modern deciphering of ancient myths has been perhaps more valuable than any direct examination of savage races, in giving us the means of realizing that early state of mind in which there is scarcely any distinct barrier between fact and fancy,—to which whatever is similar is the same. If the clouds are driven across the sky like cows from their pasture, they are not merely compared to cows, but are thought and talked of as though they really were cows; if the sun travels along its course like a glittering chariot, forthwith the wheels and the driver and the horses are there; while by treating a name as though it necessarily represented a person, it becomes possible to evolve out of the contemplation of nature those wonderful stories in which even the earth, the sea, and the sky, combine with their natural attributes a kind of half-human personality. The opinion that dreams and phantasms have an objective existence out of the mind that perceives them, and that when two ideas are associated in a man's mind the objects to which those ideas belong must have a corresponding physical connexion, are views over which the long course of observation and study of nature has brought a vast change. These things belong to that early condition of the human mind, from which, to say nothing of the special views of metaphysicians and leaders in science, the ordinary ideas of Man and Nature held by educated men differ so widely. However far these ideas may in their turn be left behind, the growth which can be traced within the range of our own observation and inference, is one of no scant measure. It may bear comparison with one of the great changes in the mental life of the individual man, perhaps rather with the expansion and fixing of the mind which accompanies the passage from infancy into youth, than with the later steps from youth into manhood, or from manhood into old age.

INDEX.

Abipones, 140, 146, 291, etc.
Adobe, 181.
Æolian flutes, living, 177.
Africa, Beast-Fables of, 10-2, 355; Stone Age in, 219-22.
Alnajah of Ethiopia, 216.
Alphabets and Syllabaria, 101-5; Finger-alphabet, 17.
America, connexion of its civilization with that of the Old World, 206, 275, 331-60.
American chroniclers, 250.
Andaman Islanders, 160.
Archimedes, his burning mirror, 248.
Architecture, evidence of progress in, 168.
Ark, 323.
Arrow-heads, stone, 209, 210, 221.
Articulation of deaf-mutes, 70-5.
Arts, transmission of, 167, etc., 365.
Aryan race, their use of metal, 212; their fire apparatus, 241, 264.
Astrology, 132.
Aubin, M., on phonetic characters of Mexicans, 84-6.
Australians, 141, 144, 176, 200, 261, 290, 363, etc.
Axes, stone, 199.

Bakalahari, 184.
Baking in hollow trees, ant-hills, pits, 260.
Balsam of Judea, 217.
Bamboo, fire produced from, 232.
Barbecue, 261.
Basques, 292.
Beast-Fables in Europe and Africa, 10-2, 355; Lion and Mouse, 342.
Bee-hunting, Australian method of, 178.
Bellows for iron-smelting, 167.
Bewitching, by images, 116-20, 125; by earth-cutting, 120; by names, 124-6; by locks of hair, parings of nails, leavings of food, etc. 127-30; by symbolic charms, 130, 133; by 'wishing,' 133; by the evil eye, 134.
Bible, tales derived from, 329-31.

Bird-trap, rudimentary, 182.
Blast-pump for iron-smelting, in East and Madagascar, 167-9, 366.
Boats, remains of, on mountains, etc., 320-4.
Boats and rafts, 102.
Boiling, 261-9; with hot stones, 262-7; vessels for, 267-9.
Bolas, 176.
Bone-caves, 196, 312; stone implements of, 196.
Bones burnt for fuel, 181.
Boomerang, 176, 198, 342.
Bread-fruit paste, 178.
Bridge of Dread, 349-52.
Bronze Age in America, 205; in Asia, 211.
Bucaros, 281.
Burnishing, 261.
Burial in canoes. etc., 352.
Burning-lens, 247.
Burning-mirror, 248-51.
Bushmen, 141.

Calculation by stones, 168.
Calendars of N. A. Indians, 91; of Mexicans, 92, 232.
Caliban, 345.
Celts, stone, 198-201.
Central America, ruined cities of, 181, 205.
Charms, 130.
Cherokees, their syllabarium, 104.
Chinampas, 171.
China, aboriginal tribes of, 207, 294.
Chinese, their clan-names, 278; their phonetic writing, 99-101.
Chocolate, 177.
Christy, Mr. H., his exploration of bone-caves of Périgord, 196; finding stone-implements in North Africa, 221.
Churn worked with cord, 240.
Circumcision: — with stone knives among Jews, 214-6; Rabbinical law as to instrument, 215; among Alnajah in Ethiopia, 216; in Fiji islands, 216; in Australia, 216.

Cistercians, their gesture-language, 40-2.

Civilisation, progress of, 2, 118, 136, 148, 150, etc., 197, 202, 240, 303, 371; decline of, 180-7, 364.

Clan-names;— in China, 278; Australia, 280; persons of same, may not marry, 277-82.

Climbing by hoops, etc., 170.

Cloth of bundles of fibre, 188-90.

Cock and Bull stories, 10.

Colour of feathers changed in live birds, 177.

Cooking, 259-60; *en papillote*, 173; roasting and broiling, 259; baking, 259; underground ovens, 260; bucaning or barbecuing, 260; boiling, 261-9; stone-boiling, 262-7.

Copper, native, used by stone-age race in North America, 204.

Cord, hand-twisting of, 188.

Corsicans, 217.

Couvade, 247-97, 309; in South America and West India, 288-94; North America, Africa, and Eastern Archipelago, 294; Asia, 294; Europe, 295; its ethnological value, 296.

Customs, 273-97, 367; tying clothes of couple in wedding, 47; fire not touched with sharp instrument, 275; sucking-cure, etc., 275-7, 290; restrictions from marriage of kindred, 277-81; Spartan marriage, 280-4; restrictions to intercourse of parents-in-law and children-in-law, 285-7; tabued relationships, 287; couvade, 287-97, 309; usages concerning sneezing, 368.

Cybele, priests of, 217.

Dasent, Dr., his argument from Beast-Fables, 10, 355.

Dead, names of, not mentioned, 142, 145.

Deaf and dumb, their mental condition and education, 17, 65-75; of themselves utter words, 72-5; their lip-imitation of words, 73.

Decline of culture, 180-7, 364; Dr. von Martius's theory of, 135; A. von Humboldt on, 186.

Deluge, 89, 317-24, 359, 310.

Devil painted white, 113; attributes of Fire-god, etc., given to, 359.

Diable boiteux, 358-60.

Digger Indians, 185.

Divination, 131.

Doing, in sense of practising magic, 136.

Dolls and toys, 107-9.

Dreams and phantasms, argument from, 5-10.

Drift gravels, stone implements in, 103-4; Mr. Prestwich on age of, 104; extinct animals of, 303-5.

Drills for boring holes and for fire-making, 187, 239-45.

Drink = river, 37.

Drum, 138.

Dumb, becomes term for foreign, barbarian, stupid, young, 34, 65.

Earrings, etc., 1.

Eclipse, 163.

Effigies, 122.

Eggs, artificial hatching of, 191.

Egypt: hieroglyphics, 97-9; Coptic alphabet, 101; decline in arts, 181; stone arrow-heads, 200; stone embalmer's knives, etc., 217.

Elephant, white, 274.

Erman, on rukh and griffin, 311.

Esquimaux, 160, 204, 241, 319, etc.

Evans, Mr. J., on wattled cloth of Swiss lake-dwellings, 188.

Evil eye, 53, 131.

Father put to bed, etc., on birth of child, *see* Couvade, 287-97, 309; parentage ascribed only to, 291.

Ferguson, Mr., on wooden forms in architecture, 168.

Fetish, 135.

Fire, myths of origin of, 228-30, 252-3.

Fire, new, 248-57;—Vestal, 248; in Peru, 249; in India, 254; on Easter Eve, 256; in Russia, 257; *see also* Needfire.

Fire, not touched with sharp instrument, 275.

Fire, races reported to be destitute of, 228-31; Guanches, 228; Islanders of Los Jardines, 229; of Fakaafo, 229; of the Ladrones and Philippines, 231; tribe in French Guiana, 233; Ethiopian tribes, 233.

Fire-drill:—simple, 237-9, 240-50; as carpenter's brace, 240; thong-drill, 240, 254; bow-drill, 243; pump-drill, 243-5.

Fire-making:—Tasmanians and Australians said to have no means of, 231; methods of, in different countries, 236-59; stick-and-groove, 236; striking fire with bamboo, 237; fire-drill, 237-45; striking fire with iron pyrites, 245, 250; with stones, etc., 246; flint and steel, 247; burning-irons, 217; burning-mirror, 248-51; lucifer matches, 251; wooden friction-apparatus, kept up to modern times, 252; evidence of early use of, in different countries, 252-4.

Flamen Dialis, 126.

Flint and steel, 217.

Floating gardens, etc., 171.

Food superstitions, 131.

Footmarks, in Mexican picture-writings, 152.

Footprints, mythic, 115-7.

Fork, eating-, 173-5.

Fossil bones, shells, etc., myths of observation connected with, 304-21.

Fountain of Youth, 352-5.

Fuegians, 162, 216, 250, 261, 264, etc.

Gaucho, 240.

Gesture-language, 14-82:—of deaf-and-dumb, 10-33; nature of, 15, etc.; arbitrary signs, 22; epithets, 21; absence of grammatical categories, 21, 62; grammar and syntax, 25-32; g. l. of savage tribes, 31-40; syntax, 29; g. l. of Cistercian monks, 40-2; the Pantomime, 42-4; g. l. as an accompaniment to speech, 41, etc.; common to mankind, 53; evidence of mental similarity, 61; compared with speech, 58-64; its dualism compared with that of speech, 59-62; prepositions, 61; theory that g. l. was the original utterance of man, 64.

Gesture-signs, 37, 45-53; translated in language, 37; nodding and shaking head, 34; kissing hand, 38; sign of benediction, 38; beckoning, etc., 45, 52; snapping fingers, 45; grasping and shaking hands, 45-7; crouching, bowing, kneeling, etc., 47; gestures of prayer, 48; uncovering head, feet, and body, 48-51; rubbing noses, etc., 51; signs of contempt, etc., 52; against evil eye, 53.

Giants, 314 ff.

Glass, legend of invention of, 151; substituted for stone in making knives, etc., 218.

Gold work of Mexico, 205.

Gourds, etc., plastered with clay, 270.

Griffins, 310-2.

Grinding and polishing stone implements, 194-201, 361.

Guanches, 224.

Guano, 177.

Hair, bewitching by locks of, etc., 127-9.

Hammers, stone, 101-3, 190, 221.

Hammock, 176.

Harpocrates, 41.

Heads, preserved, of New Zealand, 211.

Hebrides, inhabitants of, 208.

Heyne, on thought and speech, 69.

Horns, used to point weapons, etc., 221.

Hot stones, baking with, 260; boiling with, 262-7.

Hottentots, 10-2, 210.

Humboldt, A. v., on connexion of Mexicans with Asia, 92, 208, 331; on human degeneration, 180; on Mexican elephant-like head, 304.

Husband, name of, not mentioned by wife, 141.

Ichthyophagi, 207.

Ideas, association of, with images and words, 107-11.

Idiots, use of gesture-language in education of, 79.

Idols, 110-3.

Images, etc., 107-23.

Incubi and Succubi, 7.

India, stone implements in, 212; fire-making, 238, 256; marriage, 47, 77.

Indians of N. America: gesture-language, 35-40; picture-writing, 83-93.

Individuals, not held to be physically separate by lower races, 202.

Inventors and civilizers, legends of, 150-4, 208, 230, 252, 259, etc.

Iron, meteoric, used by Esquimaux, 201.

Irrigation, decline in art of, 162.

Jack and the Beanstalk, 310-9.

Japan, stone implements in, 210.

Jews, their use of stone knives, 213-4.

Jonah, 317.

Joshua, stone knives in tomb of, 214.

Jupiter Lapis, 226.

Kafirs, 141, 147, etc.

Kamchadals, 207, 238, 264, 275, 319, etc.

Kang-hi, his Encyclopædia, 208, 309, 321.

Kava or Ava, 170.

Kettles, of bark, paunch, hide, split bamboo, potstone, etc., 267-9.

Khorsabad, obsidian flake-knives under temple of, 210.

Kings' and chiefs' names not mentioned, 142-4.

Kjökkenmöddings, stone implements of, 192.

Knives, stone flake-, 194-8, 210.

Language, origin of, 15, 56-9, 64; Chinese myth of, 59; stories of attempts to discover original L. by experiments on children, 80-2; speech compared with gesture-language, 58-64; predicative and demonstrative roots compared with two classes of gesture-signs, 59-69; concretism, 62; verb-roots, 63; syntax, 63; relation of speech to thought, 68-75; deaf-and-dumb of themselves speak, 72-5; their lip-imitation of words, 73; language modified by superstitions concerning words, in Polynesia 144, Australia 145, Tasmania 145, among Abipones 146, Kaffrs 147, Yezidis 147, English and Americans 147; evidence from language as to progress in culture, 162-4, 259; as to Stone Age, 212-4.

Lartet and Christy, on bone caves of Périgord, 191.

Lazarus, Prof., 215, 289, 287.

Letters. See Phonetic Characters.

Life, future, 5-10, 293, 349-52.

Little Red Riding-Hood, 338.

Livre des Sauvages, 89.

Madagascar, 167-9, 225, 239.

Magic and sorcery, theory of, 115-39.

Malay stone-implements, 211.

Malayo-Polynesians, 167, 178, etc.

Mammoths and other extinct animals, possible recollection of, 303; myths derived from remains of, 303-12.

Man, his degeneration in size and length of life, 316; mental uniformity of, 361-3; primary condition of, 368.

Man in the Moon, etc., 326.

Man swallowed by Fish, 336-9.

Map-making, 90.

Marriage, prohibition of, among kindred, 277, etc.; in Europe, 277; Asia, 277-9; Africa, 280; Australia, 280; America, 281-3; extended to imaginary kindred, 281; wife carried off by force, 280, 281; crossing male and female lines, 277-81.

Martius, Dr. v., his theory of degeneration, 135, 364.

Massagetæ, 331.

Metal-working in Mexico and Peru, 205.

Mexico;—picture-writing, 91-7, 304; calendars, 92, 332; phonetic characters, 94-6; Quetzalcohuatl and the Toltecs, 151-4; stone implements, 191; metal-work, 205; fire-drill, 239; Humboldt on connexion of Mexican civilization with Asia, 92, 200, 275, 305, 331.

Mirrors of pyrites and obsidian, 231, 259.

Moslems, their opinion on images, 121.

Mound-builders of Mississippi Valley, 214.

Müller, Prof. Max, 61, 147.

Myths, 306-60, 370; of origin of language, 59; connected with shapes of rocks, 114; of footprints, 116; of Quetzalcohuatl, 151-4; Sun-myths, 151-4, 338-45, 354; myths relating to stone arrow-heads, 210, 223; to dolmens in North Africa, 221; of thunderbolt, 222-7; of Prometheus, 229, 254; of origin of fire in Polynesia, 230, China, 252, Phœnicia, 254; of monstrous tribes, 234; growth of, 232; permanence of, 233; of Old World transferred to New, 250; geographical distribution of, 325-60; common nature and character of, among different races, 328-9; man in the moon, etc., 326; sun and moon brother and sister, 327; Castor and Pollux in Tasmania, 327; transmission of, 329-31, 367; derived from Bible stories, etc., 329-31; of America compared with those of Old World, 332-60; World-Tortoise, 332-6; Man swallowed by Fish, 336-9; Sun-Catcher, 338-43; Tom Thumb, 336-40; Little Red Riding-Hood, 338; Jack and the Beanstalk, 340-9; ascent to heaven by the Tree, 341-9; Swan-coat, 346; Bridge of Dead, 349-52; Fountain of Youth, 352-6; Tail-fisher, 355-9; Moon taken for cheese, 355; stumpy-tailed animals, 355; Diable Boiteux, 359-60; value of myths as historical evidence, 357. See also Myths of Observation, Beast-Fables, and Traditions.

Myths of Observation, 298, 306-24:—petrified lentils, 307; sun hissing in sea, 307; rain of stones, 308; connected with fossil remains, 308-24; mammoths, mastodons, etc., 304-14; rhinoceros horns, 310-2; griffins, 310-2; animals coming out of caves, 312; creatures which die on seeing daylight, 309, 313; giants, 314-7; degeneration of man's stature, 316; bearing of fossils and remains of boats on Deluge-traditions, 317-21; bones of whales on high mountains, 319.

Names:—their association with objects, 121; their use in magic, etc., 121-7; concealed, 125; changed to deceive evil spirits, 126; exchanged in token of amity, 126; avoidance of use of certain personal names, own, of others, of husbands, of parents- and children-in-law, of other connexions, of kings and chiefs, of dead, of spirits, of superhuman beings, 130-47, 285-7.
Needfire, 243-8.
New Zealanders, 161, 188, 201, 264, etc.
North American Indians, their picture-writing, 83-8, 91, calendars, 111; syllabarium of Cherokees, 104.
Numa Pompilius, 248.
Numerals, Roman, etc., 105.

Objective and subjective impressions and connexions confused, 117-49, 252, 369.
Ornamentation of urns, 271.
Ostyaks, images of dead, 110.

Parents-in-law and children-in-law, observances concerning, 141-7; restrictions to intercourse of, 285-7.
Pellet-bow, 177.
Peru:—metal-work of, 205; New Fire, 249; Virgins of the Sun compared with Vestal Virgins of Rome, 250.
Phonetic characters, 84-106; of Mexicans, 91-6; Egyptian hieroglyphs, 97-9; of Chinese, 99-101; of Central America, 100; alphabets and syllabaria, 101-5.
Picture-writing, etc., 83-100, 159; of North American Indians, 83-91; of Mexicans, 91-7; numerals, 105.
Plants, sympathetic, 182.
Polynesians, 142-4, 161, 171, 237, 265, 299, 337, etc.
Pottery, 175, 179, 263-6; Goguet's theory of origin of, 269-72; transition vessels, 269-72; gourd-shapes, 270; ornamentation, 271.
Prometheus, 228, 254.
Puris and Coroados, 76-9.
Pygmies, 212.
Pyrites, striking fire with, 245, 250.

Quaternary deposits, 193; possible traditions of animals of, 303-5.
Quetzalcohuatl, 151-4.
Quipus, 154-8.

Rabbinical law as to circumcision, 215.
Rainmakers, 133.
Rattles, 137.

Reindeer-tribes of Central France, 106.
Reynard the Fox, 11, 355.
Rice, traditions of introduction of, 301-3, 316.
Roasting and broiling food, 259.
Ruth, 311.

Sago, 179.
Samovar, 165.
Samson, 309, 313.
Sanchoniathon, cosmogony of, 253.
Semitic race, their alphabet, 105; stone implements, 213-4.
Shell heaps, stone implements of, 192, 197.
Signatures, doctrine of, 123.
Similarity in arts, customs, beliefs, etc., in distant regions, arguments from, 5, 139, 160, 201-3, 260, 273, 290, 323, 325, etc., 361-3.
Sneezing, customs relating to, 309.
Sorcerers:—their arts, 127-39; rattles and drums, 137; cure by sucking, etc., 275-7.
Soul, future life of, 5-10, 293, 349-52.
Sound and colour, comparison of, 71.
Spartan marriage, 290-1.
Spindle, 188-90.
Spirits:—of dead affected through remains of bodies, 129; names of s. not mentioned, 143.
Steinthal, Prof., on gesture-language, 14; on thought and speech, 69.
Stick-and-groove, 238.
Stone, ornaments of hard, made by low South American tribes, 186.
Stone Age, 191-227; unground, 193-7, 369; ground, 198-209; evidence of, in different parts of the world, 209-27; evidence of language as to, 212-4.
Stone-boiling, 262-7, 302.
Stone implements, 191-227; late surviving, 191; natural stones used, 191-3; implements of Drift, 193-6; similar ones elsewhere, 196; of bone-caves, 196; of Scandinavian shell-heaps, 197; grinding and polishing, 199-201; flake-knives, 198; celts, 198-200; hammers, 199; axes, 199; special instruments, 200; high-class celts in Australia, 200; patu-patu of New Zealand and S. America, 201; general similarity of stone implements of different countries, 202; countries found under Stone Age conditions, 211; stone implements of N. and S. America, 206; Kamchatka, 207; China, 207; Tartary,

208; lightning-stones, 208; stone arrow-heads of Tuagua, 208; of Egyptians, 209; of the field of Marathon, etc., 209; stone implements of Ichthyophagi, 209; of W. and N. Asia, 210; Japan, 210; Java, Malay Peninsula, etc., 211; India, 212; Europe, 212; Aryans, 212; evidence of language as to, 212–4; use of stone implements by Jews and Al-najab, 213–8; used for circumcising, 214–6; for slaughtering beasts, 216, 222, 226; for incision of corpse to be embalmed in Egypt, 217; for extracting balsam of Judæa, 217; stone implements in Africa, 219–222; Canary Islands, 222; thought to be thunderbolts, 222–7; to be natural stones, 208, 224; used to sacrifice victims with in Africa, 223; in Rome, 224.

Stumpy-tailed animals, myths relating to, 355.

Sugar, 178.

Sun-myths, 151–4, 338–43, 354.

Supernatural beings, 110; names of, not mentioned, 143, 147.

Superstitions, 131–48, 218, 296, 360; relating to thunderbolt, 225; need-fire, 256; albino elephant, 274; seeds put with gold-dust, etc., 274; touching fire with knife, etc., 275. See also Customs.

Swan-coal, 316.

Swiss lake-dwellers, 189, 197.

Symbolic offerings, 122.

Tabu, 130, 142–5, 287.

Tail-fishing, etc., 365–8.

Tally, 168.

Tasmanians, 77–9, 195, 231, 327.

Tea-urn, 165.

Teeth, artificial, 173; stopping teeth with gold, 173.

Textile fabrics, 168–80.

Thunderbolt, 208, 211, 222–7.

Toddy, 178.

Toltecs, 152–4.

Tom Thumb, 338–40.

Tortoise-myth, 303, 332–6.

Totem, 281.

Traditions, 299–306; of inventors and civilizers, 150–4; of quipo in China, 154, 299; of Polynesia, 299; Central America, 300; in tropics, apparently belonging to high latitudes, 300; of introduction of rice, 301; first appearance of white men among N.W. American tribes, 302; possible recollection of mammoth, colossal tortoise, great ape, etc., 303–6; deluge, 317–21.

Tribes said to be deficient in speech, 75–9; degraded, 181; said to have no fire or no means of fire-making, 228–36.

Utterance, not by speech only, 14; its relation to thought, 68–75.

Veddahs, 77–9, 238.

Vei syllabarium, 104.

Vessels:—for stone-boiling, 262–7, 302; of bark, paunch, hide, bamboo, etc., for setting over fire, 267–9; of pot-stone, 268; pottery, 269–72; gourds, etc., plastered with clay, 270.

Vestal virgins, 248–50.

Wattled cloth, 188–90.

Weaving, 178, 188.

Whately, Archbishop, his theory of civilization, 160–2.

Wild fire, 252.

Words, superstitions concerning, 124–7, 139–49.

World, conception of, among lower races, 332, 340.

Writing, see Picture-writing, Phonetic characters; use of, in magic, etc., 126.

ALBEMARLE STREET, LONDON,
January, 1863.

MR. MURRAY'S

GENERAL LIST OF WORKS.

ALBERT (Prince). THE SPEECHES AND ADDRESSES on Public Occasions of H.R.H. THE PRINCE CONSORT; with an Introduction giving some Outlines of his Character. Portrait. 8vo. 10s. 6d.; or Popular Edition, fcap. 8vo, 1s.

ABBOTT'S (Rev. J.) Philip Musgrave; or, Memoirs of a Church of England Missionary in the North American Colonies. Post 8vo. 2s.

ABERCROMBIE'S (John) Enquiries concerning the Intellectual Powers and the Investigation of Truth. 15th Edition. Fcap. 8vo. 6s. 6d.

—————— —— Philosophy of the Moral Feelings. 12th Edition. Fcap. 8vo. 4s.

ACLAND'S (Rev. Charles) Popular Account of the Manners and Customs of India. Post 8vo. 2s.

ÆSOP'S FABLES. A New Translation. With Historical Preface. By Rev. Thomas James. With 100 Woodcuts, by Tenniel and Wolf. 50th Thousand. Post 8vo. 2s. 6d.

AGRICULTURAL (The) Journal. Of the Royal Agricultural Society of England. 8vo. Published half-yearly.

AIDS TO FAITH: a Series of Essays. By various Writers. Edited by William Thomson, D.D., Lord Archbishop of York. 8vo. 9s.

CONTENTS.

Rev. H. L. Mansel—Miracles.	Rev. George Rawlinson—The Pentateuch.
Bishop of Killaloe—Christian Evidences.	Archbishop of York—Doctrines of the Atonement.
Rev. Dr. McCaul—Prophecy and the Mosaic Record of Creation.	Bishop of Ely.—Inspiration.
Rev. Canon Cook—Ideology and Subscription.	Bishop of Gloucester and Bristol.—Scripture and its Interpretation.

AMBER-WITCH (The). The most Interesting Trial for Witchcraft ever known. Translated from the German by Lady Duff Gordon. Post 8vo. 2s.

ARMY LIST (The). *Published Monthly by Authority.* 18mo. 1s. 6d.

ARTHUR'S (Little) History of England. By Lady Callcott. 100th Thousand. Woodcuts. Fcap. 8vo. 2s. 6d.

ATKINSON'S (Mrs.) Recollections of Tartar Steppes and their Inhabitants. Illustrations. Post 8vo. 12s.

AUNT IDA'S Walks and Talks; a Story Book for Children. By a Lady. Woodcuts. 16mo. 5s.

AUSTIN'S (John) Lectures on Jurisprudence; or, the Philosophy of Positive Law. 3 Vols. 8vo. 39s.

—————— (Sarah) Fragments from German Prose Writers. With Biographical Notes. Post 8vo. 10s.

B

ADMIRALTY PUBLICATIONS; issued by direction of the Lords
    Commissioners of the Admiralty:—

A MANUAL OF SCIENTIFIC ENQUIRY, for the Use of Travellers.
    Edited by Sir John F. Herschel, and Rev. Robert Main. Third
    Edition. Woodcuts. Post 8vo. 9s.

AIRY'S ASTRONOMICAL OBSERVATIONS made at Greenwich.
    1836 to 1847. Royal 4to. 50s. each.

————— ASTRONOMICAL RESULTS. 1848 to 1858. 4to. 8s. each.

————— APPENDICES TO THE ASTRONOMICAL OBSERVA-
        TIONS.

    1836.—I.   Bessel's Refraction Tables. }
         II.   Tables for converting Errors of R.A. and N.P.D. } 8s.
               into Errors of Longitude and Ecliptic P.D. }
    1837.—I.   Logarithms of Sines and Cosines to every Ten }
               Seconds of Time. } 8s.
         II.   Table for converting Sidereal into Mean Solar Time }
    1842.—Catalogue of 1439 Stars. 8s.
    1845.—Longitude of Valentia. 8s.
    1847.—Twelve Years' Catalogue of Stars. 14s.
    1851.—Maskelyne's Ledger of Stars. 6s.
    1852.—I.   Description of the Transit Circle. 5s.
         II.   Regulations of the Royal Observatory. 2s.
    1853.—Bessel's Refraction Tables. 3s.
    1854.—I.   Description of the Zenith Tube. 3s.
         II.   Six Years' Catalogue of Stars. 10s.
    1856.—Description of the Galvanic Apparatus at Greenwich Ob-
               servatory. 8s.

————— MAGNETICAL AND METEOROLOGICAL OBSERVA-
        TIONS. 1840 to 1847. Royal 4to. 50s. each.

————— ASTRONOMICAL, MAGNETICAL, AND METEOROLO-
        GICAL OBSERVATIONS, 1848 to 1857. Royal 4to. 50s. each.

————— ASTRONOMICAL RESULTS. 1848 to 1858. 4to.

————— MAGNETICAL AND METEOROLOGICAL RESULTS.
        1848 to 1857. 4to. 8s. each.

————— REDUCTION OF THE OBSERVATIONS OF PLANETS.
        1750 to 1830. Royal 4to. 50s.

————— ————— ————— ————— LUNAR OBSERVATIONS. 1750
        to 1830. 2 Vols. Royal 4to. 50s. each.

————— ————— ————— ————— 1831 to 1851. 4to. 3s.

BERNOULLI'S SEXCENTENARY TABLE. London, 1779. 4to.

BESSEL'S AUXILIARY TABLES FOR HIS METHOD OF CLEAR-
    ING LUNAR DISTANCES. 8vo.

————— FUNDAMENTA ASTRONOMIÆ: Regiomontii, 1818. Folio. 60s.

BIRD'S METHOD OF CONSTRUCTING MURAL QUADRANTS.
    London, 1768. 4to. 2s. 6d.

————— METHOD OF DIVIDING ASTRONOMICAL INSTRU-
        MENTS. London, 1767. 4to. 2s. 6d.

COOK, KING, AND BAYLY'S ASTRONOMICAL OBSERVATIONS.
    London, 1782. 4to. 21s.

ENCKE'S BERLINER JAHRBUCH, for 1830. Berlin, 1828. 8vo. 9s.

GROOMBRIDGE'S CATALOGUE OF CIRCUMPOLAR STARS.
    4to. 10s.

HANSEN'S TABLES DE LA LUNE. 4to. 20s.

HARRISON'S PRINCIPLES OF HIS TIMEKEEPER. Plates.
    1767. 4to. 5s.

ADMIRALTY PUBLICATIONS—*continued*.

HUTTON'S TABLES OF THE PRODUCTS AND POWERS OF NUMBERS. 1781. Folio. 7s. 6d.

LAX'S TABLES FOR FINDING THE LATITUDE AND LONGITUDE. 1821. 8vo. 10s.

LUNAR OBSERVATIONS at GREENWICH. 1783 to 1819. Compared with the Tables, 1821. 4to. 7s. 6d.

MASKELYNE'S ACCOUNT OF THE GOING OF HARRISON'S WATCH. 1767. 4to. 2s. 6d.

MAYER'S DISTANCES of the MOON'S CENTRE from the PLANETS. 1822, 3s.; 1823, 4s. 6d. 1824 to 1835, 8vo. 4s. each.

——— THEORIA LUNÆ JUXTA SYSTEMA NEWTONIANUM. 4to. 2s. 6d.

— — TABULÆ MOTUUM SOLIS ET LUNÆ. 1770. 4to. 5s.

— —— ASTRONOMICAL OBSERVATIONS MADE AT GOTTINGEN, from 1756 to 1761. 1826. Folio. 7s. 6d.

NAUTICAL ALMANACS, from 1767 to 1833. 8vo. 2s. 6d. each.

——— SELECTIONS FROM THE ADDITIONS up to 1812. 8vo. 5s. 1834-54. 8vo. 5s.

——— SUPPLEMENTS, 1828 to 1833, 1837 and 1838. 8vo. 2s. each.

——— TABLE requisite to be used with the N.A. 1781. 8vo. 5s.

POND'S ASTRONOMICAL OBSERVATIONS. 1811 to 1835. 4to. 21s. each.

RAMSDEN'S ENGINE for DIVIDING MATHEMATICAL INSTRUMENTS. 4to. 5s.

——— ENGINE for DIVIDING STRAIGHT LINES. 4to. 5s.

SABINE'S PENDULUM EXPERIMENTS to DETERMINE THE FIGURE OF THE EARTH. 1825. 4to. 40s.

SHEPHERD'S TABLES for CORRECTING LUNAR DISTANCES. 1772. Royal 4to. 21s.

——— TABLES, GENERAL, of the MOON'S DISTANCE from the SUN, and 10 STARS. 1787. Folio. 5s. 6d.

TAYLOR'S SEXAGESIMAL TABLE. 1780. 4to. 15s.

——— TABLES OF LOGARITHMS. 4to. 3l.

TIARK'S ASTRONOMICAL OBSERVATIONS for the LONGITUDE of Madeira. 1822. 4to. 5s.

——— CHRONOMETRICAL OBSERVATIONS for DIFFERENCES of LONGITUDE between Dover, Portsmouth, and Falmouth. 1823. 4to. 5s.

VENUS and JUPITER: Observations of, compared with the Tables. London, 1822. 4to. 2s.

WALES AND BAYLY'S ASTRONOMICAL OBSERVATIONS. 1777. 4to. 21s.

WALES' REDUCTION OF ASTRONOMICAL OBSERVATIONS MADE IN THE SOUTHERN HEMISPHERE. 1764—1771. 1788. 4to. 10s. 6d.

BABBAGE'S (CHARLES) Economy of Machinery and Manufactures. *Fourth Edition.* Fcap. 8vo. 6s.

——— Reflections on the Decline of Science in England, and on some of its Causes. 4to. 7s. 6d.

BAIKIE'S (W. B.) Narrative of an Exploring Voyage up the Rivers Quorra and Tshadda in 1854. Map. 8vo. 16s.

DANKES' (George) Story of Corfe Castle, with documents relating to the Time of the Civil Wars, &c. Woodcuts. Post 8vo. 10s. 6d.

BARBAULD'S (Mrs.) Hymns in Prose for Children. With 112 Original Designs. Small 4to. 5s.

BARROW'S (Sir John) Autobiographical Memoir, including Reflections, Observations, and Reminiscences at Home and Abroad. From Early Life to Advanced Age. Portrait. 8vo. 16s.

——— Voyages of Discovery and Research within the Arctic Regions, from 1818 to the present time. 8vo. 15s.

——— Life and Voyages of Sir Francis Drake. With numerous Original Letters. Post 8vo. 2s.

BATES' (H. W.) Records of a Naturalist on the River Amazons during eleven years of Adventure and Travel. Second Edition. Illustrations. Post 8vo. 12s.

BEES AND FLOWERS. Two Essays. By Rev. Thomas James. Reprinted from the "Quarterly Review." Fcap. 8vo. 1s. each.

BELL'S (Sir Charles) Mechanism and Vital Endowments of the Hand as evincing Design. Sixth Edition. Woodcuts. Post 8vo. 6s.

BERTHA'S Journal during a Visit to her Uncle in England. Containing a Variety of Interesting and Instructive Information. Seventh Edition. Woodcuts. 12mo.

BIRCH'S (Samuel) History of Ancient Pottery and Porcelain : Egyptian, Assyrian, Greek, Roman, and Etruscan. With 200 Illustrations. 2 Vols. Medium 8vo. 42s.

BLUNT'S (Rev. J. J.) Undesigned Coincidences in the Writings of the Old and New Testament, an Argument of their Veracity : containing the Books of Moses, Historical and Prophetical Scriptures, and the Gospels and Acts. 8th Edition. Post 8vo. 6s.

——— History of the Church in the First Three Centuries. Third Edition. Post 8vo. 7s. 6d.

——— Parish Priest; His Duties, Acquirements and Obligations. Fourth Edition. Post 8vo. 7s. 6d.

——— Lectures on the Right Use of the Early Fathers. Second Edition. 8vo. 15s.

——— Plain Sermons Preached to a Country Congregation. Second Edition. 2 Vols. Post 8vo. 7s. 6d. each.

——— Essays on various subjects. 8vo. 12s.

BISSET'S (Andrew) History of England during the Interregnum, from the Death of Charles I. to the Battle of Dunbar, 1649—50. Chiefly from the MSS. in the State Paper Office. 8vo. 15s.

BLAKISTON'S (Capt.) Narrative of the Expedition sent to explore the Upper Waters of the Yang-Tsze. Illustrations. 8vo. 18s.

BLOMFIELD'S (Bishop) Memoir, with Selections from his Correspondence. By his Son. 2nd Edition. Portrait, post 8vo. 12s.

BOOK OF COMMON PRAYER. Illustrated with Coloured Borders, Initial Letters, and Woodcuts. A new edition. 8vo. 18s. cloth; 31s. 6d. calf; 36s. morocco.

BORROW'S (George) Bible in Spain; or the Journeys, Adventures, and Imprisonments of an Englishman in an Attempt to circulate the Scriptures in the Peninsula. 3 Vols. Post 8vo. 27s.; or *Popular Edition*, 16mo, 3s. 6d.

— — Zincali, or the Gipsies of Spain; their Manners, Customs, Religion, and Language. 3 Vols. Post 8vo. 18s.; or *Popular Edition*, 16mo, 3s. 6d.

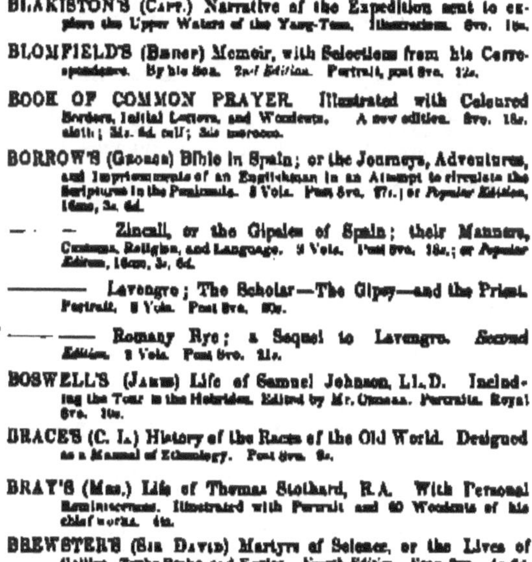

——— Lavengro; The Scholar—The Gipsy—and the Priest. Portrait. 3 Vols. Post 8vo. 30s.

——— Romany Rye; a Sequel to Lavengro. *Second Edition.* 2 Vols. Post 8vo. 21s.

BOSWELL'S (James) Life of Samuel Johnson, LL.D. Including the Tour to the Hebrides. Edited by Mr. Croker. Portraits. Royal 8vo. 10s.

BRACE'S (C. L.) History of the Races of the Old World. Designed as a Manual of Ethnology. Post 8vo. 9s.

BRAY'S (Mrs.) Life of Thomas Stothard, R.A. With Personal Reminiscences. Illustrated with Portrait and 60 Woodcuts of his chief works. 4to.

BREWSTER'S (Sir David) Martyrs of Science, or the Lives of Galileo, Tycho Brahe, and Kepler. *Fourth Edition.* Fcap. 8vo. 4s. 6d.

——— More Worlds than One. The Creed of the Philosopher and the Hope of the Christian. *Eighth Edition.* Post 8vo. 6s.

——— Stereoscope: its History, Theory, Construction, and Application to the Arts and to Education. Woodcuts. 12mo. 5s. 6d.

——— Kaleidoscope: its History, Theory, and Construction, with its application to the Fine and Useful Arts. *Second Edition.* Woodcuts. Post 8vo. 5s. 6d.

BRINE'S (Capt.) Narrative of the Rise and Progress of the Taeping Rebellion in China. Plans. Post 8vo. 10s. 6d.

BRITISH ASSOCIATION REPORTS. 8vo. York and Oxford, 1831-32, 13s. 6d. Cambridge 1833, 12s. Edinburgh, 1834, 15s. Dublin, 1835, 13s. 6d. Bristol, 1836, 12s. Liverpool, 1837, 16s. 6d. Newcastle, 1838, 15s. Birmingham, 1839, 13s. 6d. Glasgow, 1840, 15s. Plymouth, 1841, 13s. 6d. Manchester, 1842, 10s. 6d. Cork, 1843, 12s. York, 1844, 20s. Cambridge, 1845, 12s. Southampton, 1846, 15s. Oxford, 1847, 18s. Swansea, 1848, 9s. Birmingham, 1849, 10s. Edinburgh, 1850, 15s. Ipswich, 1851, 16s. 6d. Belfast, 1852, 15s. Hull, 1853, 10s. 6d. Liverpool, 1854, 18s. Glasgow, 1855, 15s.; Cheltenham, 1856, 18s.; Dublin, 1857, 15s.; Leeds, 1858, 20s. Aberdeen, 1859, 15s. Oxford, 1860, 25s. Manchester, 1861, 15s. Cambridge, 1862, 20s. Newcastle, 1863.

BRITISH CLASSICS. A New Series of Standard English
Authors, printed from the most current text, and edited with notes.
8vo.

Already Published.

I. GOLDSMITH'S WORKS. Edited by PETER CUNNINGHAM, F.S.A.
Vignettes. 4 Vols. 30s.

II. GIBBON'S DECLINE AND FALL OF THE ROMAN EMPIRE.
Edited by WILLIAM SMITH, LL.D. Portrait and Maps. 8 Vols. 60s.

III. JOHNSON'S LIVES OF THE ENGLISH POETS. Edited by PETER
CUNNINGHAM, F.S.A. 3 Vols. 22s. 6d.

IV. BYRON'S POETICAL WORKS. Edited, with Notes. 6 vols. 45s.

In Preparation.

WORKS OF POPE. With Life, Introductions, and Notes, by Rev. WHIT-
WELL ELWIN. Portrait.

HUME'S HISTORY OF ENGLAND. Edited, with Notes.

LIFE AND WORKS OF SWIFT. Edited by JOHN FORSTER.

BROUGHTON'S (LORD) Journey through Albania and other
Provinces of Turkey in Europe and Asia, to Constantinople, 1809—10.
Third Edition. Illustrations. 2 Vols. 8vo. 30s.

———————— Visits to Italy. *3rd Edition.* 2 vols. Post 8vo. 18s.

BUBBLES FROM THE BRUNNEN OF NASSAU. By an Old
Man. *Sixth Edition.* 16mo. 5s.

BUNYAN (JOHN) and Oliver Cromwell. Select Biographies. By
ROBERT SOUTHEY. Post 8vo. 2s.

BUONAPARTE'S (NAPOLEON) Confidential Correspondence with his
Brother Joseph, sometime King of Spain. *Second Edition.* 2 vols. 8vo.
26s.

BURGON'S (Rev. J. W.) Memoir of Patrick Fraser Tytler.
Second Edition. Post 8vo. 9s.

———————— Letters from Rome, written to Friends at Home.
Illustrations. Post 8vo. 12s.

BURN'S (LIEUT.-COL.) French and English Dictionary of Naval
and Military Technical Terms. *Fourth Edition.* Crown 8vo. 15s.

BURNS' (ROBERT) Life. By JOHN GIBSON LOCKHART. Fifth
Edition. Fcap. 8vo. 3s.

BURR'S (G. D.) Instructions in Practical Surveying, Topogra-
phical Plan Drawing, and on sketching ground without Instruments.
Fourth Edition. Woodcuts. Post 8vo. 6s.

BUTTMAN'S LEXILOGUS; a Critical Examination of the
Meaning of numerous Greek Words, chiefly in Homer and Hesiod.
Translated by Rev. J. R. FISHLAKE. *Fifth Edition.* 8vo. 12s.

BUXTON'S (SIR FOWELL) Memoirs. With Selections from his
Correspondence. By his Son. Portrait. *Fifth Edition.* 8vo. 16s.
Abridged Edition, Portrait. Fcap. 8vo. 2s. 6d.

BYRON'S (Lord) Life, Letters, and Journals. By Thomas Moore. Plates. 6 Vols. Fcap. 8vo. 18s.

———— Life, Letters, and Journals. By Thomas Moore. Portraits. Royal 8vo. 9s.

———— Poetical Works. Portrait. 6 Vols. 8vo. 45s.

———— Poetical Works. Plates. 10 Vols. Fcap. 8vo. 30s.

———— Poetical Works. 8 Vols. 24mo. 20s.

———— Poetical Works. Plates. Royal 8vo. 9s.

———— Poetical Works. Portrait. Crown 8vo. 6s.

———— Childe Harold. With 80 Engravings. Small 4to. 21s.

———— Childe Harold. With 30 Vignettes. 12mo. 6s.

———— Childe Harold. 16mo. 2s. 6d.

———— Childe Harold. Vignettes. 16mo. 1s.

———— Childe Harold. Portrait. 16mo. 6d.

———— Tales and Poems. 24mo. 2s. 6d.

———— Miscellaneous. 2 Vols. 24mo. 5s.

———— Dramas and Plays. 2 Vols. 24mo. 5s.

———— Don Juan and Beppo. 2 Vols. 24mo. 5s.

———— Beauties. Selected from his Poetry and Prose. Portrait. Fcap. 8vo. 3s. 6d.

CARNARVON'S (Lord) Portugal, Gallicia, and the Basque Provinces. From Notes made during a Journey to those Countries. Third Edition. Post 8vo. 3s. 6d.

———— Recollections of the Druses of Lebanon. With Notes on their Religion. Third Edition. Post 8vo. 4s. 6d.

CAMPBELL'S (Lord) Lives of the Lord Chancellors and Keepers of the Great Seal of England. From the Earliest Times to the Death of Lord Eldon in 1838. Fourth Edition. 10 Vols. Crown 8vo. 6s. each.

———— Lives of the Chief Justices of England. From the Norman Conquest to the Death of Lord Tenterden. Second Edition. 3 Vols. 8vo. 42s.

———— Shakspeare's Legal Acquirements Considered. 8vo. 5s. 6d.

———— Life of Lord Chancellor Bacon. Fcap. 8vo. 2s. 6d.

———— (George) Modern India. A Sketch of the System of Civil Government. With some Account of the Natives and Native Institutions. Second Edition. 8vo. 16s.

———— India as it may be. An Outline of a proposed Government and Policy. 8vo. 12s.

———— (Thos.) Short Lives of the British Poets. With an Essay on English Poetry. Post 8vo. 3s. 6d.

CALLCOTT'S (Lady) Little Arthur's History of England. 18th Thousand. With 20 Woodcuts. Fcap. 8vo. 2s. 6d.

CASTLEREAGH (The) DESPATCHES, from the commencement of the official career of the late Viscount Castlereagh to the close of his life. Edited by the Marquis of Londonderry. 12 Vols. 8vo. 14s. each.

CATHCART'S (Sir George) Commentaries on the War in Russia and Germany, 1812-13. Plans. 8vo. 14s.

CAVALCASELLE and CROWE'S New History of Painting in Italy, from the Second to the Sixteenth Century, from recent researches in the Archives, as well as from personal inspection of the Works of Art in that Country. With 70 Illustrations. Vols. I. and II. 8vo. 42s.

    —— Notices of the Lives and Works of the Early Flemish Painters. Woodcuts. Post 8vo. 12s.

CHAMBERS' (G. F.) Handbook of Descriptive and Practical Astronomy. Illustrations. Post 8vo. 12s.

CHARMED ROE (The); or, The Story of the Little Brother and Sister. By Otto Speckter. Plates. 16mo. 5s.

CHURTON'S (Archdeacon) Gongora. An Historical Essay on the Age of Philip III. and IV. of Spain. With Translations. Portrait. 2 Vols. Small 8vo. 15s.

CLAUSEWITZ'S (Carl Von) Campaign of 1812, in Russia. Translated from the German by Lord Ellesmere. Map. 8vo. 10s. 6d.

CLIVE'S (Lord) Life. By Rev. G. R. Gleig, M.A. Post 8vo. 3s. 6d.

COLCHESTER (The) PAPERS. The Diary and Correspondence of Charles Abbott, Lord Colchester, Speaker of the House of Commons, 1802-1817. Edited by His Son. Portrait. 3 Vols. 8vo. 42s.

COLERIDGE'S (Samuel Taylor) Table-Talk. *Fourth Edition.* Portrait. Fcap. 8vo. 6s.

COLONIAL LIBRARY. [See Home and Colonial Library.]

COOK'S (Rev. Canon) Sermons Preached at Lincoln's Inn Chapel, and on Special Occasions. 8vo. 9s.

COOKERY (Modern Domestic). Founded on Principles of Economy and Practical Knowledge, and adapted for Private Families. By a Lady. *New Edition.* Woodcuts. Fcap. 8vo. 5s.

CORNWALLIS (The) Papers and Correspondence during the American War,—Administrations in India,—Union with Ireland, and Peace of Amiens. Edited by Charles Ross. *Second Edition.* 3 Vols. 8vo. 63s.

COWPER'S (Mary Countess) Diary while Lady of the Bedchamber to Caroline Princess of Wales, 1714–20. *Second Edition.* Portrait. 8vo. 10s. 6d.

CRABBE'S (Rev. George) Life, Letters, and Journals. By his Son. Portrait. Fcap. 8vo. 3s.

    —— Life and Poetical Works. Plates. 8 Vols. Fcap. 8vo. 24s.

    —— Life and Poetical Works. Plates. Royal 8vo. 7s.

CROKER'S (J. W.) Progressive Geography for Children. *Fifth Edition.* 16mo. 1s. 6d.

———— Stories for Children, Selected from the History of England. *Fifteenth Edition.* Woodcuts. 16mo. 2s. 6d.

———— Boswell's Life of Johnson. Including the Tour to the Hebrides. Portraits. Royal 8vo. 10s.

———— Essays on the Early Period of the French Revolution. 8vo. 15s.

———— Historical Essay on the Guillotine. Fcap. 8vo. 1s.

CROMWELL (Oliver) and John Bunyan. By Robert Southey. Post 8vo. 2s.

CROWE'S and CAVALCASELLE'S Notices of the Early Flemish Painters; their Lives and Works. Woodcuts. Post 8vo. 12s.

———— History of Painting in Italy, from 2nd to 16th Century. Derived from Historical Researches as well as Inspection of the Works of Art in that Country. With 70 Illustrations. Vols. I. and II. 8vo. 42s.

CUNNINGHAM'S (Allan) Poems and Songs. Now first collected and arranged, with Biographical Notice. 24mo. 2s. 6d.

CURETON (Rev. W.) Remains of a very Ancient Recension of the Four Gospels in Syriac, hitherto unknown in Europe. Discovered, Edited, and Translated. 4to. 24s.

CURTIUS' (Professor) Student's Greek Grammar, for the use of Colleges and the Upper Forms. Translated under the Author's revision. Edited by Dr. Wm. Smith. Post 8vo. 7s. 6d.

———— Smaller Greek Grammar for the use of the Middle and Lower Forms, abridged from the above. 12mo. 3s. 6d.

———— First Greek Course; containing Delectus, Exercise Book, and Vocabularies. 12mo. 3s. 6d.

CURZON'S (Hon. Robert) Armenia and Erzeroum. A Year on the Frontiers of Russia, Turkey, and Persia. *Third Edition.* Woodcuts. Post 8vo. 7s. 6d.

CUST'S (General) Annals of the Wars of the 18th & 19th Centuries. 9 Vols. Fcap. 8vo. 5s. each.

———— Lives and Characters of the Warriors of All Nations who have Commanded Fleets and Armies before the Enemy. 8vo.

DARWIN'S (Charles) Journal of Researches into the Natural History of the Countries visited during a Voyage round the World. Post 8vo. 9s.

———— Origin of Species by Means of Natural Selection; or, the Preservation of Favoured Races in the Struggle for Life. Post 8vo. 14s.

———— Fertilisation of Orchids through Insect Agency, and as to the good of Intercrossing. Woodcuts. Post 8vo. 9s.

DAVIS'S (Nathan) Visit to the Ruined Cities of Numidia and Carthaginia. Illustrations. 8vo. 16s.

DAVY'S (Sir Humphry) Consolations in Travel; or, Last Days of a Philosopher. *Fifth Edition.* Woodcuts. Fcap. 8vo. 6s.

———— Salmonia; or, Days of Fly Fishing. *Fourth Edition.* Woodcuts. Fcap. 8vo. 6s.

DELEPIERRE'S (Octave) History of Flemish Literature. From the Twelfth Century. 8vo. 9s.

DENNIS' (George) Cities and Cemeteries of Etruria. Plates. 2 Vols. 8vo. 42s.

DERBY'S (Edward Earl of) Translation of the Iliad of Homer into English Blank Verse. 2 Vols. 8vo. 24s.

DIXON'S (Hepworth) Story of the Life of Lord Bacon. Portrait. Fcap. 8vo. 7s. 6d.

DOG-BREAKING; the Most Expeditious, Certain, and Easy Method, whether great excellence or only mediocrity be required. By Lieut.-Gen. Hutchinson. Fourth and Revised Edition. With additional Woodcuts. Crown 8vo.

DOMESTIC MODERN COOKERY. Founded on Principles of Economy and Practical Knowledge, and adapted for Private Families. New Edition. Woodcuts. Fcap. 8vo. 6s.

DOUGLAS'S (General Sir Howard) Life and Adventures; From Notes, Conversations, and Correspondence. By S. W. Fullom. Portrait. 8vo. 15s.

———— On the Theory and Practice of Gunnery. 5th Edition. Plates. 8vo. 21s.

———— Military Bridges, and the Passage of Rivers in Military Operations. Third Edition. Plates. 8vo. 21s.

———— Naval Warfare with Steam. Second Edition. 8vo. 8s. 6d.

———— Modern Systems of Fortification, with special reference to the Naval, Littoral, and Internal Defence of England. Plans. 8vo. 12s.

DRAKE'S (Sir Francis) Life, Voyages, and Exploits, by Sea and Land. By John Barrow. Third Edition. Post 8vo. 2s.

DRINKWATER'S (John) History of the Siege of Gibraltar, 1779-1783. With a Description and Account of that Garrison from the Earliest Periods. Post 8vo. 2s.

DU CHAILLU'S (Paul B.) EQUATORIAL AFRICA, with Accounts of the Gorilla, the Nest-building Ape, Chimpanzee, Crocodile, &c. Illustrations. 8vo. 21s.

DUFFERIN'S (Lord) Letters from High Latitudes; being some Account of a Yacht Voyage to Iceland, &c., in 1856. Fourth Edition. Woodcuts. Post 8vo. 9s.

DYER'S (Thomas H.) History of Modern Europe, from the taking of Constantinople by the Turks to the close of the War in the Crimea. 4 Vols. 8vo. 60s.

EASTLAKE'S (Sir Charles) Italian Schools of Painting. From the German of Kugler. Edited with Notes. Third Edition. Illustrated from the Old Masters. 2 Vols. Post 8vo. 30s.

EASTWICK'S (E. B.) Handbook for Bombay and Madras, with Directions for Travellers, Officers, &c. Map. 2 Vols. Post 8vo. 16s.

EDWARDS' (W. H.) Voyage up the River Amazon, including a Visit to Para. Post 8vo. 2s.

ELDON'S (Lord) Public and Private Life, with Selections from his Correspondence and Diaries. By Horace Twiss. Third Edition. Portrait. 3 Vols. Post 8vo. 21s.

ELLIS (Rev. W.) Visits to Madagascar, including a Journey to the Capital, with notices of Natural History, and Present Civilisation of the People. Fifth Thousand. Map and Woodcuts. 8vo. 16s.

—— (Mrs.) Education of Character, with Hints on Moral Training. Post 8vo. 7s. 6d.

ELLESMERE'S (Lord) Two Sieges of Vienna by the Turks. Translated from the German. Post 8vo. 2s.

————— Campaign of 1812 in Russia, from the German of General Carl Von Clausewitz. Map. 8vo. 10s. 6d.

————— Poems. Crown 4to. 24s.

————— Essays on History, Biography, Geography, and Engineering. 8vo. 12s.

ELPHINSTONE'S (Hon. Mountstuart) History of India—the Hindoo and Mahomedan Periods. Fourth Edition. Map. 8vo. 18s.

ENGEL'S (Carl) Music of the Most Ancient Nations; particularly of the Assyrians, Egyptians, and Hebrews; with Special Reference to the Discoveries in Western Asia and in Egypt. With 100 Illustrations. 8vo. 16s.

ENGLAND (History of) from the Peace of Utrecht to the Peace of Versailles, 1713—83. By Lord Mahon (Earl Stanhope). Library Edition, 7 Vols. 8vo. 93s.; or Popular Edition, 7 Vols. Post 8vo. 35s.

————— From the First Invasion by the Romans, down to the 14th year of Queen Victoria's Reign. By Mrs. Markham. 116th Edition. Woodcuts. 12mo. 6s.

———— (The Student's Hume). A History of England from the Earliest Times. Based on the History by David Hume. Corrected and continued to 1858. Edited by Wm. Smith, LL.D. Woodcuts. Post 8vo. 7s. 6d.

ENGLISHWOMAN IN AMERICA. Post 8vo. 10s. 6d.

ESKIMAUX and English Vocabulary, for Travellers in the Arctic Regions. 16mo. 3s. 6d.

ESSAYS FROM "THE TIMES." Being a Selection from the Literary Papers which have appeared in that Journal. Seventh Thousand. 2 vols. Fcap. 8vo. 8s.

EXETER'S (Bishop of) Letters to the late Charles Butler, on the Theological parts of his Book of the Roman Catholic Church; with Remarks on certain Works of Dr. Milner and Dr. Lingard, and on some parts of the Evidence of Dr. Doyle. Second Edition. 8vo. 16s.

FAMILY RECEIPT-BOOK. A Collection of a Thousand Valuable and Useful Receipts. Fcap. 8vo. 5s. 6d.

FARRAR'S (Rev. A. S.) Critical History of Free Thought in reference to the Christian Religion. Being the Bampton Lectures, 1862. 8vo. 16s.

——— (F. W.) Origin of Language, based on Modern Researches. Fcap. 8vo. 5s.

FEATHERSTONHAUGH'S (G. W.) Tour through the Slave States of North America, from the River Potomac to Texas and the Frontiers of Mexico. Plates. 2 Vols. 8vo. 26s.

FERGUSSON'S (JAMES) Palaces of Nineveh and Persepolis Restored. Woodcuts. 8vo. 16s.

———— History of the Modern Styles of Architecture, completing the above work. With 312 Illustrations. 8vo. 31s. 6d.

FISHER'S (REV. GEORGE) Elements of Geometry, for the Use of Schools. Fifth Edition. 18mo. 1s. 6d.

———— First Principles of Algebra, for the Use of Schools. Fifth Edition. 18mo. 1s. 6d.

FLOWER GARDEN (THE). By Rev. THOS. JAMES. Fcap. 8vo. 1s.

FONNEREAU'S (T. G.) Diary of a Dutiful Son. Fcap. 8vo. 4s. 6d.

FORBES' (C. S.) Iceland; Its Volcanoes, Geysers, and Glaciers. Illustrations. Post 8vo. 14s.

FORD'S (RICHARD) Handbook for Spain, Andalusia, Ronda, Valencia, Catalonia, Granada, Gallicia, Arragon, Navarre, &c. Third Edition. 2 Vols. Post 8vo. 30s.

———— Gatherings from Spain. Post 8vo. 3s. 6d.

FORSTER'S (JOHN) Arrest of the Five Members by Charles the First. A Chapter of English History re-written. Post 8vo. 12s.

———— Grand Remonstrance, 1641. With an Essay on English freedom under the Plantagenet and Tudor Sovereigns. Second Edition. Post 8vo. 12s.

———— Oliver Cromwell, Daniel De Foe, Sir Richard Steele, Charles Churchill, Samuel Foote. Third Edition. Post 8vo. 12s.

FORSYTH'S (WILLIAM) Life and Times of Cicero. With Selections from his Correspondence and his Orations. Illustrations. 2 Vols. Post 8vo. 18s.

FORTUNE'S (ROBERT) Narrative of Two Visits to the Tea Countries of China, 1843-52. Third Edition. Woodcuts. 2 Vols. Post 8vo. 18s.

———— Third Visit to China. 1853-6. Woodcuts. 8vo. 16s.

———— Yedo and Peking. With Notices of the Agriculture and Trade of Japan and China. Illustrations. 8vo. 18s.

FOSS' (EDWARD) Judges of England. With Sketches of their Lives, and Notices of the Courts at Westminster, from the Conquest to the Present Time. 9 Vols. 8vo. 114s.

FRANCE (HISTORY OF). From the Conquest by the Gauls to the Death of Louis Philippe. By Mrs. MARKHAM. 64th Thousand. Woodcuts. 12mo. 6s.

———— (THE STUDENT'S HISTORY OF). From the Earliest Times to the Establishment of the Second Empire, 1852. By W. H. PEARSON. Edited by WM. SMITH, LL.D. Woodcuts. Post 8vo. 7s. 6d.

FRENCH (THE) in Algiers; The Soldier of the Foreign Legion—and the Prisoners of Abd-el-Kadir. Translated by Lady DUFF GORDON. Post 8vo. 2s.

GALTON'S (Francis) Art of Travel ; or, Hints on the Shifts and
Contrivances available in Wild Countries. *Third Edition.* Woodcuts. Post 8vo. 7s. 6d.

GEOGRAPHY (The Student's Manual of Ancient). By Rev.
W. L. Bevan. Edited by Wm. Smith, LL.D. Woodcuts. Post 8vo.
7s. 6d.

————. Journal of the Royal Geographical Society of
London. 8vo.

GERMANY (History of). From the Invasion by Marius, to the present time. By Mrs. Markham. *Fifteenth Thousand.* Woodcuts. 12mo. 4s.

GIBBON'S (Edward) History of the Decline and Fall of the
Roman Empire. *A New Edition.* Preceded by his Autobiography.
Edited, with Notes, by Dr. Wm. Smith. Maps. 8 Vols. 8vo. 60s.

———— (The Student's Gibbon) ; Being an Epitome of the
above work, incorporating the Researches of Recent Commentators. By
Dr. Wm. Smith. *Ninth Thousand.* Woodcuts. Post 8vo. 7s. 6d.

GIFFARD'S (Edward) Deeds of Naval Daring; or, Anecdotes of
the British Navy. New Edition. Fcap. 8vo. 3s. 6d.

GOLDSMITH'S (Oliver) Works. A New Edition. Printed from
the last editions revised by the Author. Edited by Peter Cunningham. Vignettes. 4 Vols. 8vo. 30s. (Murray's British Classics.)

GLADSTONE'S (Right Hon. W. E.) Financial Statements of 1853,
60, 63, and 64 : also his speeches on Tax-Bills, 1861, and on Charities,
1863. *Second Edition.* 8vo. 12s.

———— Wedgwood : an Address delivered at Burslem.
Woodcuts. Post 8vo. 2s.

GLEIG'S (Rev. G. R.) Campaigns of the British Army at Washington and New Orleans. Post 8vo. 2s.

———— Story of the Battle of Waterloo. Post 8vo. 3s. 6d.

———— Narrative of Sale's Brigade in Affghanistan. Post 8vo. 2s.

———— Life of Robert Lord Clive. Post 8vo. 3s. 6d.

———— Life and Letters of Sir Thomas Munro. Post 8vo. 3s. 6d.

GORDON'S (Sir Alex. Duff) Sketches of German Life, and Scenes
from the War of Liberation. From the German. Post 8vo. 3s. 6d.

———— (Lady Duff) Amber-Witch : A Trial for Witchcraft. From the German. Post 8vo. 2s.

———— French in Algiers. 1. The Soldier of the Foreign
Legion. 2. The Prisoners of Abd-el-Kadir. From the French.
Post 8vo. 2s.

GOUGER'S (Henry) Personal Narrative of Two Years' Imprisonment in Burmah. *Second Edition.* Woodcuts. Post 8vo. 12s.

GRAMMAR (The Student's Greek.) For Colleges, and the
Upper Forms. By Professor Curtius. Translated under the Revision
of the Author. Edited by Wm. Smith, LL.D. Post 8vo. 7s. 6d.

———— (The Student's Latin). For Colleges and the
Upper Forms. By Wm. Smith, LL.D. Post 8vo. 7s. 6d.

GREECE (The Student's History of). From the Earliest
Times to the Roman Conquest. By Wm. Smith, LL.D. Woodcuts. Post 8vo. 7s. 6d.

GRENVILLE (THE) PAPERS. Being the Public and Private
Correspondence of George Grenville, including his Private Diary.
Edited by W. J. Smith. 4 Vols. 8vo. 16s. each.

GREY (EARL) on Parliamentary Government and Reform. A New
Edition, containing Suggestions for the Improvement of our Representative System, and an Examination of the Reform Bills of 1859—31.
8vo. 9s.

GREY'S (SIR GEORGE) Polynesian Mythology, and Ancient
Traditional History of the New Zealand Race. Woodcuts. Post
8vo. 10s. 6d.

GROTE'S (GEORGE) History of Greece. From the Earliest Times
to the close of the generation contemporary with the death of Alexander
the Great. Fourth Edition. Maps. 8 vols. 8vo. 112s.

———— Plato, and the other Companions of Socrates. 3
Vols. 8vo.

—— (MRS.) Memoir of Ary Scheffer. Post 8vo. 8s. 6d.

———— Collected Papers. 8vo. 10s. 6d.

GUIZOT'S (M.) Meditations on Christianity. Containing 1.
Natural Problem. 2. Christian Dogma. 3. The Supernatural.
4. Limits of Science. 5. Revelation. 6. Inspiration of Holy
Scripture. 7. God according to the Bible. 8. Jesus Christ
according to the Gospels. Post 8vo. 9s. 6d.

HALLAM'S (HENRY) Constitutional History of England, from the
Accession of Henry the Seventh to the Death of George the Second.
Seventh Edition. 3 Vols. 8vo. 30s.

———— History of Europe during the Middle Ages.
Tenth Edition. 3 Vols. 8vo. 30s.

—— Literary History of Europe, during the 15th, 16th and
17th Centuries. Fourth Edition. 3 Vols. 8vo. 36s.

———— Literary Essays and Characters. Fcap. 8vo. 2s.

—— Historical Works. Containing History of England,
—Middle Ages of Europe,—Literary History of Europe. 10 Vols.
Post 8vo. 6s. each.

———— (ARTHUR) Remains; in Verse and Prose. With Preface, Memoir, and Portrait. Fcap. 8vo. 7s. 6d.

HAMILTON'S (JAMES) Wanderings in North Africa. Post 8vo. 12s.

HART'S ARMY LIST. (Quarterly and Annually.) 8vo. 10s. 6d.
and 21s. each.

HANNAH'S (Rev. Dr.) Bampton Lectures for 1863; the Divine
and Human Element in Holy Scripture. 8vo. 10s. 6d.

HAY'S (J. H. DRUMMOND) Western Barbary, its wild Tribes and
savage Animals. Post 8vo. 2s.

HEAD'S (SIR FRANCIS) Horse and his Rider. Woodcuts. Post 8vo. 5s.

———— Rapid Journeys across the Pampas. Post 8vo. 2s.

———— Bubbles from the Brunnen of Nassau. 16mo. 5s.

———— Emigrant. Fcap. 8vo. 2s. 6d.

———— Stokers and Pokers; or, N.-Western Railway. Post
8vo. 2s.

———— Fortnight in Ireland. Map. 8vo. 12s.

———— (SIR EDMUND) Shall and Will; or, Future Auxiliary
Verbs. Fcap. 8vo. 4s.

HAND-BOOK—TRAVEL-TALK. English, German, French, and Italian. 16mo. 3s. 6d.

—— —— NORTH GERMANY, HOLLAND, BELGIUM, and the Rhine to Switzerland. Map. Post 8vo. 10s.

—— —— KNAPSACK GUIDE TO BELGIUM AND THE RHINE. Post 8vo. (*In the Press.*)

—— ——, SOUTH GERMANY, Bavaria, Austria, Styria, Salzburg, the Austrian and Bavarian Alps, the Tyrol, Hungary, and the Danube, from Ulm to the Black Sea. Map. Post 8vo. 10s.

—— KNAPSACK GUIDE TO THE TYROL. Post 8vo. (*In the Press.*)

—— —— PAINTING. German, Flemish, and Dutch Schools. Edited by Dr. WAAGEN. Woodcuts. 2 Vols. Post 8vo. 24s.

—— LIVES OF THE EARLY FLEMISH PAINTERS, with Notices of their Works. By CROWE and CAVALCASELLE. Illustrations. Post 8vo. 12s.

—— —— SWITZERLAND, Alps of Savoy, and Piedmont. Maps. Post 8vo. 9s.

—— —— KNAPSACK GUIDE TO SWITZERLAND. Post 8vo. 5s.

—— —— FRANCE, Normandy, Brittany, the French Alps, the Rivers Loire, Seine, Rhone, and Garonne, Dauphiné, Provence, and the Pyrenees. Maps. Post 8vo. 10s.

—— —— KNAPSACK GUIDE TO FRANCE. Post 8vo. (*In the Press.*)

—— —— PARIS AND ITS ENVIRONS. Map. Post 8vo. 5s.

—— —— SPAIN, Andalusia, Ronda, Granada, Valencia, Catalonia, Gallicia, Arragon, and Navarre. Maps. 2 Vols. Post 8vo. 30s.

—— —— PORTUGAL, Lisbon, &c. Map. Post 8vo.

—— —— NORTH ITALY, Piedmont, Liguria, Venetia, Lombardy, Parma, Modena, and Romagna. Map. Post 8vo. 12s.

—— —— CENTRAL ITALY, Lucca, Tuscany, Florence, The Marches, Umbria, and the Patrimony of St. Peter's. Map. Post 8vo. 10s.

—— —— ROME AND ITS ENVIRONS. Map. Post 8vo. 9s.

—— —— SOUTH ITALY, Two Sicilies, Naples, Pompeii, Herculaneum, and Vesuvius. Map. Post 8vo. 10s.

—— —— KNAPSACK GUIDE TO ITALY. Post 8vo. 6s.

—— —— SICILY, Palermo, Messina, Catania, Syracuse, Etna, and the Ruins of the Greek Temples. Map. Post 8vo. 12s.

—— —— PAINTING. The Italian Schools. From the German of KUGLER. Edited by Sir CHARLES EASTLAKE, R.A. Woodcuts. 2 Vols. Post 8vo. 30s.

—— —— LIVES OF THE EARLY ITALIAN PAINTERS, AND PROGRESS OF PAINTING IN ITALY, from CIMABUE to BASSANO. By Mrs. JAMESON. Woodcuts. Post 8vo. 12s.

HAND-BOOK—DICTIONARY OF ITALIAN PAINTERS. By A LADY. Edited by RALPH WORNUM. With a Chart. Post 8vo. 6s. 6d.

———— GREECE, the Ionian Islands, Albania, Thessaly, and Macedonia. Maps. Post 8vo. 15s.

———— TURKEY, Malta, Asia Minor, Constantinople, Armenia, Mesopotamia, &c. Maps. Post 8vo. (In the Press.)

———— EGYPT, Thebes, the Nile, Alexandria, Cairo, the Pyramids, Mount Sinai, &c. Map. Post 8vo. 15s.

———— SYRIA & PALESTINE, Peninsula of Sinai, Edom, and Syrian Desert. Maps. 2 Vols. Post 8vo. 24s.

———— BOMBAY AND MADRAS. Map. 2 Vols. Post 8vo. 24s.

———— NORWAY. Map. Post 8vo. 5s.

———— DENMARK, Sweden and Norway. Maps. Post 8vo. 15s.

———— RUSSIA, The Baltic and Finland. Maps. Post 8vo. 12s.

———— MODERN LONDON. A Complete Guide to all the Sights and Objects of Interest in the Metropolis. Map. 16mo. 3s. 6d.

———— WESTMINSTER ABBEY. Woodcuts. 16mo. 1s.

———— KENT AND SUSSEX, Canterbury, Dover, Ramsgate, Sheerness, Rochester, Chatham, Woolwich, Brighton, Chichester, Worthing, Hastings, Lewes, Arundel, &c. Map. Post 8vo. 10s.

———— SURREY, HANTS, Kingston, Croydon, Reigate, Guildford, Winchester, Southampton, Portsmouth, and Isle of Wight. Maps. Post 8vo. 7s. 6d.

———— BERKS, BUCKS, AND OXON, Windsor, Eton, Reading, Aylesbury, Uxbridge, Wycombe, Henley, the City and University of Oxford, and the Descent of the Thames to Maidenhead and Windsor. Map. Post 8vo. 7s. 6d.

———— WILTS, DORSET, AND SOMERSET, Salisbury, Chippenham, Weymouth, Sherborne, Wells, Bath, Bristol, Taunton, &c. Map. Post 8vo. 7s. 6d.

———— DEVON AND CORNWALL, Exeter, Ilfracombe, Linton, Sidmouth, Dawlish, Teignmouth, Plymouth, Devonport, Torquay, Launceston, Truro, Penzance, Falmouth, &c. Maps. Post 8vo. 7s. 6d.

———— NORTH AND SOUTH WALES, Bangor, Carnarvon, Beaumaris, Snowdon, Conway, Menai Straits, Carmarthen, Pembroke, Tenby, Swansea, The Wye, &c. Maps. 2 Vols. Post 8vo. 12s.

———— CATHEDRALS OF ENGLAND—Southern Division, Winchester, Salisbury, Exeter, Wells, Chichester, Rochester, Canterbury. With 110 Illustrations. 2 Vols. Crown 8vo. 24s.

———— CATHEDRALS OF ENGLAND—Eastern Division, Oxford, Peterborough, Norwich, Ely, and Lincoln. With 90 Illustrations. Crown 8vo. 18s.

———— CATHEDRALS OF ENGLAND—Western Division, Bristol, Gloucester, Hereford, Worcester, and Lichfield. With 50 Illustrations. Crown 8vo. 16s.

———— FAMILIAR QUOTATIONS. From English Authors. Third Edition. Fcap. 8vo. 5s.

HEBER'S (Bishop) Journey through India. *Twelfth Edition*. 2 Vols. Post 8vo. 7s.

———— Poetical Works. *Sixth Edition*. Portrait. Fcap. 8vo. 6s.

HERODOTUS. A New English Version. Edited, with Notes and Essays, historical, ethnographical, and geographical. By Rev. G. Rawlinson, assisted by Sir Henry Rawlinson and Sir J. G. Wilkinson. *Second Edition*. Maps and Woodcuts. 4 Vols. 8vo. 48s.

HESSEY (Rev. Dr.). Sunday—Its Origin, History, and Present Obligations. Being the Bampton Lectures for 1860. *Second Edition*. 8vo. 16s.

HICKMAN'S (Wm.) Treatise on the Law and Practice of Naval Courts-Martial. 8vo. 10s. 6d.

HILLARD'S (G. S.) Six Months in Italy. 2 Vols. Post 8vo. 16s.

HOLLWAY'S (J. G.) Month in Norway. Fcap. 8vo. 2s.

HONEY BEE (The). An Essay. By Rev. Thomas James. Reprinted from the "Quarterly Review." Fcap. 8vo. 1s.

HOOK'S (Dean) Church Dictionary. *Ninth Edition*. 8vo. 16s.

———— (Theodore) Life. By J. G. Lockhart. Reprinted from the "Quarterly Review." Fcap. 8vo. 1s.

HOOKER'S (Dr. J. D.) Himalayan Journals; or, Notes of an Oriental Naturalist in Bengal, the Sikkim and Nepal Himalayas, the Khasia Mountains, &c. *Second Edition*. Woodcuts. 2 Vols. Post 8vo. 18s.

HOPE'S (A. J. Beresford) English Cathedral of the Nineteenth Century. With Illustrations. 8vo. 12s.

HORACE (Works of). Edited by Dean Milman. With 300 Woodcuts. Crown 8vo. 21s.

———— (Life of). By Dean Milman. Woodcuts, and coloured Borders. 8vo. 9s.

HUME'S (The Student's) History of England, from the Invasion of Julius Cæsar to the Revolution of 1688. Corrected and continued to 1868. Edited by Dr. Wm. Smith. Woodcuts. Post 8vo. 7s. 6d.

HUTCHINSON (Gen.) on the most expeditious, certain, and easy Method of Dog-Breaking. *Fourth Edition*. Enlarged and revised, with additional Illustrations. Crown 8vo.

HUTTON'S (H. E.) Principia Græca; an Introduction to the Study of Greek. Comprehending Grammar, Delectus, and Exercise-book, with Vocabularies. *Third Edition*. 12mo. 3s. 6d.

c

HOME AND COLONIAL LIBRARY. A Series of Works
adapted for all circles and classes of Readers, having been selected
for their acknowledged interest and ability of the Authors. Post 8vo.
Published at 2s. and 2s. 6d. each, and arranged under two distinctive
heads as follows :—

CLASS A.

HISTORY, BIOGRAPHY, AND HISTORIC TALES.

1. SIEGE OF GIBRALTAR. By John Drinkwater. 2s.

2. THE AMBER-WITCH. By Lady Duff Gordon. 2s.

3. CROMWELL AND BUNYAN. By Robert Southey. 2s.

4. LIFE OF SIR FRANCIS DRAKE. By John Barrow. 2s.

5. CAMPAIGNS AT WASHINGTON. By Rev. G. R. Gleig. 2s.

6. THE FRENCH IN ALGIERS. By Lady Duff Gordon. 2s.

7. THE FALL OF THE JESUITS. 2s.

8. LIVONIAN TALES. 2s.

9. LIFE OF CONDE. By Lord Mahon. 3s. 6d.

10. SALE'S BRIGADE. By Rev. G. R. Gleig. 2s.

11. THE SIEGES OF VIENNA. By Lord Ellesmere. 2s.

12. THE WAYSIDE CROSS. By Capt. Milman. 2s.

13. SKETCHES OF GERMAN LIFE. By Sir A. Gordon. 3s. 6d.

14. THE BATTLE OF WATERLOO. By Rev. G. R. Gleig. 3s. 6d.

15. AUTOBIOGRAPHY OF STEFFENS. 2s.

16. THE BRITISH POETS. By Thomas Campbell. 3s. 6d.

17. HISTORICAL ESSAYS. By Lord Mahon. 3s. 6d.

18. LIFE OF LORD CLIVE. By Rev. G. R. Gleig. 3s. 6d.

19. NORTH-WESTERN RAILWAY. By Sir F. B. Head. 2s.

20. LIFE OF MUNRO. By Rev. G. R. Gleig. 3s. 6d.

CLASS B.

VOYAGES, TRAVELS, AND ADVENTURES.

1. BIBLE IN SPAIN. By George Borrow. 3s. 6d.

2. GIPSIES OF SPAIN. By George Borrow. 3s. 6d.

3 & 4. JOURNALS IN INDIA. By Bishop Heber. 2 Vols. 7s.

5. TRAVELS IN THE HOLY LAND. By Irby and Mangles. 2s.

6. MOROCCO AND THE MOORS. By J. Drummond Hay. 2s.

7. LETTERS FROM THE BALTIC. By a Lady. 2s.

8. NEW SOUTH WALES. By Mrs. Meredith. 2s.

9. THE WEST INDIES. By M. G. Lewis. 2s.

10. SKETCHES OF PERSIA. By Sir John Malcolm. 3s. 6d.

11. MEMOIRS OF FATHER RIPA. 2s.

12, 13. TYPEE AND OMOO. By Herman Melville. 2 Vols. 7s.

14. MISSIONARY LIFE IN CANADA. By Rev. J. Abbott. 2s.

15. LETTERS FROM MADRAS. By a Lady. 2s.

16. HIGHLAND SPORTS. By Charles St. John. 3s. 6d.

17. PAMPAS JOURNEYS. By Sir F. B. Head. 2s.

18. GATHERINGS FROM SPAIN. By Richard Ford. 3s. 6d.

19. THE RIVER AMAZON. By W. H. Edwards. 2s.

20. MANNERS & CUSTOMS OF INDIA. By Rev. C. Acland. 2s.

21. ADVENTURES IN MEXICO. By G. F. Ruxton. 3s. 6d.

22. PORTUGAL AND GALLICIA. By Lord Carnarvon. 3s. 6d.

23. BUSH LIFE IN AUSTRALIA. By Rev. H. W. Haygarth. 2s.

24. THE LIBYAN DESERT. By Bayle St. John. 2s.

25. SIERRA LEONE. By a Lady. 3s. 6d.

*** Each work may be had separately.

IRBY AND MANGLES' Travels in Egypt, Nubia, Syria, and the Holy Land. Post 8vo. 2s.

JAMES' (Rev. Thomas) Fables of Æsop. A New Translation, with Historical Preface. With 100 Woodcuts by Tenniel and Wolf. Thirty-eighth Thousand. Post 8vo. 2s. 6d.

JAMESON'S (Mrs.) Lives of the Early Italian Painters, from Cimabue to Bassano, and the Progress of Painting in Italy. New Edition. With Woodcuts. Post 8vo. 12s.

JESSE'S (Edward) Gleanings in Natural History. Eighth Edition. Fcp. 8vo. 6s.

JOHNSON'S (Dr. Samuel) Life. By James Boswell. Including the Tour to the Hebrides. Edited by the late Mr. Croker. Portraits. Royal 8vo. 30s.

———— Lives of the most eminent English Poets. Edited by Peter Cunningham. 3 vols. 8vo. 22s. 6d. (Murray's British Classics.)

JOURNAL OF A NATURALIST. Woodcuts. Post 8vo. 9s. 6d.

KEN'S (Bishop) Life. By A Layman. Second Edition. Portrait. 2 Vols. 8vo. 18s.

———— Exposition of the Apostles' Creed. Extracted from his "Practice of Divine Love." Fcap. 1s. 6d.

———— Approach to the Holy Altar. Extracted from his "Manual of Prayer" and "Practice of Divine Love." Fcap. 8vo. 1s. 6d.

KING'S (Rev. S. W.) Italian Valleys of the Alps; a Tour through all the Romantic and less-frequented "Vals" of Northern Piedmont. Illustrations. Crown 8vo. 18s.

———— (Rev. C. W.) Antique Gems; their Origin, Use, and Value, as Interpreters of Ancient History, and as Illustrative of Ancient Art. Illustrations. 8vo. 42s.

KING EDWARD VIth's Latin Grammar; or, an Introduction to the Latin Tongue, for the Use of Schools. Sixteenth Edition. 12mo. 3s. 6d.

———————————— First Latin Book; or, the Accidence, Syntax, and Prosody, with an English Translation for the Use of Junior Classes. Fourth Edition. 12mo. 2s. 6d.

KIRK'S (J. Foster) History of Charles the Bold, Duke of Burgundy. Portrait. 2 Vols. 8vo. 30s.

KERR'S (Robert) GENTLEMAN'S HOUSE; or, How to Plan English Residences, from the Parsonage to the Palace. With Tables of Accommodation and Cost, and a Series of Selected Views and Plans. 8vo. 21s.

KUGLER'S Italian Schools of Painting. Edited, with Notes, by SIR CHARLES EASTLAKE. *Third Edition.* Woodcuts. 2 Vols. Post 8vo. 30s.

————— German, Dutch, and Flemish Schools of Painting. Edited, with Notes, by DR. WAAGEN. *Second Edition.* Woodcuts. 2 Vols. Post 8vo. 24s.

LANGUAGE (THE ENGLISH). A Series of Lectures. By GEORGE P. MARSH. Edited, with additional Chapters and Notes, by WM. SMITH, LL.D. Post 8vo. 7s. 6d.

LATIN GRAMMAR (KING EDWARD VITH'S). For the Use of Schools. *Sixteenth Edition.* 12mo. 3s. 6d.

————— First Book (KING EDWARD VITH'S); or, the Accidence, Syntax, and Prosody, with English Translation for Junior Classes. *Fourth Edition.* 12mo. 2s. 6d.

LAYARD'S (A. H.) Nineveh and its Remains. Being a Narrative of Researches and Discoveries amidst the Ruins of Assyria. With an Account of the Chaldean Christians of Kurdistan; the Yezidis, or Devil-worshippers; and an Enquiry into the Manners and Arts of the Ancient Assyrians. *Sixth Edition.* Plates and Woodcuts. 2 Vols. 8vo. 36s.

————————— Nineveh and Babylon; being the Result of a Second Expedition to Assyria. *Fourteenth Thousand.* Plates. 8vo. 21s. Or *Fine Paper,* 2 Vols. 8vo. 30s.

————— Popular Account of Nineveh. *15th Edition.* With Woodcuts. Post 8vo. 5s.

LEAKE'S (COL.) Topography of Athens, with Remarks on its Antiquities. *Second Edition.* Plates. 2 Vols. 8vo. 30s.

————— Travels in Northern Greece. Maps. 4 Vols. 8vo. 60s.

————— Disputed Questions of Ancient Geography. Map. 8vo. 6s. 6d.

Numismata Hellenica, and Supplement. Completing a descriptive Catalogue of Twelve Thousand Greek Coins, with Notes Geographical and Historical. With Map and Appendix. 4to. 63s.

————— Peloponnesiaca. 8vo. 15s.

————— Degradation of Science in England. 8vo. 3s. 6d.

LESLIE'S (C. R.) Handbook for Young Painters. With Illustrations. Post 8vo. 10s. 6d.

————————— Autobiographical Recollections, with Selections from his Correspondence. Edited by TOM TAYLOR. Portrait. 2 Vols. Post 8vo. 18s.

————————— Life of Sir Joshua Reynolds. With an Account of his Works, and a Sketch of his Contemporaries. By TOM TAYLOR. Illustrations. 2 Vols. 8vo.

LETTERS FROM THE SHORES OF THE BALTIC. By a LADY. Post 8vo. 2s.

————————— MADRAS. By a LADY. Post 8vo. 2s.

————————— SIERRA LEONE. By a LADY. Edited by the HONOURABLE MRS. NORTON. Post 8vo. 6s. 6d.

LEWIS' (Sir G. C.) Essay on the Government of Dependencies. 8vo. 12s.

———— Glossary of Provincial Words used in Herefordshire and some of the adjoining Counties. 12mo, 4s. 6d.

— — —— (M. G.) Journal of a Residence among the Negroes in the West Indies. Post 8vo. 2s.

LIDDELL'S (Dean) History of Rome. From the Earliest Times to the Establishment of the Empire. With the History of Literature and Art. 2 Vols. 8vo. 28s.

———— Student's History of Rome. Abridged from the above Work. 25th Thousand. With Woodcuts. Post 8vo. 7s. 6d.

LINDSAY'S (Lord) Lives of the Lindsays; or, a Memoir of the Houses of Crawford and Balcarres. With Extracts from Official Papers and Personal Narratives. Second Edition. 3 Vols. 8vo. 24s.

— — ———— Report of the Claim of James, Earl of Crawford and Balcarres, to the Original Dukedom of Montrose, created in 1488. Folio. 15s.

— — ———— Scepticism; a Retrogressive Movement in Theology and Philosophy. 8vo. 9s.

LISPINGS from LOW LATITUDES; or, the Journal of the Hon. Impulsia Gushington. Edited by Lord Dufferin. With 24 Plates, 4to. 21s.

LITERATURE (English). A Manual for Students. By T. B. Shaw. Edited, with Notes and Illustrations, by Wm. Smith, LL.D. Post 8vo. 7s. 6d.

———— (Choice Specimens of). Selected from the Chief English Writers. By Thos. B. Shaw, M.A. Edited by Wm. Smith, LL.D. Post 8vo. 7s. 6d.

LITTLE ARTHUR'S HISTORY OF ENGLAND. By Lady Callcott. 19th Thousand. With 20 Woodcuts. Fcap. 8vo. 2s. 6d.

LIVINGSTONE'S (Rev. Dr.) Popular Account of his Missionary Travels in South Africa. Illustrations. Post 8vo. 6s.

———— — — — Narrative of an Expedition to the Zambesi and its Tributaries; and of the Discovery of Lakes Shirwa and Nyassa. 1858-64. By David and Charles Livingstone. Map and Illustrations. 8vo.

LIVONIAN TALES. By the Author of "Letters from the Baltic." Post 8vo. 2s.

LOCKHART'S (J. G.) Ancient Spanish Ballads. Historical and Romantic. Translated, with Notes. Illustrated Edition. 4to, 21s. Or, Popular Edition, Post 8vo. 2s. 6d.

———— Life of Robert Burns. Fifth Edition. Fcap. 8vo. 3s.

LONDON'S (Bishop of) Dangers and Safeguards of Modern Theology. Containing Suggestions to the Theological Student under present difficulties. Second Edition. 8vo. 9s.

LOUDON'S (Mrs.) Instructions in Gardening for Ladies. With Directions and Calendar of Operations for Every Month. Eighth Edition. Woodcuts. Fcap. 8vo. 5s.

LUCAS' (Samuel) Secularia; or, Surveys on the Main Stream of History. 8vo. 12s.

LUCKNOW: a Lady's Diary of the Siege. *Fourth Thousand.* Fcap. 8vo. 4s. 6d.

LYELL'S (Sir Charles) Elements of Geology; or, the Ancient Changes of the Earth and its Inhabitants considered as illustrative of Geology. *Sixth Edition.* Woodcuts. 8vo. 18s.

———— Geological Evidences of the Antiquity of Man. *Third Edition.* Illustrations. 8vo. 14s.

LYTTELTON'S (Lord) Ephemera. Post 8vo. 10s. 6d.

LYTTON'S (Sir Edward Bulwer) Poems. *New Edition.* Revised. Post 8vo. 10s. 6d.

MAHON'S (Lord) History of England, from the Peace of Utrecht to the Peace of Versailles, 1713–83. *Library Edition.* 7 Vols. 8vo. 93s. *Popular Edition.* 7 Vols. Post 8vo. 35s.

———— "Forty-Five;" a Narrative of the Rebellion in Scotland. Post 8vo. 3s.

———— History of British India from its Origin till the Peace of 1783. Post 8vo. 3s. 6d.

———— Spain under Charles the Second; 1690 to 1700. *Second Edition.* Post 8vo. 6s. 6d.

———— Life of William Pitt, with Extracts from his MS. Papers. *Second Edition.* Portraits. 4 Vols. Post 8vo. 42s.

———— Condé, surnamed the Great. Post 8vo. 3s. 6d.

———— Belisarius. *Second Edition.* Post 8vo. 10s. 6d.

———— Historical and Critical Essays. Post 8vo. 3s. 6d.

———— Miscellanies. *Second Edition.* Post 8vo. 5s. 6d.

———— Story of Joan of Arc. Fcap. 8vo. 1s.

———— Addresses. Fcap. 8vo. 1s.

M'CLINTOCK'S (Capt. Sir F. L.) Narrative of the Discovery of the Fate of Sir John Franklin and his Companions in the Arctic Seas. *Twelfth Thousand.* Illustrations. 8vo. 16s.

M'CULLOCH'S (J. R.) Collected Edition of Ricardo's Political Works. With Notes and Memoir. *Second Edition.* 8vo. 16s.

MacDOUGALL (Col.) On Modern Warfare as Influenced by Modern Artillery. With Plans. Post 8vo. 12s.

MAINE (H. Summer) On Ancient Law: Its Connection with the Early History of Society, and its Relation to Modern Ideas. *Second Edition.* 8vo. 12s.

MALCOLM'S (Sir John) Sketches of Persia. *Third Edition.* Post 8vo. 5s. 6d.

MANSEL (Rev. H. L.) Limits of Religious Thought Examined. Being the Bampton Lectures for 1858. *Fourth Edition.* Post 8vo. 7s. 6d.

MANSFIELD (Sir William) On the Introduction of a Gold Currency into India: a Contribution to the Literature of Political Economy. 8vo. 3s. 6d.

MANTELL'S (Gideon A.) Thoughts on Animalcules; or, the Invisible World, as revealed by the Microscope. *Second Edition.* Plates. 16mo. 6s.

MANUAL OF SCIENTIFIC ENQUIRY, Prepared for the Use of Officers and Travellers. By various Writers. Edited by Sir J. F. Herschel and Rev. R. Main. *Third Edition.* Maps. Post 8vo. 9s. *(Published by order of the Lords of the Admiralty.)*

MARKHAM'S (Mrs.) History of England. From the First Invasion by the Romans, down to the fourteenth year of Queen Victoria's Reign. *154th Edition.* Woodcuts. 12mo. 6s.

———— History of France. From the Conquest by the Gauls, to the Death of Louis Philippe. *Sixtieth Edition.* Woodcuts. 12mo. 6s.

———— History of Germany. From the Invasion by Marius, to the present time. *Fifteenth Edition.* Woodcuts. 12mo. 6s.

———— History of Greece. From the Earliest Times to the Roman Conquest. By Dr. Wm. Smith. Woodcuts. 12mo. 6s. 6d.

———— History of Rome. From the Earliest Times to the Establishment of the Empire. By Dr. Wm. Smith. Woodcuts. 12mo. 6s. 6d.

———— (Clements, R.) Travels in Peru and India, for the purpose of collecting Cinchona Plants, and introducing Bark into India. Maps and Illustrations. 8vo. 16s.

MARKLAND'S (J. H.) Reverence due to Holy Places. *Third Edition.* Fcap. 8vo. 2s.

MARRYAT'S (Joseph) History of Modern and Mediæval Pottery and Porcelain. With a Description of the Manufacture. *Second Edition.* Plates and Woodcuts. 8vo. 31s. 6d.

———— (Horace) Jutland, the Danish Isles, and Copenhagen. Illustrations. 2 Vols. Post 8vo. 24s.

———— Sweden and Isle of Gothland. Illustrations. 2 Vols. Post 8vo. 28s.

MATTHIÆ'S (Augustus) Greek Grammar for Schools. Abridged from the Larger Grammar. By Blomfield. *Ninth Edition.* Revised by Edwards. 12mo. 3s.

MAUREL'S (Jules) Essay on the Character, Actions, and Writings of the Duke of Wellington. *Second Edition.* Fcap. 8vo. 1s. 6d.

MAXIMS AND HINTS on Angling and Chess. By Richard Penn. Woodcuts. 12mo. 1s.

MAYNE'S (R. C.) Four Years in British Columbia and Vancouver Island. Its Forests, Rivers, Coasts, and Gold Fields, and Resources for Colonisation. Illustrations. 8vo. 16s.

MELVILLE'S (Herman) Typee and Omoo; or, Adventures amongst the Marquesas and South Sea Islands. 2 Vols. Post 8vo. 7s.

MEREDITH'S (Mrs. Charles) Notes and Sketches of New South Wales. Post 8vo. 2s.

MESSIAH (THE): A Narrative of the Life, Travels, Death,
Resurrection, and Ascension of our Blessed Lord. By a Layman.
Author of the " Life of Bishop Ken." Map. 8vo. 18s.

MICHIE'S (Alexander) Siberian Overland Route from Peking
to Petersburg, through the Deserts and Steppes of Mongolia, Tartary,
&c. Maps and Illustrations. 8vo. 16s.

MILLS' (Arthur) India in 1858; A Summary of the Existing
Administration. Second Edition. Map. 8vo. 10s. 6d.

——— (Rev. John) Three Months' Residence at Nablus, with
an Account of the Modern Samaritans. Illustrations. Post 8vo. 10s. 6d.

MILMAN'S (Dean) History of the Jews, from the Earliest Period,
brought down to Modern Times. New Edition. 3 Vols. 8vo. 36s.

——— ——— Christianity, from the Birth of Christ to the
Abolition of Paganism in the Roman Empire. New Edition. 3 Vols.
8vo. 36s.

——— ——— Latin Christianity; including that of the Popes
to the Pontificate of Nicholas V. New Edition. 9 Vols. 8vo. 54s.

——— ——— Character and Conduct of the Apostles considered as
an Evidence of Christianity. 8vo. 10s. 6d.

——— ——— Life and Works of Horace. With 300 Woodcuts.
2 Vols. Crown 8vo. 30s.

——— ——— Poetical Works. Plates. 3 Vols. Fcap. 8vo. 18s.

——— ——— Fall of Jerusalem. Fcap. 8vo. 1s.

——— ——— (Capt. E. A.) Wayside Cross. A Tale of the Carlist
War. Post 8vo. 2s.

MILNES' (R. Monckton, Lord Houghton) Poetical Works. Fcap.
8vo. 6s.

MODERN DOMESTIC COOKERY. Founded on Principles of
Economy and Practical Knowledge and adapted for Private Families.
New Edition. Woodcuts. Fcap. 8vo. 6s.

MOORE'S (Thomas) Life and Letters of Lord Byron. Plates.
6 Vols. Fcap. 8vo. 18s.

——— Life and Letters of Lord Byron. Portraits. Royal 8vo. 9s.

MOTLEY'S (J. L.) History of the United Netherlands: from the
Death of William the Silent to the Synod of Dort. Embracing the
English-Dutch struggle against Spain; and a detailed Account of the
Spanish Armada. Portraits. 2 Vols. 8vo. 30s.

MOUHOT'S (Henri) Siam, Cambojia, and Lao: a Narrative of
Travels and Discoveries. Illustrations. 2 Vols. 8vo. 32s.

MOZLEY'S (Rev. J. B.) Treatise on Predestination. 8vo. 14s.

——— Primitive Doctrine of Baptismal Regeneration. 8vo. 7s. 6d.

MUNDY'S (General) Pen and Pencil Sketches in India.
Third Edition. Plates. Post 8vo. 7s. 6d.

———— (Admiral) Account of the Italian Revolution, with
Notices of Garibaldi, Francis II., and Victor Emmanuel. Post 8vo. 12s.

MUNRO'S (General Sir Thomas) Life and Letters. By the Rev.
G. R. Gleig. Post 8vo. 3s. 6d.

MURCHISON'S (Sir Roderick) Russia in Europe and the Ural
Mountains. With Coloured Maps, Plates, Sections, &c. 2 Vols.
Royal 4to.

———— Siluria ; or, a History of the Oldest Rocks containing Organic Remains. *Third Edition.* Map and Plates. 8vo. 42s.

MURRAY'S RAILWAY READING. Containing :—

WELLINGTON. By Lord Ellesmere. 6d.
NIMROD ON THE CHASE. 1s.
ESSAYS FROM "THE TIMES." 2 Vols. 8s.
MUSIC AND DRESS. 1s.
LAYARD'S ACCOUNT OF NINEVEH. 5s.
MILMAN'S FALL OF JERUSALEM. 1s.
MAHON'S "FORTY-FIVE." 3s.
LIFE OF THEODORE HOOK. 1s.
DEEDS OF NAVAL DARING. 3s. 6d.
THE HONEY BEE. 1s.
JAMES' ÆSOP'S FABLES. 2s. 6d.
NIMROD ON THE TURF. 1s. 6d.
ART OF DINING. 1s. 6d.

HALLAM'S LITERARY ESSAYS. 2s.
MAHON'S JOAN OF ARC. 1s.
HEAD'S EMIGRANT. 2s. 6d.
NIMROD ON THE ROAD. 1s.
CROKER ON THE GUILLOTINE. 1s.
HOLLWAY'S NORWAY. 2s.
MAUREL'S WELLINGTON. 1s. 6d.
CAMPBELL'S LIFE OF BACON. 2s. 6d.
THE FLOWER GARDEN. 1s.
LOCKHART'S SPANISH BALLADS. 2s. 6d.
TAYLOR'S NOTES FROM LIFE. 2s.
HAMILTON'S WANDERINGS. 1s.
PENN'S HINTS ON ANGLING. 1s.

MUSIC AND DRESS. By a Lady. Reprinted from the " Quarterly
Review." Fcap. 8vo. 1s.

NAPIER'S (Sir Wm.) English Battles and Sieges of the Peninsular
War. *Third Edition.* Portrait. Post 8vo. 10s. 6d.

———— Life and Letters. Edited by H. A. Bruce, M.P.
Portraits. 2 Vols. Crown 8vo. 28s.

———— Life of General Sir Charles Napier; chiefly derived
from his Journals and Letters. *Second Edition.* Portraits. 4 Vols.
Post 8vo. 48s.

NAUTICAL ALMANACK. Royal 8vo. 2s. 6d. (*By Authority.*)

NAVY LIST. (*Published Quarterly, by Authority.*) 16mo. 2s. 6d.

NEW TESTAMENT (The) Illustrated by a Plain Explanatory
Commentary, and authentic Views of Sacred Places, from Sketches
and Photographs. Edited by Archdeacon Churton and Rev. Basil
Jones. With 110 Illustrations. 2 Vols. Crown 8vo.

NEWDEGATE'S (C. N.) Customs' Tariffs of all Nations; collected
and arranged up to the year 1855. 4to. 30s.

NICHOLLS' (Sir George) History of the English, Irish and
Scotch Poor Laws. 4 Vols. 8vo.

———— (Rev. H. G.) Historical Account of the Forest of
Dean. Woodcuts, &c. Post 8vo. 10s. 6d.

———— Personalities of the Forest of Dean, its successive
Officials, Gentry, and Community. Post 8vo. 3s. 6d.

NICOLAS' (Sir Harris) Historic Peerage of England. Exhibiting the Origin, Descent, and Present State of every Title of Peerage which has existed in this Country since the Conquest. By WILLIAM COURTHOPE. 8vo. 30s.

NIMROD On the Chace—The Turf—and The Road. Reprinted from the "Quarterly Review." Woodcuts. Fcap. 8vo. 3s. 6d.

O'CONNOR'S (R.) Field Sports of France; or, Hunting, Shooting, and Fishing on the Continent. Woodcuts. 12mo. 7s. 6d.

OXENHAM'S (Rev. W.) English Notes for Latin Elegiacs; designed for early Proficients in the Art of Latin Versification, with Prefatory Rules of Composition in Elegiac Metre. Fourth Edition, 12mo. 3s. 6d.

PARIS' (Dr.) Philosophy in Sport made Science in Earnest; or, the First Principles of Natural Philosophy inculcated by aid of the Toys and Sports of Youth. Ninth Edition. Woodcuts. Post 8vo. 7s. 6d.

PEEL'S (Sir Robert) Memoirs. Edited by EARL STANHOPE and MR. CARDWELL. 2 Vols. Post 8vo. 7s. 6d. each.

PENN'S (Richard) Maxims and Hints for an Angler and Chess-player. New Edition. Woodcuts. Fcap. 8vo. 1s.

PENROSE'S (F. C.) Principles of Athenian Architecture, and the Optical Refinements exhibited in the Construction of the Ancient Buildings at Athens, from a Survey. With 40 Plates. Folio. 5l. 5s.

PERCY'S (John, M.D.) Metallurgy of Iron and Steel; or, the Art of Extracting Metals from their Ores and adapting them to various purposes of Manufacture. Illustrations. 8vo. 42s.

PHILLIPP (Charles Spencer March) On Jurisprudence. 8vo. 12s.

PHILLIPS' (John) Memoirs of William Smith, the Geologist. Portrait. 8vo. 7s. 6d.

———— Geology of Yorkshire, The Coast, and Limestone District. Plates. 4to. Part I., 20s.—Part II., 30s.

———— Rivers, Mountains, and Sea Coast of Yorkshire. With Essays on the Climate, Scenery, and Ancient Inhabitants. Second Edition, Plates. 8vo. 15s.

PHILPOTTS' (Bishop) Letters to the late Charles Butler, on the Theological parts of his "Book of the Roman Catholic Church;" with Remarks on certain Works of Dr. Milner and Dr. Lingard, and on some parts of the Evidence of Dr. Doyle. Second Edition. 8vo. 16s.

POPE'S (Alexander) Life and Works. *A New Edition.* Containing nearly 500 unpublished Letters. Edited with a New Life, Introductions and Notes. By Rev. WHITWELL ELWIN. Portraits. 8vo. (*In the Press.*)

PORTER'S (Rev. J. L.) Five Years in Damascus. With Travels to Palmyra, Lebanon and other Scripture Sites. Map and Woodcuts. 2 Vols. Post 8vo. 21s.

———— Handbook for Syria and Palestine: Including an Account of the Geography, History, Antiquities, and Inhabitants of those Countries, the Peninsula of Sinai, Edom, and the Syrian Desert. Maps. 2 Vols. Post 8vo. 24s.

PRAYER-BOOK (The Illustrated), with 1000 Illustrations of Borders, Initials, Vignettes, &c. Medium 8vo. 18s. cloth; 31s. 6d. calf; 36s. morocco.

PRECEPTS FOR THE CONDUCT OF LIFE. Extracted from the Scriptures. *Second Edition.* Fcap. 8vo. 1s.

PUSS IN BOOTS. With 12 Illustrations. By OTTO SPECKTER. Coloured, 16mo. 1s. 6d.

QUARTERLY REVIEW (The). 8vo. 6s.

RAMBLES in Syria among the Turkomans and Bedaweens. Post 8vo. 10s. 6d.

RAWLINSON'S (Rev. GEORGE) Herodotus. A New English Version. Edited with Notes and Essays. Assisted by SIR HENRY RAWLINSON and SIR J. G. WILKINSON. *Second Edition.* Maps and Woodcut. 4 Vols. 8vo. 48s.

———— Historical Evidences of the truth of the Scripture Records stated anew. *Second Edition.* 8vo. 14s.

———— Five Great Monarchies of the Ancient World. Illustrations. 4 Vols. 8vo. 16s. each.
Vols. I.—II., Chaldæa and Assyria. Vols. III.—IV., Babylon, Media, and Persia.

REJECTED ADDRESSES (The). By JAMES AND HORACE SMITH. Fcap. 8vo. 1s., or *Fine Paper,* Portrait, Imp. 8vo. 6s.

RENNIE'S (D. F.) British Arms in Peking, 1860; Kagosima, 1862. Post 8vo. 12s.

———— Pekin and the Pekinese: Narrative of a Residence at the British Embassy. Illustrations. 2 Vols. Post 8vo.

REYNOLDS' (SIR JOSHUA) His Life and Times. Commenced by C. R. LESLIE, R.A., and continued by TOM TAYLOR. Portraits and Illustrations. 2 Vols. 8vo.

RICARDO'S (DAVID) Political Works. With a Notice of his Life and Writings. By J. R. M'CULLOCH. *New Edition.* 8vo. 16s.

RIPA'S (FATHER) Memoirs during Thirteen Years' Residence at the Court of Peking. From the Italian. Post 8vo. 2s.

ROBERTSON'S (CANON) History of the Christian Church, from the Apostolic Age to the Concordat of Worms, A.D. 1123. *Second Edition.* 4 Vols. 8vo. 54s.

ROBINSON'S (REV. DR.) Biblical Researches in the Holy Land. Being a Journal of Travels in 1838 and 1852. Maps. 3 Vols. 8vo. 42s.

———— Physical Geography of the Holy Land. Post 8vo. 10s. 6d.

ROME (THE STUDENT'S HISTORY OF). FROM THE EARLIEST TIMES TO THE ESTABLISHMENT OF THE EMPIRE. By DEAN LIDDELL. Woodcuts. Post 8vo. 7s. 6d.

ROWLAND'S (DAVID) Manual of the English Constitution; Its Rise, Growth, and Present State. Post 8vo. 10s. 6d.

———— Laws of Nature the Foundation of Morals. Post 8vo.

RUNDELL'S (MRS.) Domestic Cookery, adapted for Private Families. *New Edition.* Woodcuts. Fcap. 8vo. 5s.

RUSSELL'S (J. Rutherford, M.D.) Art of Medicine—Its History
and its Heroes. Portraits. 8vo. 14s.

BUXTON'S (George F.) Travels in Mexico; with Adventures
among the Wild Tribes and Animals of the Prairies and Rocky Mountains. Post 8vo. 3s. 6d.

SALE'S (Sir Robert) Brigade in Affghanistan. With an Account of
the Defence of Jellalabad. By Rev. G. R. Gleig. Post 8vo. 2s.

SANDWITH'S (Humphry) Siege of Kars. Post 8vo. 3s. 6d.

SCOTT'S (G. Gilbert) Secular and Domestic Architecture, Present and Future. Second Edition. 8vo. 9s.

——— (Master of Balliol) University Sermons. Post 8vo. 8s. 6d.

SCROPE'S (G. P.) Geology and Extinct Volcanoes of Central
France. Second Edition. Illustrations. Medium 8vo. 30s.

SELF-HELP. With Illustrations of Character and Conduct.
By Samuel Smiles. 50th Thousand. Post 8vo. 6s.

SENIOR'S (N. W.) Suggestions on Popular Education. 8vo. 9s.

SHAFTESBURY (Lord Chancellor); Memoirs of his Early Life.
With his Letters, &c. By W. D. Christie. Portrait. 8vo. 10s. 6d.

SHAW'S (T. B.) Student's Manual of English Literature. Edited,
with Notes and Illustrations, by Dr. Wm. Smith. Post 8vo. 7s. 6d.

——— Choice Specimens of English Literature. Selected from
the Chief English Writers. Edited by Wm. Smith, LL.D. Post 8vo. 7s. 6d.

SIERRA LEONE; Described in Letters to Friends at Home. By
A Lady. Post 8vo. 3s. 6d.

SIMMONS on Courts-Martial. 5th Edition. 8vo. 14s.

SMILES' (Samuel) Lives of British Engineers; from the Earliest
Period to the Death of Robert Stephenson: with an account of their Principal Works, and a History of Inland Communication in Britain.
Portraits and Illustrations. 3 Vols. 8vo. 63s.

——— George and Robert Stephenson; the Story of their Lives.
With Portraits and 70 Woodcuts. Post 8vo. 6s.

——— James Brindley and the Early Engineers. With Portrait
and 50 Woodcuts. Post 8vo. 6s.

——— Self-Help. With Illustrations of Character and Conduct.
Post 8vo. 6s.

——— Industrial Biography: Iron-Workers and Tool Makers.
A companion volume to "Self-Help." Post 8vo. 6s.

——— Workmen's Earnings—Savings—and Strikes. Fcap. 8vo.
1s. 6d.

SOMERVILLE'S (Mary) Physical Geography. Fifth Edition.
Portrait. Post 8vo. 9s.

——— Connexion of the Physical Sciences. Ninth
Edition. Woodcuts. Post 8vo. 9s.

SOUTH'S (John F.) Household Surgery; or, Hints on Emergencies. Seventeenth Thousand. Woodcuts. Fcp. 8vo. 4s. 6d.

SMITH'S (Dr. Wm.) Dictionary of the Bible; its Antiquities, Biography, Geography, and Natural History. Illustrations. 3 Vols. 8vo. 105s.

———— Greek and Roman Antiquities. 2nd *Edition*. Woodcuts. 8vo. 42s.

———————————— Biography and Mythology. Woodcuts. 3 Vols. 8vo. 5l. 15s. 6d.

————————————— Geography. Woodcuts. 2 Vols. 8vo. 80s.

———— Classical Dictionary of Mythology, Biography, and Geography, compiled from the above. With 750 Woodcuts. 8vo. 18s.

———— Latin-English Dictionary. 3rd Edition. Revised. 8vo. 21s.

———— Smaller Classical Dictionary. Woodcuts. Crown 8vo. 7s. 6d.

———— Dictionary of Antiquities. Woodcuts. Crown 8vo. 7s. 6d.

———— Latin-English Dictionary. 12mo. 7s. 6d.

———— Latin-English Vocabulary; for Phædrus, Cornelius Nepos, and Cæsar. 2nd Edition. 12mo. 3s. 6d.

———— Principia Latina—Part I. A Grammar, Delectus, and Exercise Book, with Vocabularies. 6th Edition. 12mo. 3s. 6d.

———————————— Part II. A Reading-book of Mythology, Geography, Roman Antiquities, and History. With Notes and Dictionary. 3rd Edition. 12mo. 3s. 6d.

———————— Part III. A Latin Poetry Book. Hexameters and Pentameters; Eclogæ Ovidianæ; Latin Prosody, &c. 2nd Edition. 12mo. 3s. 6d.

———————————— Part IV. Latin Prose Composition. Rules of Syntax, with Examples, Explanations of Synonyms, and Exercises on the Syntax. Second Edition. 12mo. 3s. 6d.

———— Student's Greek Grammar. By Professor Curtius. Post 8vo. 7s. 6d.

———————— Latin Grammar. Post 8vo. 7s. 6d.

———————— Latin Grammar. Abridged from the above. 12mo. 3s. 6d.

———— Smaller Greek Grammar. Abridged from Curtius. 12mo. 3s. 6d.

STANLEY'S (Dean) Sinai and Palestine, in Connexion with their History. Map. 8vo. 16s.

———— Bible in the Holy Land. Woodcuts. Fcap. 8vo. 2s. 6d.

———— St. Paul's Epistles to the Corinthians. 8vo. 18s.

———— Eastern Church. Plans. 8vo. 12s.

———— Jewish Church. Vol. 1, ABRAHAM TO SAMUEL. Plans. 8vo. 16s.

————————————— Vol. 2, SAMUEL TO THE CAPTIVITY. 8vo. 18s.

———— Historical Memorials of Canterbury. Woodcuts. Post 8vo. 7s. 6d.

———— Sermons in the East, with Notices of the Places Visited. 8vo. 9s.

———— Sermons on Evangelical and Apostolical Teaching. Post 8vo. 7s. 6d.

———— ADDRESSES AND CHARGES OF BISHOP STANLEY. With Memoir. 8vo. 10s. 6d.

SOUTHEY'S (ROBERT) Book of the Church. *Seventh Edition.*
Post 8vo. 7s. 6d.

————. Lives of Bunyan and Cromwell. Post 8vo. 2s.

SPROETER'S (OTTO) Puss in Boots. With 12 Woodcuts. Square
16mo. 1s. 6d. plain, or 2s. 6d. coloured.

— — — . Charmed Roe; or, the Story of the Little Brother
and Sister. Illustrated. 16mo.

ST. JOHN'S (CHARLES) Wild Sports and Natural History of the
Highlands. Post 8vo. 3s. 6d.

———— (BAYLE) Adventures in the Libyan Desert and the
Oasis of Jupiter Ammon. Woodcuts. Post 8vo. 2s.

STANHOPE'S (EARL) Life of William Pitt. With Extracts
from his M.S. Papers. *Second Edition.* Portraits. 4 Vols. Post 8vo.
42s.

————. Miscellanies. *Second Edition.* Post 8vo. 5s. 6d.

STEPHENSON (GEORGE and ROBERT). The Story of their
Lives. By SAMUEL SMILES. With Portraits and 70 Illustrations. Post
8vo. 6s.

STUDENT'S HUME. A History of England from the Invasion
of Julius Cæsar to the Revolution of 1688. By DAVID HUME, and
continued to 1858. Woodcuts. Post 8vo. 7s. 6d.
  ₊ A Smaller History of England. 16mo. 3s. 6d.

———— HISTORY OF FRANCE; from the Earliest Times
to the Establishment of the Second Empire, 1852. By W. H. PEARSON,
M.A. Woodcuts. Post 8vo. 7s. 6d.

— HISTORY OF GREECE; from the Earliest Times
to the Roman Conquest. With the History of Literature and Art. By
WM. SMITH, LL.D. Woodcuts. Crown 8vo. 7s. 6d. (Questions, 2s.)
  ₊ A SMALLER HISTORY OF GREECE. 16mo. 3s. 6d.

———— HISTORY OF ROME; from the Earliest Times
to the Establishment of the Empire. With the History of Literature
and Art. By DEAN LIDDELL. Woodcuts. Crown 8vo. 7s. 6d.
  ₊ A SMALLER HISTORY OF ROME. 16mo. 3s. 6d.

———— GIBBON; an Epitome of the History of the Decline
and Fall of the Roman Empire. By EDWARD GIBBON. Incorporating the Researches of Recent Commentators. Woodcuts. Post 8vo.
7s. 6d.

MANUAL OF ANCIENT GEOGRAPHY. By
Rev. W. L. BEVAN, M.A. Woodcuts. Post 8vo. 7s. 6d.

———— ENGLISH LANGUAGE. By GEORGE P. MARSH.
Post 8vo. 7s. 6d.

ENGLISH LITERATURE. By T. B. SHAW,
M.A. Post 8vo. 7s. 6d.

—— - SPECIMENS OF ENGLISH LITERATURE.
Selected from the Chief Writers. By THOMAS B. SHAW, M.A. Post
8vo. 7s. 6d.

STOTHARD'S (THOS.) Life. With Personal Reminiscences.
By Mrs. BRAY. With Portrait and 60 Woodcuts. 4to. 21s.

STREET'S (G. E.) Gothic Architecture in Spain. From Personal
Observations during several journeys through that country. Illustrations. Medium 8vo.

———————— Brick and Marble Architecture of Italy in the
Middle Ages. Plates. 8vo. 21s.

SWIFT'S (JONATHAN) Life, Letters, Journals, and Works. By
JOHN FORSTER. 8vo. (In Preparation.)

SYME'S (PROFESSOR) Principles of Surgery. 5th Edition. 8vo. 12s.

TAIT'S (BISHOP) Dangers and Safeguards of Modern Theology.
8vo. 9s.

TAYLOR'S (HENRY) Notes from Life. Fcap. 8vo. 2s.

THOMSON'S (ARCHBISHOP) Lincoln's Inn Sermons. 8vo. 10s. 6d.

THREE-LEAVED MANUAL OF FAMILY PRAYER; arranged
so as to save the trouble of turning the Pages backwards and forwards.
Royal 8vo. 2s.

TRANSACTIONS OF THE ETHNOLOGICAL SOCIETY OF
LONDON. New Series. Vols. I. and II. 8vo.

TREMENHEERE'S (H. S.) Political Experience of the Ancients,
in its bearing on Modern Times. Fcap. 8vo. 2s. 6d.

TRISTRAM (H. B.) The Great Sahara. Wanderings South of the
Atlas Mountains. Map and Illustrations. Post 8vo. 15s.

TWISS' (HORACE) Public and Private Life of Lord Chancellor Eldon,
with Selections from his Correspondence. Portrait. Third Edition.
3 Vols. Post 8vo. 21s.

TYLOR'S (E. B.) Researches into the Early History of Mankind,
and the Development of Civilisation. Illustrations. 8vo.

TYNDALL'S (JOHN) Glaciers of the Alps. With an account of
Three Years' Observations and Experiments on their General Phenomena. Woodcuts. Post 8vo. 14s.

TYTLER'S (PATRICK FRASER) Memoirs. By Rev. J. W. BURGON,
M.A. 8vo. 9s.

VAUGHAN'S (Rev. DR.) Sermons preached in Harrow School.
8vo. 10s. 6d.

VENABLES' (REV. R. L.) Domestic Scenes in Russia. Post 8vo. 5s.

WAAGEN'S (DR.) Treasures of Art in Great Britain. Being an
Account of the Chief Collections of Paintings, Sculpture, Manuscripts,
Miniatures, &c. &c., in this Country. Obtained from Personal Inspection during Visits to England. 4 Vols. 8vo.

WALSH'S (SIR JOHN) Practical Results of the Reform Bill of
1832. 8vo. 6s. 6d.

VAMBERY'S (ARMINIUS) Travels in Central Asia, from Teheran
across the Turkoman Desert, on the Eastern Shore of the Caspian to
Khiva, Bokhara, and Samarcand in 1863. Map and Illustrations. 8vo. 21s.

WELLINGTON'S (The Duke of) Despatches during his various Campaigns. Compiled from Official and other Authentic Documents. By Col. Gurwood, C.B. 8 Vols. 8vo. 21s. each.

———————— Supplementary Despatches, and other Papers. Edited by his Son. Vols. I. to XII. 8vo. 20s. each.

———————— Selections from his Despatches and General Orders. By Colonel Gurwood. 8vo. 18s.

———————— Speeches in Parliament. 2 Vols. 8vo. 42s.

WILKINSON'S (Sir J. G.) Popular Account of the Private Life, Manners, and Customs of the Ancient Egyptians. New Edition. Revised and Condensed. With 600 Woodcuts. 2 Vols. Post 8vo. 12s.

———————— Handbook for Egypt—Thebes, the Nile, Alexandria, Cairo, the Pyramids, Mount Sinai, &c. Map. Post 8vo. 15s.

———————— (G. B.) Working Man's Handbook to South Australia; with Advice to the Farmer, and Detailed Information for the several Classes of Labourers and Artisans. Map. 18mo. 1s. 6d.

WILSON'S (Bishop Daniel) Life, with Extracts from his Letters and Journals. By Rev. Josiah Bateman. Second Edition. Illustrations. Post 8vo. 9s.

———————— (Genl. Sir Robert) Secret History of the French Invasion of Russia, and Retreat of the French Army, 1812. Second Edition. 8vo. 15s.

———————— Private Diary of Travels, Personal Services, and Public Events, during Missions and Employments in Spain, Sicily, Turkey, Russia, Poland, Germany, &c. 1812-14. 2 Vols. 8vo. 26s.

———————— Autobiographical Memoirs. Containing an Account of his Early Life down to the Peace of Tilsit. Portrait. 2 Vols. 8vo. 26s.

WORDSWORTH'S (Canon) Journal of a Tour in Athens and Attica. Third Edition. Plates. Post 8vo. 8s. 6d.

———————— Pictorial, Descriptive, and Historical Account of Greece, with a History of Greek Art, by G. Scharf, F.S.A. New Edition. With 600 Woodcuts. Royal 8vo. 28s.

WORNUM (Ralph). A Biographical Dictionary of Italian Painters: with a Table of the Contemporary Schools of Italy. By a Lady. Post 8vo. 6s. 6d.